SYDNEY AND HIS PLANTATION FRIENDS.

NORTHWOOD;

OR,

LIFE NORTH AND SOUTH:

SHOWING THE

TRUE CHARACTER OF BOTH.

BY

MRS. SARAH JOSEPHA HALE.

Illustrated.

"HE WHO LOVES NOT HIS COUNTRY CAN LOVE NOTHING."

SECOND EDITION.

NEW YORK:
H. LONG & BROTHER,
43 ANN-STREET.

Entered, according to Act of Congress, in the Year One Thousand Eight Hundred and Fifty-two, by MRS. SARAH J. HALE, in the Clerk's Office of the District Court, for the Southern District of New York.

A WORD WITH THE READER.

Twenty-five years ago the book you are about to read was written; and thus commenced my literary life. To those who know me, it is also known that this was not entered upon to win fame, but a support for my little children. Northwood was written literally with my baby in my arms—the "youngling of the flock," whose eyes did not open on the world till his father's were closed in death!

The Reader who has suffered, or who is struggling to perform sacred duties, will rejoice that this work not only succeeded, but that the mode of its success proved it was not unworthy of public favor.

Northwood was published in Boston, where I was not then personally known to a single individual. The MS. was sent to a stranger; in less than a month after the book appeared I had received many letters of congratulation and promises of friendly aid. Among these letters was one from a publishing firm in that city, proposing to establish a periodical for Ladies, and offering me the editorship, if I would remove to Boston. This proposal was accepted, and the "Ladies' Magazine" established, the first literary work exclusively devoted to women ever published in America. Its success led to others of a similar spirit. Among these was Godey's "Lady's Book," published at Philadelphia. With this work my Magazine was united in 1837, and ever since I have continued editor of the "Ladies' Book."

Furthermore, the success of my literary life has enabled me to educate my children liberally, as their father would have done—and I hope the influence of the various productions I have sent forth has been in some dedegree beneficial to my own sex, and to the cause of sound literature and of pure morality.

Thus the kind Reader will see why this, my first novel, should be referred to as an era in my life.

Moreover, Northwood received commendations where no personal motives could have held sway. Under the title of "A New England Tale," it was republished in London—at that time a very remarkable compliment to an American book,—and honored with favorable notices in some of the leading Metropolitan Journals. In short, the author had no reason to feel dissatisfied with the success of her book. The portraitures of American character were pronounced excellent—particularly that phase generally known as *the Yankee.* The habits and tone of feeling characterizing the real yeomanry of this class are nowhere so clearly marked as in New Hampshire. There, the Farmers are really lords of the soil, — loving their country next to their God, and holding talents and learning in higher estimation than wealth or rank. And from the glorious old Granite State, where the scenes of this novel begin, have come forth those great men, "Defenders of the Constitution,"—who "know no North and no South,"—but wherever the sacred Charter of Union stretches its cordon of brotherhood, and the Eagle and the Stars keep guard, is their country. In the same spirit our book goes forth. Northwood was written when what is now known as "Abolitionism" first began seriously to disturb the harmony between the South and the North. In the retirement of my mountain home, no motives save the search for truth and obedience to duty prompted the sentiments expressed in this work; nor has a wider sphere of observation, nor the long time for examination and reflection changed, materially, the views I had then adopted. These views, based on the conditions of the compact the framers of the Constitution recognized as lawful, and the people of the United States solemnly promised to observe, have been confirmed by a careful study of the word of God, as well as of human history.

It is, therefore, a proud satisfaction to know that my own "Granite State," during all the fury of a sectional strife, has stood firm for the Constitution and the Union, like the pine on her hills, gathering strength of root from the storm that shakes its strong arms and even rends some of the noble branches from the parent tree.

One cheering proof of the world's progress is the earnestness of those who are now working in the cause of humanity. Men and women, too, are seeking for light to guide them in the way of duty. That it is easier to burn a temple than to build one, and that two wrongs never make one right, are points conceded by all; yet all seem not to have considered what is quite as sure, that fraud and falsehood never promote the cause of goodness, nor can physical force make or keep men free. The chain may be broken in one direction, only to be more firmly riveted in another, unless Love and Truth act as solvents, and destroy the fetters altogether. The great error of those who would sever the Union rather than see a slave within its borders, is, that they forget the *master* is their brother, as well as the *servant;* and that the spirit which seeks to do good to all and evil to none is the only true Christian philanthropy. Hoping that Northwood might, in some degree, aid in diffusing this true spirit, I have consented to its republication at this time. The few additions made to the original work are only to show more plainly how the principles advocated may be effectually carried out. Fiction derives its chief worth from the truths it teaches. I have aimed to set forth some important truths—their worth I leave to be estimated by the Reader.

PHILADELPHIA, September 9th, 1852.

CONTENTS.

NORTHWOOD:

OR,

LIFE NORTH AND SOUTH.

CHAPTER I.

A HOME IN THE OLD GRANITE STATE.

Domestic bliss, that like a harmless dove,
Can centre in a little quiet nest
All that Desire would fly for through the earth;
That can, the world eluding, be itself
A world enjoyed; that wants no witnesses
Save its own sharers, and approving heaven.

KENNEDY.

SIDNEY ROMILLY, the eldest of a numerous family, was a native of New Hampshire. The local situation of the little village in which he was born, offered few temptations to the speculator, and the soil promised no indulgence to the idle; but it abundantly repaid the industrious cultivator. It was therefore inhabited, almost exclusively, by husbandmen, who tilled their own farms with their own hands, laboring actively six days in the week, and on the seventh, offering, to that Being who alone could crown their labors with success, the unfeigned homage of contented minds and grateful hearts.

In short, some twenty or thirty years since, the inhabitants of this retired place displayed, in the simplicity and purity of their manners and morals, a model, which Jeremiah Belknap, when describing so admirably what constituted a "happy society," might have quoted as an illustration of his "picture."

Among this unsophisticated people, where men are esteemed more for merit and usefulness, than rank and wealth, James Romilly, Esq., the father of our hero, was a very honorable man; yet it was not wealth which gave him consideration, for he was only what is called in middling circumstances, and the deference with which he was treated was the more gratifying as he knew it to be an unpurchasable tribute paid by freemen to his abilities and integrity.

He, like almost all the New England yeomanry, married young, and lived most happily with his wife; for she was the woman of his choice, and truly and faithfully a helpmeet for him in his labors, and a tried and discreet friend, in whose sympathy and counsels he found he might always rely.

When they first came to reside on their farm, it was almost a wilderness; but unremitting industry soon altered its appearance—the thrifty orchard occupied the place of the maple forest, the garden bloomed where the wild briar had sprung, and a comfortable house quite eclipsed the log hut, which had, at first, afforded them shelter.

But the complacency with which Mr. Romilly surveyed the outside of his new habitation, was nothing to the pleasure he enjoyed while contemplating the beloved and happy faces within; and among a family of fine promising children, his dearest hope, perhaps unconsciously, rested on the eldest.

There is an emotion of the soul awakened at the birth of the first-born, which seems to place that child in a nearer connexion with the parents than any subsequent offspring; and in most civilized countries, the laws give the eldest some peculiar privileges, as the right of birth.

The wisdom or justice of such regulations, however, it is not now my intention to discuss. I would only remark, that if parental partiality was ever justifiable, the parents of young Sidney might well be excused for selecting him as their favorite. He was very handsome, and although personal beauty is of little consequence to the man, it gives much interest to the child. In the spring, who does not like to gaze on the most beautiful flowers? But yet it is the intelligence and vivacity displayed in the countenance that create the strongest interest, as the odor of the flower is prized more than the beauty of its tints, because we know it will longer continue.

Sidney, even from infancy, exhibited uncommon aptitude for learning, and it is not strange if his parents, at least, should think his large, luminous eyes and expansive forehead gave promise of uncommon genius; he was, besides, very docile and sweet-tempered; what was considered most remarkable, his father often declared he never heard him tell an untruth, nor even attempt the least prevarication.

Falsehood may be termed the besetting sin of infancy, and the child who has the mental courage to adhere strictly to truth, even when it may expose his own faults to punishment, certainly deserves our warmest admiration, and gives the most unequivocal promise of future excellence.

Indeed, the only fault of our little hero, (which in a child would scarcely appear one) was the facility with which he yielded his own opinions and inclinations to the perseverance or persuasions of others. A boy of this facile, generous temper, which melts like wax, is liable to every impression, and requires more constant watchfulness, and unremitting restraint, than those sturdy, stubborn, self-willed varlets, who, by turbulent opposition to necessary regulations, perhaps often require punishment. The former is always liable to adopt the faults of others, which the latter from his very stubbornness resists.

It must not, however, be inferred from this, that a condescending temper is a misfortune; it only becomes so by mismanagement. Chiefly because parents or guardians, weary of the task of rational discipline and instruction, relax whenever they can without immediate inconvenience; and although they may be sufficiently assiduous to drive out the *evil* spirit, seem to forget it is necessary to be equally alert to prevent its re-entering.

The tree that grows straight of itself, seems to require no care of the gardener, yet its very luxuriance often prevents its becoming fruitful; while the crooked, crabbed shrub, that requires constant pruning and grafting, becomes at length a sightly tree, producing abundantly, and of the best quality. "But these observations are out of place here," says the novel reader; "reserve them for a treatise on education."

Mr. Romilly was well read in English history, and from admiration of the splendid talents and devoted patriotism of the famous Algernon Sidney, selected the same name for his own son. He would have given him both names, but Mrs. Romilly objected seriously to Algernon. It sounded, she said, too much like "Algerine," and she detested it.

Her husband, laughing, told her he had no fear of their son turning pirate; "but," added he, "I dislike double names myself, and so, if you please, we will call him only Sidney."

And Sidney he was called; and although Mr. Romilly was a man of too much sense to imagine a certain combination of letters would impart qualities to the mind of his boy, yet the noble sentiments and exalted character of the British statesman were so inwoven in his memory with the name of *Sidney*, that, at times, when pronouncing it, he would almost feel an assurance of his own son's future usefulness and distinction.

Indeed, few conditions in this world of care can be imagined more enviable than that of Mr. Romilly, when of a winter evening, with every chore done, he seated himself before a "rousing fire," "monarch of all he surveyed," and listening to the roaring of the tempest without, contrasted it with the peace, plenty, and security reigning within.

The ample fire-place, piled with wood, soon sent forth a blaze which illuminated every corner and object in a neat and comfortably-furnished apartment; his wife, with her knitting-work in her hand, or work-basket beside her, looked the presiding genius of domestic felicity, and his children, their little faces bright and beautiful as animated innocence could make them, sported around him; all eager to share his caresses, or listen to the stories he related. It was at such seasons, he often repeated those lines from Cowper, (for Cowper was his favorite poet):

> "Domestic happiness, thou only bliss
> Of Paradise that has survived the fall."

Thus smoothly passed the years over the happy dwelling of the Romillys, bringing no changes save those quiet and expected ones which the heart anticipates and blesses, and affording no diversity except in the occasional absences from home, which, to Mr. Romilly, public business made necessary.

The bustle of political life was not at all congenial to his disposition or habits; but he considered every freeman under sacred obligations to serve his country whenever and in whatever manner she required his services; and the confidence of his own townsmen placed him, almost every year, in some office, which, had he consulted his inclination or interest, he would unhesitatingly have refused. These separations from his family and farm, were the only interruptions to the domestic happiness of Mr. Romilly, which occurred till Sidney had entered his twelfth year, beloved and praised not only by his own parents, but the whole neighborhood.

But there always "lurks some wish in every heart," and many who can truly estimate the world for themselves, will yet overrate it for their children; and thus Mr. Romilly, although he was indifferent to public honors for himself, and felt convinced that happiness seldom resided in the bosoms of the ambitious and celebrated, yet he ardently desired to give Sidney an opportunity of distinguishing himself. For this purpose he was daily planning how to bestow on him a liberal education.

Literature is the star and garter of a Yankee. It claims precedence and gains privileges to which wealth alone is not entitled. This Mr. Romilly well knew. His own education had, in youth, been neglected; but good, natural sense, a sound judgment, and uncommon taste for reading, in a great measure supplied the deficiency; at least, it enabled him to discharge much of the public business of his own town to the entire satisfaction of his employers, and he had twice sat in the Legislature of New Hampshire, as a representative. But there he met with superiors, and although he was, by nature, remarkably free from an envious or repining disposition, yet he could not avoid feeling some mortification while comparing his own acquirements with those of "College learned" men; and he resolved to hazard suffering almost any inconvenience, rather than Sidney should thus be cast into the shade for the want of understanding a Latin quotation, or a reference to the customs of antiquity.

CHAPTER II.

FRIENDS FROM THE SOUTH.

Maidens, like moths, are ever caught by glare,
And Mammon wins his way where Seraphs might despair.
[CHILDE HAROLD.

ABOUT this time, Mr. Romilly was visited by a sister, whom he had not seen for nearly twenty years.

This lady, for reasons which the reader will ultimately discover, must be introduced somewhat particularly. She was the only daughter of her parents, and in her youth a celebrated beauty; two very unfortunate circumstances for the happiness of a woman. An only daughter is sure to be humored by her family; a beautiful girl will be flattered by her admirers; either of these is sufficient to turn a young and giddy brain, and requires to be counteracted by good sense and a strictly judicious education, or the object of such attentions will be pert and vain while they are continued, peevish and unreasonable when they are withdrawn.

Those who have the superintendance of young girls, cannot too often nor too forcibly impress on their tender minds, those lessons of prudence, forbearance and humility, which the world is sure, sooner or later, to force upon them. The art of self-government is indispensable to woman's felicity.

But Miss Lydia Romilly was never taught this lesson beneath the paternal roof. All there was subservient to her wishes or whims; and it was the common saying of the neighborhood, that she ruled the whole family. Yet she was neither ill-natured nor passionate; her greatest fault was that self-estimation which made her imagine her own happiness ought to be the first consideration with all who approached her.

Lovers without number bowed before this rural belle, and at length she did what few belles ever do, bestowed her affections on one of the most worthy. He was not rich, but possessed what is preferable, industry to acquire wealth, and capacity to preserve it; good health, good habits, and good morals; but (the truth must be told) it was not to those requisites he was indebted for the favor of Miss Lydia, but to his manly form and fine face, which, when set off by a handsome military dress, (he was a militia captain) she declared was quite irresistible. She loved him, however, as sincerely as one whose standard of reference was ever *self,* could love another; and her parents willingly sanctioned her choice, though they would have been better pleased could Reuben Porter have added one round 0 to the sum total of his fortune.

But the match was settled. Reuben, who already owned a farm, set about building a house, and old Mrs. Romilly, full of bustling importance, began in earnest to prepare her daughter's furniture.

While these operations were going on, Lydia took an opportunity of visiting an acquaintance who resided in Boston. She was induced to go partly to see the capital, but more especially to procure her wedding dress and ornaments in a style superior to what the country afforded. She was determined her wedding should be the most splendid her native town ever witnessed.

While in Boston, she was, at a party, introduced to a young gentleman by the name of Brainard; he was from South Carolina, reputed immensely rich—as all southern people are—he was highly accomplished, and was, of course, very much caressed in the polite circles of the metropolis. Although he had been heard to declare he felt himself perfectly impenetrable to female charms, in a climate where the arrows of Cupid must, at least two-thirds of the year, be tipped with frost, yet at first sight he fell deeply in love with Miss Romilly.

He was informed of her engagement; yet considering

a Yankee rival as no very formidable obstacle to his success, he did not hesitate to declare his passion. He was not half as handsome as her plighted swain, but he was far more fashionably dressed, and had that air of easy elegance and winning confidence in his deportment, which can only be acquired by mixing much with good company, and seeing what is called the world.

These accomplishments could not fail of making some impression on a girl of nineteen, who, notwithstanding her engagement, still felt at liberty to do as she had ever done, consult her own feelings only. Still in her heart she preferred Reuben; but she wished him to know what a fine gentleman her charms had captivated; and this female vanity of seeking to multiply admirers, made her, at last, yield to the importunities of Mr. Brainard, and consent he should accompany her home.

The town of S—— was instantly in an uproar. A proud beauty must never expect friends among her own sex. It requires the utmost suavity of manners on the part of a handsome girl, to make the less favored ones tolerate the superiority which nature has bestowed.

But Miss Lydia Romilly had always carried a very high head, and sure of gaining lovers, had taken no pains to attach friends, or conciliate enemies. Fortunate circumstances more than her own prudence had hitherto prevented her giving much cause for censure; but an opportunity was now presented which nearly all seemed willing to improve.

Mothers harangued their daughters on the monstrous wickedness of thus trifling with a solemn engagement, always concluding with the observation that "Lydia Romilly would never prosper."

The young ladies affected to hold her conduct in the utmost abhorrence; while the young men, who had nearly all bowed to Lydia, felt chagrined and enraged, that the girl, whom they had so eagerly and vainly sought, should be thus easily won by a stranger.

To Reuben Porter the intelligence of her levity was speedily conveyed; no less than fourteen of his very kind friends contriving, in the course of two days, to inform him of the whole transaction, condole with him on the disappointment of his hopes, and offer him all the counsels of their wisdom and experience. Two opposite modes of procedure were, by his lady friends, recommended in the case. One was, to abandon Lydia immediately and utterly, as forever unworthy of his love or confidence.

This advice was offered in the belief that the addresses of the Southern gentleman were only prompted by gallantry; that he had no serious intention of marrying her; and that, if the breach between her and Reuben could be rendered irreconcilable, she would at Brainard's departure, suffer a complete mortification, and verify the old adage, that between two stools, one was sure of coming to the ground.

The other party thinking Brainard's intentions were really serious, and that Lydia was equally anxious to wed him, urged Reuben to assert his claim, and thus prevent the accomplishment of their wishes.

So much for the advice of *disinterested* friends!

But there was one good old lady who really loved both Reuben and Lydia.

"Reuben," said she one day, as he breathed a low sigh, "don't be cast down; all may end happily yet. Lydia loves you, I know she does, and perhaps she is not so much to blame as has been represented. Stories, you know, lose nothing by being carried, and though I would not have you imposed upon, yet let me warn you not to form any hasty resolutions. I always thought you were made for each other, and so I think still, notwithstanding what has happened."

Reuben had hitherto listened, apparently unmoved, to the surmises, guesses and exhortations of his officious friends; but now he started from his seat, grasped the old lady's hand, and pressed it fervently, while a tear moistened his eye, and his voice quivered as he pronounced—"Thank you!" So touching is real sympathy.

Reuben loved Lydia as his life, but he had a good share of Yankee independence in his spirit; and although her unfaithfulness pierced him to the soul, yet he prudently resolved to put a good face on the matter. To compel her to fulfil her engagement, was revolting to his love, and pride forbade his appealing to her compassion. So smothering his emotions, he appeared calmly to await the result of her coquetry. And his conduct was an example of stoicism, which Zeno himself might have acquired credit by imitating.

Lydia, meanwhile, was not without anxiety and self-reproach. Her sense of justice she might perhaps have stifled, but she had not yet brought her mind to contemplate an eternal separation (to use the lover's language) from Reuben, without emotion; and her pride was sorely piqued at the apparent indifference with which he received the intelligence of her defection. But Brainard pressed his suit with so much earnestness, and his riches pleaded his cause so powerfully, that Lydia's parents were much inclined to favor him. True they had the reputation of being very pious people, and no considerations would have induced them to advise a breach of a solemn engagement. Thus far their consciences admonished them. So they just allowed their daughter to do as she pleased in the affair; and when she applied to them for counsel, secretly hoping they would advocate the cause of Reuben, they merely observed—

"That it was for her to decide. Her happiness was at stake. And as Reuben, by not more manfully asserting his right, had tacitly relinquished her, they thought she was at liberty to consult her own inclinations."

In short, to give the result of the affair as concisely as possible, three weeks from the time of Lydia Romilly's return from Boston, saw her the wedded wife of Horace Brainard, and journeying with him to his home in South Carolina!

Poor Reuben! she left thee, but I shall not; and will a single reader, who has a heart of any compassion, grudge to accompany an unfortunate lover a few lines further?

Reuben Porter neither cursed the fickleness of his lost love, nor thanked God he was rid of her: he kept quietly at work on the house he was fitting for her reception; and, although the woman where he boarded thought his eyes, for several successive mornings, looked red and swollen, as if he had passed sleepless nights, and his appetite nearly failed him, yet he never complained. So no one dared insult him by a show of compassion, which is, on such occasions, to a refined or sensitive mind, the most exquisite cruelty.

In a few months he paid his addresses to a very amiable girl. She was not a beauty, but sufficiently pretty to be agreeable, and in every requisite for a good wife, far superior to Lydia Romilly. They married, acquired a handsome property, lived very happily together, and were much beloved by all their acquaintance. Reuben was never heard to allude to his own disappointment but once. His wife bore him several girls in succession —and some one was observing to him, they thought a family of sons far preferable for a farmer, and that one girl was quite sufficient for any family.

"No," he replied, "give me a dozen rather." Then added, laughing—"I am not partial to only daughters. You must remember I was jilted by one."

From this observation people inferred he attributed the fickleness of Lydia's conduct more to her injudicious education than to her heart.

CHAPTER III.

NORTH AND SOUTH.

The lily's hue, the rose's dye,
The kindling lustre of an eye,
Who but owns their magic sway—
Who but feels they all decay!—BURNS.

MRS. BRAINARD, as in future we must call her, did not bid adieu to New England without emotions of regret, and even some feelings of compunction. The parting from her parents, from whom she had experienced nothing but kindness and indulgence, was painful in the extreme—she felt she had liberty to weep; and when the carriage reached the last height that overlooked the village where she had passed so many bright days, and which she was now leaving perhaps forever, she leaned forward to catch another look, and a torrent of tears bedewed her cheeks. They did, indeed, owe some of their bitterness to the remembrance of Reuben—she thought of his affection, his disappointment, and her heart reproached her for the part she had acted.

From the height where she then was, the house Reuben had been building for her was plainly visible. She had assisted him to design it, or alter it rather, and she now recollected how cheerfully he had complied with all her suggestions. One window in particular, she knew he altered to please her, when no other inducement would have prevailed. That window she now beheld, and the train of feeling it awakened, was almost too painful for her undisciplined mind to endure.

Without sufficient stability of principle to guide, she had just piety enough to torment her; and the fear that, for her broken vows, some punishment awaited her in the strange land to which she was going, took immediate possession of her weak fancy.

Her husband, who thought all her grief proceeded from the necessity of separating from her home and parents, tried the usual methods of consolation practiced on such occasions—kissed the tears from her fair cheek, talked of his love, and gratitude, and constancy, all eternal of course; and told her of the thousand amusements awaiting her in a gay city, where his wealth would enable her to command every pleasure she desired.

This last consideration gave her some comfort. Persons who dare not commune with their own hearts, are not only dependent on society for their pleasures, but must seek it as a refuge from anxiety and remorse.

It may be thought strange, Lydia should give her hand to Brainard, when in her heart she really preferred her first love. But one wrong step usually makes many others inevitable. The love of admiration first induced her to admit the addresses of Mr. Brainard; then the cool behavior of Reuben Porter made her fear he would not forgive her levity without concessions, which she disdained to make; and thus she was compelled either to wed the former, or risk being considered a forsaken damsel, a character she abhorred above all things.

It cannot then excite wonder, if Mrs. Brainard's ideas of future felicity, instead of centering in the dear domestic circle over which she was so soon to preside, should borrow many of their tints of happiness from the fashionable and gay diversions to which her husband inconsiderately directed her attention.

That she now felt far from being completely happy, her heart acknowledged; but willing to attribute it to anything rather than her own folly, she complained of the tediousness of traveling, the inconveniences of hotels, and scarcely seeing an object that gave her any satisfaction in the whole way, impatiently urged her husband to hasten his journey.

Mr. Brainard was a gay man, and one who sometimes

yielded his reason to the influence of violent passions, as he had done in his hasty marriage; but he possessed, nevertheless, a generous heart and a cultivated mind.

He was particularly fond of fine scenery, and his principal inducement to visit the North was to examine and take views of some of the sublime prospects nature exhibits in this part of the Union. Often, when alone, had he lingered on the way, and his solitary excursions had afforded him exquisite satisfaction; but he now anticipated an increase of pleasure, when he had such a loved and lovely one by his side, to whom he might whisper his observations, and who, by the delicacy and refinement of her taste and feelings, would correct and improve his own.

What an oversight, that before taking her "for better for worse," he did not ascertain whether she had taste, and how far it was in unison with his own!

However, he soon found she had little admiration to bestow on any object except herself. She must be the fairest flower in every parterre, the object of unceasing solicitude and attention, or she felt neglected and unhappy. Sometimes, in a fit of sudden enthusiasm, he would call on her to admire with him a sublime or beautiful prospect, or endeavor to introduce rational conversation; but the impatience of her countenance and her listless answers, soon convinced him he must change his subject.

Before reaching Charleston, he had become heartily weary of the insipid, common-place chat which only could entertain her, and something very much like a sigh heaved his bosom when reflecting he must travel the journey of life with such a companion.

But he felt certain her face would, in the opinion of the world, excuse him for marrying her; and he determined to become her preceptor, and doubted not, but with a little assiduity on his part, she would become as agreeable a companion as she already was a beautiful mistress.

He had, with all his learning, yet to learn that the woman who has from infancy been accustomed to a constant course of adulation and indulgence, seldom exerts her talents, because she thinks such exertion unnecessary; and the person who presumes to arouse her from this supineness, is sure to excite her displeasure.

Mr. Brainard was the owner of a large plantation about twenty miles from Charleston, and an elegant house in the city. It was to his city residence he first conducted his bride, and there introduced her to his pleasant circle of fashionable acquaintance.

The women allowed she was very pretty, yet each had objections to urge against particular features. One thought her nose too long; another said her forehead was too low; a third disliked blue eyes; and a fourth was quite sure the brilliancy of her complexion was heightened by art; but they all joined in condemning her air and manners as absolutely rustic if not dowdyish.

The men, however, uninfluenced for once by the ladies, unanimously voted her an angel. Whatever was abrupt in her conversation, or ungraceful in her address, was, by them, termed *naiveté*, and, had not the days of chivalry been past, the Northern lass might, in a Southern city, have boasted many a champion of her charms.

It was even rumored that a number of young gentlemen had vowed to go on a pilgrimage to New England before selecting their wives; nay, it was absolutely asserted *one* had departed; but the result of his expedition was never, I believe, made public.

What Mrs. Brainard thought of the new scene to which she was thus introduced, will be best understood by the perusal of two letters which she addressed to her mother soon after her arrival. To explain how these letters fell into my hands, would be a long and needless story; but the reader may depend on their authenticity. Yet the veracity of a historian obliges me to acknowledge they have undergone some alterations. The orthography needed many corrections, and the punctuation had to be entirely supplied. The capital letters, also, were distributed with the utmost impartiality throughout the whole, as often ending a word, as beginning a sentence.

Indeed, no one who saw the crooked, blotted, mis-spelt scrawls, would have imagined a delicate hand had penned, and bright eyes overlooked them. These facts are not recorded for a libel against Mrs. Brainard, but merely as a warning to beautiful young ladies, lest, like her, they should depend on the graces of their persons, and neglect the cultivation of their minds.

For her there was some excuse. Female education had not, at that time, been well provided for even in New England. True, the common schools were open to girls as well as boys; but it was often very difficult for the former to attend. The school-house would be distant and uncomfortable, the roads generally bad; and, though boys could rough it through all ways, winds and weathers, and were sent off as a matter of duty, the delicate little girl was allowed to stay at home—if she chose.

And Lydia Romilly had chosen to stay at home. In summer she complained of the heat, in winter of the cold; and as such a lovely child really seemed to her parents, as our first mother did to Adam,

——— "In herself complete,"

they had indulged her idleness in study, till it was too late to correct the habit. Thus she passed her early youth without any taste for reading, one of the very few among the Yankee girls who never fell in love with the hero of a novel; for, truth to tell, Lydia Romilly never read a work of fiction. Her letters will, I fear, show also that she had not much acquaintance with the facts of authentic history.

* * * * * * * * * *

[LETTER FIRST.]

Charleston City, Dec. 17, 17—.

My Dearest Mother,—I now take my pen to inform you I am well, and hope this letter will find you enjoying the same blessing. We had a very uncomfortable journey, jolting along over the rough roads, up hill and down; but we reached the end of it in safety, which I take to be a special interposition of Providence, considering the great length of the way, and my being totally unused to traveling. Mr. Brainard has a fine house, the prettiest I have seen in Charleston; and I like the house well, and I should like the place very well if it were not for the black people—*niggers* they call 'em here. Oh! dear mother, you know how frightened I always was at a negro—how I used to run behind your chair when old Sampson came to the door, and always screamed when he offered to step in. But, mercy! here the negroes are as thick as bees; the streets are full of 'em. I am sure I did not imagine there were so many in the universe. When our carriage drove up to the gate, out bolted a great black fellow, and Mr. Brainard shook hands with him, and was as glad to see him as could be; but I trembled all over, for I began to remember the stories I had read of slaves murdering their masters and mistresses, and many such bloody things. I guess Mr. Brainard saw I was pale, for he told me not to be frightened at Tom, who was one of the best creatures living. But when we entered the hall, there stood a row of blacks, laughing till their mouths were stretched from ear to ear, to welcome us. They all crowded round my husband, and I was so frightened, thinking some of them might have knives in their hands to kill us, that I could not help shrieking as loud as I could; and the slaves ran away, and Mr. Brainard looked angry, and I hardly know what happened next, for I believe I fainted. I am sure if I had only known this was a negro country, I never would have come here. They have a great many parties and balls here. I don't go to the balls, for I never learned to dance, and I think they are sinful; but I go to all the parties, and dress just as rich and fine as I please. I have a new head-dress, the prettiest thing my eyes ever beheld; I wish you could see it. My husband buys me every thing I ask for, and if I did not eternally see them black people about me, I should be quite happy. Every single day I am urging Mr. Brainard to send them off.

He always tells me it is impossible, and would be cruelty to them, as they are contented and happy, and have no other home or country where they could be received. But I intend to tease him till he does. I don't care where the creatures go to, nor much what becomes of them, if they can only be out of my sight. Pray give my love to Betty Baily, and tell her I wish she would come and live with me, and then I should want no other help. I often tell my husband I could do my work alone, but he laughs, and says, "What a ridiculous thing it would be to see you in the kitchen." And besides, he says, no white person will live long if they attempt to labor in this warm climate. What to do, I know not, but I am determined to get the black creatures away.

Your dutiful daughter,

LYDIA BRAINARD.

[LETTER SECOND.]

" *Charleston City*, *May* 3*d*, 17—.

MY DEAREST MOTHER—I received your kind letter of February first, and I should have answered it immediately, but I have had a world of trouble of late. I do not know how to tell you what I have discovered; but yet I must, that you may pray for me, that my faith may be strengthened, and that I may be kept from temptation. I have often heard you say, the children of professors were especially protected by divine grace; and I am sure I need such protection—for, don't you think Mr. Brainard is a pope, or a papist, I forget which they call 'em, and he goes to a chapel and calls it a meeting, when it is no more like our meetings than it is like a ball. I have been twice, but I am determined to go no more, and I say everything I can against it, for it is so different from our christian worship I am sure it must be wrong. I am sure you will be very much shocked to hear of this, and I was when I discovered it; and I have a thousand times wished myself in New England. But don't say a word about it—you know who I would not have hear of it for all the world.

I have everything money can command to content me; and if Mr. Brainard would only send away his *servants*, as he calls them, and go to a congregational meeting, I think I should be quite happy. But these blacks are always at my elbow. Here's one just been into the room to see if I wanted anything, but I bade her to go about her business. If my husband will keep them he may order them—I will not, for they frighten me out of my senses. Mr. Brainard is very kind to them, and they love him like a brother, though he will keep them in slavery; while they hate me, I know they do, yet I tell them every day I wish they were in Guinea. But they are a stupid, ungrateful race, and I detest them perfectly.

I have a new carpet for my parlor—very beautiful indeed. Father would say it was too handsome to walk on; but yet, I don't know how it is, such fine things, now I have them so common, are not half so pleasing as I expected they would be. I have to sit about, with nothing to do, till I am quite low spirited; and then I think how I used to enjoy myself when at home—how I could work and sing the whole day. Oh! I shall never be so happy again. Give my love to all my friends.

Your dutiful daughter,
LYDIA BRAINARD."

CHAPTER IV.

THE HERO CHOSEN.

Will fortune never come with both hands full?
She either gives a stomach, and no food—
Such are the poor in health; or else a feast,
And takes away the stomach; such the rich,
That have abundance and enjoy it not.
[KING HENRY IV., PART 2d.

FROM the letters in the foregoing chapter, the domestic management of Mrs. Brainard may be easily understood. Educated from her infancy to consult her own feelings only, neither the interest, the happiness, nor the wishes of her husband, could induce her to yield to the necessity of the case, and endeavor to conquer her antipathy to the blacks. It was not principle but prejudice that actuated her conduct. She cared little for their fate if removed from her sight. She feared and detested them, and they reciprocated her dislike. They had rather be whipped than hated.

It was in vain her husband attempted to reason with her—told her that his father, on his death bed, in consigning to his care the servants, had solemnly charged him to treat them kindly, and never to sell or alienate those who conducted well. He told her, moreover, that no one could hold the system of slavery in greater abhorrence than himself; but the peculiar circumstances under which the slaveholders were placed, rendered a relinquishment of their right over their slaves, for the present, impracticable. But that he, with every noble minded gentleman, inhabiting the south, anticipated the day, when the necessity for slavery would cease to exist, and when their country, in being freed from its curse, would wipe off the only blot that stained her character.

His arguments were given to the winds. The usual answer of Mrs. Brainard was, that there were no slaves in New England, and there was no need of having any in South Carolina.

Then the discovery that her husband was a Roman Catholic, was a still more serious affair. His belief, like that of the generality of men, was more the effect of habit and education, than of reflection or serious examination. His parents, who lived as Christians ought to live, and died as Christians must wish to die, were Catholics; and the remembrance of their virtues and piety, hallowed, in the heart of their son, the religion they professed. Yet he was *not* bigoted to its particular tenets, and his kindliness of disposition always inclined him to think favorably of the motives of human conduct, and of the religions that differed from his own.

Mrs. Brainard's piety, however, was of quite a contrary spirit. Elected to salvation, she had nothing to do but accept, and then there was no possibility of her failing to gain the crown, however she might loiter by the way, or deviate from the prescribed course. And she could not believe any one would be saved who had not an experience to relate, and who had not been convicted and converted in the regular way. She had faith, but forgot to add to her faith patience, or charity, which is the greatest of all. Having naturally a timid mind, and being inclined to superstition, she imagined her husband's infidelity, for so she termed his liberal principles, was to punish her for her unfaithfulness to Reuben Porter.

But the history of matrimonial infelicity is an unpleasant subject, especially when, as in the present case, it seems to be owing more to what may be termed fate and necessity, than folly or vice.

The truth was, the habits, opinions, and tastes, of the husband and wife were totally dissimilar, and neither was willing to make concessions, or relinquish their favorite theories.

He thought, as husbands are apt to think, that it was his prerogative to rule, and his wife's happiness must consist in studying and contributing to his.

She rarely reasoned much on any subject. Her wishes had, beneath the paternal roof, been laws to all who approached her; and the transition from a goddess receiving adoration to an obedient wife, was a falling off to which, as she had never anticipated, she did not submit with a very good grace.

Those whom Providence seems to favor by bestowing the means of luxury without the necessity of labor, are often the least enviable of our species. If they have much leisure, they will soon find it a heavy commodity on their hands, and be willing to exchange it even for the most trivial amusements and unprofitable pursuits. None, save a judiciously disciplined mind, is fitted to properly enjoy and dignify leisure.

It was certainly very unfortunate for Mrs. Brainard, that no necessity existed for the exertion of her industry. She was naturally industrious; and had they been poor, the efforts to procure a livelihood would have prevented that melancholy vacuity of mind she experienced while sauntering from apartment to apartment in her splendid mansion, where nothing required her care, and nothing interested her feelings.

She soon found it was possible to be very rich and very wretched; while Mr. Brainard became convinced, that the personal beauty of a wife added little to her husband's felicity.

The consequences may be easily divined. Instead of passing his happiest hours beneath his own roof, Mr. Brainard sought his pleasures in the circles of dissipation. The race ground, billiard table and theatre, were his favorite places of diversion; yet his good sense and natural prudence prevented his falling a victim to vice, although he was fast becoming a votary of folly.

His wife, who had fewer resources for killing time, was

soon the prey of ennui and discontent. Had they been blest with children, their story would doubtless have been a different one. A common offspring hallows the union of a wedded pair far more than the benediction of the priest. They then sympathize in the same hopes, fears and affections, and each day draws closer and closer the bonds of interest and self-love; for they love themselves in their race, till their union becomes inseparable by any thing save death.

This bond, however, did not operate in the case of Mr. and Mrs. Brainard, for children they had none; and the disappointment of their wishes sensibly diminished their tenderness for each other. There were not, to be sure, any gross insults or outrages against propriety, offered by either; but there was a constant clashing of sentiments, a perpetual disagreement in tastes and opinions, a kind of querulousness on the part of the wife, and contempt on that of the husband, which rendered their domestic society irksome and unpleasant to all who joined it; to themselves it must have been most disagreeable and repulsive.

In this manner they passed nearly twenty years, Mrs. Brainard often entreating her husband to take her to New England; but as she scrupulously insisted on the fulfilment of a promise he had given her mother, to go the whole journey by land, he had a good excuse for declining her request. And perhaps she never would have had an opportunity of revisiting her native state, had not a severe fit of sickness come opportunely to her aid. Her physician pronounced traveling indispensable to the perfect recovery of her health; and her emaciated countenance awakening, in the heart of her husband, pity and remorse, rekindled in some measure his first tenderness for her.

He could not forbear reflecting that by promises of enduring love and unwearied care, he had prevailed on her to leave the home of her childhood, and the dear friends who delighted to cherish and indulge her. Nay, more; for him she had forsaken a lover, who would doubtless have made her a far more fitting husband than he had done. It was not probable her life would continue long, and Brainard, with the generosity natural to his disposition, when his better feelings predominated, determined to gratify her wishes.

Accordingly they started for New Hampshire, and, traveling by easy stages, arrived without accident at the end of their monotonous journey. But twenty years had wrought strange changes. Both parents of Mrs. Brainard were in their graves; her brothers had all, James excepted, emigrated to other states, and of her early companions and friends, but very few remained in her native village.

"I came to the place of my birth, and said, 'the friends of my youth, where are they?'—and echo answered, 'where are they?'"

Mrs. Brainard had never read the sentiment, but her heart felt its force; and, feeble and melancholy, she entreated her husband to take her to the town where she understood her brother James, now dignified by the title of James Romilly, Esq., resided.

She had left him a lad of sixteen, lively, ardent, and unfearing; she found him an enterprising, intelligent, and respectable man, happily employed on a farm, which he had purchased with his own earnings, and now cultivated with his own hands. A neat, commodious house, a pleasant, happy looking wife, and half a dozen lovely children, were the pledges of his felicity.

"We have but a small house to receive you in," said Mr. Romilly to his splendidly dressed visitors, "but your welcome is as sincere as though we could usher you into a palace."

"I doubt it not," returned Mr. Brainard, "and you have all that is really necessary to happiness—health, a competency, and those dear ones," glancing his eyes on the group of little laughing faces which were stretching forward, eager to catch a peep at the strangers.

The children were immediately called forward; their names repeated, and the good qualities and promising abilities of each enumerated and dilated upon somewhat at length by their delighted mother, who, though a very sensible woman, had yet the mother's weakness of being dotingly fond of her children.

Mrs. Brainard beheld her brother's happiness with feelings very much like envy; certainly with deep repinings at her own less favored lot. She had wealth to gratify every whim, but finding its enjoyment did not satisfy her heart, she considered it worthless, and often thought she would willingly part with it all, could she only have one sweet child to call her by the endearing name of "mother," and embrace her as affectionately as the children did her sister-in-law. She could not bear the thought of returning to her desolate home and living in the cheerless domestic solitude which had so long preyed on her spirits.

"I shall never have a child of my own," said she to herself one day, as she sat tracing in the infantile features of her brother's children the resemblance of her deceased parents; "but I will beg one of these—my brother cannot refuse me—and then I will have something to live for."

No sooner had this idea taken possession of her mind, than she hastened to impart it to her husband, hoping he would aid her in the accomplishment of a plan which now seemed indispensable to her happiness, and almost necessary to her existence.

Mr. Brainard had secretly formed the same wish. He had no near relative who needed his property, and flattered himself, if he could obtain a son of Mr. Romilly, and educate him as his own, he should then transmit his immense wealth to one who, grateful for the gift, would, by his assiduity and filial respect, endeavor to merit the favor.

Seldom had the husband and wife been so well agreed on any subject as in the design of obtaining one of the little rosy checked urchins, who now bounded by them, all frolic and happiness; as unconscious and uncaring of the proud fortune which awaited one of their number, as

MR. BRAINARD SELECTING AN HEIR.

were the children of Jesse, when the prophet came to select from among them a king to reign over Israel. But the motives of choice in the two cases were widely different. The prophet did not regard the outward appearance, nor the age; Mr. Brainard and his wife were almost entirely influenced by these considerations.

Sidney was the eldest, and would soon be a companion for them; he had a fair countenance, and would do honor to their selection.

These were the first requisitions; then Mrs. Brainard recollected his mother had told her how sweet-tempered and docile he was, and what an excellent scholar.

"And," said she, "any one may know he is amiable, by only looking on his face; and for genius, there never was a Romilly deficient in that."

Mr. Brainard smiled. He might, perhaps, have named one exception, but his good nature, or good breeding, prevented, and he only remarked, he wished they might obtain the child.

Mrs. Brainard undertook to procure her brother's consent, while her husband was to try his rhetoric on Mrs. Romilly, from whose maternal tenderness they apprehended the most serious opposition to their plan.

It would be too tedious to detail all that was said and thought on this occasion. I will not believe it would be uninteresting; for can the deep emotions of parental love, contending with the powerful temptations of ambition and interest, be an uninteresting exhibition to those who would analyze the human mind, by tracing the operations of its most potent passions?

The parents hesitated long, and not till a few days before the time fixed by Mr. Brainard for the conclusion of his visit, did they give a decisive answer to his proposal of taking Sidney to South Carolina, adopting him for his own son, educating him in the best manner, and making him sole heir to his vast possessions.

"What answer shall we give?" said Mr. Romilly to his wife, as they were discussing the matter after the family had retired for the night. "I wish to subdue my own feelings, and act wholly for the best interests of our child."

Mrs. Romilly sighed. She thought the boy's interest would certainly be promoted by going, and that such was the conclusion at which his father was intending to arrive.

"If I thought it was the will of heaven," said she, in a low tone, "I would submit. I have often thought something singular would happen to that child. Don't you remember what strange dreams I have had about him?—that, in particular, which I thought portended his death?"

"No, I do not recollect it," replied her husband.

"Well, perhaps I never told it you," returned she; "but I dreamed I was looking out of our east window, and I saw a man riding up the lane, full speed, on a coal black horse. The man was a stranger to me then, but since I have seen brother Brainard, I think he did resemble him. Well, he came up to the door, took Sidney by the hand, and placed him on the horse, and galloped off as fast as he could, and they were soon out of sight. I told the dream to Mrs. Watson, and she said a black horse always betokened prosperity, and she should think Sidney would have good fortune."

"I hope it may prove so," answered her husband, who had listened to his wife's dream and Mrs. Watson's interpretation thereof without a single smile or "pshaw!"—(would all husbands be as well bred?)—"but I own I have not much faith in presages; still, I have always, myself, cherished the idea, that Sidney was born to be distinguished; and I have been forming every plan I could devise to give him a liberal education, yet, I fear, I shall not be able. We have a number of children already, and shall probably have more; and the income of my farm will only give us a comfortable support. May not this offer of our friends be an interposition of Providence to fulfill my anxious wishes? And now, shall we murmur, and refuse the blessing, because it is not bestowed in just the way we desire? And I know

Sidney has been our idol. May not his removal from us, for a time, be in mercy, lest by rejoicing in the gift, and forgetting the giver, we merit a more severe trial?"

There was a long pause. Both felt Sidney must go; yet neither had courage to express their feelings.

"How can I bear the separation?" said Mrs. Romilly, at length.

"We must endure separation from those we love," replied her husband, pressing her hand in his. "Even we must part! and in that solemn day our sweetest consolation will be, that we have, to the best of our abilities, discharged faithfully the duties incumbent on us, even though their performance was painful."

Mrs. Romilly wept; but she urged no more objections, and the departure of Sidney was considered certain, and preparations were accordingly made.

Had Mr. and Mrs. Romilly known exactly the situation and principles of those to whose care they were consigning their darling child, they would never have consented to his departure. But happy themselves, blessed and blessing each other, they hardly thought family disagreements possible; and shame and pride had operated on the minds of their visitors, and prevented them from revealing their domestic troubles.

How could Mrs. Brainard, while displaying her rich satins and laces, and costly jewels, to her admiring sister-in-law, acknowledge they were worn to conceal the throbbings of a discontented and despairing heart, and that with all her riches and splendor she was a prey to grief? No, she could not humble herself so far. Had her mother been living, she would have poured into her pitying ear the tale of her distresses; but now she endeavored to appear as cheerful as possible, and her altered countenance was ascribed altogether to the ravages of time and disease.

She had made a profession of religion when very young, before she was married, and from her conversation her brother ascertained she still held fast her hope. It was true he did not see in her that spirit of humility so lovely in a Christian; but he considered her situation and habits of living were very different from his, and charity bade him make many allowances. He knew also, that Mr. Brainard was far from being an orthodox believer, but the affability of his manners, and the generosity and kindness of his temper, seemed pledges of his tender care to the child he was adopting; and Mr. Romilly, who always saw the good in every character, and excused, if possible, the evil, hoped he would yet be won by the pious conversation of his wife, to embrace religion.

The day of separation at length came, and passed, as every day will, whether brightened by joy or saddened by grief; and the evening found Mr. Romilly and his wife seated in their accustomed places before the fire. A small table stood between them, on which lay her work and an open Bible, in which he was preparing to read a chapter, as a part of his evening devotions. It was a custom he never omitted, always taking the chapters in succession, till he had read the whole Bible, and then again turning to the beginning.

The chapter which came in rotation that evening, was the forty-sixth of Genesis, and when reading the particulars of the meeting of Jacob with his son Joseph, Mr. Romilly came to that affecting exclamation of the aged father,—

"Now let me die, since I have seen thy face, and thou art alive, my son!" his voice quivered, and he paused. A moment of affecting silence ensued, which was broken by the hysterical sobs of his wife.

"Mary—my dear Mary," said he, taking her trembling hand, "we must be calm. God can restore our child, and I have faith to believe He will, in His own good time, grant us to see that dear boy's face again. Let us rely on His goodness, and seek His protecting grace for ourselves and children."

So saying he arose, and leaning over his chair, (a position in which the descendants of the puritans usually addressed the throne of grace,) he breathed forth the feelings of his soul in a most fervent petition to the Being whom he loved and trusted. He prayed for fortitude, faith, and resignation, for himself, and her who was dearer than himself; and he prayed for his absent child, that he might be kept from temptation, and preserved from every snare; and oh! how earnestly he entreated that, although they might be denied the happiness of seeing him again on earth, they might all meet in that glorious world where there are no changes to dread, no separations to grieve!

From that time the parents were resigned to the destination of Sidney: true, his name often trembled on the lips of his mother, but it was only to wish they might hear he had reached the end of his journey in safety.

And in due time her desire was gratified. A letter arrived, filled with Sidney's praises, and the thanks of his uncle and aunt for such a good boy. This letter was a treasure, especially to Mrs. Romilly. She read it at least fifty times in the course of the week, and every person who called, being supposed interested in the intelligence it conveyed, had to listen to its contents. And her kind heart was not mistaken in her friends and neighbors. Nearly all rejoiced with her; yet truth must be told, however it may shame poor human nature. There were, even in that secluded and friendly place, a few good ladies who made visiting the business of their afternoons, and talking that of their lives. These tea-drinking veterans did not, in their hearts, love Mrs. Romilly; she was too strict a "keeper at home" to obtain their favor; yet they usually contrived to spend an afternoon with her every two or three weeks, just to scold her for not returning their visits.

And when, with all the mother in her voice and countenance, she read to them the letter she had received concerning Sidney, one remarked, that "his uncle might give him a great fortune, and make a gentleman of him, but, for her part, no earthly consideration should ever tempt her to let one of her children go such a distance."

Another said, "the climate was very unhealthy, and she should not be surprised if the boy didn't live a year."

While a third observed, that "if she had let one of her children go to such a far away place, and he did die, she should never forgive herself;" adding, "there is no one will take care of a sick child like an own mother."

Mrs. Romilly's heart sunk within her at these suggestions. She feared she had done wrong in giving her consent to Sidney's departure, and could scarcely speak without weeping the whole afternoon.

"Ah!" said her husband, when, to his eager inquiries of what disturbed her, she had related the conversation of the gossips, "Ah! Mary, you are too good and benevolent yourself to suspect envy or ill-will in others; but do you really think those women are kinder mothers, and love their children better than you do yours? No, it is all fudge; and when they read you another lecture on maternal tenderness, tell them to evince theirs by staying at home and taking care of their families."

Another and another letter succeeded, filled with good tidings concerning Sidney; and for a whole year, scarce a fortnight passed without bringing intelligence of his health, growth, and progress in literature and in the hearts of his friends. Then the letters began to be more rare, and finally became much like "angels' visits," owing, no doubt, to the multiplicity of engagements in which Mr. Brainard was involved.

So, at least, thought Mr. Romilly, and his wife was more easy under the neglect than might have been expected. But besides the effect which time naturally has in diminishing our concern, and diverting our thoughts from the absent, there was another reason which reconciled Mrs. Romilly to at least a partial suspension of the correspondence from South Carolina.

Mr. Brainard never paid the postage on his letters. Rich people rarely do: a shilling is of so little consequence to them, they think it as trifling to others. But the postage on his letters to New Hampshire being then twenty-five cents per letter, amounted, in the course of a year, to a pretty round sum for a Yankee farmer to pay, who was not much in the habit of corresponding, and Mrs. Romilly felt willing it should be lessened. Accordingly, when her messenger returned from the post office with tidings of "no letter to-day," although she felt disappointed, it was a consolation to reflect they had "no postage to pay."

"Should anything serious befall our child," said she to her husband, "they will inform us; and my mother always used to say, 'no news is good news.'"

And thus, in peace, sufficiency and content, lived this good and happy pair.

> "Retirement, rural quiet, friendship, books,
> Ease and alternate labor, useful life,
> Progressive virtue and approving heaven,
> These are the matchless joys of virtuous love."

And these, for nearly thirteen years following the departure of their son, they enjoyed in as perfect a degree as the nature of humanity will permit. In that space of time, they had added four fine children to their household, which, with their former ones, made altogether a pretty round number.

Yet Sidney was not forgotten. Often did his father, in a particular manner, allude, in his evening devotions, to the dear absent one; and never did a Thanksgiving pass without his saying, as he looked on his plentifully-supplied table, surrounded by smiling, happy faces, "Oh! if Sidney were only here, my joy would be complete." Then the sigh or tear from his wife reminding him he must check his own feelings to support her's, he would add, "But it is best as it is; we have as many children as we can provide for, and Sidney is well off."

During the last four years, they had received but two letters, both from Sidney: the first reporting the decease of his aunt, Mrs. Brainard; the other giving an account of a tour he had made through Virginia, and describing in particular Mount Vernon and the tomb of Washington. Both letters were warmly admired as well as welcomed;

yet Silas and James, the two brothers next in age to Sidney, contended the handwriting was not equal to theirs, and thought it strange that a scholar, who had nothing to do but study, should write no better than Yankee lads, whose education had been solely acquired by attending a district or common school a few months in each year. Their mother, however, warmly supported the cause of her first born, asserting his superiority, especially in flourishes, of which, it must be admitted, he had been very profuse.

Mr. Romilly was called upon to settle, by his opinion, the point in controversy. After examining the specimens quite as attentively as do literary committees the addresses submitted for the New Year's prize, he finally decided in favor of the two younger claimants, adding, by way of appeasing his wife:

"Sidney does, indeed, write well, but so many flourishes are unnecessary. It is utility, and not show, we should encourage. A good handwriting requires no ornament, and a vile one no ornament can conceal."

From this decision and these remarks, we may safely infer that Mr. Romilly was, in practice as well as theory, a real republican.

CHAPTER V.

THE RETURN.

What recollections memory's power restores,
Home of my childhood, thy beloved shores!
Fair bursting through oblivion's mist appear
Thy deep-green vales, bold hills and fountains clear:
Again the crag abrupt I climb, and now
Pluck the wild berries purpling o'er its brow:
Days of untroubled joy! yet why deplore
Days fled forever, joys that come no more?
[HOME, A POEM.

AUTUMN in New England! The idea is fraught with glory and beauty indescribable. To-day, the forest is green and full-leaved, as when Spring left her work to the warm hand of Summer. Over the wide panorama of mountain and valley shines the clear October sun, bright, but not warm; for the north wind is abroad, sweeping the clouds from the sky, and chilling the dews gathering in upper air.

The sun goes down; and the wind, as if weary, sinks to rest; and through the long night the stars seem watching the change of nature. Sleep reigns over the earth; the trees are motionless; the frost only is abroad. His cold breath has chilled the heart of the forest, and its life-blood no longer flows. The finger of Death passes over the foliage, and the touch has left a lustre life never displayed.

Go forth when the morning rises, and the old woods stand before you in gorgeous robes, as though rainbows had been lavishing their colors as a pledge of the return of life and spring!

These wonderful changes of the autumnal forest are

seen nowhere in such beauty and variety as in the Old Granite State; and the wild scenery of that mountain-land is then gorgeous in its magnificence. But the charm soon passes. Winter storms are gathering, and the rich garniture of leaves is torn off by the blast, and scattered, trodden down, destroyed, illustrating the fate of all human glory.

But the glory of nature never departs; and to the eye that sees the Great Architect in his work,

"Though all the gay foppery of nature is flown,"

the earth is still beautiful. And our autumn has a period of peculiar and mysterious loveliness, called the "Indian summer." This brief season, of about twelve days in the whole, though rarely following in consecutive order, is most beautiful and most distinctly marked in New England. The softness of the atmosphere is then indescribable. The sun looks down as though dreaming of June and its roses; while some "tricksy spirit" throws over the faded earth a veil that, mirage-like, gives a charm beyond the brightness of summer noon. This is most perfect in November.

It was perfect when our story opens.

The turnpike leading from Concord, N. H., to Portsmouth, passes directly through the retired, but *romantically*-situated town of Northwood, in the county of Rockingham. On this route, and near where the turnpike entered the western part of the town, Landlord Holmes had, some twenty-five or thirty years ago, established himself: he had just opened a new tavern, and all his thoughts were employed in contriving how to obtain customers, or how to please them. The seasons rolled round without bringing any pleasure to him, except they brought company; and on that account he considered the winter as far the most agreeable part of the year.

So now, although he stood calmly smoking his pipe under the "Sign of the Eagle," (which, by the way, very much resembled a turkey,) and gazing attentively around, let no one imagine he was delighted with the prospect. And yet the prospect was delightful, when the sun, suddenly bursting forth from behind a dark cloud, which had, for the last half hour, totally obscured his brightness, threw his rich beams on the leafless forest trees and seared fields, till the russet covering assumed a silvery hue, as the flood of light quivered over its surface.

But the landlord thought not on the beauty of the afternoon, except to wonder more heartily at the unaccountable delay of the stage, which usually reached his house two hours earlier.

"The dinner will be totally spoiled," cried his wife, in a shrill voice, from within.

"How can I help it," replied her husband gruffly, "except I eat it myself? But look! yonder they come, as sure as eggs—very carefully, though—some accident has certainly happened."

The stage drove slowly up; and while the passengers were alighting, the landlord inquired the reason of the delay.

"Oh! it was all on account of a sick man, who could not bear to be driven fast," answered the driver; "but he has paid me well for the delay, and now, landlord, I shall leave him with you to provide for."

"Provide for!" eagerly ejaculated the landlord. "Why, does he intend staying here?"

"No longer than while you can harness your horses," answered the other. "He and another gentleman are intending to go somewhere to the south part of the town, to visit some relations, I guess; and I told them you could doubtless furnish them with a carriage."

"But I can't," replied the landlord; "I have no carriage at home, except the old wagon, and none to drive it but little Zeb."

"Why, where the deuce are all your carriages?" inquired the driver.

"Oh, the boys have taken the new wagon and gone off to the shooting-match," said the landlord; "to-morrow is Thanksgiving day, you know, and the *gals* are gone in the chaise to the store, to buy some furbelows for the ball; and none of 'em will be at home till pitch dark, I dare say. There's nothing done here the day before nor day after Thanksgiving."

"Well, well," replied the driver, "you can see the gentlemen, and then conclude what to do. I shall leave 'em here, and they may take care of themselves, which they can do pretty well, I guess, for they have money plenty."

This last item of information brightened the landlord's countenance, and his step was quick and light as he entered his house to reconnoitre the strangers.

Whether, like our own statesmen, they merely exerted their eloquence, or whether, like British ministers in the olden times, they offered a bribe, I am not able to say, but it seems the means they employed were successful. The corpulent landlord was soon seen puffing and bustling about, exerting himself to clean and repair his old wagon for an expedition. Zeb, too, came out, habited in his Sunday suit, with his hat set smartly on his head, and cracking his whip with all the importance of a veteran postillion. Everything was planned to make the worse appear the better—a large buffalo-skin covered and concealed, in part, the decayed seat of the crazy vehicle; but the sagacious landlord could devise no expedient which would conceal the defects of a steed, that in appearance and qualities very nearly resembled the Vicar of Wakefield's old blackberry. Soon all was pronounced ready, and the two gentlemen appeared to take their seats.

One, whose countenance bore traces of recent and severe illness, had doubtless been a stout man, for his clothes hung loosely on him, and there were wrinkles on his face which did not appear to be the effect of years. He was very pale, but the brightness of his eye told that his heart was glad with the hope of returning health, although its current had not yet sent the glow to mantle on his sunken cheek. His stature was rather below the middle size, yet he had an air of conscious superiority, usually imparted by high rank, that added dignity to his figure, and his address and manners bore ample evidence of the refinement and elegance to which he had been accustomed; and, on the whole, though there was nothing peculiarly striking or interesting either in his face or form, yet whoever looked on him would wish to look again.

The other gentleman, on whose arm he leaned, was of a very different appearance. Tall and symmetrically formed, his figure was a model of elegance united with the appearance of strength and activity; and nature, as if disdaining, for once, the assistance of art, in striking him off, had stamped on every lineament, and impressed on every movement, the perfect gentlemen. His eyes were dark hazel, yet when agitated by emotions of any kind, either of pleasure or anger, the lighting up of his countenance gave to them such a lustre that they were almost always mistaken for black, and several wagers had been lost in deciding on their color. His dark hair clustered thickly around a high forehead, whose polished whiteness proved the original tincture of his skin to have possessed all the delicacy of a lady's. True, the climate in which he had resided, or the exposure of a journey had bronzed it a little, and his cheek did not wear the northern freshness; yet his was a face that would excite curiosity and admiration, and the eye that rested on him would be loath to withdraw its gaze.

Neither did his countenance lose any of its interest from a shade of melancholy which, at times, passed over his fine features; for the beholder always felt an involuntary sympathy in his fortunes, and it will, I believe, be generally found that the world sympathizes more willingly and sincerely with the sorrowful than the gay. But the smile that now hovered on his lip seemed to speak only of felicity, and the mellow tones of his clear voice, while making inquiries of the landlord, were kind as the accents of a friend, rejoicing to meet and learn the welfare of beloved objects after a long separation.

The landlord was minute in his directions, and his last words, as they started, were an order to Zeb, to "drive slowly, remember and keep the right-hand road, and be sure and take a long sweep when he turned."

Phæton's example was an evil one, no doubt, but he has found many imitators. There never yet was a youthful hand entrusted with the reins, that always guided them steadily, and Zeb was not exempt from the ambition of wishing to display his skill as a coachman, now he had mounted the box—or chair rather, such being the substitute for the driver's seat.

Exerting all his strength, therefore, he applied his long-lashed whip with such good will that he succeeded for once in starting the lazy beast upon a furious trot, which, as the road was none of the smoothest, and the wagon seat had no springs, was rather too stirring an exercise for the nerves of an invalid. The gentlemen loudly ordered him to stop; and, prompt to obey the order, the boy pulled the reins violently, and the horse, much more willingly obeying the rein than whip, stopped so suddenly, that the shock nearly threw them both from their seats.

"What the devil did the fellow mean, Romilly," cried the sick man, as soon as he could recover himself, "by giving us such a rumbling old ark as this? Or, perhaps," added he, seeing his companion's mirth, "perhaps this is your real Yankee style."

"True Yankee style," replied the other, who was, indeed, Sidney Romilly, and who had been nearly convulsed with laughter. "Now, boy, drive on, but slowly;" and then composing his countenance, and turning to his friend, he added, gravely, "you will, doubtless, Mr. Frankford, in a short time learn to appreciate our fashions."

"Not at the expense of my bones, I hope. Oh! they are half dislocated already. Pray, how far have we to ride in this manner?"

"About two miles, or perhaps three."

"And all the way over such an execrable road?"

"Why, the road that leads towards my own native home cannot seem execrable to me," answered Sidney.

"The objects begin, already, to look familiar. See yonder mountain, where the rays of the sun are now striking! I have climbed that mountain many a time, and it looks like a friend."

"And those ragged rocks and stumps, black as if they had just risen from the infernal pit, are your old acquaintances, I presume," replied Frankford. "Come, Romilly, you must confess your Yankee farmers are the most slovenly people on earth that pretend to civilization. Look at the half cleared fields, and fences falling down before they are finished, and timber houses placed plump in the highway; what would an English farmer say to such management?"

"Mr. Frankford," replied Sidney, "perhaps I might show you the unreasonableness of expecting to find the appearance of a country, which scarcely fifty years ago was an unexplored wilderness, corresponding in agricultural improvements and neatness of appearance with one settled and cultivated for nearly twenty centuries. But we have not time, neither do I now feel an inclination for argument. My mind has sweeter fancies, and I shall not even attempt to defend my country from your criticism. I wish only to enjoy its beauties."

He spoke with energy, and the Englishman, who really possessed the candor and generosity which many of his countrymen only affect, although so deeply imbued with the national contempt for everything American, that he sometimes forgot his good breeding and good feelings while expressing his sentiments, immediately asked pardon for what he had said.

"'Tis granted," replied Sidney, smiling; "the jolting you have just undergone, was certainly a sufficient provocation for your severity; and it has diverted your attention from our carriage, which, I confess, deserves all your anathemas. But now which road do we take?"

"The straight forward one," said the boy.

"But we are going to the south parish," said Sidney, and must certainly turn south to reach it."

"I know it, sir," replied the pertinacious Zeb, "but we go half a mile further before we turn."

"Look at the roads, Romilly!" cried the Englishman, "and be sure take the best. 'Tis always my maxim. I like to travel in a smooth road, and I have always found such led to the most agreeable places."

"Take that turning to the left," said Sidney.

"You are certainly wrong, sir," said Zeb, still holding fast the reins, "and so you will find, for that road goes to the mill."

"Then to the mill we will go," replied Frankford: "turn, I say."

The boy slowly obeyed the order.

"A true slip from the Puritan stock, I'll warrant him," continued the Englishman, "determined to have his own way—that was their liberty of conscience."

"Yes," said Sidney, "and to that unconquered and unconquerable spirit, we owe the settlement, independence, and glory of America."

"And its republicanism, you may add," replied the Englishman; "and that I like in theory but not in practice. I like to hear and to read of liberty. It is a glorious thing to repeat a 'nation is free,' if we did not find the tyranny of the people to be far more galling than that of the prince. In a country where men boast of equality, where there are no distinctions of rank, no established customs, no certain forms of respect instituted towards superiors, there the rabble rule, for there is always a rabble in every community. And whose pride is most insupportable, that of the upstart, covered with filth, or the gentleman, who, feeling secure of his own dignity, is not constantly puffing it about your ears?"

"If I receive a kick," replied Sidney, "I care little whether the foot which bestowed it be covered with a shoe of leather or prunella. One, to be sure, may inflict a deeper wound than the other, but a blow is a blow. Yet I think, sir, you mistake the organization of our society. Nor is it at all strange, as no age nor country can produce a parallel. We really enjoy what the Greeks and Romans, with all their boasts, never did—rational freedom; and every person is equally protected by mild and equitable laws; but laws which he can neither defy nor evade. As men wish to be treated, so they must treat others; and thus the principle of self-love operates to prevent insults from being offered. And this intercourse between equals is marked by a courtesy of demeanor, equally free from fawning servility or overbearing arrogance, which you will in vain seek where distinctions of rank are organized and supported."

"At least," returned Mr. Frankford, "you must allow that, for the rich and superior classes, the intercourse with the world is more agreeable and refined where those little observances are attended to. There can be no community where all are precisely on a level. The superiority of wealth, intelligence and virtue, even the differences of age, and distinctions of sex, render a different address to different persons proper and necessary. In this particular, I think your countrymen are deficient. For instance, this little urchin here, whose answers, I confess, now awakened these ideas—why, he speaks to us with just the same *sang froid* he would to a school fellow. What he says is pertinent and intelligent enough, but there is wanting that preface of respect with which, in every other civilized country, we should be addressed. He has not once said 'your honor,' or 'your worship,' nor do I believe he ever heard those terms used when speaking to a superior."

"Did you ever call any man 'your honor,' or 'your worship,' Zeb?" asked Sidney, settling his countenance with all the gravity in his power.

The boy, glancing round his roguish eye with an expression which showed not a syllable had been lost on him, said, "I never saw any gentleman with such names in my life."

The arch simplicity of his manner made the Englishman smile, and Sidney, laughing heartily, was about to reply, when his attention was diverted by the appearance of a man coming towards them, to whom Zeb desired they would speak, and inquire if that road did not lead to the mill. There was not, however, much room for doubt, as the man was then evidently returning from such a place. He was driving a horse before him, laden with bags, whistling the air of "Yankee Doodle," and looking around him with perfect unconcern.

"There," said Sidney; "now, Frankford, you may see a genuine Yankee; I know by his whistle he is a true one. You have often enough heard him described and beheld him caricatured; now look at the original."

The age of the man might be about five and thirty; he was nearly six feet in height, and rather spare; but showed such an athletic and vigorous form as might well entitle him to the character of being the "bone and muscle" of the land. He was habited in a dark colored suit, made of what is termed "home manufactured;" for the celebrated Lucretia herself could not spin with a more becoming grace than *did*, at that time, the fair wives and daughters of the New England farmers; and, not to keep their families comfortably clothed, would have reflected great discredit on their industry, and consequently on their characters. His clothes were fitted nearly in the London fashion, though the fashion of a year gone by; for every individual being ambitious to appear well dressed, and antiquity not having sanctioned any particular form for the habit, nor necessity obliging our citizens to appear in the suits of their ancestors, "the fashions" are, by all classes and ages, more universally followed throughout the United States, than by any other nation in the world. A red bandanna handkerchief was tied around his neck, above which rose his shirt collar, white as the driven snow; boots and a good hat completed his array, which appeared to unite comfort and economy with a tolerable degree of taste, and showed the wearer was one who thought something of himself, and meant to appear in such a manner as to claim attention and respect from others. As they drew nearer he ceased his whistling, and taking his horse by the bridle, led him on one side of the road to allow the wagon to pass more conveniently.

Zeb's steed stopped the moment he came opposite, as if anticipating his young master's desire to learn the route.

"Is this the direct road to the south parish?" inquired Sidney, bowing to the stranger.

The man, raising his hat, returned the salutation, and replied with a pleasant though inquisitive look, "No, it is not the direct road, and you have come a little out of your way; but you may get there by making a circuit."

Zeb turned round and smiled.

"And which way must we go?" said the Englishman.

The farmer let go his horse and came up close to the wagon.

"There are," said he, "two ways which lead there, but you will do best to take the first, turning to the left; then go about fifteen or twenty rods and turn short round by a guide-board, and that will bring you to Pleasant Pond, and then the road is strait forward."

"Yes, I shall know the way well enough, if I can once reach the pond," said Sidney, his eyes glistening with emotion, "and the distance is not quite a mile."

"Then you have been hereabouts before, I guess, sir?" said the farmer, regarding him earnestly.

"Yes, I have," replied Sidney; "but might not now have found the way, without your direction. Good-bye, sir."

The farmer responded the farewell; Zeb snapped his whip, and they set off.

The road, and a bad one, too, for more than a mile led through a thick wood. Frankford made many observations on the state of the highways and the multitude of forest trees growing in the uncultivated parts of America; while Sidney's mind was occupied with the idea of the approaching meeting with his family, and he scarcely listened to the invectives of the Englishman against the horrid roads, nor replied to the arguments he used to prove the country would never be a pleasant place of residence till it was better cultivated and more tastefully adorned.

But soon, on turning the corner, the beautiful sheet of water, called, significantly, "Pleasant Pond," appeared, expanding before them. Its surface, just dimpled by the passing breeze, rose in trembling undulations; and as the quivering water caught the last glow of the setting sun, it shone, like Loch Katrine,

"One burnished sheet of living gold."

Beyond the lake or the pond, and near its eastern edge, rose a high mountain, whose bold peak reflected the light in strong contrast to the shadows that were already gathering at its base. The mountain was clothed nearly to its summit by a growth of evergreens, intermingled with sumac and white birch; the straight, white trunks of the latter, appearing through the dark green of the firs and spruce, like pillars still standing, while the edifice they had supported was overthrown. Common willows and dwarf pines grew around the edge of the pond, but the leaves of the former were nearly fled, and the naked branches drooping over the water, looked like the arm of age, still stretched to screen the loved one from danger, although the strength that had made such defense effectual, was withered.

The feelings of Sidney could no longer be restrained. He started nearly upright, and extending his hand toward the water, exclaimed:

"O, that I may find the hearts of my friends as unchanged as the face of that lovely lake! Years have made no alteration here—just so I have seen it look a hundred and a hundred times. Here was my holiday resort; fishing in the summer, and sliding in the winter. And on that mountain—how many times have I rambled over it in search of blueberries, or climbed on yonder high peak and rolled down huge rocks, listening, as they bounded thundering from crag to crag, till they fell dashing in the waters below! Ah, those were blessed times! But they are passed, and the change that has come over me will forbid their return. The lake and the mountain are beautiful and sublime as ever—the blight of time falls only on the human heart."

Zeb had reined in his steed, and was listening with wondering attention to this burst of sentiment; but Frankford, who really felt greatly fatigued, did not relish it quite so well; and his voice was peevish as he inquired how much farther they had to go.

"When we reach the top of yonder hill, we shall see my father's house," said Sidney, still keeping his eyes fixed on the water.

"You are certainly more romantic than I imagined, Romilly," said the Englishman, "and this meeting with your friends after so long a separation, will be a real novel scene. I have a great mind to describe the thing. Suppose I should write a book, and put the speech you have just spoken in the mouth of some hero returning from an expedition, or some saint from a pilgrimage, or even a discarded lover from self banishment, how apposite it would appear! And what answering sympathy it would awaken in the bosoms of my fair readers. Oh, that I possessed the skill of a ready writer!"

"Perhaps it might do," returned Sidney, smiling. "I have often been told I had many traits of a novel hero in my character, and an old sibyl once predicted I would die for love. And so, if you wish to make your tale truly pathetic, you must wait till that catastrophe overtakes me."

"Which will be shortly, I presume," replied the other. "You say New England is the native land of female beauty; and some Dulcinea will soon ensnare your susceptible heart. A lady's fair face must certainly overpower you, if you are thus moved at the face of a lake."

They had now gained the height overlooking the village, if it deserved that name, consisting of about a dozen or so of dwelling houses, built on a street running east and west, with a meeting-house, as it was called, on a rise of ground at its angle with a road from the south; the one by which Sidney should have entered the village.

The tall steeple, whose spire was ornamented with a fish (doing duty as a weathercock), that still reflected the brightness of the western sky, looked like a sentinel guarding the humble abodes beneath and around it, and by the associations its sacred purposes inspired, served as a memento to lift the gazer's thoughts to heaven. What the fish was designed to represent, I am unable to say; but from the known protestantism of the builders, I presume it had not the most remote allusion to St. Anthony, or his mission to the aquatic tribe.

"Which is your father's house?" said Frankford.

Sidney looked earnestly around.

"I do not recognize it," replied he. "The road, or the village, or both are altered. The church and half the houses have been built since I left the village. I cannot see a familiar object. Oh, yes, there is the school-house; that was erected the year before I left home. Do you know, Zeb, where Mr. Romilly resides?"

"Squire Romilly, you mean," said the boy,

"Yes."

"Well, I don't know exactly," answered Zeb, "I never was here but once, and that was to a muster, and then there was so many folks I did'nt see any body. But I guess it is pretty near that are store."

"The store!" said Sidney—"there was no store there when I left home. What an alteration a few years will produce!"

"In such a new country," replied Frankford, "and where the number of inhabitants is doubled once in fifteen or twenty years, there must, of necessity, be great and rapid changes."

"They don't double only once in twenty-five years, sir," said Zeb, looking up with an air of much self-complacency.

"And how should you know anything about statistics?" said Frankford, regarding the boy with astonishment.

"I didn't read it in stactics, sir," replied Zeb; "I read it in our almanac."

Both gentlemen laughed so heartily, that the boy, abashed, hung his head, fearing he had said something wrong; then brightening up as he saw an opportunity of diverting the conversation. "Yonder," said he, "comes Harvey Romilly, now, riding on that are horse," pointing to a lad about his own age, on horseback, without saddle or hat, and urging his spirited looking pony to a full gallop.

As he drew nearer, the Englishman exclaimed, "He is your relative, Romilly, without doubt. See, he is your perfect miniature, and has your features exactly."

And so he had, only his were blended with infantile softness. His brown curling hair was flung back from his fair forehead by the rushing wind that met his career; the smile of rapture seemed issuing from his parted lips; and his laughing eye and flushed cheek completed a picture of innocent and wild delight, on which even a misanthrope could not have gazed without acknowledging there was a season when the children of men are happy.

Before they met him, he had reached a small house which was erected close by the road ride, and bounding from his horse, he gave the bridle to a man who stood at the door watching the approaching wagon, and then turned himself to gaze on the strangers.

"Now," whispered Frankford, "there is an excellent opportunity, Romilly, for you to establish your favorite doctrine of sympathy. Speak to that little fellow, and see if his spirit will claim kindred with yours."

"Can you inform me in which of those houses Mr. Romilly resides?" inquired Sidney of the man who was regarding him.

"He lives in that large yellow house, yonder," replied the man, pointing to a dwelling about a quarter of a mile distant, "and here is a son of his just going home, who can be your company."

"Come into the carriage, my little man," said Sidney, extending his hand towards him. The boy hesitated, and put his hand on his head; his countenance saying, I feel the want of my hat. "Come, step in," continued Sidney, "here is plenty of room."

The kindness of his voice and manner seemed to penetrate the heart of the child; he bounded lightly in, but then his bashfulness returned, and refusing the offer of Sidney's knee, he took a seat on the side of the wagon.

No one, except him who has been long separated from his near relatives, and who has felt the chill of unreciprocated affection and that vacancy in the bosom which nothing but the consciousness of kindred love can fill, is competent to judge of the feelings of the elder brother, while he fixed his admiring and tender gaze on the sweet face of the little fellow now seated beside him. How his soul yearned towards him, and how he longed to clasp him to his heart and call him brother! But he could not articulate a word, and taking his hand, pressed it in silence.

"You are a fine boy," said Frankford, who saw his friend's emotion, and wished to divert it, "pray how old are you?"

"Nine, sir, last June."

"And how many brothers have you?" continued Frankford.

"I have four, sir, Silas, and James, and Sam, and Oliver," answered the child.

"And have you no more?" asked Frankford.

"O! yes, sir, I've one more, Sidney; but he is in Carolina, and I never saw him in my life."

"Should you like to see him?" inquired the Englishman.

"O! yes, sir, indeed I should," answered the child, with emphasis; "and ma' says she knows he will come home soon, and then we shall all be so glad! But there, see Oliver now, after that old turkey!—he ha'nt catched him yet, and he said he should before I got back. I threw off my hat to chase him,"—and a flush passed over his bright cheek, as if glad of an opportunity to apologize for thus appearing bare-headed,—"but I'll help catch him now."

"And what are you intending to do with him?" asked Sidney.

"Oh, kill him for dinner to-morrow. It will be Thanksgiving day." And he sprung from the wagon and joined in the pursuit of the bird.

"We have come in an excellent time," said Frankford. "Now, I presume, the fatted calf will be killed as well as the turkey. Don't you think, Romilly, the return of the prodigal was on the eve of a Thanksgiving?"

"Shall I drive up to the back door?" inquired Zeb, as they drove near the house.

"No," replied Sidney, "we will alight here, and you may now return, or you will be late home. I paid your father," he continued, as they alighted, "for our passage; but here is something for your good behavior."

"And here is a trifle," said Frankford, "to buy you an almanac for the ensuing year. Study it, and I have no doubt but you will hereafter become a statesman."

Zeb bowed and smiled his hearty thanks for the money, or the compliments, then turning his wagon with a long sweep, his horse seemed to know instinctively the road homewards, and set off with a furious clatter.

CHAPTER VI.

HOME AS FOUND.

All hail, ye tender feelings dear!
The smile of love, the friendly tear,
The sympathetic glow. BURNS.

THE house before which our travelers now stood was a two-story building in front, with a range of low buildings behind; the whole painted yellow, with white window sashes and green doors, and everything around looked snug and finished. The house stood about five rods from the highway; and this fact deserves to be recorded, as a genuine, old-school Yankee, living twenty-five years ago, seldom left so many feet before his habitation. Indeed, they usually appear to have grudged every inch of ground devoted merely to ornament; the mowing lot, cow pasture and corn-field being all the park and lawn and garden they desired.

A neat railing, formed of slips of pine boards, painted white, and inserted in cross pieces, which were supported by wooden posts, ran from the highway to the house, on each side, and stretched across the front, enclosing an oblong square, to which was given the name of the "front door yard." Around this square were set Lombardy poplars, an exotic, which was then cherished in New England, to the exclusion of far more beautiful indigenous trees, as foreign articles are considered more valuable in proportion to the distance from whence they must be imported. It appeared, however, that the Romillys had discovered their error, and were endeavoring to correct it. This was evinced by the young elms and maples planted between the poplars, evidently with the design to have them for the guard and ornament of the scene, whenever their size would permit their tall, straight neighbors to be displaced. A graveled walk led up to the front door steps, which were formed of hewn granite, and wrought to appear nearly as beautiful as marble, and much more enduring. Clumps of rose bushes and lilacs were set around the paling, and, intermingled with evergreen shrubs, guarded, on each side, the graveled walk; but the pride of the parterre was the mountain ash. Several of these beautiful native trees, throwing up their heads as though proud of their coral clusters, now looking so bright in the absence of flowers, were scattered over the ground. It was evident that the forming hand of taste had been busy in disposing all to the best advantage; and had it been the season of sweets, the senses and imagination of even the most refined might have found full gratification.

On the east side of the railing, a gate opened into the back yard; and there was a carriage-way to drive round to the kitchen door, beyond which the barns, sheds, corn house, and all the various offices of a thriving and industrious farmer's establishment, were scattered about, like a young colony rising around a family mansion.

The last gleams of the setting sun yet lingered on the distant mountains, the village lights were beginning to appear, and a strong gleam, as of the blaze from a fire, illuminated the windows of one of the front apartments in the house of Mr. Romilly.

"What if this worshipful father of yours should not acknowledge you?" said Frankford. "We seem to be thrown entirely on his mercy."

"He will, at least, entertain us for the night," replied Sidney, opening the gate and going forward, "as we have money sufficient to clear our score."

"Yes," replied the Englishman, "I have been told a Yankee will sell any civility for cash; and it is usually on that alone we must depend for favors in our intercourse with them."

The last remark was uttered in a low tone, and did

not reach the ear of Sidney, who was just knocking at the door for admittance. A masculine voice was heard, bidding him "walk in;" and immediately obeying, they entered what in Europe is called the hall, here the front entry. It was about ten feet wide, and ran through the building, and at its termination was a door leading to the kitchen. A flight of stairs, painted to imitate marble, conducted to the chambers; and doors, opening on either side below, led to apartments called the parlor and "keeping room."

As they entered the hall, the door of this keeping room was thrown open by a little girl, with her knitting work in her hand, who, in a soft tone, said, "Walk in here, if you please."

They followed her, and entered an apartment about eighteen feet by twenty, and eight feet in height, finished in the style of the country. The floor was painted yellow; the wainscoating, reaching to the windows, blue. Above this and overhead, it was plastered and whitewashed.

There were no paper hangings, nor tapestry, nor pictures; but some itinerant painter had exerted his skill, probably to the no small admiration of the wondering community, to ornament the room, by drawing around on the plaster wall a grove of green trees, all looking as uniform in appearance as Quakers at a meeting, or soldiers on a parade, excepting that here and there one would tower his head above his fellows like a commander.

Over the mantel-piece, the eagle spread his ample pinions, his head powdered with stars, his body streaked with white and red alternately, his crooked talons grasping an olive branch and a bundle of arrows; thus significantly declaring, that although he loved peace, he was prepared for war; and in his beak he held a scroll, inscribed with the talisman of American liberty and power —*E pluribus unum.*

A very long, wide sofa or couch, (in truth, a large, old-fashioned *settle*, well stuffed and covered with chintz,) was ranged on one side of the room. A deep writing desk, that seemed designed for an *official bureau*—so multitudinous were its drawers and compartments—was surmounted by a book-case, whose open door showed it nearly filled with well-worn volumes. A large cherry table, a small work table, a wooden clock, and about a dozen chairs, completed the furniture of the apartment.

There was no candle burning; perhaps the precise time to light it had not arrived; but a large wood fire sent forth a bright blaze from the hearth; and before it, in an arm chair, was seated a serious but happy-looking man. In one hand he held a newspaper, which he had probably been perusing; and with the other he was pressing to his bosom a rosy-cheeked girl of three or four years, who sat on his knee.

Rising at the approach of the strangers, he set down his child, and offered them his hand with a "how d'y do?"—and then bidding Mary set some chairs, he resumed his own, while his little daughter immediately regained her station on his knee.

Sidney at once recognized his father, and his heart beat violently.

"A fine evening for the season!" said Squire Romilly—as he was always called, contracting his real title. He was, in fact, "justice of the peace and quorum" for the county; therefore legally an "esquire;" and I shall so designate him, to avoid confusion, though I do hate titles.

"It is quite cold, I think," replied Frankford, moving his chair towards the fire.

"You have been riding, I suppose," returned the Squire, "and that makes you feel the cold more sensibly. I have been at work all day, and thought it very moderate."

While he spoke, he gave the fire a rousing stir, and threw on some wood that was standing in the corner of the fire-place. He then looked several times from one to the other, as if endeavoring to recollect them, and, bidding Mary draw a mug of cider, again addressed himself to entertain them.

"Do you find the roads pretty good the way you travel?"

"Not the best," replied Sidney, who determined to speak, though the effort was a painful one.

"There ought to be better regulations respecting the highways, I think," said the Squire. "Where every man is permitted to work out his own tax, the public are but little benefited. I was telling Deacon Jones the other day—he is our surveyor this year—that I would take half the money and hire workmen, who should repair the roads better than they are done by collecting the whole in the manner it is now managed."

"Then Deacon Jones is living yet?" said Sidney, glad to hear a familiar name.

"Yes, he is living," answered the Squire, surveying Sidney attentively; "are you acquainted with him?"

"I have seen him many times, but it is now some years since," replied Sidney.

"I expect he will call here this evening," observed the Squire.

"He would not probably recollect me now," answered the other, "yet I have been at his house often."

"Then you once lived in this neighborhood?"

"I have."

"And how long since?" said the Squire, whose curiosity seemed powerfully awakened.

"It is nearly thirteen years," replied Sidney, raising his hat from his head and turning his fine eyes full on his father's face.

The truth flashed on his mind.—"My son!" exclaimed he, starting from his seat.

"My father!" replied his son, and they were locked in each others' arms.

Just then Mary entered with her pitcher of cider; she caught the last words, and, setting down her pitcher, darted out of the room, and

"Sidney's come! Sidney's come!" resounded through

the house in a moment. In the next, the room was filled. Mother, brothers and sisters crowded around the long absent but never forgotten Sidney.

Oh! it was a meeting of unalloyed joy—one of those sunlit points of existence, when the heart lives an age of rapture in a moment of time.

Mr. Frankford, who often described the scene thus far, always declared it would be in vain for him to attempt more. And I must follow his example, leaving it to the reader's imagination, and those who have the best hearts will best portray it.

When the first burst of affectionate exclamations and interrogatories was over, Sidney introduced Mr. Frankford, as an Englishman, and his particular friend, with whom he had traveled from the south, and made a tour to Saratoga Springs, and north as far as Montreal. At the latter place, Mr. Frankford had been confined nearly three months, with the typhus fever, from which he was now recovering, and Sidney wished them to consider him with particular attention.

Mr. Frankford had hitherto sat entirely unnoticed, though not unnoticing; for he there learned a lesson from the exhibition of natural feelings, which made him ever after disgusted with the heartlessness and frivolity of the fashionable world. And whenever he wished to dwell on a holy and touching picture of nature, he always recalled that scene to his remembrance.

He was not, however, suffered to be any longer a stranger or a spectator. The friend of Sidney was the friend of the family, and every one seemed anxious to render him attentions. Mr. Romilly immediately resigned his arm-chair, in which one of the little girls officiously placed a cushion; and having persuaded Frankford to seat himself in it, Mrs. Romilly brought from her closet a cordial of her own preparation, which she recommended as "the best thing in the world to prevent a cold after riding;" and bidding the girls hasten supper, she told him that before going to bed he must bathe his feet in warm water, and then a good night's rest would restore his spirits at once; adding, "you must, sir, endeavor to be at home and enjoy yourself, for I cannot bear to think any one is sad while I am so happy."

She was a goodly looking woman of five-and-forty, perhaps dressed as if she had been engaged in domestic affairs, but still neatly. She had on a black flannel gown, a silk handkerchief pinned carefully over her bosom, and a very white muslin cap, trimmed with black ribbon—her mother had been dead more than a year, but she still wore her mourning. Her apron she would doubtless have thrown off before entering the room, had she thought of anything save her son; for when she returned, after leaving the apartment to assist her daughters in their culinary preparations, it was laid aside.

The dress of the daughters, which their mother observed was "according to their work," it may perhaps be interesting to describe, and then, a century hence, when our country boasts its tens of millions of inhabitants, all ladies and gentlemen arrayed in satins and silk velvets, muslins and Mecklin laces, chains of gold and combs of pearl, this unpretending book may be a reference, describing faithfully the age when to be industrious was to be respectable, and to be neatly dressed, fashionable.

Both sisters, who were of the ages of seventeen and fifteen, were habited precisely alike, in dresses of American calico, in which deep blue was the prevailing color. The frocks were fitted closely to the form, fastened behind with blue buttons, and displaying the finely rounded symmetry of the shape to the greatest advantage. The frocks were cut high in front, concealing all the bosom but the white neck, which was uncovered and ornamented—when does a girl forget her ornaments?—with several strings of braided beads, to imitate a chain; and no eye that rested on those lovely necks would deem they needed richer adornments. The only difference in their costume was in the manner they dressed their hair. Sophia, the eldest and tallest, confined hers on the top of the head with a comb, and Lucy let hers flow in curls around the neck. Both fashions were graceful and becoming, as not a lock on either head seemed displaced; both were combed till the dark hair resembled fine glossy silk. Around their foreheads the curls clustered lovingly, and those who gazed on their sweet faces, glowing with health and happiness, where the soul seemed beaming forth its innocence and intelligence, and the smile of serenity playing on lips that had never spoken, save in accents of gladness and love, would feel no regret that they were uninitiated in the fashionable mysteries of the toilet.

Mr. Frankford often declared he never, before seeing them, felt the justness of Thompson's assertion, that

> ——————"Loveliness
> Needs not the foreign aid of ornament,
> But is, when unadorned, adorned the most."

They were, indeed, beautiful girls—the Romillys were a comely race—and every fair reader who honors these pages with a perusal, and does not think them, at least, as handsome as herself, may be certain she possesses either a vain head or an envious heart.

The supper was now in active preparation. The large table was set forth, and covered with a cloth as white as snow. Lucy placed all in order, while Sophia assisted her mother to bring in the various dishes. No domestics appeared, and none seemed necessary. Love, warm hearted love, supplied the place of cold duty; and the labor of preparing the entertainment was, to Mrs. Romilly, a pleasure which she would not have relinquished to have been made an empress, so proud was she to show Sidney her cookery; and she tried to recollect the savory dishes he used to like, and had prepared them now in the same manner. At length all was pronounced ready, and after Squire Romilly had fervently besought a blessing, they took their seats.

The supper consisted of every luxury the season afforded. First came fried chicken, floating in gravy; then broiled ham, wheat bread, as white as snow, and butter so yellow and sweet, that it drew encomiums from the Englishman, till Mrs. Romilly colored with pleasure while she told him she made it herself. Two or three kinds of pies, all excellent, as many kinds of cake, with pickles and preserves, and cranberry sauce—the last particularly for Sidney—furnished forth the feast. The best of young hyson, with cream and loaf sugar, was dispensed around by the fair hand of Sophia, who presided over the department of the tea pot; her mother being fully employed in helping her guests to the viands, and urging them to eat and make out a supper, if they could.

Sidney's feelings were too much occupied to allow any great appetite for mere corporeal food. He wanted every moment to gaze on the loved faces smiling around him, or listen to voices whose soft tones, when calling him *son* or *brother*, made every fibre of his heart thrill with rapture.

But Frankford was as hungry as fasting and fever could make him. He was just in that stage of convalescence when the appetite demands its arrearages with such imperious calls, that the whole mind is absorbed in the desire of satisfying its cravings. He did honor to every dish on the table; till Sidney, fearing he would injure himself by eating to excess, was obliged to beg he would defer finishing his meal till the next morning; "for you know, Mr. Frankford," added he, laughing, "the physician forbade your making a full meal till you could walk a mile before taking it."

"If that be the case," said Squire Romilly, "I hope you will exert yourself to-morrow. It is our Thanksgiving, and I should be loath to have the dinner of any one at my table abridged. It will, indeed, be a day of joy to us, and Sidney could not have come home at a more welcome season."

While he spoke, he directed a glance towards Silas, whose cheeks, fresh as they were, showed a heightened color, and his black eyes were involuntarily cast down. Sidney observed it, and asked his father if there was to be any peculiarity in the approaching festival.

"Do you," said he, "still have your plum-pudding and pumpkin-pies, as in former times?"

"O yes," replied his father, "our dinner will be the same; but our evening's entertainment will be different."

A wink from Mrs. Romilly, who evidently pitied the embarrassment of Silas, prevented further inquiries or explanations, and they soon obeyed her example of rising from the table.

Mr. Frankford, who they feared would exert himself too much, was now installed on the wide sofa, (or *settle*) drawn up to the fire, and all the pillows to be found in the house, as he thought, were gathered for him to nestle in. When he was fairly arranged, like a Turk on his divan, half sitting, half reclining, he addressed Squire Romilly, and inquired the cause of the Thanksgiving he had heard mentioned.

"Is it a festival of your church?" said he.

"No; it is a festival of the people, and appointed by the Governor of the State."

"But there is some reason for the custom—is there not?" inquired the Englishman.

"Certainly; our Yankees seldom do what they cannot justify by reasons of some sort," replied the Squire. "This custom of a public Thanksgiving is, however, said to have originated in a providential manner."

Mr. Frankford smiled rather incredulously.

The Squire saw the smile, but took no heed, while he went on.

"Soon after the settlement of Boston, the colony was reduced to a state of destitution, and nearly without food. In this strait the pious leaders of the pilgrim band appointed a solemn and general fast."

"If they had no food they must have fasted without that formality," said Frankford.

"True; but to convert the necessity into a voluntary and religious act of homage to the Supreme Ruler they worshiped and trusted, shows their sagacity as well as piety. The faith that could thus turn to God in the extremity of physical want, must have been of the most glowing kind, and such enthusiasm actually sustains nature. It is the hidden manna."

"I hope it strengthened them: pray, how long did the fast continue?"

"It never began."

"Indeed! Why not?"

"On the very morning of the appointed day, a vessel from London arrived laden with provisions, and so the fast was changed into a Thanksgiving."

"Well, that was wise; and so the festival has been continued to the present day?"

"Not with any purpose of celebrating that event," replied the Squire. "It is considered as an appropriate tribute of gratitude to God to set apart one day of Thanksgiving in each year; and autumn is the time when the overflowing garners of America call for this expression of joyful gratitude."

"Is Thanksgiving Day universally observed in America?" inquired Mr. Frankford.

"Not yet; but I trust it will become so. We have too few holidays. Thanksgiving, like the Fourth of July, should be considered a national festival, and observed by all our people."

"I see no particular reason for such an observance," remarked Frankford.

"I do," returned the Squire. "We want it as the exponent of our Republican institutions, which are based on the acknowledgment that God is our Lord, and that, as a nation, we derive our privileges and blessings from Him. You will hear this doctrine set forth in the sermon to-morrow."

"I thought you had no national religion."

"No established religion, you mean. Our people do not need compulsion to support the gospel. But to return to our Thanksgiving festival. When it shall be observed, on the same day, throughout all the states and territories, it will be a grand spectacle of moral power and human happiness, such as the world has never yet witnessed."

Here Mrs. Romilly interrupted her husband, to ask, in a whisper, which was rather loud,—

"Was that basket of things carried to old Mrs. Long?"

"Certainly; I sent Sam with it."

"She will have a good Thansgiving then; for Mrs. Jones has sent her a pair of chickens and a loaf of cake," said Lucy.

"Every one ought to have a good dinner to-morrow," said Sophia.

"Is the day one of good gifts as well as good dinners?" inquired Mr. Frankford.

"So far as food is concerned," replied the Squire. "Everybody in our State will be provided with the means of enjoying a good dinner to-morrow: paupers, prisoners, all, will be feasted."

Mr. Frankford now confessing he felt wearied, was persuaded to retire, Mrs. Romilly all the time lamenting he had not reached Northwood before his sickness, and repeatedly saying, "If you and Sidney had only come here instead of going on to Montreal, how much better it would have been! I would have nursed you, and we have the best doctor in the country. I don't believe you would have been half as sick here."

"Nor do I," replied he, gratefully smiling. "And to have been a witness and partaker of so much goodness and benevolence, would have made disease not only tolerable, but pleasant; the sympathy and interest I should have awakened in such a kind heart as yours, would have more than indemnified me for my sufferings."

Squire Romilly attended him to his chamber. It was directly over the sitting-room, and finished nearly in the same style. The ornament of the eagle, however, was wanting; but its place over the mantel-piece was supplied, and, in Frankford's estimation, its beauty excelled, by a "Family Record," painted and lettered by Sophia Romilly.

There was an excellent looking bed in the chamber, with white curtains and counterpane; a mahogany bureau, half a dozen handsome chairs, a mirror, and a dressing-table, covered with white muslin and ornamented with fringe and balls. Everything was arranged with perfect neatness, order and taste—yes, taste; nor let the fashionable belle flatter herself that she monopolizes the sentiment. The mind of a rural lass may be possessed of as just conceptions of the sublime and beautiful, and less trammeled by fashion; she consults nature in selecting the appropriate, which is sure to please all who have good sense, whatever may be their refinement or station.

A glowing fire on the hearth, and a large deeply-cushioned rocking-chair (Mrs. Romilly's own chair) drawn up before the fire, looked as if inviting the stranger; a foot-bath and plenty of warm water was near; on a small table was a pitcher of hot chamomile tea, (a favorite specific with Mrs. Romilly in diseases of all kinds), and also a small bottle of cordial.

Squire Romilly set down the light, and was about leaving the chamber, when Mr. Frankford, laying his hand on the door, remarked there was no lock nor fastening.

"We don't make use of any," said the Squire. "I never in my life fastened a door or window; you will be perfectly safe, sir."

"Why, have you no rogues in this country?" asked Frankford.

"None here that will enter your dwelling in the night with felonious intentions," replied the other. "I suppose you might find some in the cities, but they are mostly imported ones," he added, smiling.

"And can you really retire to rest," reiterated Frankford, with a look of incredulity, "and sleep soundly and securely with your doors unbarred?"

"I tell you, sir," replied the Squire, "I have lived here twenty-five years, and never had a fastening on a door or window, and never was my sleep disturbed except when some neighbor was sick and needed assistance."

"And what makes your community so honestly disposed?" asked Frankford.

"The fear of God," returned the Squire, "and the pride of character infused by our education and cherished by our free institutions."

"But I should think there might be some strolling vagrants," said Frankford, "against whom it might be prudence to guard."

"We seldom think of a shield when we never hear of an enemy," answered the Squire. "However, if you feel insecure, I will tell Sidney—he will sleep in this chamber," pointing to the open door of a small bed-room adjoining—"I will tell Sidney to place his knife or some fastening over the door, before going to bed."

"I hope," said Sidney to his mother, after his father and the Englishman had withdrawn, "that Mr. Frankford will have a good bed. He complains bitterly of his lodgings since he came to America."

The matron drew herself up with a look of exultation.

"He will find no fault here, I'll warrant him," said she. "My beds are as soft as down; indeed, those two in the chamber where you and he will sleep, are nearly all down. I made them for the girls, though I keep them now for spare beds; and I told your father I could afford to give each of the girls a down bed when they were married, as I have always had such capital luck with my geese."

Sidney bestowed a kiss on the blushing cheeks of each of his fair sisters, telling his mother he thought it much easier to provide beds for such sweet girls, than find husbands worthy to share them.

The idea of matrimony, however, awakened a desire in Mrs. Romilly's mind to communicate the intelligence her significant looks had prevented her husband from relating while at supper. With true feminine delicacy, she did not wish to have Sidney first apprised of it in the presence of Silas; nor did she feel willing a stranger should hear the remarks and interrogations which Sidney might make. These objections were now removed, as Silas had gone out and Mr. Frankford retired to bed; and so she ventured to say that "to-morrow evening Silas is to be married to Priscilla Jones; and," said she, "it is an excellent match for him. Deacon Jones is very rich, and has only three daughters; the other two have already married and moved away, and so your brother will go there to live and have the *homestead*."

Squire Romilly now returning to the room, they drew their chairs around the fire and entered into a confidential family conversation. And the *conversaziones* of Italy offer no entertainment like that which the Romillys enjoyed—the interchange of reciprocal and holy affection. A thousand mutual inquiries were made, and Sidney listened, delighted, to many an anecdote of his boyish acquaintance, or the history of many an improvement in his native village. The clock struck twelve before they thought the evening half spent, and then, after a most fervent prayer from the father-priest, so full of gratitude and joy that all were melted to tears of thankfulness, Sidney was suffered to retire and dream over the scene he had just enjoyed.

CHAPTER VII.

A THANKSGIVING SERMON.

All has its date below; the fatal hour
Was registered in heaven ere time began.
We turn to dust, and all our mighty works
Die too; the deep foundations that we lay,
Time ploughs them up, and not a trace remains.
COWPER.

THE first sound that saluted the ear of Sidney, on awaking next morning, was the voice of Harvey, who entered the chamber bearing a large pitcher of fresh water: he informed the gentlemen breakfast was ready. The sunbeams were shining brightly through the thin muslin window curtains, and Harvey, to their interrogatories, replied it was past eight o'clock; "but ma'," said he, "would not have you called before, though we always breakfast at seven."

"She is a blessed woman," said Frankford, "and I do not wonder, Romilly, you wished me to accompany you home. The only strange thing is, that when you had such a good, affectionate, and lovely family to welcome you, you could stay so many years from their embraces."

"I think myself it is strange," replied Sidney; "but till my education was completed, my uncle would never consent to my coming, and since that period he has always seemed unwilling; yet I will not blame him entirely. Till within a few months, pleasure has been the idol of my pursuit; and I have, I believe, sought it in every place except where alone it is to be found—in a virtuous home." He sighed as he concluded.

"You seem to be spiritually minded this morning,"

said Frankford, stretching himself and yawning. "And so all your follies are to be given to the winds, I suppose; at least, while you are here. It is best, perhaps, for I have been told that politics and religion are the only subjects which excite an interest in Yankee society."

On descending to the sitting room, where the breakfast table was spread—that apartment serving for many purposes—they found all the family assembled, every eye bright with benevolence, and every face looking like the personification of happiness.

To the inquiries of "how they rested?" and "how they liked their accommodations?" the Englishman expressed his entire satisfaction; and launching forth in encomiums on his bed, he declared it was the very best he had found in America, and fully equal to any in his own country.

Mrs. Romilly, a good but a true woman, was not insensible to flattery; at least, it might have been thus inferred from the delight which diffused itself over her comely countenance on hearing these praises; and it was afterwards often remarked by her neighbors, that they never knew Mrs. Romilly so taken with any stranger as she was with that Englishman.

Their table was, if possible, more plentifully supplied than on the preceding evening; and Sidney observed, that he feared they had forestalled their dinner, as he did not see how they could be gratified with a greater variety.

"Your mother will answer for that," replied the Squire; "she has a plenty of niceties still in store for us, I presume; but we must all attend church to-day, and endeavor to fit our hearts, as well as appetites, to enjoy with advantage to ourselves the blessings a kind Providence is continually bestowing."

This speech led to inquiries concerning the clergyman, and Sidney was glad to hear Mr. Cranfield still continued to officiate.

"And what has become of George?" he inquired.

"Well," replied his father, "he has been through college, and, as I hear, was called an excellent scholar. He is now at home studying divinity with his father, and promises to be an ornament to his profession."

"You will see him this evening," said Mrs. Romilly, nodding to Sidney; "he is to be the bridesman."

Mr. Frankford now made some inquiries concerning who was to be married, which elicited an account of the arrangements for the evening, and a cordial invitation to join the festivity and witness the marriage.

"Nothing," said he, "could give me greater satisfaction, except being myself the principal on such an occasion;" and he gazed so earnestly at Sophia, that her face, which happened at the moment to be turned towards him as she handed him some cakes, was crimsoned to her forehead.

As he withdrew his eyes, they met Sidney's—their keen glance seeming to say, "Beware of trifling here; we are proud as you!"—and Frankford, abashed, resumed his breakfast.

"These Yankees," thought he, "intend to be very dignified."

Just as they had risen from the table, Harvey, who was standing by the window, exclaimed—"There! Dr. Perkins is coming now; he said he should call this morning and see brother Sidney."

"And who is Dr. Perkins?" asked Sidney.

"Why, don't you remember Warren Perkins?" inquired his father.

"To be sure I do," returned Sidney: "he and George Cranfield were my dearest friends. But is he really metamorphosed into a doctor of physic?"

"Indeed he is," replied Mrs. Romilly, "and an excellent one too. He has all the practice, now old Dr. Rodgers is dead; and I never heard a word of fault found with him, except by Mrs. Watson, and she always has something to say against every one."

"And every one against her, of course," said Sidney. "Your slanderers are the Arabs of society; their hand against every one, and every one's hand against them. And though they deprive many of character, they are still destitute themselves; as the descendants of Ishmael live in wretchedness while the plundered wealth of caravans is scattered around them."

Here he was interrupted by the entrance of Dr. Perkins, a robust, florid complexioned, happy looking fellow, with a sort of comical shrewdness in his small blue eyes, that instantly revealed the lover of fun and frolic; yet the child of misfortune would have addressed him, confident of succeeding in any request that appealed to his heart.

It is useless to attempt a description of these meetings. Those who have souls will understand what they must have been; and those who have none are requested to lay down this volume—it was not written for them. If, after this fair warning, they will read on, I shall not think myself amenable to their criticism. To the dull, all books will be dull.

"You are altered, Sidney," said Dr. Perkins, "besides your growth, for which I was prepared. You have lost much of that fairness of complexion which used to make you so handsome. And I may be allowed to remember it, for, to confess the truth, I used to think, when we were at school together, that the teachers, school-mistresses in particular, were always partial to you; but what it could be for, except your good looks, I never could divine."

"Then you attributed nothing to his superior industry and application to his book," said Squire Romilly, who still remembered that Sidney was always allowed to be the best scholar.

"I think, sir," replied Dr. Perkins, "there must be a *cause* before an *effect;* and that it is encouragement and attention on the part of the teacher which makes good and attentive scholars. I was always called an unlucky rogue; they knew by my countenance I was one, and accordingly I was watched and punished; and thus the faculties of my mind were more directed to deceive them and escape punishment, than to acquire learning. Sidney, on the contrary, had such a pleasant, amiable looking face, that he was patted on the head, called a fine fellow, and had full confidence placed in his integrity, and this animated him to deserve it. Whatever you wish to make a child, treat him as such, and you will seldom be disappointed."

"But, Warren," said Sidney, "it don't appear that you have suffered at all for your juvenile follies. You are now a physician, with a diploma, and I have no such honors to boast."

"You never sought them," answered Perkins. "Wealth and distinction were yours without exertion; but I have been compelled to save every sixpence, or go without my dinner, and force my way upward by main strength, or run the risk of being precipitated to the bottom by some jostling competitor. And thus, partly necessity and partly competition, have operated to make me what I am—a poor physician, who will do his best for any patient that pays him well; yet nature has still a nook in my heart, and I can love and serve a friend without pay."

"I wish I could give as good an account of myself," said Sidney, laughing; "but mine has been a kind of life more pleasant to pass than profitable to relate. I have seen much, and studied little; resolved great things, and done nothing at all—nothing, at least, that I can claim any merit for having performed."

"And do you call saving my life a performance of no merit?" asked Frankford. "I never knew before how low you rated me."

"Then he did save your life?" repeated Mrs. Romilly, her countenance brightening. "I knew Sidney had done some good; it is his disposition; and now Providence has given him the means, he would be criminal to do otherwise. And 'tis just so with all my children; I never knew one of 'em that would ever hurt a fly. There's Silas, now," and she looked around to assure herself he was absent, "he will make one of the best husbands in the world."

"And to-night is his wedding," said Dr. Perkins; "faith, I had forgotten it."

"You are going?" said Mrs. Romilly.

"Certainly," he replied, "I would not miss this wedding for the fees of a month. There will be the old Deacon, puffing and preaching, all smoke and original sin. Have you forgotten, Sidney, how the school-master flogged me for robbing the Deacon's pear tree? That was the last flagrant breach of the eighth commandment I was ever guilty of. The master's ferule, or the Deacon's lecture, effectually convinced me of my fault, and induced a thorough reformation."

"I have entirely forgotten the circumstance," said Sidney. "Indeed, I recollect but very little about Deacon Jones, except his sour looks, and how my mother once scolded me for saying he resembled a crab apple. I believe it was the only witty thing I ever attempted."

The conversation now became more desultory, if possible; and though many things were said, at which the party laughed heartily, readers might not be so humorously inclined. Indeed, to relish a good thing, the hearer must sympathize with the speaker; and jests that convulse an audience with merriment, often appear exceedingly silly when published as *bon mots.* For these reasons I shall omit many conversations, which, as they actually occurred during the visit of my hero, I had taken down with all an author's accuracy, for publication; but the difficulty of making them understood, and the fear of swelling the work beyond fashionable limits, prevented their insertion.

At length, after the most urgent invitations to Mr. Frankford and Sidney to visit him and spend a month, if possible, and see his wife and two boys, and telling them that they should meet again in the evening, Dr. Perkins took his leave.

"A doctor, you call him!" said Frankford; "I should sooner think him a Merry Andrew."

"You will find, sir," said Squire Romilly, "that notwithstanding this appearance of careless humor, which is constitutional, he is a man of strong talents, and sound judgment; and he has not only a practically useful, but even a classical education, though almost entirely self-acquired. And a more honest man, or sincere friend, or better citizen, I do not believe exists! He and Deacon Jones are often at variance on religious opinions; but I tell the deacon, if Warren Perkins' principles are unsound, his practice might be an example for the most rigid professor."

"What is he," asked Frankford carelessly, "a deist?"

"A deist!" repeated the Squire, "no, indeed; there never was a deist in this town, I guess. He only objects to the doctrine of the decrees and election; and to confess the truth, I don't think them subjects of very profitable discussion. But the deacon thinks otherwise; and if our minister followed his advice, we should have nothing but doctrinal discourses. However, Mr. Cranfield manages to satisfy the deacon tolerably well; and, indeed, it is impossible for any one to dislike him. Even the most opposite in sentiment are equally charmed with his preaching, and his spotless life bids defiance to censure. But you will have an opportunity of hearing him to-day, and then he will not need my praises to recommend him."

Mr. Frankford smiled *almost* contemptuously, that a Yankee puritanical preacher should be considered an object of any interest to him, who had heard the most eloquent and learned doctors of divinity declaim without any sensations save of weariness, and had thought the conclusion far the best division of the discourse.

"I believe," said he, "I shall hardly feel in health to attend to-day."

At this declaration the whole family appeared so distressed for fear he needed some remedy which they had not yet provided; and their inquiries and solicitude about his disorder, and sorrow and disappointment that he was not to hear their Thanksgiving sermon, were so overwhelming and sincere, that the apathy of the Englishman was overcome.

"I cannot," thought he, "refuse to make these kind creatures happy when it depends only on appearing so myself. I will go to their meeting, and, if possible, refrain from ridiculing the oddities and absurdities I shall undoubtedly see and hear."

The whole family, Sophia excepted, were soon arrayed in their best, and ready for church. She was left at home to superintend the various operations of stewing, roasting, baking, &c., which were in the full tide of successful experiment, and required careful attention.

"Sophia," said her mother, "can manage such matters better than Lucy, though she would do them nicely. But Sophia is going to the ball to-morrow evening, and so is willing to stay at home to-day."

"Then you dance in this country," said Frankford. "I thought that was a prohibited amusement with your religionists."

"It has been so, in particular places," replied the Squire, "but there is now less of opposition. For my own part, I never could see any enormous wickedness in dancing, when managed with decorum and followed with moderation. I have always permitted my children to attend, and should have made no objection to their taking a few lessons in the art, had there been an opportunity; but some of my brethren in the church were so bitterly opposed that no school for teaching it could be established in this town."

"Deacon Jones, in particular," said Mrs. Romilly, "thinks it the unpardonable sin, and he has been here to give me and the children many a lecture, and argued the matter with my husband till I have been vexed beyond measure—he is so unreasonable, and so set in his way."

"And probably honest in his opinion now," replied the Squire, "whatever he was when adopting it. Men cannot, for any length of time, defend a system without becoming convinced of its truth, especially if its tenets are much controverted. The arguments they advance may fail to convince an opponent, but are not lost on themselves; they strengthen their zeal, till creeds, which at first were adopted without reflection or consistency, shall become the polar star of their existence. How carefully should we examine a proposition that affects our morals or happiness, before we admit its truth, or advocate its requirements!"

All were now assembled, and the bell had ceased ringing as they set off. Squire Romilly was arrayed in a suit of black, *home made* merino, and Silas in one of deep blue—*bran* new for the wedding. Mrs. Romilly wore a black satin dress, Lucy a changeable silk, and the children looked not only neat, but handsomely attired.

The church stood about eighty rods from Squire Romilly's, but so punctual were the parishioners to be "in season," that all had entered before he arrived. His seat was the second in the middle aisle, an excellent one for observation; its situation enabling the occupants to see, to the best advantage, not only the clergyman, but nearly all the congregation.

Mr. Frankford had the best corner assigned him, and Sidney sat by his mother, who experienced a triumph which a queen might have envied, in seeing the eyes of her acquaintance so often turned towards him. It was the triumph of maternal feeling.

Frankford had determined to be entirely at ease, and look about him, as such an opportunity for commenting on the real Yankee phiz, especially when lengthened by the solemnity of his severe devotions, might never again occur.

The psalm was performing when they entered. The tune was "Old Hundred," with a bass viol for an accompaniment. They sung with energy, and made up in tone what they lacked in harmony; yet there were some fine tenor voices, and the Englishman allowed the performance to be tolerable, but he said there was wanting the full, swelling peal of the organ, to lift the soul to heaven; and nothing could in church music, he thought, supply the place of that instrument.

Mr. Cranfield had been reclining in the pulpit, so as

4*

not to be visible, but a moment after the singing ceased, he arose, and the whole congregation, by a simultaneous movement, arose with him, "and stood up." When, clasping his hands, he raised his eyes towards heaven, where the prayer he poured forth seemed ascending, Mr. Frankford admitted the possibility that his talents might merit the praises they had received.

Not a foot was moved nor a loud breathing heard; all seemed to realize that they were in the presence of a holy God; and when the *amen* was pronounced, there was not a heart in the assembly that could not have responded, "so be it!"

Again they sung, and then Mr. Cranfield, who had been industriously turning over the leaves of his Bible as if searching for his text, arose, and looking around, a profound silence was maintained, while, with a slow and solemn pronunciation, he "invited their serious attention to what might be offered from that portion of the sacred scriptures recorded in the prophet Isaiah, twenty-sixth chapter and fifteenth verse:

'Thou hast increased the nation, O Lord, thou hast increased the nation: thou art glorified; thou hast removed it far unto all the ends of the earth.'"

That the whole sermon is not inserted is no fault of mine, and well was it worthy of being so; but the copy could not be obtained. Mr. Cranfield, with the usual modesty of pulpit orators, refusing it for publication, I can give only such an imperfect sketch as the recollection of one of the audience could supply.

After an appropriate exordium, descriptive of the happiness and security of that "nation whom God increased," the orator adverted to America, succinctly mentioning its settlement by the pilgrims; their persecutions in the old world, and the perils they braved in the new, and the influence which their character had exerted in fashioning the minds of their descendants.

From thence the transition was easy to the war of our revolution, which was waged in resistance of oppression; and in detailing some of its most trying scenes, he showed plainly that "if the Lord had not been on our side when men rose up against us, we should indeed have been swallowed up."

Then he noticed our excellent institutions, securing the liberty and happiness of the people on the broad foundations of intelligence and public virtue; and drawing a picture of the prosperity of our country, he anticipated its probable increase, power, and glory, by an estimate of its hitherto rapid growth, and unparalleled and almost inexhaustible resources.

No eye was closed during the sermon, nor was a nod, or even a look or action, expressive of weariness, seen throughout the assembly. With eyes riveted on the speaker, old and young sat motionless; except, at times, a half curious, half gratified glance was directed towards the pew where sat the Englishman, to learn, if possible, how he relished such sentiments.

And he afterwards acknowledged, that never, during his life, had he experienced such a variety of emotions. His contempt for itinerant or uneducated clergymen, among whom he supposed were ranked all in America, excepting a few in the cities, had led him to expect nothing more than a rhapsody in favor of some exclusive dogma, or a rant against some prevailing sin. Little had he anticipated the beauties of a chaste and classical composition; the polished period; the clear and concise, yet animated description; the pathetic appeal; the lofty sentiment; and the soul-stirring patriotism, that seemed, like a shock of electricity, to thrill the nerves of the audience, and even, in spite of his prejudices, made his own tremble.

He knew very well, that America had been discovered and settled, and that the States had gained their independence; but he seemed now to learn it for the first time. He knew, too, that his countrymen had been beaten by these *rebels,* and little had he recked of the matter; but now, when the orator, in describing the tremendous struggle, alluded to Bunker Hill and the little band of patriots who, fighting their first fight in defense of their liberties, met and defied the proud power of Britain, when he told of the twice routed foe, and the wasteful carnage before succeeding to dislodge the Americans, Mr. Frankford shaded his face with his hand, and internally vowed never to listen to another Yankee Thanksgiving discourse.

The orator did not stop at the point where his hearers naturally concluded he would, the acme of the prosperity and glory of his own country; he glanced at the probable consequences such an event would have on the nations of the old world, and particularly on that from which we were descended. He dwelt on the advantages which would accrue to England from an intercourse with independent America, proving it to promise far more important benefits than could have been realized from colonies; that the community of language, similarity of laws, customs, habits, and religion, formed a bond of union between the two countries, which nothing but the most pernicious policy or absurd prejudices on the part of Great Britain, would prevent from operating to increase her resources, and perpetuate the grandeur of her name and character.

"Great Britain," said he, "once called herself our mother, and though far from being an indulgent one, we do not deny her maternity; but there is a period when nations, as well as individuals, quit their minority, and if the parent country would continue the parallel of relationship which subsists in families, she will not consider her independent offspring as her natural enemy."

"Suppose a mother had a daughter who was, on some occasions, self-willed, and finally married against her consent, would she, breathing a malediction against her child, endeavor to accomplish her ruin? Would she not, rather, secretly rejoice in her prosperity, and, taking the first decent opportunity for a reconciliation, renew those offices of kindness and generosity which those of the same blood should ever be ready to reciprocate? And do we not see instances where a mother finds, not only a useful friend in the child she once discarded, but even a supporter in the imbecility of age, and one who will afford an asylum when no other protector is to be found?

"When Alexander sacked Tyre, and made that haughty city a heap of ruins, the Carthagenians who were present conveyed many of the Tyrians to a place of safety; they remembered they were the descendants of a Tyrian colony. 'The things which have been, are those which shall be.' Where are the mighty empires and proud cities of antiquity? They have passed away like the chaff of the summer threshing floor, or left only memorial ruins to waken the sigh of the traveler, or to gratify the researches of the antiquary! And will Great Britain, think ye, be exempted from the operation of those universal laws of nature which have governed all created things on this globe, and all their works? Will not luxury enervate her spirit as it did that of Greece? Will not the extension of her empire weaken her power, as it did that of Rome? Will she not, like them, have her period of growth, of maturity, and of decay?

"Yes, I repeat—her period of decay—though heaven forbid she should, like the heathen nations, fall to rise no more! The word of God is in her homes, and the light of the hallowed Sabbath on her hills and pleasant places. But her haughty pride must be humbled, and her power will suffer an eclipse. The nations of Europe will band against her, for she has trampled them down in her day of triumph; and she has the light of freedom, which tyrants hate. The nations will gather against her, and she will be sorely beset.

"And then will America remember her; and here shall her exiles and her fugitives find a refuge and a home. Here, mingling with a people descended from the same stock, speaking the same language, inheriting the same passion for liberty, and worshiping the same God—brothers and christians—they will feel that they yet have a country.

"I consider the settlement of the United States by Englishmen, and its separation from the mother country, as two of the most fortunate events which could have occurred to the kingdom of Great Britain. A young and mighty nation is here rising, a nation which the 'Lord has increased,' and whose borders 'are far removed, even unto all the ends of the earth,' and this nation will perpetuate the names and achievements of Englishmen—even should the monuments of that now glorious land be crumbled into dust!"

Frankford looked up during this, and every word fell on his heart. He could not forbear thinking it was purposely designed for him; others were likewise of the same opinion. And perhaps they were right in their conjectures, as Mr. Cranfield had, late on the preceding evening, been informed of the arrival of Sidney Romilly and his English friend; and he might—his office was to win souls and teach good-will to the children of men—take the only but doubtful method of giving the whole view of the subject, to soothe the feelings of the stranger, after listening to an eulogium on a country which he had probably been taught to execrate as ungrateful, or despise as insignificant.

A short and impressive prayer closed the services of the day, which will never be forgotten, either by the Romilly family or the Englishman—they connect it with the return of a beloved son or brother; he refers to it as an original exhibition of piety, patriotism, and eloquence.

CHAPTER VIII.

THANKSGIVING DINNER.

Thine, Freedom, thine, the blessings pictured here.
GOLDSMITH.

As they quitted the house, the old friends of the Romillys and boyish acquaintances of Sidney thronged about him to shake hands and congratulate his return; and those who had never seen him, being anxious to watch the meeting between such friends, he was very soon surrounded by nearly all the assembly.

A considerable portion of the attention, however, was directed towards Mr. Frankford, who, fatigued, both from the length of the services and the crowd, gladly accepted the invitation of Mrs. Romilly to walk home with her. "For there is no telling," said she, "when Sidney will get away, so many want to see him, and I am afraid the turkey will be over-roasted."

Together, therefore, they walked homeward, but Mrs. Romilly's mind being so intent on her preparations for dinner, that she could talk of nothing else, the Englishman found no opportunity of censuring, as he had intended, the sentiments of the preacher, and criticising his style and manner.

About half an hour elapsed before the return of Squire Romilly and his sons, and in that time every thing had been arranged for the dinner.

Although the description of a feast is a kind of literary treat, which I never much relished, and hope my readers do not, yet as this was a thanksgiving entertainment, one which was never before, I believe, served up in style to *novel* epicures, I may venture to mention some of the peculiarities of the festival, without being suspected of imitating those profound and popular writers who make a good stomach the criterion of good taste; and instead of allowing their characters to display their sentiments in conversation, make them eat to display their appetites. Such authors might very well dispense with all but two characters in their books—a cook to dress their dinners, and a hero to devour them.

And now for our Thanksgiving dinner. A long table, formed by placing two of the ordinary size together, was set forth in the parlor; which being the best room, and ornamented with the best furniture, was seldom used, except on important occasions. The finishing of the parlor was in a much better manner than that of any other apartment in the house; the wood work was painted cream color, and the plaster walls ornamented with paper hangings of gay tints and curious devices.

Over the mantel-piece hung two paintings, executed by Sophia and Lucy, representing scenes from the Shepherdess of the Alps. A connoisseur in the art would undoubtedly have seen faults in both pieces, on which he might have displayed his critical acumen to advantage. He might have objected that the shepherd was nearly black, and the shepherdess very *blue*—her *nose*, and not her stockings—that the sheep resembled wolves, and the rocks coffins; but such profane things never had been said of them, for they had been examined only by those who, having the landscape of nature always before their eyes, require something both strange and new in an exhibition of art. They had therefore not only escaped all censure, but even excited rapturous praise.

The furniture of the parlor consisted of a mahogany sideboard and table, a dozen handsome chairs, a large mirror, the gilt frame covered with green gauze to prevent injury from dust and flies; and on the floor was a substantial, home-manufactured carpet, woven in a curious manner, and blended with all the colors of the rainbow. Seldom were the junior members of the family allowed the high privilege of stepping on this carpet, excepting at the annual festival; and their joy at the approaching feast was considerably heightened by the knowledge that it would be holden in the best room.

The table, covered with a damask cloth, vieing in whiteness, and nearly equaling in texture, the finest imported, though spun, woven and bleached by Mrs. Romilly's own hand, was now intended for the whole household, every child having a seat on this occasion; and the more the better, it being considered an honor for a man to sit down to his Thanksgiving dinner surrounded by a large family. The provision is always sufficient for a multitude, every farmer in the country being, at this season of the year, plentifully supplied, and every one proud of displaying his abundance and prosperity.

The roasted turkey took precedence on this occasion, being placed at the head of the table; and well did it become its lordly station, sending forth the rich odor of its savory stuffing, and finely covered with the froth of the basting. At the foot of the board, a sirloin of beef, flanked on either side by a leg of pork and loin of mutton, seemed placed as a bastion to defend innumerable bowls of gravy and plates of vegetables disposed in that quarter. A goose and pair of ducklings occupied side stations on the table; the middle being graced, as it always is on such occasions, by that rich burgomaster of the provisions, called a chicken pie. This pie, which is wholly formed of the choicest parts of fowls, enriched and seasoned with a profusion of butter and pepper, and covered with an excellent puff paste, is, like the celebrated pumpkin pie, an indispensable part of a good and true Yankee Thanksgiving; the size of the pie usually denoting the gratitude of the party who prepares the feast. The one now displayed could never have had many peers. Frankford had seen nothing like it, and recollected nothing in description bearing a comparison, excepting the famous pie served up to the witty King Charles II., and containing, instead of the savory chicken, the simple knight.

Plates of pickles, preserves and butter, and all the necessaries for increasing the seasoning of the viands to the demand of each palate, filled the interstices on the table, leaving hardly sufficient room for the plates of the company, a wine glass and two tumblers for each, with a slice of wheat bread lying on one of the inverted tumblers. A side table was literally loaded with the preparations for the second course, placed there to obviate the necessity of leaving the apartment during the repast.

The Romillys had no domestic, properly speaking; their only *help* was a pauper maiden, known as "old Hester." She was blind of one eye, utterly shiftless, and with such a crooked temper that her relations could do nothing with her. They were poor and shiftless too; so "old Hester" had to be supported by the town. She was the only pauper in Northwood, and made as much trouble for the public, and more talk, than would a work-house of paupers in England; because there paupers are of no consequence. Old Hester made herself felt in every department; and Squire Romilly had been so annoyed with her complaints, and complaints about her, that he told her one day she might come and live with Mrs. Romilly a month or two, and he should then know who was in fault. So Hester came; and partly because she wished to prove her accusers had been wrong, but chiefly because the Romilly family always called her "Miss Hester," and treated her with much respect, she had done her very best, and so improved her ways, that Squire Romilly informed the town officers "he would keep her for the present without any charge on the public;" and so Northwood had no pauper.

This had happened about five years before our Thanksgiving dinner, and Miss Hester was still in the family, but had gone to eat her dinner with her sister, as every one must go to their own on Thanksgiving Day; and so the Romillys had to wait on themselves.

There was a huge plum-pudding, custards and pies of every name and description ever known in Yankee land; yet the pumpkin pie occupied the most distinguished niche. There were also several kinds of rich cake, and a variety of sweetmeats and fruits.

On the sideboard was ranged a goodly number of decanters and bottles; the former filled with currant wine, and the latter with excellent cider and ginger beer—a beverage Mrs. Romilly prided herself on preparing in perfection. There were no foreign wines or ardent spirits, Squire Romilly being a *consistent* moralist; and while he deprecated the evils an indulgence in their use was bringing on his countrymen, and urged them to correct the pernicious habit, he *practiced* what he *preached*. Would that all declaimers against intemperance followed his example.

Such, as I have attempted to describe, was the appearance of the apartment and the dinner when Mr. Frankford, ushered by his host, and followed by Sidney and the whole family, entered and took their stations around the table.

The blessing which "the saint, the father, and the husband" now fervently besought, was not merely a form of words, mechanically mumbled over to comply with an established custom, or perform an irksome duty. It was the breathings of a good and grateful heart acknowledging the mercies received, and sincerely thanking the Giver of every good gift for the plenteous portion he had bestowed. And while enumerating the varied blessings with which the year had been crowned, Squire Romilly alluded to the return of the long absent child, and expressed his joy in thus, once more, being permitted to gather all his dear family around his table, his voice quivered;—but the tear which fell slowly down his cheek was unnoted by all save Frankford; the others were endeavoring to repress or conceal their own emotion.

The eating of the dinner then commenced in earnest. There was little of ceremony, and less of parade; yet the gratified hospitality, the obliging civility and unaffected happiness of this excellent family, left on the heart of the foreigner a lasting impression of felicity, while the recollection of many a splendid *fete* in gorgeous halls had passed away.

The conversation during the repast, though chiefly

employed in comparing the respective qualities of the several dishes, and explaining the manner of their preparation, was more interesting than a discussion of the same subjects would have been at a nobleman's table; because those who supported or listened to the discourse, were more immediately concerned in the decision of the various questions proposed, and more gratified by the eulogiums which the quality of the provisions and the perfection of the cookery received from the two guests. Mrs. Romilly attended particularly to them, helping them to the choicest bits, and replenishing their plates so often and so bountifully that the appetite of the Englishman, craving as it had been, was completely satiated. Yet he could not forget how hungry he had been, and while refusing the "pudding which Lucy had made," and the "custard Sophia had prepared," he looked around on the still loaded table, with a kind of sorrowful disappointment that he must leave so many good things untasted.

"Our wine," said Squire Romilly, smiling, while he placed a decanter of his currant preparation before Mr. Frankford, "is not the precise kind to which you have been accustomed. For your sake, I wish it were champagne or old Madeira."

"Thank you," replied Frankford, "and why not for your own sake? You have undoubtedly sufficient discrimination to prefer the best."

"If what we prefer be the best," replied the Squire, "I shall certainly give the palm to my currant. The fashionably discriminating taste of appetite is entirely acquired. And the fastidiousness which rejects the wholesome because it is common, and prizes only the rare, dear and far-fetched, is the offspring of whim or vanity."

"It may be so," returned the other, "yet I think it no small privilege to have been taught that fashionably discriminating taste, as you term it. It always accompanies refinement of manners. The Greenlander may prefer his draught of oil, or the Highlander his whisky; their preferences are as much acquired tastes as my own, yet

I fancy you, sir, would sooner conform to mine than theirs."

"Their tastes are acquired by necessity," said the Squire; "they have no choice. Their situation or their poverty deprives them of all opportunities of discriminating. No such necessity governs us. But I think it becomes the people of a great and free country, to consider well the effect which the indulgence in foreign luxuries may have on their own character, and the high privileges committed to their trust. The Greek and Roman legislators frequently enacted sumptuary laws, restraining the extravagance of fashion and the excesses of appetite. We depend for decency, sobriety, order, and economy, on the good sense, cultivated reason, and enlightened patriotism of our citizens. Excessive luxury and rational liberty were never yet found compatible."

All true born and bred Americans, Yankees in particular, are fond of argument. Their reasoning faculties are constantly excited by canvassing the merits of rival candidates for their frequent elections, and sharpened by the necessity they find or make of often engaging in political controversies; add to this their liberty of conscience, which gives every man full power to form or defend his own religious creed by the light and strength of his own understanding, and we shall be convinced that the force of circumstances alone would operate to give them dexterity and *tact* in supporting their own opinions, or refuting those of an antagonist.

The circulation, too, of newspapers and other periodicals throughout every part of the country, and their perusal by almost every individual, diffuse a knowledge of all passing events, and impart a tone of intelligence to the society even of the humblest orders, which the mass of European inhabitants do not display.

Men are fond of doing what they are conscious of performing well, and Squire Romilly, although of a most liberal and conciliating temper, had been too often victorious in the war of argument not to feel he had strength for the encounter; and he was probably more gratified with the turn the conversation had unexpectedly taken, than he would have been, had the Englishman, by complimenting his currant wine, and preferring it to champagne or old Madeira, precluded the necessity of reply.

"And do you imagine, sir," said Frankford, laughing heartily, while he set down the glass he had just emptied, "that currant wine or ginger-beer are at all connected with the preservation of your liberties?"

"If you had been in this country forty years ago," answered the Squire, with equal good humor, "would you have imagined the article of *tea* could have had any influence in accelerating our independence? Yet, had your East India company kept their tea at home, or your parliament possessed *three pennyworths* more of wisdom, we might, till this day, have been a colony of Great Britain. Small causes often produce great effects; and the fate of nations, as well as individuals, is decided or materially altered by such trifles as we scarcely think worthy notice."

"But your clergyman proved to-day, and plainly, as he thought, I presume, that the separation of these states from the mother country was an excellent affair for us Englishmen. By a parity of reasoning, I can demonstrate that the introduction of foreign luxuries, will advance your prosperity. It will increase your trade, and by that means augment the revenue of your government; these surplus revenues may be expended in public improvements, and thus your country, by becoming more polished and respectable, will offer greater inducements to our *fugitives and exiles* to make it their *asylum and home.*"

There might have been a little acrimony in the emphasis which Mr. Frankford laid on particular words in the last observation, but the gay laugh with which it concluded, seemed to pledge that it was not spoken in anger nor intended as an insult; and the Squire proceeded, without noticing it, to descant on temperance and industry, and on the necessity of inculcating the practice of these virtues on the rising generation, till Mr. Frankford archly interrupted him.

"You must then," said he, "abolish your Thanksgivings entirely, for who can practice temperance when set down to such a table as this? If you were a hermit, and our meal had been roots and water, I might have listened, much edified, to your discourse; but now, sir, I confess my excellent dinner has totally disqualified me from receiving any benefit from a homily on temperance; nor can you, while placing me in the midst of temptation, wonder if I fall into the snare."

"Well, well," replied the Squire, laughing, "I may at least recommend industry, for all this variety you have seen before you on the table, excepting the spices and salt, has been furnished from my own farm and procured by our own labor and care."

"If that be the case," returned Frankford, looking around on the various and complicated dishes with a half incredulous stare, "you are privileged to enjoy them. The fruits of his own labor every man may surely partake. You think the indulgence in domestic luxuries perfectly innocent?"

"No; but I think them less dangerous and less apt to be indulged to excess. And the exertion to procure them cherishes a spirit of patriotism, independence, and devotion. We should love our native land were it a sterile rock; but we love it better when to our cultivation it yields an ample increase; and the farmer, instead of sighing for foreign dainties, looks up to heaven, and depends on his own labors; and when they are crowned with a blessing, he thanks God, as tens of thousands throughout our State are doing this day. Let us join our voices with theirs."

"So saying, he arose, and the whole family with him. The thanks of the Romillys were sincere, but the Englishman, who had never, at a dinner party, been accustomed to quitting the table in such an abrupt manner, and had expected—though he knew there was nothing to drink but currant wine and ginger-beer—to sit an hour or two after the ladies had withdrawn, was too much surprised to listen to thanks. He stood stock still in his place till the family were all in motion removing the dishes, Mrs. Romilly all the time hurrying and bidding the girls "make haste and clear away the things and do up the *chores*, or we shall certainly be late at the wedding."

Mr. Frankford then walked to a window to conceal the mirth he could not suppress at the unfashionable ending of the feast.

"But," thought he, "they have done as well as they know how, and better than I could have expected in this wild place."

After the removal of the things, coffee was brought in and served round by Oliver and Harvey. This was an innovation—coffee not being usually taken after a Yankee dinner. Mrs. Romilly explained the matter by telling the foreigner, who had taken a seat beside her, that it was done at Sidney's desire: "and really," said she, "I think I shall like the fashion very well, for coffee always settles my head so nicely."

They then began to arrange for the wedding. The distance from Squire Romilly's to the dwelling of Deacon Jones, was about half-a-mile, and the evening being a beautiful one, with a *good moon*, they all preferred walking. Mrs. Romilly, however, insisted that Mr. Frankford must ride.

"You have been to meeting," said she, "and you look pale, and if you get too fatigued and catch cold, it may bring on a relapse. No, no, you must ride. James, get out the chaise, and Sophia may ride too—she is tired."

Sophia's cheeks were crimson, while she declared she "should walk with Sidney."

"Well, then," replied the good mother, "I'll ride with Mr. Frankford myself, and carry Lydia; the poor child wants to see the wedding as much as any of us."

The Englishman was fain to acquiesce in this arrangement, but the look he directed towards Sophia declared, unequivocally, that he would willingly have exchanged *two* for *one*.

It was dusk when they started. Silas had been gone an hour, and Mrs. Romilly more than once regretted that they were so late. It was not that she feared the ceremony would commence before their arrival, but her habits of industry made her always feel in a hurry to have every thing performed, in which she was at all concerned, immediately.

Such promptness is an excellent thing in a housewife, but when it degenerates into teasing impatience, it is very uncomfortable in a companion.

CHAPTER IX.

A COUNTRY WEDDING.

Though fools spurn Hymen's gentle powers,
Those who improve his golden hours
By sweet experience know,
That marriage, rightly understood,
Gives to the tender and the good
A Paradise below. COTTON.

THE house of Deacon Jones was a tolerably fair specimen of Yankee architecture. A genuine Yankee consults no *order* save the order of his own will; and to suit himself and build as large a house as possible, is the rule of every New England farmer. Should his means confine him at first to small dimensions, he never fails improving the first favorable opportunity of enlarging his tenement by building what he significantly terms *additions*—they are rarely improvements—till either age or poverty compels him to desist. And it was in this manner the dwelling of Deacon Jones had acquired most of its size, and, in his judgment, all its importance.

It was originally a one story building, with two square rooms in front and several small rooms back, and accommodated his family very well. But when Mr. Jones, as he was then called, found his substance increasing, he could think of no better method of displaying his wealth than by enlarging his dwelling; so he reared what he denominated "a back kitchen," joining his old house, and extending back about forty feet. Here was a capacious dairy room, cheese closet, and every *convenience*—a significant term, and much better understood by a thrifty New England farmer than the *sublime*—for his large dairy. Yet still he was not satisfied. Some of his less wealthy neighbors were already residing in their two story houses, and it galled his pride to see the eyes of strangers who visited the village attracted towards their showy buildings, while his were passed carelessly by, when he numbered so many more head of cattle, and sold so much more butter and cheese than they did. These reasons determined him to erect a wing, or body, rather, to his lowly dwelling.

The new building was of two stories, of course, but to make it appear more elevated, he directed the posts to be made two feet longer than the usual dimensions. The wing was thirty feet by twenty-four; the upper story being divided into two chambers, with ample closets, finished handsomely and designed for his daughters.

The lower story formed but one room, and many were the conjectures of the good and inquisitive people in the neighborhood, concerning the use for which such a huge apartment could be designed. Some guessed Mr. Jones was intending to open a tavern, and designed it for a bar-room; others surmised that he was about turning merchant, and would convert it into a store; and the young lads, who hated him for his opposition to their amusements, declared that they knew he was preparing it for a ball-room. One wag actually wrote tickets for a house-warming in Mr. Jones' behalf, inviting all the young ladies and gentlemen in Northwood to meet at his new *hall* and celebrate its accomplishment.

The worthy proprietor deigned no explanation to any of these surmises. He kept his workmen busily employed in finishing it after the pattern he had shown them, and on the Sabbath following its completion, after the services were closed and a conference appointed at the school-house, he arose in his place and communicated to his brethren, in a solemn tone of voice, the important information, that he had provided a room in which they might for the future hold their conferences!

The circumstance caused quite a sensation in the little community, and many who had formerly accused Mr. Jones of worldly-mindedness, now acknowledged, that if he had been a little too anxious to obtain property, he seemed willing to improve it for useful and pious purposes. He was soon after elected deacon, by an almost unanimous vote of the church, a station he had long coveted, and no doubt often sincerely prayed for, but which, had he not made himself useful to his brethren, might not have been so readily or spontaneously granted him.

Selfishness is an insidious passion, mingling itself with motives, and inspiring actions which claim to proceed from holy and benevolent feelings. And—I would not teach uncharitableness—when Deacon Jones surveyed his spacious conference room, completely finished, with a row of seats around, and furnished with a table, chairs, and candlesticks, and appurtenances requisite for the accommodation of his brethren, and was remembered publicly in their prayers, as one who "had opened his doors" for the reception of God's children, he felt quite secure of the divine favor, and ever after attributed his worldly prosperity to the particular approbation of the Most High.

I have, perhaps, been more minute in the description of this conference-room than the subject required. The reader will pardon it when informed it was there the wedding was to be celebrated, and there the guests were received and seated.

Among those assembled when the Romillys arrived, were Dr. Perkins and lady. The Doctor immediately joined them, and after introducing his wife, a sweet looking young woman, to Frankford and Sidney, he proceeded to point out to the notice of the latter each particular person in the room, describing their characters and humors in his own lively manner. Sidney remembered the names of many of the families, for nearly the whole neighborhood was invited and assembled: of the individuals he had but a faint recollection.

After some lively rattle on Sidney's inquiries respecting one particular young lady, Perkins said, "Romilly, if you have really returned here with the patriarchal intention of taking a wife from among the daughters of your own land—by the way, could you ever seriously think of a patriarch being in love?—why, I can promise you the sight of a girl worthy to captivate an emperor."

"Where is she?" inquired Sidney, looking round.

"She has not yet entered the room," replied the doctor; "she is the bridesmaid, and will, on that account, be easy for you to distinguish, though her own loveliness will distinguish her far better."

"Am I acquainted with her name or family?" asked Sidney, continuing the conversation more on account of the interest it appeared to excite in his companion, than from any he felt himself.

"No, I rather think not," replied the doctor; "her mother was sister to the old deacon there, and married a merchant of Boston. They lived in high style for a few years, when Mr. Redington—that was her husband's name—dying suddenly, his affairs were found insolvent. It was rumored at the time, that the widow and infant daughter were defrauded by the villany of his partner; but nothing could be proved, and Mrs. Redington, after every thing was settled, found herself entirely destitute. It has been said that her brother, the deacon, wrote to her, offering her an asylum in his house; but his letter contained so many reproaches for her former extravagance, as he termed it, that she declined accepting his benevolence, and resolved to obtain her own support by her needle.

"She is represented as being a very extraordinary woman, uniting the fortitude and energy of our sex with the sensibility and meekness of hers; and she succeeded in supporting herself and child in competency. Her patient endurance of misfortune, and perseverance in performance of her duties, gained her many valuable friends; and when she died, which was when her daughter was about twelve years old, a lady of the first respectability, who was childless, took Annie Redington, and adopted her for her own child. Here she was educated in every accomplishment; but death, as she once observed to me, seemed determined to deprive her of protectors, and at the age of eighteen, she followed Mrs. Eaton, her second mother, to the grave.

"Mr. Eaton was a very fashionable man, and although he had always called Annie his daughter, yet very soon after the decease of his wife, he was glad to recollect she was not within the degrees of affinity which by Scripture and law are forbidden to marry together. In short, he was over ears in love with the fair orphan, and had Annie possessed the vanity or ambition of many of her sex, she would certainly have accepted his splendid alliance; but, no—she was astonished, frightened, and grieved, and having no relation except the deacon, was forced, in the terrible dilemma, to apply to him for advice and assistance. The old man bestirred himself most manfully in the affair; he hurried to Boston, and notwithstanding the entreaties, reproaches, and threats of the widower lover, succeeded in freeing the lady from duress. Eaton, when he found Annie determined to depart, offered her money to any amount she wished; but she refused accepting it, and the deacon practiced what I call a most heroic act of self-denial, for he actually told Eaton his gold might perish with him; adding, with a sneer, that he felt quite able to maintain his own niece without assistance.

"This happened about two years ago, and since then Annie has resided constantly in Northwood. Indeed, she is absolutely confined, having no relatives in any other place, and no acquaintance excepting in Boston, which she dares not visit for fear of encountering Mr. Eaton. He remains unmarried, and perseveres in declaring his determination yet to obtain her hand."

"Indeed!" said Sidney, "and do you think it probable he will succeed?" suppressing, though with difficulty, a yawn. Should the reader feel the same inclination, it must excite no wonder—the power of sympathy is proverbial.

"Why, no," answered Perkins; "I think his case is

hopeless. But there comes George Cranfield; he is master of the ceremonies this evening, and we shall now be marshalled round the room with all the formality of a battalion at a muster. The etiquette of the ceremony will assign us different stations; but don't forget to look at the bridesmaid."

"I should imagine the bride would be the more interesting object," said Sidney.

"No, by no means," eagerly replied the other. "She is pretty enough, but no more to be compared with Annie Redington than I——to you, sir. Hercules would be a borrowed simile, and I like to manufacture my own comparisons."

George Cranfield now approached, and affectionately taking Sidney's hand, told him his seat was next to Mr. Frankford.

After the bustle of a few minutes, the company was arranged, all conversation hushed or carried on in low whispers, and a stranger, who had not been apprised of the cause which had assembled such a goodly number together, might have thought the *conference room* was occupied for its original destination.

Both Frankford and Sidney improved this interval in a critical survey of the apartment and the company. The room has been already described; and the company were, even in the Englishman's opinion, a very decent, clever, civil-looking set, and considering there were none who had any pretensions to noble extraction, or had received the polish which travel and good society bestows, they seemed to understand how to behave themselves with propriety.

At the head of the apartment was seated the Deacon and his wife; he in his elbow chair, with his head reclining backwards, eyes raised and half closed, as if in the act of imploring a blessing on the approaching solemnity. His thin and sharp visage, wrinkled and receding forehead, whose baldness was shaded only by a few snow-white hairs, made his appearance quite saintly; and it was not till you caught the shrewd glance of his little grey eye, cautiously peeping from its thick and overhanging eyebrow, that you would imagine him engaged in any earthly speculations, or interested by any sublunary spectacle.

His wife was really his "better half," being fat enough for a Chinese beauty, and possessing that contented, kind, benevolent countenance, which constitutes the beauty of *age* in all countries.

Next were seated Squire Romilly and lady; then Mr. Frankford, and either to honor him as being a stranger from a far country, or else in consideration of his recent illness, he was placed in a large easy chair, furnished with a high cushion, the covering of patch-work, and formed of as many *stars* as are displayed in the flag of our country.

Sidney came next; then the sisters of the bride, each with her spouse, then the remainder of Squire Romilly's family, while friends and neighbors filled the remaining seats.

These were all arrayed in their best; the young ladies in white, the married in silks or crapes, and the men mostly in suits of dark-colored cloth, which, although *homespun*, would not, in some instances, have suffered much by a comparison with foreign manufacture.

Nearly in the middle of the apartment was seated the Rev. Mr. Cranfield, a clear space before him being left for the bridal party. A wood fire blazed brightly in the ample chimney, and a number of candles and lamps disposed around the apartment, made the whole appear to the best advantage.

It was evident from the glances of the assembly, that they were quite as much interested with the appearance of the strangers as the latter could be with them; and they continued to reconnoitre each other till the sound of approaching steps directed all eyes towards the door to see the *entrée* of the bride. The door being thrown wide open by young Cranfield, Silas Romilly entered, leading by the hand a very amiable-looking girl, whose downcast eye and blushing cheek told at once her history.

Sidney looked not at her; a young lady walked beside her, apparently anxious, by assiduity, to save her from all embarrassment. It was Annie Redington; and Sidney, while he steadfastly regarded her, internally exclaimed, "Perkins, you did not exaggerate!"

But now is no time to describe her, for the ceremonies are commencing; and who would delay a wedding to read the description of the most beautiful woman on earth?

The marriage ceremony is the most interesting spectacle social life exhibits. We see two rational beings, in the glow of youth and hope, which invests life with the halo of happiness, appear together, and, openly acknowledging their preference for each other, voluntarily enter into a league of perpetual friendship, and call heaven and earth to witness the sincerity of their solemn vows—we think of the endearing connexion, the important consequences, the final separation—the smile that kindles to ecstasy at their union must at length be quenched in the tears of the mourning survivor!—but while life continues, they are to participate the same joys, to endure the like sorrows, to rejoice and weep in unison. Be constant, man; be confiding, woman, and what can earth offer so pure as your friendship, so dear as your affection!

The couple who now approached the altar of Hymen, came in the simplicity of virtuous love, and the vows they breathed were dictated by the truth as well as fervency of their feelings. There was a slight embarrassment visible in the countenance and manner of the bridegroom, but it probably proceeded from his concern for the timidity of his trembling bride. Silas Romilly had never been called handsome, yet now when his coal-black eyes were lighted up with animation, giving a deeper glow to his healthy, though rather dark complexion, his thick black hair combed back from a finely formed forehead, his tall and manly figure, and the serious yet happy air of his deportment, formed a portrait which no observer could survey with indifference.

Priscilla Jones, to whom he was about to plight his faith, was, in appearance, entirely his reverse. She was a small, slender, delicate girl, and the wreath of white roses entwined amidst her fair hair, was hardly paler than her cheek. Her dress was a frock of plain white muslin, trimmed around the bosom and sleeves with lace; the only ornament she wore, was a gold chain around her neck, to which was attached a small miniature picture of a brother who had been drowned.

After a short pause, Mr. Cranfield inquired if they were ready to proceed; and on George's replying they were, he arose, and all obeyed his motion. He made a short, but solemn prayer, fervently imploring a blessing on the lovers; then addressing himself first to the bridegroom and then to the bride, he recapitulated, in a pertinent and impressive manner, the duties which the marriage covenant imposed, and asked if they promised to perform them. A bow and courtesy answered in the affirmative, —no vocal response is necessary,—and he pronounced them "lawfully married," &c.; and the ceremonies, the whole occupying fifteen or twenty minutes, were concluded.

After they were all again seated, a deep silence ensued, which was first broken by Mr. Cranfield. He made some observations, and addressed a few words of advice to the young married pair;—but soon whispers began to be heard in the distant parts of the room—and finally, on the appearance of the assistants, who were the neighbors, —one bearing a large waiter filled with tumblers and glasses containing wine (the real juice of the grape), and another with a still larger waiter filled with cake,—the god of silence (if such a deity ever presides at an assembly) resigned his charge, and a burst of loquacious gaiety effectually prevented his return.

There were several kinds of cake, all *very nice;* and it would have puzzled any one, except a professor in *goût*, to have decided which was best. But what was significantly termed the *wedding cake* was conspicuous by being iced, covered with sugar plums of all colors and forms, and tastefully decorated with myrtle and evergreen.

Of this cake all the young ladies, and, by their persuasions, nearly all the young men, preserved a small slice for the purpose of placing it beneath their pillows when retiring to rest—it being the popular opinion, that, in consequence of its peculiar virtues, they should be favored with dreams revealing their future destiny.

Who would wish to be always wise or grave? Not the young while celebrating a wedding. The evening passed delightfully to most of the party, and many an ardent wish was breathed for the felicity of the wedded pair.

In the changes of place which now occurred, Dr. Perkins soon elbowed his way to a seat near Sidney.

"You are obeying my instructions," were his first words to Sidney, the direction of whose eye made them perfectly understood.

"Why, yes. You did not imagine I would be indifferent to your panegyrics, did you?" replied Sidney.

"No, no, I had no fear of that; and now tell me honestly, have you, at the South, any beauties who surpass her?"

"Who?—the young lady now presenting the cake to the bride? I think not,—one, perhaps,—yet it is seldom we find a more faultless face."

"And her mind, her disposition, Sidney, is as fair and faultless. And after all our admiration of a perfect outside, it is the perfection within which must perpetuate our esteem."

"You are enthusiastic in her praise, and a married man too!" answered Sidney, laughing.

"And does being married," said Perkins, "destroy all perceptions of beauty or virtue, except in the individual to whom my vows are pledged? You need not be jealous, however, or imagine I feel any emotions in gazing on the face of that fair girl which would not be awakened by the sight of any similar piece of perfection. Yet where is such n one to be found? There is nothing in creation on which the eye of man can rest so lovely as woman in her Eden charms of youth and innocence; and I never look on such a one without thinking of the pure pleasures there must be in heaven, where none but agreeable objects meet the sight, and where we can feel assured they will forever retain their loveliness. The recollecting how soon our terrestrial beauties fade, is a melancholy drawback to me—I regard them as fair flowers, which the first cold blast will wither."

"Yet, notwithstanding you are assured that beauty is so evanescent, you appear to prize it very highly," said Sidney.

"And so does every man and every woman; and for this reason, that we associate, in our imaginations, excellence of mind and character with excellence of person. After a few disappointments, we acknowledge the injustice of the criterion; yet still we look and admire, and it is not till tardy reason has confirmed experience that we are fully convinced the worth of the jewel must not be estimated by the casket that contains it." Perkins paused, and then added, laughing, "I have given you a longer sermon on beauty than I intended; but George will, I believe, give a longer one to Annie. See how attentive he is. George is her undisguised admirer."

"Is he a favored one?" asked Sidney.

"Why, no; I think not. She esteems him undoubtedly, but I guess there is not much love in the matter; however, it is the general opinion here that she will marry him."

"Marry him!" repeated Sidney, looking rather blank.

"Yes, marry him," re-echoed Perkins, laughing at the earnestness of Sidney's manner; "and should you have any objection to urge against the fitness of the union? George is an excellent young man, and liberally educated—a large item, you know, in his favor, especially with the ladies. Then his father has a pretty good property, to which George is sole heir, and you can see he looks very well."

"There is nothing under heaven to prevent his success," said Sidney, peevishly, "as I suppose he has ample opportunity to cultivate her good graces."

"O yes, I believe, between ourselves, that the old deacon would give his consent with all his heart. Yet I will give him his due; he has been very kind and indulgent to Annie since her residence with him."

"And who could be otherwise?"

"Why, no one who saw with your eyes," replied Perkins, regarding Sidney archly; "but the deacon's eyes require more substantial charms. A good farm, a fine horse, or even a fat cow, have beauties more congenial to his taste than had Helen herself."

"Can you not introduce me to your belle?"

"With pleasure; and now your brother has married her cousin you may claim some intimacy as a relation. O, how I wish you would woo and marry her, and settle here among us!"

A sigh was the answer to this remark.

"I shall love no more," thought Sidney, as he followd the doctor.

"Miss Redington, Mr. Sidney Romilly, the brother of your friend Silas," said Dr. Perkins.

The usual compliments ensued, and the doctor contrived, by displacing a couple of stout yeomen, and interrupting one or two confidential communications, to seat Sidney and himself immediately within the bridal circle.

The conversation soon became very lively; and Sidney supported his part with that ease and elegance which an acquaintance with the world and with the manners of good society alone imparts. Miss Redington had not, since her residence in the country, met with a gentleman of such varied information and winning deportment. Time fled noiselessly on, unheeded by any in that circle, and none of them seemed to remember they were ever to separate. But a bustle began to arise at length among the elderly part of the company, and Sidney heard the unwelcome intelligence that it was time to retire.

Now was the time for the display of true Yankee politeness and hospitality. The people, especially in the interior towns, were not, twenty-five years ago, accustomed to the courtly manner of sending cards to invite their guests. Verbal invitations were then the compliments mostly used. And on the present occasion, there were very urgent invitations tendered from *all* to *all;* but Sidney in particular, was overwhelmed with their civilities.

Nor did the Englishman depart unnoticed. He was invited over and over to "come with young Romilly"—to "come at any time"—to "come and see how poor folks live"—and assured he should "find a welcome if he found nothing else."

And even after they had left the house and, as Sidney thought, were fairly clear from the good company, one farmer-looking fellow came up, and, taking Sidney by the hand, said,—

"I 'spose you've most forgotten me, but that makes no odds: I remember you well enough, and want you should come and see me and be acquainted. I have made some improvements on my farm I should like to show you. And pray bring this gentleman too," turning to Frankford. "I have read of the fine breed of cattle they raise in old England, sir, but if you will take pains to come and see me at my poor house, I guess I can show you some that will match 'em."

"He has a good house, I am certain," said Sidney, as he walked with Frankford to the chaise. "You may easily tell a rich Yankee farmer—he is always pleading poverty."

"For what reason?" inquired Frankford: "I should think he would rather boast."

"It is boasting in disguise. He knows that his wealth is of a kind which will display itself; and the more he disclaims the more minute he hopes will be your survey, wonder, and admiration."

When they had reached home, and all drawn their chairs around a good fire, kindled by Harvey, who had been sent forward for that purpose, Sidney asked Frankford how he liked the wedding and the appearance of the people.

"Shall I answer you on my honor, and in sincerity?" said the Englishman.

"Yes—sincerely," replied Sidney.

"Well, your wedding ceremony was very interesting, and your people appeared better than I expected, and—I will speak truth—better than I wished: all except your deacon—he is a most confounded *bore*,—although now connected with your family."

"Make no difference on that account," replied Sidney; "say of him what you please, we will resign him entirely to your mercy."

"I should show him but little if his destiny depended on me," said the Englishman, "for I received none at his hands. Did you see our encounter?"

"No; nothing particular. I thought, however, you and the deacon were engaged in some interesting discussion."

"As agreeable as you were enjoying by the side of that beautiful girl! Strange, with what delusive coloring imagination invests objects! When we are happy ourselves, we think no one need complain. I wish you had been compelled to exchange seats with me for one half hour, at least."

"Why, you had the best seat in the apartment," remarked Squire Romilly, "and was treated with marked attention, I thought."

"That I willingly acknowledge," said Frankford. "My chair was a good one, and the cake and wine, both excellent, were almost forced upon me by that motherly-looking deaconess, in quantities sufficient to have satisfied the appetite of a Milo."

"Of what, then, do you complain?" inquired Sidney.

"Of your cursed long-winded deacon," replied Frankford. "He was resolutely bent on coercing my admiration, and I have had to listen to every minutiæ of his history, from the hour of his birth, up to this twenty-fifth of November, 18—."

"And have been much edified, I presume," said Sidney, laughing heartily, "or you would have contrived to have escaped him."

"Escape him, Romilly!" ejaculated the Englishman, "the thing was impossible; I might as well have escaped from Newgate. He drew his chair opposite mine, and so close that our noses were more than once absolutely in contact. And then he poured forth his tribulations, and he has undergone more perils than ever did St. Paul. I have been through the wars to some purpose. First the old French war, as he called it, where, at the age of thirteen, he made his *debut* in arms; and then the war of the Revolution, where, if we credit him, the British were sorely beaten, and chiefly by his invincible valor. Then he commenced his civil life,—moved into the wilderness—felled forest trees—and fought wolves; till, finally, he had succeeded in bringing his farm into the best state of cultivation of any one in the town of Northwood; as was evident from his having obtained the premium for the best calf at the last cattle show."

"And so ended his history?"

"No, indeed, I found it only the exordium. Then came an eulogium on his wife's talents for managing a dairy; next the marriages of his daughters, and the death of his son. And I congratulated myself on having arrived near the conclusion, for death, as I thought, was the end of all; but my joy was soon turned to sorrow, for from the decease of that child he dated his experience; and very minutely he related the travail of his soul, I assure you; from thence the transition was easy to the state of the church, and the zeal with which he had labored in its formation; and finally, and lastly, I found he had been deacon thereof for the space of nine years."

The mirth of Sidney, and indeed of the Squire and family, at this recital, was too violent to be restrained, and the room echoed with their peals of laughter.

Frankford's countenance, at first, betrayed some chagrin; but the sympathy of good humor at length conquered, and he joined heartily in the mirth.

"You will probably, Mr. Frandford, report this conversation, as a perfect specimen of Yankee manners and character," said Squire Romilly.

"And if I should, sir," replied the Englishman, "could you tax me with being guilty of much error or exaggeration? I shall make exceptions," continued he, looking round on the family, till his eye rested on Sophia; "but exceptions, you know, do not invalidate a general rule."

"Yet in fixing the standard of national character and manners," said the Squire, "we consider the influence which wisdom and talent exert in the state, and not the wisdom and talents of every individual who composes it. Your nation is renowned for literature and arts; yet the number of educated persons bears no proportion to the ignorant. And your national character is decided by the influence men of honor and abilities exercise over public sentiment. We ask a like indulgence. It is true we have citizens who are and deserve to be ridiculed by Europeans; but they are not those who possess most of the esteem and confidence of their own countrymen. Shall I conclude, because I find you, sir, an accomplished gentleman, that of such is the majority of your inhabitants? And should I make the tour of England, would such expectations be realized? You smile, and I presume would not wish me to measure the intelligence, manners and morals of the farmers of Yorkshire, the manufacturers of Birmingham, and miners of Cornwall by such a standard. Neither must you decide, because you find among us those who are egotists in conversation and bigots in religion, that egotism and bigotry are therefore characteristics of Americans.'

CHAPTER X.

A WALK AND A TALK.

And this our life, exempt from public haunt,
Finds tongues in trees, books in the running brooks,
Sermons in stones, and good in every thing.
AS YOU LIKE IT.

WHEN Frankford entered the breakfast room next morning, the first object that presented itself was Sidney, sitting on a low seat at the farthest part of the room, and surrounded by the junior members of the family, all talking in the loud and animated tones of eager exultation.

"What do you find so very delightful, Romilly?" said the Englishman to Sidney, who was laughing heartily.

"I am showing brother Sidney my cyphering book," said Harvey, his bright eyes sparkling with conscious importance, "and I told him I could repeat every word in my geography."

"And here is my writing book," cried Mary, the rose waxing deeper on her round cheek, "and I had this premium for being at the head of my class the last day."

"I have read this here story book twenty times," said little Lydia, lisping so as almost to need an interpreter, "and ma' gave me this pretty picture to reward me."

Mr. Frankford advanced and examined the specimens of these infant competitors for literary honors; then turning to Harvey,

"You understand geography, you say?"

"Yes, O yes, every question in it," exclaimed the child.

Mr. Frankford opened the map of the world;—"I am an Englishman," said he, "now show me my country."

Harvey immediately pointed to Great Britain.

"And where am I now?"

"Here, sir, right here in New Hampshire," replied the boy, laying his finger on the little mark distinguishing that state.

"Am I far from my country?" inquired Frankford.

"O yes, sir three thousand miles; I should not like to be so far off," replied Harvey; and a shade of concern passed over his smiling countenance.

"And what rout must I take when I wish to return home?" continued the Englishman.

"O, you must sail across the Atlantic, and through the Brittish Channel, and up the Thames, and so to London, if your home is in London?" And he looked up inquiringly in the face of his questioner.

Mr. Frankford smiled.

"I do live there, my little fellow; and when you grow a man, if you should ever sail across the Atlantic, and through the British Channel, and up the Thames, and so to London, come to my house and I will welcome you."

Then taking from his pocket a handful of money, he presented a crown to each of the children, telling them to purchase a Christmas box with it, when the time came, as he should not be there to make them presents.

Squire Romilly and his wife were spectators of this scene; the latter, who had just placed her toast and coffee on the table, seemed to forget they were cooling. They looked at each other, then at their children;—a tear of delight dimmed the eye of the mother—a smile lighted up the benevolent features of the father. It was a happy and proud moment in their lives; such as only is enjoyed when we see our fond exertions crowned with success, and feel that virtue approves the means we have taken to secure it.

When they were seated at the table, Mr. Frankford inquired if it were really true that the whole population of New England was educated.

"If by being educated," replied the Squire, "you mean a knowledge of reading, writing, arithmetic, grammar and geography, or what we term a common school education, the whole population is educated. Every child in the New England States has the privilege of attending our free schools; a noble institution, and unparalleled in the annals of the world."

"Yes," replied the Englishman, "I have heard something about your free schools. If I remember rightly, you usually have one in every township."

The parents smiled, and the children, who were attentively listening to this conversation, were heard to titter.

"Your information," said the Squire, "is hardly correct. The number of free schools in a town depends on the number of inhabitants. The towns are divided into districts, each containing usually from twenty to sixty children under age, or minors, as you would express it. Every district is required, by law, to furnish a school-house; and whenever a district becomes too populous to allow the children to be accommodated in one building, or by the superintendence of one teacher, it is subdivided, on an application of the freemen of that district to the authorities of the town, and after a vote in the affirmative is taken on the question. We now have seven school districts in Northwood, and in a few years shall probably have more."

"And do you maintain schools constantly in every part of your town?" inquired the Englishman.

"No, not constantly in any part. Our public money, which is raised by a tax on our polls and ratable estates, is proportioned among the several districts; in some towns, according to the number of scholars; in others, of property, each district usually receiving sufficient to support a school six months in a year. Thus every child—the poor equally with the rich—from the ages of four to twenty-one, have the privilege of attending school six months in each year. They do not all avail themselves of the extent of this privilege; but none dare neglect it entirely, as the person who could not at least read and write, would almost be thought infamous. Nothing, except gross vices, renders one so completely contemptible, among us, as ignorance. And it is to this general diffusion of knowledge, and the influence it possesses in moulding the character and directing the passions, that we owe most of the moral and political blessings we enjoy. Universal education, sir, is the broad foundation on which we are rearing the imperishable structure of our liberties and national glory."

The good Squire was now in his element, as every free born American is when the independence and glory of his country are the themes of discussion; and he might have launched forth in encomiums, which the fastidious pride of the Englishman would have styled a rhodomontade, had he not luckily been interrupted by the hasty entrance of Doctor Perkins.

"I have come," said the Doctor, addressing himself to Sidney, "commissioned to give you and your friend, Mr. Frankford, an invitation to join our ball this evening. I will not promise you the brilliancy of a London rout, or a Charleston assembly; but you shall see many happy faces, and some handsome ones, and receive a cordial welcome from generous men, and amiable women."

"What say you, Mr. Frankford," said Sidney to the Englishman, who was scrutinizing his card as if willing to find some blunder—"shall we attend?"

"I shall not probably be able to join the festivity," replied he, "but I will go with pleasure, unless Deacon Jones is to be there."

"The Deacon!" exclaimed Perkins; "why, he would sooner attend a levee of Pluto. But Miss Redington will be there, and I feel in duty bound to give Sidney the information, although I fear it will prevent him from attending."

"Annie Redington!" cried Mrs. Romilly; "I don't see how that should hinder Sidney from going. She is the best girl in the world—always so pleasant to every one, and as industrious as if she had lived all her life in the country, instead of being at the top of Boston."

"Will George Cranfield join you?" inquired Sidney.

"No," replied the Doctor; "he never dances. It is a deference to his father's profession, which it becomes him to pay, as he is also qualifying himself for the desk. Yet he does not condemn dancing, when enjoyed with moderation, and on suitable occasions."

"He thinks with me," said the Squire, "that there is a time to dance. I have come to that conclusion after a serious, and, as I believe, a candid examination of the arguments on both sides of the question. My liberality has drawn on me severe censures from some of my brethren, but I cannot place my conscience in the keeping of any mortal, however honest he may be in his opinion. I must judge and act according to the light imparted me, and, until I am convinced of the evil of a practice, I shall not condemn it to gratify others."

"Then we have your approbation for this evening's amusement?" said Sidney.

"Certainly; and my best wishes that you may be happy while enjoying it."

It was soon settled they would attend; and then Doctor Perkins departed, after enjoining it on Frankford and Sidney to dine with him the ensuing day.

"Would you not like to walk out this morning," said the Squire to his son, "and look about the farm to see what improvements we have made during your absence?"

"Yes, I should," replied Sidney: "it is the proposal I was just intending to make. But how will Mr. Frankford be entertained in the meantime? If he go with us, he will probably have to listen to pretty much such a discourse as the deacon gave him last evening."

"It will, at least," said the Englishman, smiling, "be free from religious cant. The good sense of your father ensures me that; and I can tolerate anything better than the puritanical zeal which exalts itself at the expense of every social virtue and innocent enjoyment; which knows no pleasure save that of getting money, and acknowledges no excellence except in a particular and exclusive mode of faith."

"You seem to forget," replied the Squire, "that our country is the only one in which liberty of conscience is fully and perfectly enjoyed. And while no one denomination can claim pre-eminence except what purer principles or better arguments afford, is it a wonder each should endeavor, as far as possible, to uphold its own purity and truth? The discipline of our churches is more strict, and the walk of our professors obliged to be more circumspect, than with you; and this severity and strictness doubtless has a tendency to nourish spiritual pride. But where do you find excellence without a foil? In judging of each other, we should never forget that "Charity hopeth all things." Charity is the virtue for which there is no substitute: if we are deficient in that, *mene, mene, tekel, upharsin*, will be written upon us. I am of Pope's opinion:

> "In *faith* and *hope* the world may disagree;
> But all mankind's concern is *charity*."

They were now prepared for their walk. The morning was beautiful for the season, though the night had been cold, and the frost yet remained where the beams of the sun had not penetrated.

"The autumn has been an extraordinary mild one," said the Squire: "we commonly calculate on a fall of snow about Thanksgiving, and intend, if possible, to have our crops gathered in, and everything snug and secured by that time. I hurried the boys very much, fearing we should have a storm; but it don't come yet."

"Your winters commence early," said the Englishman.

"And continue late," replied the Squire. "We have a cold climate and rough soil to contend with; but the certainty of enjoying the fruits of their industry will animate men to encounter and overcome almost every obstacle. We labor hard, sir but we labor for ourselves;

and Sidney will, I presume, acknowledge there is some difference between voluntary and forced exertion."

"Yes, indeed," replied Sidney. "I recollect perfectly well, when I first went to the South and saw the slaves at labor, I used to think my father would never allow his workmen to be so idle; and many times have I wanted to show them how to work; but their implements were so uncouth, I could not blame them entirely."

As they passed the farm yard, they saw Harvey busily employed in driving forth the cows, that they might obtain a scanty supply of food from the adjoining field.

To some inquiries of Frankford's, the Squire observed he did not keep a great number of cattle.

"My usual number," said he, "is about twenty head of horned cattle, two horses and a flock of sheep. Some of my neighbors winter a much larger stock; but I do not intend any shall have a better one. I always take care to winter no more than I can feed well, and by that means my oxen are able to do much more work, and my cows give double the quantity of milk they would do if poorly fed. But I will not tire you," he continued, turning to Frankford with a smile, "by relating all my history at one time. I am more fortunate than Deacon Jones. As you stay longer with me, I shall be able to communicate it by degrees, and thus save you from being entirely overcome."

As he concluded, Harvey, mounted on a high-spirited colt, galloped past them, and rode a little distance to open a gate for his flock. "That boy rides like a Cossack," said Frankford. "I should think it dangerous, however, to allow him such a pastime."

"His mother is of your opinion," said the Squire; "but I tell her if we run no risk, we can expect no reward. Courage and skill are not to be taught by lectures, Mr. Frankford; they must be acquired by practice, and improved by braving danger; and the younger we begin our lessons the better. An axe, a horse and a gun, were among the first indulgences my boys coveted; and I always gratified them when reason did not absolutely forbid. My wife says I have often violated prudence."

In such conversation they beguiled their walk, till they had proceeded about half a mile, and reached a brook, as we call it; but which in Europe would have been dignified with the name of a river.

This brook, issuing from the pond Sidney had so much admired, and taking an easterly course, watered the fields on the south of the village, and formed a strip of meadow land which only wanted better cultivation to be very productive.

The land on the opposite side of the stream had never (to use the phrase of the country) been cleared; and black alders, and evergreens, intermingled with berry-bearing bushes, hung over the water, and extended back some distance till they were met by taller trees. These soon thickening to a forest, stretched away to the base of a mountain, whose broken ridges and unequal eminences, now softened with a covering of shrubbery, and now rearing their bold and rocky foreheads to the clouds, bounded the horizon of the village, and seemed to forbid access from that quarter.

Along this brook, which the heavy rains usually preceding winter in North America had swelled to a rapid stream, Squire Romilly now proceeded. There was nothing apparent to excite or gratify curiosity, and Frankford more than once wondered why such a route had been chosen. But the Squire had a motive. He wished to discover whether Sidney would recollect a place in the stream, where he had once narrowly, and, as it were, providentially, escaped drowning. Nothing had been mentioned of the circumstance, and when they came opposite the spot, which, ever since the accident, had gone by the name of the "deep holes," Squire Romilly paused and entered into conversation with the Englishman, to allow Sidney full time for the examination of the scene.

The incidents which befall us in childhood and youth, are well and long remembered; and it is then the habits and principles, which through life influence our actions and determine our characters, are almost always imbibed.

In childhood the seed is sown; its growth may be stinted by circumstances; its maturity retarded by situation; its fruit materially altered by culture; yet it will still partake, in a degree, the qualities and flavor of its original stock.

Here was the spot where Sidney, when snatched from the water, had kneeled to thank God for sending him rescue; and here his father had often, during the absence of his son, retired to meditate on the goodness which had then so singularly interposed, and strengthen his faith that the same Providence was still watchful and able to preserve his child though plunged in the chilling stream of affliction, or hurried away by the more dangerous, because insidious current of pleasure.

Squire Romilly had never made or allowed any alterations in this spot, and he could not doubt but Sidney must recollect it.

He did so, but the emotions and train of thought it wakened, were too painful for communication; and turning from his father and Frankford, he stood silent with his eyes fixed on the stream. He thought of the feelings he had there experienced; the wild terror, the struggle for life, the agony when the remembrance of his mother, and how she would weep, came over him; and then he shrieking called on his father: he knew not that he was near, but his father came and snatched him from the waters!

Oh! the joy to escape from death! and his father held him to his breast, and he felt the warm tears bedew his cheek.

He remembered, too, how, while he was endeavoring to thank that kind parent, his father interrupted him and bade him thank God, for He it was who had preserved him. Then his father kneeled and he with him, and he remembered how he there mentally promised never to forget the Being his father adored with such gratitude.

But he had forgotten Him, and there arose in his mind confused images of many scenes in which he had participated, that his father's prudence and piety would have condemned; and he dreaded, so powerful is conscience when first awakened, to meet his eye, lest its expression should convey a reproach that the life he thus preserved had been devoted to folly.

There is a sacredness in the emotions of early piety, for gratitude to God is piety, which hallows its recollections even to the heart which has been enervated by pleasure, or hardened by an intimacy with selfishness and vice; and Sidney, while his mind wandered backward and dwelt on the innocent and happy days of his childhood, was tempted to wish he had then resigned his life; even then when his spirit would have returned to heaven pure as when breathed by the goodness of his Creator.

"That stream interests you much," said Frankford. "I should think it recalled recollections similar to the pond that we passed in our way hither."

Sidney raised his head—his eye met his father's;—there was something in its expression which seemed to say,—

"My son, is your heart yet pure? Can you still, when in danger, look confidently to Him who must save, or you will perish forever?"

"This spot," said Sidney, striving to speak cheerfully, "has not much claim to my admiration, although a deep place in my memory. It was here when, about nine years old, in attempting to swim I once went beyond my depth, and should not now have related the story had not my father unexpectedly come to my aid."

"Yet it was not to me I told you to ascribe the favor," said his father, watching with anxiety his son's varying countenance.

"Am I certain it was a favor?" returned Sidney. "I have sometimes thought long life was not greatly to be desired."

"To those who improve it as they ought, it is undoubtedly a blessing. I have lived nearly fifty years, and never did one pass without bringing comforts and mercies in its train; and not one that I cannot reflect on with satisfaction and gratitude," said the Squire.

"Then the fault must be mine, I suppose," returned Sidney; "but I confess I have, even in my short career, at times thought life was a dear purchase, and that those only who were fools or cowards coveted it."

"I fear, my son," replied the affectionate father, while the tears of parental concern filled his eyes, "I fear your acquaintance with the world has not contributed to your happiness."

"Do you think, sir," inquired the Englishman, "that an acquaintance with the world, as it is termed, that is, with its follies and vices, is ever productive of happiness? Some philosophers have asserted that man can be happy only in proportion to his removal from a civilized state, and that of all nations now existing, the savage are the best entitled to pretend to innocence and happiness."

"And I wish," replied the Squire, "that all such philosophers were compelled to test the truth of their theories by an actual residence of a few years with the people they so much admire."

The subject of conversation had changed, and neither Sidney nor his father seemed disposed to renew it. Leaving the brook, therefore, they walked on in silence, and, ascending a rising ground, passed a very large thrifty-looking orchard, when Squire Romilly interrupted the meditations of his guests, by descanting on the goodness and quantity of fruit it produced, assuring them that, "take one year with another, he made forty barrels of cider; and," continued he, "the cider I sell, or the greater portion,—five or six barrels of cider, with plenty of home-brewed beer, and my wife's currant wine, are all the liquors we use in our family, and all we find necessary to enable us to support fatigue, or enjoy a social visit of our friends.

After walking a little farther, they reached an eminence which the Squire told them commanded a view of his whole farm, and indeed most of the neighborhood, and they turned to examine the prospect.

Before and below them lay the village, with its irregular buildings, of all sizes, shapes and colors, which the owners thereof could devise or obtain, each wishing to give some distinguishing characteristic to his own dwelling. Above all, rose the meeting-house, with its towering spire and cunning fish, catching a brilliancy from the morning beams, which every inhabitant of the briny deep might have envied.

North and south stretched the cultivated fields of the villagers, all now brown and seared; but from their situation, and the degree of cultivation they exhibited, there was no doubt but they well rewarded their owners for the industry which had thus made the harvests wave on the site of the wilderness.

And to the honor of this little community, most of whom were farmers, it shall be recorded, that nearly all the stumps—I wish I could write *all*—were removed. It is the appearance of these stumps which, to the eye accustomed to the neatness of European cultivation, particularly the English, so much disfigures the scenery throughout most of New England, and, indeed, of all North America. But in this pleasant village, the stumps had disappeared, and the stones, too, had been mostly removed, and used in forming enclosures around the fields. Many cattle and sheep were scattered over these fields, picking a scanty meal from the withered herbage, and their unsatisfied hunger keeping them continually shifting their places, gave to the scene an appearance of animation and interest which Frankford remarked with admiration.

"Why, yes," said the Squire, "those cattle stirring so, make everything look alive. And, indeed, I think men never appear more happy or more honorable than when surrounded by their natural dependents, those animals which are willingly subjected to their sway, and glad to receive protection from them. Their brethren are not thus easily subdued."

"And yet," said the Englishman, "there are, in your free country, human beings, brothers I suppose you would call them, in a condition which degrades them to a level with yonder brutes."

"I acknowledge it," returned the Squire, "and I feel it is a stain on our national character, and none could more heartily rejoice to see the evil removed. But the sin of introduction, Mr. Frankford, is not on the Americans. They did not wish it; indeed they zealously opposed it. It was forced upon them by Great Britain, whose colonies we then were; and Englishmen should not reproach us with the system of slavery, when the power of England alone effected its introduction."

The good Squire spoke with warmth, and in an elevation of tone he seldom used. Frankford carelessly replied.

"Your statements are undoubtedly true, yet your southern planters seem willing enough to continue the system. I presume they find it a very useful and convenient thing, and doubt not it would require a much greater exertion of power to suppress slavery than it did to introduce it."

"And of necessity it must," said the Squire. "We all know that habits, when once formed, even though they may have been adopted with reluctance or aversion, are often thought necessary to our happiness and sometimes to our existence. It is this principle in human nature which should make us very sedulous to guard our hearts and lives from the approaches of evil. I have no doubt many of the slave-holders would rejoice to have the southern states entirely freed from slaves, and cultivated in the same manner we Yankees do at the north. They cannot be blind to the evils of the system—they certainly are not blind to its dangers; but the difficulty is to provide a remedy. I have thought much on the subject, especially since Sidney's residence at the south, and I own I do not see how the masters can, at present, do better by their slaves than treat them humanely; but I hope and pray the time may come when they can be emancipated without danger to themselves or the country."

"You may *hope*, but do you seriously *believe* such a time will ever come in this country?"

"I do," replied the Squire, firmly.

"When?"

"Times and seasons are known only to the Most High."

"It is very easy to prophesy a good time coming, and leave it for Providence to bring about," said Frankford, dryly. "Now the British people and parliament are in earnest; our West India slaves will soon be freed, whether the right time has come or not."

"Well, try the experiment. We may learn something from its workings, though I do not anticipate any favorable results to the cause of freedom and humanity from such a step," said the Squire.

CHAPTER XI.

THE DAY AFTER THANKSGIVING.

'Tis liberty alone that gives the flower
Of fleeting life its lustre and perfume,
And we are weeds without it. All constraint,
Except what wisdom lays on evil men,
Is evil. COWPER.

THE Squire would probably have expatiated at length on the topic of slavery, for it was one, in all its bearings with which he was better acquainted than most of his neighbors, having been often compelled by the animadversions of some of his less prosperous neighbors, and above all, from the fiery abolition zeal of Deacon Jones, to defend his conduct, in placing Sidney in a slaveholding country; but they were interrupted by the report of a gun a few paces off, in a wood on their left.

They had heard the same a number of times during their walk, and Frankford had been on the point of inquiring the cause of its frequency, but had been prevented, at the moment, by some conversation which it was difficult to interrupt. He now inquired, but before he could receive an answer, a lad appeared issuing from the wood, his gun supported on his shoulder with one hand, and in the other was a quantity of game. As he sprung over a tree which had been blown down, and which had prevented his seeing the party, he stood directly before them.

"You are hunting, then, this morning, Luther," said the Squire; "do you have good luck?"

"O, pretty considerably good, sir," replied the youth; "I have killed these here five squirrels, two patridges and a blue-jay. I was out as soon as 'twas light, but the game a'nt half so plenty as 'twas a month ago, when your Jim and Amos Winter had their squirrel hunt."

"Are you fond of hunting, young man?" asked Mr. Frankford, attentively surveying the stripling who was standing so erect before them. His hat was set smartly on his head, and he was neatly though plainly dressed; while the exercise the pastime he was enjoying required, gave a deeper glow of health to his ruddy countenance, now lighted up with the keen animation of the sportsman. But what rendered him most peculiarly an object of interest to the foreigner was, that air and look of fearless confidence, blended with an expression of civility and a willingness to oblige, which, in this land of equality, distinguishes the poorest of our free citizens from the peasantry of every other country in the world.

"Fond of hunting?" repeated the youth, "I guess I am, sir. When my gun is good and game plenty, I love it better than eating when I am hungry."

"And how is your gun now?" inquired Sidney, laying his hand on the neat fowling piece.

The lad instantly resigned it.

"O, it is a capital one," he replied; "I don't believe there ever was a better, though my father is always praising his old Queen Anne rifle, and telling how many times he fired it without missing at the battle of Bennington, and how General Stark praised him; but I tell him I know I could fire this as many times without missing."

"You endeavor to keep alive the memory of your battles, I see," said the Englishman, turning to the Squire with a look of affected indifference.

"Why, yes," replied he, "the war of our revolution was too important in its consequences to allow its details to be soon forgotten. *We*, at least, shall preserve them."

"What are you intending to do with your game?" inquired Frankford, addressing the young hunter; "do you eat these animals?" and he pointed to the squirrels and the jay.

"Eat them," repeated the lad, laughing, yet looking full in the stranger's face with a glance of keen inquiry, as if endeavoring to ascertain whether the question were prompted by pleasantry or contempt; "no, I guess not. Why, sir, John Watson and I are captains of the hunting match, and we have agreed to carry all the whole squirrels we kill; sometimes they carry only the heads, but then they cheat plaguily, for they'll kill 'em a week beforehand, sir, and they can keep heads better than whole squirrels. But we intend to have everything fair and square, and so we carry whole ones; and every partridge and blue jay counts one, and the side that is beaten pays for the supper and toddy."

Frankford, when asking his question, which was prompted merely by the wish of changing a conversation in which he found he could obtain no laurels, little anticipated such an animated reply; and the effect was entirely to dispel his chagrin for the allusion to the Bennington battle; and his countenance, from an expression of mortified vanity and a little contempt, relaxed during the harangue of Luther Merrill to the merry pleasantry of broad good humor, while again addressing Luther.

"You say you are a captain—pray how many men do you command?"

"We have twelve on each side, sir, besides boys to carry the game. I engaged a boy to go with me, but he did'nt come. But yonder comes Harvey—now Squire, I wish you'd let him go with me."

This request was eagerly backed by Harvey, who came bounding up the hill to tell his father he had "done all the *chores* himself, for Sam and Oliver went off early to the shooting match, and now," continued he, "I want to go and play, for it is the day after Thanksgiving."

"Well, go," said the indulgent father, "but mind my boy, and keep out of the way of the guns, and take care, Luther, and do no mischief in your fun."

Both promised to be careful, and striking into the woods, were out of sight in a moment; in the next, the report of the gun, followed by the loud laugh of Harvey, and the shout, "he's dead, he's dead, Luther!" justified the encomiums the latter had bestowed on his fowling piece.

"Have you any laws for the securing of your game?" inquired the Englishman; "or do your people hunt wherever they please?"

"Just where they please," returned the Squire. "The beasts of the forest, the birds of the air, and the fish of the sea, are not protected by our institutions. We, sir, make laws for freemen, and no statutes assimilating their condition to that of slaves would be endured."

"But your laws ensure to every citizen his rights of property," rejoined the other. "Now, on my estate, I consider the game as the most valuable part of my property."

"That," returned the Squire, "is because you have been accustomed to such considerations. But reason, if we consult it, will tell us that whatever we have bestowed cost or labor upon, or have received by transmission from those who possessed by such a right, is the only property we can rightfully claim the exclusive privilege of enjoying or transmitting to others. The animals which own no master, and subsist without any care from man, being dependent on nature alone, cannot belong to any individual."

"Well, if I were the owner of an estate here," said Frankford, "I would endeavor to have some regulations, giving me the exclusive right to game on my own estate. Do you not think such a statute, if enacted, could be enforced?"

"No, not for any length of time."

"What! would your Yankees take the field and oppose it with their rifles?"

"No, I think not; but with weapons you would find quite as efficient—with their votes at the poll. You gentlemen, accustomed to monarchical institutions, are apt to confound our liberty with licentiousness; but no people, as a people, are more submissive to the laws than the freemen of our United States; every good citizen holding himself responsible for the execution of those wholesome regulations he has either directly or indirectly contributed to make, and for the observance of the constitution. No, sir, I do not think there would be any hostile measures used until we had exhausted all pacific ones. We should probably forbear trespassing on your grounds till the next meeting of the legislature; taking good care, in the meantime, to elect such members as would, then and there, repeal your exclusive statute."

"Yes, I presume so," returned the Englishman. "The rabble here have entirely the ascendancy, and every man who can contrive to get himself nominated is eligible to office. I think, in New Hampshire, you require no qualifications of rank, property, character or religion: a proper *age* is all the requisite."

"We acknowledge no rank," observed the Squire, "and perfect liberty of conscience is enjoyed by all; consequently, the rank or religious creed of an individual can have no influence on his election. That we pay no deference to property, is not certainly a reproach: we cannot be taxed with selling our votes to the highest bidder; but character is very essential. I do not believe a man guilty of gross and notorious vices would consent to become a candidate for any office. The press, sir, is with us perfectly free; and the opposition would drag every hidden sin to light; and public opinion, when rightly directed, exercises a censorship more appalling to vice than any punishment a tyrant could inflict."

"And is no mischief to be apprehended from the expression and influence of popular sentiment? Is the voice of the people always the voice of justice? You, sir, are well read in ancient history, and will recollect Aristides was banished by the vote of the people! In the hands of upright and intelligent men like yourself, Squire Romilly, power may be safely trusted: it is the preponderance of the rabble which will prove your destruction."

"While public opinion is enlightened by universal

education," answered the Squire, "there is but little cause to fear injustice from popular sentiment, or the subversion of our institutions. Had all the Athenians who voted for the banishment of Aristides been capable of *writing* their own names on the shells, the ostracism against him might not have been obtained. Nor have we, in the New England States, many such persons as you designate by the appellation of *rabble.* There may be, in the cities, a few worthy of that ancient and significant name; yet not many of these are native-born American citizens. We are an industrious, sober, quiet and orderly people, generally reflecting before we act, and examining before we decide; and this our history, if you should ever think it worth your examination, will abundantly prove."

During this long (and rather dull, is it not?) conversation, Sidney had remained silent, and apparently absorbed in no very pleasant meditations; and the anxiety with which his father frequently regarded him, manifested a suspicion that all was not well with this still favorite child.

But the bustling importance with which Mrs. Romilly welcomed their return, and the anxiety she expressed lest Mr. Frankford should have caught cold, or be too much fatigued by his walk, allowed Sidney time to recover his wonted flow of spirits and usual serenity of countenance.

The day passed pleasantly away; to Sidney and his family it was rendered exquisitely delightful by the interchange of interesting communications, and the confidence of mutual inquiries; to the Englishman it was *unique* at least. It displayed human nature in a light which he had never beheld nor considered probable.

Here was the father of a family living in all the simplicity of retirement, inuring his children to habits of prudence and laborious industry; yet cultivating in them a taste for the refinements of literature and the love of science, and cherishing in their minds hopes of obtaining the highest honors and privileges their country could bestow, by superior merit alone, without the subterfuges of artifice or the favor of the great.

Squire Romilly was a man exactly calculated to win on the mind of prejudice, and remove those unfavorable impressions which arise more from misapprehension than actual dislike. His good sense and extensive information on every subject connected with the history and political situation, not only of his own country, but of Europe, made his conversation at once interesting and instructive; but what rendered it more agreeable to the stranger, was the candor with which he listened to objections Frankford sometimes urged against particular customs or institutions of the Americans; the deference and admiration he expressed for the English character and literature, and above all, the entire suppression of that boasting spirit which, to foreigners, is often disgustingly visible in our countrymen.

The hour for attending the ball, seven o'clock, had arrived, and they were all assembled in the sitting-room, waiting the coming of the carriage—a stage coach, hired by the managers for the occasion, and driven round to collect the company—when Harvey came running, almost breathless, into the apartment, to tell that the squirrel-hunt was over, and they had just counted the game.

"And has Captain—I forget his name—conquered?" asked Frankford.

"O no, no, sir!" replied Harvey, "Luther hunted and hunted, and killed twenty-nine himself; but his side is beaten for all that. John Watson has five the most; but Luther says he knows he cheated, and I know he did."

"Harvey," said his father, in a mild but reproachful tone, "should you like to be accused of cheating?"

The child felt the rebuke; he hung his head and cast down his bright eyes with a look of shame.

"I *guess* he cheated," said he; "I am sure Luther ought to have beaten."

"How soon," said Squire Romilly, turning to Frankford, "our feelings will warp our sense of justice! Because Harvey has attended Luther Merrill to-day, he en ters entirely into his interest, and that so warmly, he can see no merit in his competitor. It is of the first importance to impress on the minds of children and youth, the precept of doing as they would be done by—no other principle will preserve their integrity at the age when reason is feeble and appetite and passion strong."

"Yet I cannot much blame my little friend here for his preference," said Frankford; "to confess the truth, I entered very heartily into the interest of that Merrill. He looked so frank, so confident of success, and so happy, that I feel really sorry disappointment has overtaken him."

"What if we try to mitigate his misfortune," said Sidney; "I suppose it is mostly of the pecuniary kind."

"O no," replied the Squire; "our young hunters feel heavily the disgrace of being beaten. Not, perhaps, so much as your Wellington would have done at Waterloo, but enough to mortify them very sensibly."

"He shall feel no other inconvenience at this time," said Sidney, taking out his pocket book. "Pray, Harvey, do you know what the bill for supper was expected to be?"

"I heard brother Oliver say," replied the child, "it would be as much as fifty cents a-piece."

"And there are twelve of them," said his father; "how much, Harvey, will be the amount of the whole bill?"

"How much?—why, just six dollars, sir," he replied, after a moment's hesitation.

"You allow no opportunity of instructing your children to pass unimproved, I see," said the Englishman.

"I endeavor to give them advice and information at the moment they feel its need," replied the Squire; "they will then appreciate its value. The formality of lectures is of but little importance in correcting imprudences of practice, or imparting practical knowledge."

Sidney had now taken out his pocket book. "Allow me to go shares in your liberality," said the Englishman.

"No, sir, no," replied Sidney; "I have taken this

affair wholly on myself. We will only, in our behalf, tax you with a generosity of spirit in judging of our character and customs; on your purse we need make no demands."

He then delivered the money to Harvey, with directions, and Frankford, notwithstanding Sidney's objections, would add a crown to defray, he said, any extra expense which might arise. Harvey having received the cash and orders, scampered off, happier than ever was a candidate for political honors in obtaining the object of his ambition; for his happiness arose solely from the pure benevolent idea of the felicity he was commissioned to impart to others.

CHAPTER XII.

THE BALL AND THE BELLE.

On with the dance! let joy be unconfined;
No sleep till morn, when youth and pleasure meet
To chase the glowing hours with flying feet.

CHILDE HAROLD.

THE ball which our visitors were invited to attend, was given at the public hotel, the room appropriated to this amusement being always designated "the hall."

This hall, a spacious room, in the estimation of the company, had been splendidly fitted up for the occasion. Branches of pine, and spruce, and festoons formed of a species of evergreen called ground laurel, ornamented with artificial roses, were disposed around the apartment, which was lighted by a handsome chandelier, depending from the middle of the vaulted roof, and numerous lamps, tastefully arranged among the evergreens around the room. At one side of the apartment, and on seats raised several steps from the floor, sat the musicians. These were three in number, two playing the violin, the other the clarionet.

The ball had been opened before the arrival of our party, and the dancers were jigging with spirit. The strangers were met at the street door by one of the managers, conducted up stairs, ushered to the head of the hall, and seated in a convenient place to reconnoitre the company. Dr. Perkins was immediately beside them.

"I had got to the bottom," said he, striving to recover breath, "but I would have left the middle of the dance to welcome you. Mr. Frankford, I hope you will have no reason to regret the honor you do us by joining our party to-night;—for my friend Romilly here, I presume he will be unhappy when I inform him I have arranged for his dancing the next figure with Annie Redington."

Mr. Frankford, bowing, made the usual compliment of the happiness it gave him to witness theirs; and Sidney inquired why he was thus supposed predetermined to be wretched.

"Because," replied Perkins, "I cannot doubt but your affections are already engaged. With your advantages of person and fortune, you must have excited the sensibility of some fair creature; and with your warm heart, she would certainly have met a return: it must be so," he continued, while a half stifled sigh and a whole blush, swelled the heart and crimsoned the cheek of Sidney; "and now how can you help feeling miserable when dancing with such a beautiful girl, whom you cannot but admire, and yet know you have not a heart to give her?"

"And why is he considered the only susceptible man?" inquired the Englishman: "do you think me wholly formed of ice?"

"I suppose your heart is impenetrable here," answered the doctor; "not by nature—heaven forbid I should ever think so ill of the countryman of Byron—but by—prejudice. Pardon the word, sir, I could not soften it."

"And so I have been, I confess, doctor; but my armor is fast dissolving. A few days spent in your hospitable society have taught me how to appreciate your character better than would an age of study; and I shall certainly regret to leave your country, although to visit my own."

The doctor listened to this compliment with a smile of more than pleasure—it was pride. There is no people whose good opinion is more gratifying to Americans than that of the English; and although we shall never fawn or stoop to obtain it, we justly appreciate it when generously offered.

But the doctor was prevented from replying, by a summons to his place, and Mr. Frankford continued silent and attentive till the dance was finished. The doctor then again appeared, and inquired of him if he would join in the next dance.

"Not now," replied the other; "and indeed my health ought to excuse me for the whole evening; yet, perhaps, before its close, inclination will overcome prudence."

"And remember," said the gay doctor, laying his hand familiarly and kindly on the shoulder of the Englishman, "should bad effects ensue, I am in the commission of health here, and shall claim the privilege of attending you."

Then taking Sidney's arm he led him to another part of the hall and presented him to Miss Redington, communicating, at the same time, the request of the managers, that they would call the figure.

After some demurring and excuses, such as usually occur, this was finally assented to; and then, seeing the floor filled and the dance commenced, Perkins returned and seated himself by the Englishman.

The history of Annie Redington, now the partner of our hero, has been briefly, yet perhaps sufficiently sketched; but the influence her rather singular fortune had had on her mind and disposition, may not be uninteresting to those who like to have a reason rendered for every appearance, and a cause ascribed for every effect.

It has already been said she was beautiful, and I think personal appearance has a decided influence on female character. Yet, let not the lady who has a fair face look up with an exulting smile, thinking the palm of excellence is to be awarded to beauty; neither let her of homely features heave a sigh, while reflecting on the inferiority to which nature has doomed her.

They would both mistake my meaning.

The eye is delighted with fair proportions: symmetry, delicacy, and grace, have a charm over the senses of the beholder, directly communicating with the heart, and often imposing on the understanding.

"There's nothing ill can dwell in such a temple," is a

suggestion involuntarily arising when we first gaze on a being whom nature has delighted to honor. And were such impressions realized—were beauty of person always an index of mental excellence—the hard-favored and ill-featured ones would indeed be in a sad predicament.

But nature is not thus partial in the distribution of her favors. To those who boast but little of her fashioning skill without, is often imparted as much symmetry of mind—I will hazard the expression—as much delicacy and beauty of soul, as ever went to the formation of a Helen or a Rosamond; and the chances for the improvement of those spiritual graces are certainly in her favor. She has not the admiration of the world to seduce her attention from her studies or duties; the syren voice of the flatterer does not arrest her progress while striving for perfection, by whispering she is already an angel. She soon learns the necessity of being useful if she would be respected, and good if she would be loved; and thus, to the desire of obtaining the approbation of heaven and the applause of her own conscience, is added the powerful motive of obtaining the favor of men to accelerate her proficiency in those qualifications which must ultimately fix the standard of her excellence in both worlds.

A fair face does not long retain its fairness; and there are few beings more unhappy or contemptible than the antiquated belle or coquette, with no charm of mind to prevent the beholder from dwelling on the alteration of her person, and no loveliness of heart to repair the ravages of time or disease.

It is the bane of beautiful women to trust in their beauty; yet while they are continually receiving homage for their charms, how difficult it is to convince them it will not always be thus! Nothing, under such circumstances, except the most watchful discretion and assiduous care on the part of those entrusted with her education, or the grace which cometh from on high, can prevent such a lady from becoming vain.

Vanity and envy are the besetting sins of women.

The handsome are inclined to the former, the plain to the latter. Vanity sullies the charms of the person, and envy withers the excellences of the mind; but as the plain are necessarily obliged to be more assiduous in cultivating their understandings and regulating their tempers, there is more hope that they will correct those errors and foibles which are common to humanity.

To sum the whole, as in the library of the student, the books he most values are usually the plainest bound; so in the female world, excellence, and merit, and talents, are oftenest found beneath a plain covering; yet when the pure page is enclosed in a beautiful binding, it is then most perfect.

And Annie Redington was such a one. Circumstances beyond human control or agency had undoubtedly contributed to this result; yet worth is not the less to be prized because it has been formed by culture.

Few are born with such happy dispositions as make discipline unnecessary. And Annie certainly was not; but she had that docile temper which lends a willing ear to instruction, and endeavors to profit by the lessons of wisdom and experience.

The death of her father, and the consequent indigence of her mother, prevented her childhood from being indulged in the supineness and selfishness which so often injure the children of the rich; while the elegance of her mother's manners, and the refinement of her sentiments, equally removed her from the contagion of vulgarity and meanness, to which the poor are exposed.

Her mother was the magnet of her young heart and affections. To imitate her example, and contribute to her happiness, were the first wishes she formed. And if sometimes, with the thoughtlessness of the child, she enumerated the pretty playthings and costly ornaments of her little mates, and asked for like indulgences, her mother had but to say—"Annie, you have no father to provide for you, and are you not contented to live as your mother must?"

Then the sweet girl, throwing her arms around her

mother's neck, and kissing the tears from the face she so much loved, would declare she had enough, all she wanted, and was sorry she had asked for a single thing.

Thus early was taught the lesson of self-control. And from pitying her mother, she felt the desire, and formed the resolution to assist her; happy under every task imposed, and asking only to beguile it, that her mother would talk about her father.

This was a theme on which Mrs. Redington could dwell with that fond melancholy which the joys that are past inspire. Her husband she had loved with that deep, devoted, confiding affection, which merit only inspires and virtue only feels; and to trace his character and impress his sentiments on the heart of their child, was the dearest earthly pleasure her widowed soul could enjoy. It encouraged her piety when reflecting on his, and she was reconciled to endure the crosses of earth when confiding in hope that she should shortly meet him in heaven to part no more.

Thus the pleasures of the world never obtained a prominence in any picture of future felicity which Mrs. Redington presented before her darling child. She was taught that our earth is what all will find it—a place where much *may* be enjoyed, and also a place where much *must* be suffered; and her fortitude was strengthened by the lessons of patience, prudence, resignation, and self-denial which her mother's example always exhibited—a much more efficient method of impressing truths on the human mind, than the most eloquent or elaborate lectures.

Yet they did not dwell in a state of melancholy seclusion from the world, or in peevish repining at their own situation. Annie's temperament was gay as the birds when first welcoming the spring flowers; and Mrs. Redington, naturally of a cheerful disposition, did not wish to depress that happy buoyancy of spirit which sits so gracefully on youth and innocence. She only carefully watched, lest gaiety should approach levity; and by awakening her reason, and sometimes by gentle expostulations, she directed to the performance of her duties, those energies which are often allowed to expend themselves on frivolous fashions or selfish gratifications.

Whenever the art of education can make duties pleasures, the grand obstacle in the path of human improvement is removed.

But her mother died; and to Annie's young heart the world then appeared as wide and lonely as it did to our first parents when driven from Eden.

Yet there is One who careth for all; and in Him the dying Christian trusted. She committed, in faith, the care of her destitute child to her God, and He did provide. The hearts of all who knew the little orphan were softened to pity; and the lady who finally adopted, and for six years treated her with all the tenderness of a mother, was a woman capable of performing tne duties she had thus voluntarily assumed. Beneath her forming care, the fair child grew a lovely, intelligent, and accomplished young lady, realizing those expectations her docility and early industry had inspired.

There can be no excellence attained without industry. The mind of the idle, like the garden of the slothful, will be overgrown with briars and weeds; and indolence, under whatever fashionable name it may assume, sensibility or nervous affections, delicacy or dyspepsia, is a more dangerous enemy to practical goodness, and to moral and intellectual improvement, than even dissipation or luxury. Those who tread a devious path, may possibly retrace their steps, or by a circuitous route finally reach the goal; but those who never stir, how can they win the race!

It is a good thing to have habits of industry formed early, and to be able to connect our first exertions with the happiness or benefit they imparted to those we loved. This Annie Redington could do, and the pleasure it gave her made employment, ever after, a privilege instead of a burden; and when she was released from the necessity of labor, she was still ready to receive every order, and attentive to fulfill every wish of her benefactress. Her warm and grateful heart would indeed have incited her to do all this, but she could now perform it with dexterity and satisfaction to herself; and Mrs. Eaton, to the pleasure of having protected the destitute, soon found she might add the convenience of having obtained an excellent assistant. And she soon loved Annie better, for the useful must combine with the agreeable, in the character of one whom we love well and love long. Accomplishments are like costly apparel, elegant, but sometimes cumbrous or useless appendages; while usefulness, like a plain suit, is always becoming and often indispensable.

To a superficial observer, Annie might have been thought to owe her education entirely to Mrs. Eaton; but it was her mother who bent the twig to the right inclination — whose lessons imparted perseverance and energy to genius and delicacy, and infused patience and fortitude in a bosom naturally possessing the keenest and most trembling sensibility.

It was this disciplined disposition which made her so soon and so easily conform to the simple arrangements of her uncle's family. She was never once heard to repine at her altered style of living, nor ridicule the inconvenient house and old fashioned furniture, nor squeamishly affect a distaste for her aunt's plain cookery; but she exerted herself to please and serve them in every way she could devise, and was, by her own desire, very soon initiated in all the mysteries of the dairy, and even learned of her cousin Priscilla to spin!

Perhaps it would gratify those who do not delight in perfect characters, if I tell them Annie did weep and even fret a little at the necessity of parting with her beloved piano. But her uncle would not be persuaded to allow the "rattling thing," as he called it, "to enter his sober dwelling." He had no ear for the concord of sweet sounds, and told Annie "he hoped she would find something better to do than to be flourishing and twiddling away at *sich* a rate; any way, Priscilla would not have time to listen."

So the sweet girl played her farewell air, kissed the

instrument which had so often afforded her ecstatic delight, wiped her eyes, and with a smile followed her uncle to his carriage.

She did not think, because her uncle had offered to protect her, he was therefore bound to gratify all her whims or wishes; and she was never heard to complain of the cruelty which had separated her from her piano; nor indeed did she name the instrument at all, till when learning to spin she one day told Priscilla the noise of the wheel reminded her of the music of that instrument.

But the wheel did that for Annie which the harp of Apollo would never have effected. It entirely removed the pain in her side, from which she formerly suffered, and restored the circulation of her blood to its original briskness; and when she was introduced to Sidney, the glow and animation of perfect health, joined with youth, beauty, and intelligence, to complete a picture of loveliness rarely surpassed. And the person who could have gazed on her finely rounded form and expressive face, where every grace seemed united, and thought her less delicately attractive because she owed the bloom on her cheek, and the happy gayety of her manner, mostly to the health and cheerfulness which industrious exercise bestows, must have been fastidious indeed.

As Sidney gazed, his heart acknowledged she was worthy to be loved; yet he did not fall in love. There is a kind of credulous fervency, a glow of the imagination, which can make deities of mortals and heaven of earth, necessary to constitute a *lover at first sight*;—this glow, like April sunshine, is bright and brief, and when it has once been clouded, it rarely burns again with its original warmth or intensity. The cloud had passed over Sidney, and he was "a sadder and a wiser man;" but here is no place to relate his history.

Annie Redington, however, was more susceptible. She had never before beheld a man who at all realized the idea she had formed of her father. Mrs. Redington would often describe him to her child, and when the affectionate creature would simply ask if he was as hand some as her mother, she always received an answer in the spirit, if not in the words, of Lady Randolph's affecting language to her son:

> ———————"In me thou dost behold
> The poor remains of beauty once admired;
> The autumn of my days is come already,
> For sorrow made my summer haste away;
> Yet in my prime I equaled not thy *father*."

And thus Annie, from her mother's description and her own imagination had formed an ideal picture of perfection—"where every god did seem to set his seal," and with which every man who approached her had to be compared. And no wonder they should suffer by such a comparison! Even the merits of George Cranfield were obscured, and although Annie esteemed him, and felt she could love him dearly if he were her brother, yet she would never for a moment admit the idea of marrying him.

But Sidney Romilly was a very different being; he had such a very striking and noble countenance, was so graceful in his manners, so polite and attentive, and spoke so kindly, she thought he must be like her father, and while listening to him was almost tempted to wish with poor Desdemona, "that heaven had made her such a man;" or rather that she might appear as amiable in his eyes as he did in hers.

Had he been an utter stranger, the timid delicacy of her nature would have shrunk from his attentions, but his family were her best and most valued friends, and she had so often heard him described and extolled that she thought his merit undoubted, and in conversing with him felt all the freedom which approved worth and intimate acquaintance inspire.

But their apparent satisfaction with each other did not pass unnoticed; many significant smiles were seen, and some knowing winks exchanged, yet none seemed to disapprove, or be jealous of their intimacy, except one little pert looking fellow, who kept continually hovering around Annie, watching every movement and endeavor ing to catch every syllable of their conversation. His impertinence in following them to their seat when the figure was ended, and crowding as near as possible, did not escape the notice of Dr. Perkins, who remarked to Mr. Frankford "that there was a fellow he heartily wished was in Constantinople."

"For what reason?" inquired the Englishman.

"Because he would immediately turn Turk and then might possibly go to Mahomet's paradise—to the christian's heaven he never will."

"Are his sins unpardonable by your creed?"

"Why, sir," replied Perkins, "he is a compound of meanness, selfishness, and hypocrisy; one of those characters who deserve a prison daily for violations of humanity, honesty, and decency; and yet he calculates so warily that the law can have no hold on him, and he gains property so fast he has his adherents and flatterers even among the respectable and well-meaning. But I hope," added he, eyeing the little gentleman who appeared to be edging still closer to Sidney and Annie, "I hope, if he offer an insult to Romilly he will have to answer it;—I should like to be Sidney's second on such an occasion."

A movement among the company prevented farther explanation; and the floor was soon occupied for another cotillion.

Perkins again asked the stranger if he wished to join; he declined for that time, but added, "Don't let me detain you, doctor; I shall be well entertained by seeing your performance."

"No," said Perkins, "I am not in a humor for jigging to-night. My wife is not here, and I can never enjoy such a scene without her to partake it. She was detained at home by the sudden illness of our babe, and I should have staid with her, had I not expected to meet you and Romilly."

The Englishman received this domestic intelligence with a kind of comical stare; and he could not help thinking how such a speech, delivered as this was, in the perfectly natural tone of native feeling, would be greeted by the fashionable husbands of his own fashionable metropolis.

The figure now called was an intricate but very graceful one when well executed, and the dancers acquitted themselves handsomely. After regarding their movements for some time with earnest and silent attention, Mr. Frankford suddenly burst into a laugh which appeared wholly involuntary.

Dr. Perkins started, and a slight embarrassment, half ludicrous, half alarmed, might be perceived shading his good humored countenance, as he turned his eyes on the Englishman with a look which demanded explanation.

Frankford, the moment he could speak, explained the whole by saying,

"Excuse me, doctor, I was not laughing at your countrymen, but at my own. I was thinking of the ridiculous prejudices the English as a nation, have imbibed respecting America. There are individuals, and honorable ones too, who do you ample justice; and to such should I describe the scene I am now witnessing, they would credit me, and rejoice in your happiness and social refinement. But the mass of my countrymen would account it as much a fable as the discoveries of Gulliver. They think you half savage, wholly selfish, and possessing nothing which assimilates you to Englishmen except the tatters of their language. Should I tell them that, in the interior of New Hampshire, I attended a ball, where the ladies and gentlemen were dressed in the same materials (I don't say as rich,) and, nearly in the same fashions as would be found in a London assembly; that the music was tolerable, (though I think it the worst part of the performance,) and all the arrangements conducted with civility, good taste, and even elegance, why they would think me either jesting or dreaming; either intending to deceive them, or laboring under a deception myself. It was the wonder my narrative would create that caused my mirth."

"Then you intend to do us justice," said the doctor,

with a little trepidation, yet affecting to look unconcerned.

"Yes, indeed, I do," returned the other, "you need not fear my travels being a second edition of the scoundrel Faux. But he described what he wished to find, and what he knew would be acceptable to his employers. We have not, sir, quite forgiven you the sin of acquiring your independence. It galls our pride, it mortifies our self-love;—but we are becoming better acquainted with your character, and shall in time surmount our prejudices."

"And we shall gladly meet you half way. We have never forgotten our ancestors were Englishmen; and we trust the time will come when even your proud Islanders shall acknowledge we do not shame the stock from whence we sprung."

"And with such a sample before me, I shall not hesitate to acknowledge it now. Your ladies, sir, have more symmetry of form, and nearly as much delicacy of complexion as our own. And what is more remarkable, yours cannot owe these advantages to the delicacy of their education; for I suppose but few now before me are exempted by their wealth or station from industry."

"No, not one," returned Perkins; "but their labor is entirely domestic. I presume you will not find, should you travel throughout the United States, scarcely a single female engaged in the labors of the field, or any kind of out-door work, as it is called. And the manner in which women are treated is allowed to be a good criterion by which to judge of the character and civilization of a people. Wherever they are oppressed, confined, or made to perform the drudgery, we may be sure the men are barbarians. But I do not believe there is now or ever was a nation which treated their women with such kindness and consideration, tenderness and respect, as we Americans do ours. Here they are educated to command esteem, and considered as they deserve to be, the guardians of domestic honor and happiness, friends and companions of man. 'And to study household good,' and rear and educate their children, is all the labor we wish them to perform. But see, the dance is ended, and by the bustle of the managers, I think we may expect supper; you shall eat in peace, sir; I will not trouble you with as long an eulogium on our cake as I have on our ladies."

The supper tables were spread in a long dining-hall below stairs, and covered with every dainty and delicacy the season afforded, or the occasion would justify. And Frankford, while partaking the plentiful and excellent entertainment, asked Perkins, by whom he was seated, if the Thanksgiving feast lasted as many days as the Passover.

"You shall be feasted as many days," replied the Doctor, "and more, if you will spend them in our society."

"I should not need the promise of a feast to induce me to prolong my visit; but my evil genius will, I suppose, drive me hence on Monday."

"What! so soon? Then you must come to my house to-morrow."

This Frankford said he should be happy to do, if Sidney Romilly's engagements permitted.

When they returned to the ball-room, at his own request, he led the dance with Sophia Romilly. That the Englishman did not acquit himself entirely to his own satisfaction, nor fulfil the expectations of superior grace and elegance of movements, the Yankees had expected, was ascribed by him to the musicians, and by them to his illness; so he sat down with as much credit, though not entirely as happy as he would have felt could he have flattered himself he had excelled.

After enjoying the festivity till about one o'clock, the Romillys, among whom were included Frankford and Annie Redington, retired; leaving the company, who were expected to prolong their pleasure till nearly morning. The carriage called at Deacon Jones' house, and Sidney had the honor of handing Annie out, but had also to undergo the penance of being unmercifully rallied the remainder of his ride. Even after they had retired to their chambers, Frankford did not desist, till Sidney almost angrily declared, there was not a woman on earth to whom he would offer his hand.

"Then the proposal will come from the fair lady," said Frankford, looking very grave, "for I know you will marry her. I have spent some time in studying the laws of fate, and if you two are not made for each other, I will forswear my art."

"Are the designs of fate always fulfilled?"

"Always; so make up your mind for the noose."

"Not to-night," replied Sidney, enveloping himself in the ample bed-clothes. "I shall sleep soundly, without once dreaming of Miss Redington."

Whether he did sleep as soundly as he would have done had Annie never crossed his path, the lover's muse hath never recorded; but certainly the fair lady did not. Again and again Sidney's image, combined with the imaginary likeness of her father, arose before Annie; every word of his conversation was recalled, and when she thought of his riches and the style in which he had been educated, she sighed deeply that he should see her thus, a poor, dependent orphan.

It was the first time poverty had drawn a sigh from her happy heart; but she checked all repining at her destiny, and folding her hands on her innocent bosom, meekly murmured,—"Father in heaven, thy will be done," and sunk calmly to repose.

CHAPTER XIII.

A YANKEE DOCTOR.

These are kind creatures. Gods, what ties I've heard!
Our courtiers say, all's savage but at court.

SHAKSPEARE.

"WE shall hardly visit Dr. Perkins to-day," said Frankford, as they entered the breakfast-room. "What a terrible storm you have—why, the snow is a foot deep already."

"O, yes," replied the Squire, "it snows pretty fast, but I think it will soon be over, and we are not at all frightened, as we always expect a storm at Thanksgiving."

The conversation then continued respecting the climate of New England, and the good Squire displayed much philosophical research in accounting for the difference of heat and cold in countries within the same latitude, and considerable acumen in deducing particular facts from general causes.

The storm, however, increased, notwithstanding the Squire's prediction, and the Englishman's impatience, who really wanted to spend the day with Perkins. As they were contriving where to obtain a carriage, Silas Romilly having taken his father's the day before, and gone with his bride, to accompany her sister to Nottingham, her place of residence, Dr. Perkins drove up to the door.

"I have come to fetch you both," said he, shaking the snow from his feet as he entered, "for otherwise I might have been disappointed of the pleasure I have promised myself in your society to-day. Sidney was not always to be daunted by a northeaster, but a southern sun has doubtless enervated him a little, and Mr. Frankford's health would be a sufficient apology for his neglect. But I was resolved that no excuse should be left you, so get your hats and overcoats instantly."

The gentlemen gladly complied with this very frank invitation, for they both felt the languor and ennui which are apt to steal on the body and mind after the excitement of a night's revel, and these were now heightened by a severe and gloomy storm. Such feelings we know are not local, yet the eagerness with which all seek a change of place as a relief would imply it.

A ride of something less than a mile, brought them to the door of a neat, snug, one story house, painted white; a color which looks well in summer, but has, during the winter, an appearance of coldness rather uncomfortable to gaze upon. However, when the door opened, the gentlemen found the cheerlessness was all without. The doctor ushered them into his parlor, where a rousing fire, carpeted floor, and cushioned chairs, promised them all of comfort an Englishman could desire.

Mrs. Perkins came forward and gave them a smiling welcome. Her very pretty face was rendered more interesting by that air of maternal kindness and concern called forth by the illness of the infant she held in her arms, and which, to her husband's eager inquiries, was reported much better. Another sweet little boy, of between two and three years, sat on the carpet playing with his kitten; but the moment his father entered, his playthings were abandoned, and he sprung to embrace him.

Mr. Frankford, at first, almost fancied himself introduced into the nursery, but he soon found the children were entitled to all the privileges of place enjoyed by any of the family, and that no separate apartment or confinement with nurses and servants was found necessary in this land of "equal rights." So the Englishman sat down, having Mrs. Perkins and babe on one hand

and the doctor in his arm-chair, with his boy on his knee, at the other.

The doctor, after again welcoming them, and stirring the fire, began to rally Sidney on the speculations which his gallantry at the ball had excited. "We all think Annie an angel," continued he; "and were our religion Catholic, she would most certainly be worshiped: and you must be very clever or we shall not resign her even to a Romilly, though that is an honored name among us."

"I noticed, last evening, a little man who betrayed quite an anxious interest for Miss Redington," said Sidney; "pray, who is he?"

"O, it was Skinner," replied Perkins;—"Ephraim Skinner, by name, and a *skinner* by nature, also. I never observed the least sensibility in that man except what Annie has awakened, and I believe she is the only human being for whom he feels any tenderness."

"Is he her lover?" asked Sidney.

"No—only a dangler; yet, I really think the fellow would love her if he had a heart. My wife always looks as if she wanted to check me when I utter censure; but indeed, gentlemen, I am not given to evil speaking. I am much happier in praising than condemning, when truth will warrant it; nor will I wantonly expose faults when the offender shows by his conduct that he regrets them. But the man who glories in mischief deserves no mercy."

"What is his profession?" inquired Frankford, who seemed interested by the ardor his host displayed.

"He is a merchant, a money-lender, and a miser," replied Perkins,—"three vocations in which he labors unceasingly."

"Skinner?" repeated Sidney; "I have no recollection of such a name. Is he a native of Northwood?"

"O, no; he is from Connecticut, the land of steady habits; and he certainly has the habit of being steady in the pursuit of his own interest. He came here about five years since, and, always taking advantage of the times, and when he can, of his customers, he has realized a handsome property."

"But riches will not surely recommend such a character to the favor of Miss Redington?" said Sidney.

"No, indeed," replied Mrs. Perkins; "she would not marry him if he had an ocean of gold. I think she detests him as much as her generous heart will permit her to detest a human being; but Deacon Jones thinks him an excellent man and an excellent match."

"To the deacon's perception," said the doctor, "riches not only cover a multitude, but *all* sins; and there is another bond of sympathy between him and Skinner—they think exactly alike on religious subjects."

"I should not imagine," said the Englishman, smiling, "from your representations of Skinner, he would be very particular about his religious tenets."

"But he is, sir," replied the Doctor, "very particular to adopt the theory he finds most popular; and perhaps it is not so difficult for him to believe in total depravity as it would be for a better man; and certainly his salvation, if he ever attain to such a glorious state, must, unless he alter his practices, be a matter of *free grace*, and wholly by faith, as he has no good works on which to depend. So you perceive his interest and his habits both conspire to make him a sound orthodox believer; and that consideration, added to his increasing wealth, gives him great importance in the opinion of Deacon Jones, and indeed of many others."

"Yet these convenient qualities or qualifications—I hardly know which to call them—have not, it seems, obtained your favor," said Frankford, laughing as much at the manner of the speaker as the matter spoken.

"I have too often unmasked the villain to be deluded by his vizor. My profession introduces me to families of every grade and every situation, and much of their private history is necessarily unfolded to me. And almost every instance of poverty, intemperance and wretchedness, which has for the last three or four years fallen beneath my observation in this vicinity, I have found to be either directly or indirectly the work of Skinner. It would be disagreeable and tedious for me to relate, or you to hear, these histories of debts, and mortgages, and suits, and executions."

"I should suppose," said Sidney, "people would be apprised of his artifices, and become wary of putting themselves in his power."

"Experience does not always teach wisdom," replied Perkins. "The man in want is usually weak, or at least credulous to believe those professions which have his interest or convenience for their ostensible object. Skinner is a plausible creature, one who 'can smile and smile and be a villain;' in short, a hypocrite, a word including almost every term of reproach."

"I thought Connecticut was your stronghold of morality and piety, a fountain that always sent forth pure streams," said the Englishman.

"You doubtless recollect the pathetic language of poor Job to his wife," said the Doctor. "The world and men are still the same; we receive no good without a mixture of evil—no garden is free from weeds—no society exempt from pests and traitors. Connecticut is an excellent State, and has given birth to excellent men, but all are not such; and one restless, intriguing fellow, shall go forth and do more mischief than a dozen good ones can repair. We have, in our town, a number of deserving men, who were natives of Connecticut, and it was in a great measure owing to their character for probity, that Skinner first obtained the confidence of our people. Neither is he destitute of talents; and his industry is unwearied. But the love of money—not merely the root of evil, remember, but of *all* evil—has taken such entire possession of his heart and soul, that it deadens or destroys every kindly feeling of his nature. There is no passion so engrossing as the love of money, when it thoroughly possesses the whole man, and certainly none which renders him so contemptible. The thirst for fame, the pursuit of glory, may be indulged till they become criminal, yet there is still an apology in the magnitude and grandeur of the objects pursued; even the votaries of pleasure exhibit, at intervals, a romantic tenderness or generosity which palliates their follies or faults; but your man of cent. per cent. has no feeling but for himself, and can see no excellence but through the medium of yellow dust. Alfred, my boy," he continued, raising his child from his knee, where he had been stationed for some time, watching his father's rapid utterance with pleased attention, "Alfred, I have given you a glorious name, may you never sully it by making gold the idol of your worship."

The conclusion of this harangue, so different from what the gentlemen expected, made them both smile, and Frankford, following the last idea, inquired why the name of Alfred was entitled to such an eulogium?

"I should not have expected that question from an Englishman," replied the Doctor. Frankford blushed. "Your Alfred has immortalized the name, and that is what few kings do."

"And did you really name this pretty boy in reference to our Alfred the Great?" asked Frankford, taking the little fellow's hand.

"I did. I have, perhaps, rather peculiar ideas about the propriety of given names. I think we too often neglect a significancy in the appellation. Among the ancients it was not thus an unmeaning sound; it excited ideas of former incidents, or roused hopes of future blessings. When we give our children the names of dear or departed relatives or friends, there are sentiments of affection and respect produced while repeating them; when we call them for the good or illustrious, we are reminded of the virtues and deeds which made the name celebrated; but when we merely select a pretty sounding word, we display neither refined taste, warm feelings, nor just perceptions. I was the youngest of twelve children, and born an uncle, and my brothers and sisters had monopolized all the family names before I had an opportunity of using them. My father had a half score of grandsons called Josiah, for himself, and all my uncles and grand uncles had been remembered, and so I concluded to resort to history."

"Have you given your other son as proud an appellative?" asked the Englishman, surveying with a smile of admiration the fair little creature, who was now playing with the ringlets of his mother's hair, and every few moments pressing his dimpled cheek to hers; while she regarded him with a look of unutterable fondness and delight.

> "I know not whether is most fair,
> The mother or her child,"

thought Frankford, as he gazed upon them.

"That boy bears the name of my favorite Latin poet, Horace," said Perkins.—"Horace," continued he with a loud whistle; the child started, stared at him a moment, and then began to bound and laugh, all ecstasy at receiving his father's attention; "Horace, you will never touch the lyre like the Roman satirist; but you may manage a farm as well as he did his Sabine villa, and live as happily."

The conversation then turned on the beauties of Latin and Greek poetry—the site of Troy—which Frankford had visited—Alexander and Bonaparte—Roman eloquence—aborigines of America—British manufactures—culture of turnips—American literature—Shakspeare—Milton—British Navy—Irish patriots—Emmet—character of Washington—and the study of physic in Europe.

The discussion of these dissimilar subjects seemed to follow each other naturally, without a designed introduction by either party; and being interspersed with common topics, and lively anecdotes related mostly by Perkins with infinite humor, and enlivened by a dinner bearing ample evidence of its thanksgiving fraternity; excellent wine, cider and fruits—the apples blushing a beautiful red without requiring the presence of Apollo, engrossed and entertained them so happily, that the shades of night began to descend, before Sidney or the Englishman could believe the day had departed.

"I shall send my boy to drive you home," said Perkins, as he assisted Frankford to adjust his over-coat. "I must mount my horse and ride twenty miles before to-morrow morning."

"What, to-night in such a storm, and on horseback too!" said the Englishman.

"O yes, in the mountainous road I must travel, a carriage would not be convenient; and for riding in the evening, why, sir, I rode twelve miles last night after leaving the ball; and dealt out to my patients a pretty good supply of medicine, I assure you, in order that I might have this day of leisure to enjoy with you and Sidney."

"And we have enjoyed it," replied Frankford; "but I little thought you would be subjected to such a penance for your hospitality."

"I should not value submitting to perform penance, if by that means I might pass another day as pleasantly; but business is not usually a penance to me, yet now I should rather be excused, as my absence must, I fear, be prolonged till after your departure on Monday. I have patients, or rather *im*patients in the next town who have sent requiring my attendance to-morrow, and I must not return home without seeing them. So I thank you for the pleasure of your society to-day, and wish you a prosperous voyage to the land of your fathers; and sometimes when your thoughts wander to America, may I hope you will remember the Yankee doctor?"

As he concluded he took Frankford's hand, and pressed it cordially.

The Englishman returned the pressure.

"I shall remember you while I live, and I hope meet you again. Why do you not come to England? My friend Romilly has promised to visit me next spring; come with him. A tour abroad would to your strong and inquisitive mind afford materials for much pleasure and lasting improvement. Few men could see the world with the advantages you possess: because your sound judgment and practical education qualify you to make a just estimation of men and things; and the gloss of novelty would not deceive you. Come, then, and I will aid your researches all in my power; I need not say how gladly I should welcome you."

"Sidney can go without any inconvenience," replied the doctor, "and were I in a similar situation I should not hesitate. Yet I do not repine because he possesses the means of gratifying all his wishes, while I am compelled to bound mine by the distance my patients may happen to reside. I believe our duties and happiness are so closely connected that the better we fulfil the one, the more perfectly we enjoy the other. And when you are a married man, Mr. Frankford, and have a home rendered dear by the presence of those you most love, you will see all the world necessary to your felicity beneath your own roof."

As he ended, his eyes rested on his wife and children, who returned his glance with those affectionate smiles that so richly repay the toil of labor and the anxiety of care.

"I shall note you down for the most perfect philosopher I ever met with," said Frankford.

"Not a silent one, nor a cynic, I hope," replied Perkins, laughing.

"No, indeed—I shall describe you as one whose life illustrates the philosophical portion of your favorite Horace: 'that the happiness of life consists in serenity of mind and virtuous enjoyments.' And I think there is more sound philosophy in that ode than in many a huge volume of jargon miscalled ethics. You are just the character I have often wished yet never expected to see —a man of an independent mind, enlightened yet unshackled by education, and with an understanding governed by reason alone."

"And instructed by Revelation, you may add," replied Perkins, seriously. "I laugh at Deacon Jones' absurdities, and I detest his prejudices; but I honor religion. There can be no abiding excellence of character unless it has a principle of piety for its basis. The glory of

Great Britain is more effectually supported by her Bible Societies than her standing armies."

Perhaps Frankford would willingly have spared this unexpected burst of enthusiasm, as he felt inclined to call it; but it was spoken so unaffectedly and sincerely he felt a sentiment of respect for the candor which had prompted the avowal.

They again shook hands, and after seeing them seated in the carriage, Dr. Perkins bade the boy drive on, and bowed his last adieu.

"Shall I never see that man again?" said the Englishman to Sidney, bending from the carriage, as Perkins entered his house. "And very soon I must part with you and your amiable family. What a melancholy drawback on the pleasure of traveling, that we either go over the world without forming attachments with the deserving, or abandon them almost as soon as we have learned their value."

To the inquiries of Squire Romilly, Mr. Frankford replied, he had seldom passed a more agreeable day.

"Your doctor is a most original fellow," said he, "and possesses the happy talent of nicely discriminating character, and readily applying principles, which is the charm of intelligent conversation. And he is tolerably well informed too; with every subject discussed, and they were numerous, he appeared sufficiently familiar to be agreeable, although I perceived he was not profoundly erudite on any."

"If you would consider the desultory manner in which his education has been acquired," replied the Squire, "and the round of business in which he is now engaged, you would cease to wonder he was not profound."

"Perhaps so; but when a man pretends to knowledge, we are, I think, at liberty to test his pretensions; we do not require the display, yet when made it must be supported or he cannot expect credit for his intelligence. Your American mode of education is generally conducted in a miscellaneous manner, and your scholars too often verify the old adage of Pope, that 'a little learning is a dangerous thing.' Yet I am not applying these remarks to Dr. Perkins. He is really a man of information, and his learning sits so easily on him, there is amusement as well as instruction in the display. I never saw a person who could more readily adapt his conversation to the taste or capacity of his company. I have before observed your countrymen possessed a flow of ideas and fluency of language no other people with whom I am acquainted can boast. The French talk more, perhaps, but they are triflers;—one Yankee would out-reason a dozen Frenchmen could he make them listen to his arguments. But the doctor, I was intending to observe, is at home on every subject; one moment he converses professionally, then he is the farmer, then the scholar, the antiquary, the politician, and perhaps playing with his children, or playing the buffoon immediately afterwards. And all appears perfectly natural. Did you notice Mr. Romilly, when his little boy hurt his head against the table, Perkins was eagerly engaged in drawing an ingenious parallel between Alexander and Bonaparte? but he stopped, hushed the child by telling him the story of the cat and the fiddle, and then proceeded in his parallel without the least embarrassment or hesitancy."

"Yes, I noticed it," replied Sidney; "but Warren could always wield any instrument or any argument, and succeed in any study or business when he chose to exert himself. He was born a Jack at all trades."

"I think you Yankees all are," said Frankford smiling; "certainly I now find manual labor and mental refinement more compatible than I ever imagined they could be, and their united effects on the human character are very favorable. Activity of body prevents the mind from becoming the prey of ennui, while the cultivation of the mind corrects that grossness and selfishness which are so disgusting in the ignorant; and thus the mind and body being preserved in a healthy and vigorous tone, there is here, a freshness of intellect and feeling, a kind of human spring, which is as delightful in the moral, as the natural spring is to the physical world."

"You could not have read our character more rightly had you studied it a century," exclaimed Squire Romilly, starting from his seat and grasping the Englishman's hand.

"Should I study it a century I should probably read it differently," replied Frankford, smiling with the most winning kindness. "The season of youth for nations, as well as individuals, will soon pass; what character your country will finally attain I am not qualified to decide. But I think there is reason to fear that what it gains in glory will be lost in purity."

"Ours is an experiment," said Sidney, "yet with our advantages there is not much fear but the result will be favorable to human nature."

"Hope everything—hope is the privilege of youth," said the Englishman, rising and laying his hand on his bosom, "and from my heart I wish you success."

CHAPTER XIV.

THE DESTINY OF AMERICA.

I see the living light roll on,—
  It crowns with fiery towers
The frozen peaks of Labrador,
  The Spaniard's land of flowers;
It streams beyond the splintered ridge
  That parts the northern showers,—
From eastern rock to sunset wave
  The continent is ours!

DR. HOLMES.

THE Sabbath proved a rainy day, and the sudden dissolving of the snow made the walking so very bad, that Mr. Frankford excused himself from attending church.

He passed the day in his own apartment, engaged, as it was thought, in making notes on Northwood and its people—but his volume has never been published. Perhaps he slept.

In the evening, however, he appeared eager for information about the settlement and history of the old Granite State, and seemed much gratified to find its people were descended, chiefly, from English parentage.

"Your family name is similar with that of our late distinguished philanthropist and statesman, Sir Samuel Romilly," said he to the Squire. "Are you from the same stock!"

"According to our traditions, we are—but the relationship is now rather remote. We are descended from the younger brother—there were two, Pierre and Jacques Romilly, who fled from France on the revocation of the edict of Nantes. The elder settled in London; the younger came to America and settled first in Boston, but afterwards removed to New Hampshire, where his descendants, or most of them, remain."

"Then you claim fraternity with the French?"

"Yes—but a stock engrafted on several other nations. My children inherit, on my side, the blood of France and Britain—my great grandmother was an Englishwoman: on the side of my wife there is Irish and Spanish blood; but it is now all united in one patriotic current—the American."

"I have heard it asserted that from such an intermixture of races, the most perfect and beautiful one would be derived;" remarked the Englishman, reflectively.

His gaze was fixed on Sophia Romilly, who sat by the table reading. He saw her *en profile* and to great advantage, as she had put her curls behind her ear, and thus revealed not only the exquisite perfection of that little member, but also the delicate outline of her cheek and her beautiful throat. Her skin was of that pure, clear, lily white which seems as though it would never be sullied. She had very dark hair, eyebrows and eyelashes, while her eyes were the soft blue of summer skies. In truth, she seemed as fair a specimen of the mingled beauty of the races as one could hope to look upon, and it was not strange if Mr. Frankford so regarded her.

He was aroused from his reverie, which an æsthetic philosopher can only understand, by a remark of Sidney Romilly's.

"That emigrants from Europe were now flocking to our land in such numbers he feared the old Puritan stock would be blotted out."

"No fear of that, my son," said the Squire, cheerfully. "Let them come. We have room for all, and food, too; besides, we want their work, and they want our teaching. We shall do each other mutual good."

"Is there no danger to your peculiar institutions from this influx of foreigners?" inquired Frankford. "These people are not accustomed to your liberty."

"I don't think they will try to destroy it though;

they have suffered too much from oppression in the old world to wish it introduced here," returned the Squire.

"They may destroy it by their ignorance," observed Sidney; "at least such is the fear of our Southern states men."

"We must enlighten them—the emigrants, I mean," said the Squire. "The destiny of America is to instruct the world, which we shall do, with the aid of our Anglo Saxon brothers over the water," he added with a smile, as he turned to Mr. Frankford.

"We shall be much obliged for such a permission," said Mr. Frankford. "Where shall we begin?"

"At home. Let both nations be faithful there. Great Britain has enough to do at home and in the East Indies to last her another century. We have this continent and Africa to settle and civilize, besides keeping open school for people of all nations, tongues and sects that choose to come here and enjoy its privileges."

Mr. Frankford looked a little amazed, but after a moment's reflection he said, pleasantly—"I thought Great Britain held a small portion of this continent?"

"Over which the stars will yet wave."

"Why? what reason have you to believe this?"

"Because in the first place our title covers it. 'The United States of North America' is the title given our Republic by the wise framers of our Constitution, and will be fulfilled. In the second place, we have already more than doubled our original territory. We shall gain other additions as we have gained Louisiana and Florida."

"Oh! you are intending to buy the world. That alters the case. I thought you were anticipating Roman triumphs," said Frankford.

"The triumphs of peace are greater than Roman; they are Christian. We may have to draw the sword, but I hope not."

"Well," said the Englishman, after reflecting a little, "you have laid out work enough at home for your citizens during another century, I think; and you spoke of having something to do in Africa. Perhaps you are intending to free all your slaves and send them there to accomplish their destiny."

"Yes, that is the greatest mission of our Republic, to train here the black man for his duties as a Christian, then free him and send him to Africa, there to plant Free States and organize Christian civilization."

"Degraded as he is by slavery," said Frankford.

"Elevated as he is by American slavery," returned the Squire, "the most miserable slave you can find at the South is an enlightened and civilized man compared with his heathen brothers in Africa, who have never heard of a Saviour. The evils of the system bear heavily on our land—but the negro race have been and will be, eventually, greatly benefited from their contact with American institutions. And this point should never be forgotten. The white race here endures the heaviest burden of the evils of slavery. Look at Virginia! Absolutely a century behind Massachusetts in agriculture, arts and manufactures. Yet the former has every advantage of soil, climate and mineral wealth, and the latter nothing indigenous except granite and ice! Slave labor keeps Virginia poor: free labor makes Massachusetts rich. So it is throughout our whole land. Everywhere the free states are the most prosperous."

"Why then do the southern states keep their slaves, if they are injured by them?"

"What shall be done with them?"

"Why, give them freedom! Your Constitution declares all men are entitled to that."

"And have equal right to life, liberty, and the pursuit of happiness"—put in Harvey, who was sitting on a stool by his father's knee, and looking earnestly at each speaker in his turn.

They all smiled, and Frankford said inquiringly, laying his hand on the boy's head—"You will never be a slaveholder?"

Harvey was quite abashed, for he had heard Deacon Jones speak contemptuously of Sidney—as a "southern slaveholder"—and the little boy, looking on his eldest brother, would not believe it was so very wicked—yet it seemed that Mr. Frankford thought it was bad too. He was puzzled. Before he had settled his doubts, his mother changed the subject. She had, for some time, been looking, alternately, at the clock and little Lydia, who seemed in a very sleepy condition. Touching her husband's arm, Mrs. Romilly whispered something in his ear: he nodded, and turning to his guest—

"I must beg your indulgence, Mr. Frankford, we hold our family devotions early on Sunday evening, so that the little ones may be with us. We have singing, too, and that, I fear, may annoy you."

"Oh! not at all. I shall be happy to listen and heartily wish I could join; but psalmody is not one of my accomplishments."

"It is the only musical accomplishment of my children," returned the Squire; "at least, the only one in which they have been instructed. Nature gives the voice."

By this time the arrangements mere made. The big Bible and several hymn books were laid on the table—the candles set in order, and the family circle waiting in silent attention. The father, glancing his eye around and finding all prepared, opened reverentially THE BOOK, and selecting the *twentieth chapter* of that sublime and mysterious "Revelation," yet to be revealed, read in a very impressive manner:

"And I saw an angel come down from heaven, having the key of the bottomless pit and a great chain in his hand.

"And he laid hold on the dragon, that old serpent, which is the Devil and Satan, and bound him a thousand years.

"And cast him into the bottomless pit, and shut him up, and set a seal upon him, that he should deceive the nations no more till the thousand years should be fulfilled," &c.

The whole chapter was read, and listened to with devout seriousness. Mr. Frankford was struck with the scene. He seemed to hear the strange passages for the first time. Hitherto he had considered the whole as a myth—but it appeared that this family believed in the actual coming of the events foretold. "Will they come?" was his thought.

After the Bible was laid down, the Squire took the hymn book offered by his wife, saying—"Well, Mary, you have chosen the song, I see. Children, sing the 282d hymn of the collection;" and he read it—

1. "For a season call'd to part,
Let us now ourselves commend
To the gracious eye and heart
Of our ever-present Friend.

2. "Jesus, hear our humble prayer,
Tender Shepherd of thy sheep;
Let thy mercy and thy care
All our souls in safety keep.

3. "In thy strength may we be strong,
Sweeten every cross and pain;
And our wandering lives prolong,
In thy peace to meet again.

4. "Then if thou thy help afford,
Ebenezers shall be reared;
And our souls shall praise the Lord,
Who our poor petitions heard."

"We have lost our best bass voice, now Silas is gone," said Mrs. Romilly, softly, "unless Sidney will join. I hope you sing, my son; you had a fine voice."

"I do sing a little, mother, and I will try now," answered Sidney, tenderly.

The strain was raised; the Squire led the household choir, and every one, even little Lydia, joined.

Mr. Frankford had listened at operas and concerts, where the first musical geniuses of the age had displayed their powers; but no one, not even Malibran herself, had so moved his soul as did the voice of Sophia, a soprano of great clearness, naturally, and now, by her feelings, modified to a softness touchingly sweet. She paused at the close of the third verse, and did not resume. As she sat, still as a statue, the long dark eyelashes drooping till they entirely shaded the downcast eye, and no sign of emotion visible, except the ebb and flow of color on her fair young cheek, he thought, "Oh, that I could read her heart! Fool that I am—it beats for her brother! She thinks only of the parting with him!"

And so—perhaps—she did.

Then they all knelt, the Englishman beside Mrs. Romilly—who often, afterwards, mentioned it as a proof that he was a real good man,—and the prayer of faith, hope, and love ascended to Him who blesses the family altar. It was a touching petition, and so appropriately as well as fervently worded, that the Englishman quite forgot, while listening to its earnest breathings for his own safety and happiness, his prejudices against extempore prayers in general.

After the children had retired, Mrs. Romilly asked Sidney what church he attended in Charleston.

"The Episcopal."

"Ah, well; I am glad you go there, and not with your uncle."

"He goes often to the Episcopal church."

"Indeed! How long has he gone there?"

"Since the death of my aunt. My Uncle Brainard is quite a different man from what he was when I first went to the South," added Sidney.

"There is something to me quite inexplicable in this strife of sects in America," said Mr. Frankford. "Where all religions are exactly on the same footing in the state, I don't see the use of trying to make proselytes. Besides, your religious people spend so much strength and time in controversies, they can have very little for Christian duties."

"You are right," returned the Squire. "And these dissentions about points that all concede are not material to our salvation, are doubtless the 'tares sown by the enemy'—the temptations of that Evil One who would, if possible, deceive the very elect. It is cheering to reflect that his power will end when the millennium begins."

"Do you really, sir, believe such a time of peace and happiness is coming on this earth?" inquired Frankford, earnestly.

"I do, because God has promised it."

"I should like to believe it; but is there any reason for such hope? Men have changed very little since the time of Cain, of Nimrod, or of Solomon. Hatred—power—pleasure—these move the master minds, and selfishness governs the multitude. Christianity seems to have caused some improvement; but when we examine closely, we find selfish motives apparent among those styled the most pious men. It has taken eighteen hundred years, almost, to make a few real Christians; the great mass, nearly the whole world in fact, is still heathen, or little better. It seems, therefore, hopeless to look for any great improvement in the future."

"Reasoning from the past, entirely, you are, perhaps, right in your conclusions," returned the Squire. "But you leave out of account the two great elements of human progress which the millennium will introduce."

"I don't understand."

"You have shown, Mr. Frankford, that men have not improved much; morally speaking, this is true. And you conclude, therefore, they never will improve, forgetting that God has promised to do for man what he cannot do for himself. Now, to bring about the 'good time coming,' God has promised to do two things."

"What are they?"

"To change man's heart, and to chain the devil!"

"God must certainly do the last, if it is ever done. But do you believe what you read this evening about chaining the devil, is to become a literal fact?"

"So far as this—the temptations of the enemy of God and goodness will cease. The devil will not have power to deceive. Revenge, ambition, selfishness, will appear as they really are—foul, mean, monstrous. Men will see the truth, their hearts will be changed to love the truth, and the truth will make them free!"

"And then American slavery will cease, I suppose," said Frankford, shrugging his shoulders.

"It will; and slavery will cease in India also. Asia is now a den of oppressions of all kinds, to which American slavery is freedom. The greater portion of Europe is under despotic power;—the people are slaves. Our country has made the greatest progress in the true principles of liberty; our government was the first to prohibit the slave trade; our nation will be the first to find out the *right* way—the Christian way is good and peaceable—of converting slaves into free men."

"Should the States continue united, your people will, doubtless, prosper; but the Union may be dissolved."

"Heaven forbid! The evil would be so disastrous to the world, so crushing to the cause of humanity and religion, that God, surely, will never permit the enemies of truth and freedom such a triumph."

"You believe the devil will be chained?" said Frankford.

"Yes; and I also believe that 'the knowledge of the Lord will cover the earth, as the waters doth the sea,' and that peace and brotherhood will be universal," said the Squire.

Early on Monday morning the chaise was in readiness, and Sidney prepared to accompany Mr. Frankford to landlord Holmes', where the stage to Boston was taken.

There were warm wishes breathed, and warm tears shed at the parting, though the acquaintance had been but for a few days. Confidence is soon established and esteem won, where all are deserving and all sedulous to appear agreeable.

Mr. Frankford kissed the younger members of the family; to the elder ones he proffered his hand, and the blush that crimsoned Sophia's cheek was, by her brother James, always attributed to a very tender pressure, and with many a sly jest he afterwards reminded her of the circumstance.

Mrs. Romilly said, as she wiped the tears from her

eyes, after the carriage was fairly out of sight,—"Well, I never thought I should cry at parting with an Englishman; but there, he don't seem like a stranger; he talks, and thinks, and feels, just as we do. I wonder he don't stay here in America—I'm sure it must seem just like his own country; but I shall always remember him, because he's our Sidney's friend."

The stage was drawn up at the door of the tavern, and the baggage of the Englishman being soon transferred, all was ready for his departure. He came up to Sidney and took both his hands in his. There was evidently a struggle in his bosom, and the dignified stateliness of his manner seemed assumed to conceal the weakness of feelings he was ashamed to indulge.

Tears started in the eyes of Sidney. "You will write soon, Mr. Frankford. I shall wait anxiously to hear of your safe arrival in England."

"With not more anxiety than I shall wait your promised visit there," replied the Englishman. "I shall never feel at peace till I can have an opportunity of repaying some of the obligations with which you have loaded me. It was to you I owed my favorable reception at Charleston; it is to your care at Montreal I owe my life. Now give me an opportunity of proving how highly I esteem your generous character. You have often heard the English people were proud: you shall find we are grateful. Farewell!"

Sidney returned home very low spirited, and all the exertions of his family were insufficient to dispel his sadness. He had, for the last ten or twelve months, passed most of his time in the society of Frankford, and felt, on parting with him, perhaps forever, that vacuity of heart which all feel on the first separation from favorite and familiar friends.

The day appeared long, and soon as tea was over he retired to his chamber, notwithstanding Deacon Jones had called with the avowed design of having "a talk with Mr. Sidney, and learning something about how he had spent his time away there to Carolina."

The deacon, indeed, attempted to indemnify himself for his disappointment by closely questioning the Squire and Mrs. Romilly, but all the particulars he gathered did not satisfy his mind; and as I hope some of my readers will feel a like anxiety, though from different motives, we will go back to the period when Sidney Romilly first left the home of his childhood for the house of strangers.

CHAPTER XV.

THE STORY GOES BACKWARD.

Youth might be wise. We suffer less from pains
Than pleasures.
FESTUS.

THE characters of Mr. and Mrs. Brainard, those relatives whom Sidney Romilly accompanied to South Carolina, have been briefly sketched, and a greater dissimilarity between persons, considered respectable, can scarcely be imagined than between them and his own kind parents.

In the home he had left, resided peace, the brightest angel of domestic bliss. There, no forced smiles were necessary to conceal real sorrow; no words of honey issued from hearts of gall; no feigned compliances were extorted to save appearances; but sincere affection inspired the wish to please, and gratified affection still blessed the loved face, whose smiles even time, the destroyer of beauty, could not mar. And the flowers of love, to be worth gathering, must be perennial; but none are so, except rooted in the soil of virtue, discretion, and mutual esteem, and moistened with the soft falling dews of confiding truth, delicacy, and piety.

Shame, however, will sometimes teach decorum when even a sense of duty would not inspire forbearance; and a married couple, whose constant bickerings have been a disagreeable annoyance to their neighbors and intimate friends, will often live very decently together in the presence of a stranger.

And thus Mr. Brainard and his wife were, for a time, awed by the presence of the child, into something very much like conjugal tranquillity. They both knew the manner in which Sidney had been educated; the examples of kindness, benevolence and self-control to which he had always been accustomed, and they shrunk from exhibiting angry or petulant passions before him.

But the vexed spirit, like the raging sea, is difficult to be restrained. Nothing but the voice of the Almighty can hush the one, and nothing but the grace inspired by waiting on Him can give us wisdom to subdue the other.

Mr. Brainard and his wife did disagree, and after a few faint apologies for the first contentions, they became regardless of Sidney's presence, and very soon required him to arbitrate between them in their trifling, yet obstinately managed disputes. His aunt, thinking he belonged especially to her as being of her own blood, now unfolded to him all her trials and sorrows; his uncle claiming the affinity which, in many respects, a similarity of disposition engenders, related the story of his disappointment; each endeavoring to win his confidence and sympathy, and infuse into his young heart their own illiberal and bitter prejudices.

But there was one subject on which they perfectly agreed, and that was to grant Sidney every indulgence he desired. They both adored him, and looked to him as the sweet minstrel whose soothing strains were to bring to their troubled bosoms the peace they had so foolishly forfeited.

Sidney was formed to be happy. His gay and unbroken spirits imparted to every object he beheld a portion of his own felicity; and even the evident unhappiness of those with whom he resided had but a passing remembrance in his innocent bosom.

Indeed he could not sympathize with his aunt in her abhorrence of the negroes; he was delighted with them when they came around him, smiling with obsequious attention to greet his arrival; and he had not yet learned the immeasurable inferiority a shade of the skin can impart to beings of the same human family.

They were told he was to be their master, and exerted themselves to obtain his favor.

He was informed what rights the laws of men had given him over them, but nature was not obliterated in his heart, and instead of claiming their services as a right, he yielded his love as a recompense.

His aunt could not endure this, and labored to shame or pique him out of his partiality for the blacks.

His uncle was a good master, and from particular circumstances, being anxious, in the event which all must expect, to consign his slaves to a kind owner, he saw the amity subsisting between them and his heir with much satisfaction.

Perhaps, too, the idea that it vexed his spouse, might make him more willing to encourage it; certainly he permitted his nephew to frolic and ramble about his estate in company with two or three favorite servants, who soon initiated him in the arts of hunting and fishing, and all those games and pastimes in which unlettered leisure is sure to find amusement.

While Sidney had resided with his father he had been accustomed to constant employment, working on the farm, except when attending school, and never considered play as necessary to his happiness; but the descendants of Adam are always willing to escape his penalty of eating bread gained by hard labor; and the little republican was soon familiar with the idea of his own privilege of exemption from the degradation of work, which he was now taught to consider a menial employment.

His uncle had stipulated and indeed intended to bestow on him a liberal education, but he felt loath to part with him for the length of time necessary to complete it. His house seemed insupportable without one happy face, and so he postponed, month after month, the beginning of his Latin studies, excusing his neglect by the difficulty of finding a competent instructor.

At length, after more than a years' delay, a tutor was obtained, and as Mr. Brainard could not endure the thought of sending Sidney to college, he determined to have him educated at home, beneath his own eye.

The advantages of a public education have been often asserted, and notwithstanding many objections, the majority of sensible people have, I believe, given their suffrages in its favor. Certain it is that Sidney's proficiency will not be creditable to the private manner of instructing. He had no competitor to excel, and no reward to obtain, which he might not by other means have acquired. He was still docile, but his mind wanted a stimulus which the pedantic and formal lectures of his master, an old-fashioned birch pedagogue, never could impart.

His love of study was now languid, and progress in learning slow compared with what they had been in the district school of his own native village. There, his reward for application was certain, immediate, and what is best of all, while it satisfied his ambition, it still cherished the generous and kindly feelings of his nature. To walk home with the medal suspended on his bosom, and receive a smile from his mother as her glance rested on the proof of his scholarship; to have his father lay his hand on his head, and inquire the particular manner of excelling by which it had been obtained, and listen while the little fellow, with a most exalted tone, repeated his perfect lesson, or spelt his hard word; these were the honors he had coveted, and to gain them he had been urged to the most unwearied exertions.

Nor was there any punishment he dreaded like the loss of his station in the class, and the censure of his parents.

But now his uncle was engrossed by pleasure or business, and had no leisure for such trifles, and his aunt had neither taste nor capacity for the task of instructing. True they were both anxious Sidney should be a scholar, and to have insured him such they would willingly have offered a large premium. Money to almost any amount they would freely have given, but their own time, or personal inspection or encouragement, they could not afford.

The consequence was, as it ever is when study is made an irksome duty, Sidney's book was neglected for play whenever it could be without incurring severe reprimands, and these his uncle's affection and indulgent temper rarely permitted to be employed. Once, it is reported, the master threatened correction, but Mr. Brainard soon gave him to understand nothing of that kind must be attempted with his heir, and so *Cornelius Nepos* and *Virgil* slept quietly and unthumbed, while the *Latin* scholar was taking his lessons at marbles or ninepins.

How I wish I had a more perfect hero. One of those patent made creatures, who either by nature or intuition are possessed of every virtue, art and accomplishment. It mortifies me to record, that after seven years' instruction, Sidney Romilly was still ignorant of those languages, which, by being called *learned*, we are taught no one can be learned without understanding; and, what I consider far worse, that for all kinds of mathematical studies he had the most invincible aversion. Should these deficiencies, which truth compels me to make public, be considered as depreciating from his merits, let those who aspire to the character of heroes carefully avoid an imitation of his errors.

But though the classics and mathematics held but a slight tenure in his memory, he was not wholly idle. The French language he studied; philosophy and belles lettres possessed charms to interest his feelings and fancy, and to these he devoted his attention.

His tutor for some time struggled against the inclinations of his pupil; but as he declaimed only against those studies which Sidney found intelligible and agreeable, without endeavoring to render those he recommended equally so, his pupil paid no attention to his remonstrances. And finally, as he found resistance vain, the faithful tutor contented himself with a good salary, and let Sidney have his own way, quieting his conscience by laying all the blame on Mr. Brainard's indulgence and the boy's obstinacy.

At the age of twenty his education was declared complete, his tutor was dismissed, and Mr. Sidney Romilly introduced into society as a young gentleman whose scientific attainments entitled him to a high rank in the learned world, while his polite accomplishments assured him a flattering reception in the fashionable one.

He was handsome and agreeable; his uncle had riches and influence, and his pretensions to learning were never questioned; nor did he suffer more inconvenience for his lack of Greek, than did the professor at the university of Louvain.

His time was passed in a continued series of amusements, and for two years his only occupation seemed to be the discovery and enjoyment of some new pleasure. Wherever he appeared, a welcome awaited him; his taste was the fashion, his applause excellence, and the gay and accomplished Yankee became the pride and ornament of a southern city.

But, though he drank deep of the cup of luxury, he was not the votary of vice. The natural benevolence of his feelings prevented him from indulging in pleasure at the expense of another's happiness; and his acquired prudence kept him from such as would grossly injure himself.

But, above all, those early lessons of sobriety and virtue which he had, as it were, drawn in with his mother's milk, those pure and pious precepts instilled into his soul before one blight of the world had stained its innocence, still clung around his heart, still visited his imagination in dreams by night, when he would find himself again beneath that roof where folly and repentance were alike unknown.

His father's revered form, while lifting his hands in holy prayer, was often before his eyes; and the expression of the last petition which he had ever heard from his lips, was an entreaty to Him who can keep us from temptation, to preserve and return spotless the dear one who was about to quit the paternal roof; and the remembrance of that scene often came over him in the midst of gaiety, and never did it fail of having a restraining and salutary effect.

But his mother's tears were still more admonitory. He

never recalled her to his mind without thinking how, with the last kiss bestowed on his then innocent cheek, raising her streaming eyes to heaven, she said, "Oh! my God, I commit him to Thy care, for thou only canst preserve him."

And that Sidney Romilly, in the midst of the pleasures which a gay city presented, with wealth to gratify every wish, should yet, in a great measure, preserve the integrity of his heart and his love of virtue, must doubtless be ascribed to the lessons of his childhood and the example and prayers of his parents.

It has undoubtedly been already anticipated that Sidney had been a lover—for what *hero* is not—and strange it would have been, if amidst the bright circles in which he moved, and where he was an acknowledged favorite, his susceptible feelings should not have been awaked.

Yet his heart was not an easy conquest. The unhappiness he had witnessed in his uncle's family had prejudiced him against marriage, and his libertine companions had treated it with ridicule. His course of reading was mostly novels and poems, and although they usually ended by placing their best characters in the honorable state of wedlock, yet they terribly magnified the perplexities and dangers besetting the path which leads to the temple of Hymen.

However, from the recollection of the happiness enjoyed by his kind parents, and the whispers of his own heart, he felt assured the most perfect felicity earth witnesses, is theirs, "whose hearts, whose fortunes, and whose beings blend." Yet he imagined this felicity was attained only by the wedded pair who loved each other solely and individually, without any alloy of worldly considerations to sully the purity of their affection; and he fully determined never to marry, unless assured his fair one loved him for himself alone.

This was a difficult problem to solve, and cordially as he hated Euclid, he would willingly have sat down to the study of angles and triangles, if he might thereby have obtained a result by which to calculate the sentiments of the lady on whom he might fix for a bride.

His appearance, rank, and fortune, made his alliance a prize not lightly to be rejected by people of fashion; and he had nothing of that vanity which converts civilities offered to the station into marks of personal esteem.

This refinement, as most men would call it, made him distrust exceedingly the friendly and affectionate notices bestowed on him by mothers who had unmarried daughters, and aunts who had unportioned nieces. Perhaps if he had really loved any of the fair or fine ladies of his acquaintance, he might have fancied a return; the coolness of his reasoning certainly argued insensibility to their attractions, as none but an uninterested spectator can make such rational and unbiased reflections.

At length, however, his philosophy was tested. He was sitting at the theatre one evening, his eye wandering unsatisfied over brilliant beauties and dazzling dresses, when an elderly gentleman entered a box on his right. His appearance and air bespoke him a man of mighty consequence in his own opinion, yet he attracted none of our hero's homage. Sidney looked, but it was at a beautiful young creature who accompanied him.

How many sensations a single glance can awaken how much the heart can grasp in a moment of time—how soon the affections expand when warmed by real love!

Sidney gazed and loved, and in imagination wooed and married; nor did the brother of Orlando and the cousin of Rosalind come to the conclusion of the matter sooner than he.

The features of this unknown charmer were not regularly handsome—the fascination of her countenance was its expression; so sweet, so innocent, so feminine, it seemed as if the softness and harmony of her soul had diffused their influence over her form and face, giving to one the most exquisite symmetry, to the other that indescribable grace which breathes the soul of love and tenderness.

Sidney's eyes were riveted; and with his romantic feelings it is no wonder that

> "In every secret glance he stole,
> The fond enthusiast sent his soul."

One would, indeed, be reminded of Ellen Douglas, while gazing upon her. There was a likeness between the creation of the bard and the fair creature before him which immediately occurred to Sidney. The same lightness of figure, the same raven tresses, the same dark eye; but the heightened bloom which "sportive toil" had imparted to the complexion of the Highland *lassie* did not mantle the cheek of the fair stranger. She was pale, and sometimes Sidney fancied a shade of sadness passed over her mild features like a soft cloud over the brightness of the summer moon. Yet so young, so lovely, apparently so affluent, whence could her sorrows arise!

She bestowed no attention on the many curious observers who regarded her, being apparently absorbed in the scenes of the drama, or in her own reflections.

The play was Douglas, and during the representation of some acts she appeared affected even beyond what the most refined tragic-loving grief could warrant. Through the first scene she shaded her face entirely; and when towards the last of the play Lady Randolph sighs forth in the bitterness of her spirit,

> ————————"Alas! a little time
> Was I a wife; a mother not so long!"—

the tears fell in large drops down the colorless cheeks of that sweet being, who appeared totally unconscious of the remarks her conduct excited, and sympathizing only in the sorrows of the wife and mother.

"Pshaw!" said a dandy, who was regarding through an opera glass the same interesting object, "pshaw! how I do detest to see a lady playing off her airs of sensibility and always expecting some compliment for tender feelings, and to be told how well her grief becomes her. It is only, take my experience for it, to gull our sterner race by making us believe what kind, affectionate, managable wives they will make; but marry them, and the soft cloud that seemed to distil only tears is soon changed to one surcharged with thunder and lightning, and we may think ourselves fortunate if we escape being prostrated by a devil of a whirlwind."

Here he paused, to laugh at his own wit.

It did not strike Sidney as wit; but he felt there might be truth in the observation. His acquaintance with the world had taught him how often men are deceived by appearance; "and yet," thought he, "who can suspect artifice in one so young and apparently so innocent?"

He intended to follow her and discover her lodgings, but as she left the theatre the crowd retarted his progress, and she was gone he knew not whither. No one could answer his inquiries concerning her, and after a fruitless search he returned home to dream of the vision he had seen.

CHAPTER XVI.

FIRST LOVE.

Thou hast the secret of my heart;
Forgive, be generous, and depart.
LADY OF THE LAKE.

THE moment breakfast was finished on the following morning, Sidney seized his hat and hurried into the street, and continued sauntering through the city during the whole forenoon. He would not have acknowledged, even to himself, the motive which prompted him to this singular display; yet, from the eagerness with which he surveyed every lady he met, and the disappointment of his air as he turned from each fair face, unequivocally declared the object he wished to meet did not reward his search; and restless and sad he entered the dining room where his uncle was already seated.

"A fine afternoon we shall have," said Mr. Brainard; "I hope, Sidney, you are not engaged?"

"Why so?"

"Because, I have promised to spend the evening with an old friend of mine, just come to town—a worthy gentleman from Savannah, rich as Crœsus, and generous as rich; and I have engaged you shall accompany me. He is very anxious to cultivate your acquaintance."

"I don't know," answered Sidney, with as vacant a look as hopeless love could well assume, "as I wish for the introduction. I had rather forget half-a-dozen old acquaintances than form one new one."

"You will be interested this evening, or I'll forfeit a cool hundred," said his uncle; "so make no more objections, for you must go."

Sidney never opposed any serious wish of his uncle, and he prepared to go, although he had no inclination for the visit, and would much have preferred spending the evening at home, musing, like a faithful Quixotte, on the unparalleled perfections of that unknown damsel who had captivated his heart.

They went at an early hour, and were conducted into an elegant drawing-room, where Mr. Atkinson waited to receive them. He embraced Sidney with all the ardor of friendship, telling him that his uncle's commendations had prepared him to be pleased with Mr. Romilly; "but," added he, "your appearance and manners would have been a sufficient passport to my favor."

Sidney listened to all his compliments without being able to answer one word; and Mr. Brainard, wondering at his silence, almost cursed his stupidity, and resolved to scold him heartily when they reached home.

But the truth was, Sidney at once recognized in Mr. Atkinson, the old gentleman he had seen at the theatre as the protector of that lovely girl, and surprise and joy held him mute.

"Where is your daughter?" inquired Mr. Brainard; "shall we not see her this evening?"

"She will attend us soon," replied Mr. Atkinson. "Ah! she comes now. Zemira, my love, let me introduce you to Mr. Romilly, the nephew of Mr. Brainard, my good friend here. You two must be friends as we are."

Zemira blushed deeply; yet it was only maiden bashfulness at the appearance of a stranger; but poor Sidney felt as if every drop of his blood were rushing back to his heart. He hardly respired; and the sudden paleness of his countenance alarmed his uncle, who hastily inquired what ailed him.

The event was a fortunate one for our hero, as the exertions he was obliged to make to convince them he was "perfectly well—never better in his life," enabled him to conquer his surprise, and collect his thoughts. He was soon convinced Zemira did not recognize him, probably had not noticed him, and he determined to keep his own counsel, and let no one know the impression her first appearance had made on his heart.

"They shall not know I was so weak as to fall in love," thought he: "I will first ascertain whether she is worthy to be loved; and in the second place, whether she will return my affection. Love at first sight, my uncle has often told me, a declaration the first opportunity, and a marriage without reflection, were the three grand errors of his life, which no subsequent prudence or sagacity on his part could remedy."

So Sidney resolved to be circumspect, and guard his heart, but armor is useless when we have already surrendered; and so much did his passion speak in his eyes when gazing on Zemira, and in the tremulous tones of his voice when addressing her, that the old gentlemen both perceived it, and with many sly winks and knowing smiles, expressed their satisfaction at the attachment which promised a consummation of their fondest wishes.

They had been friends from infancy, and wished to perpetuate the friendship of their families; what better method could be devised than to join in wedlock those who were nearest and dearest to each? They both had large estates: how could they be better preserved than by uniting them? For several preceding years, the nephew of the one, and the daughter of the other, had always been mentioned in their letters to each other; but it was only a short time since any explanation of the views and hopes both had secretly entertained had been suggested.

The ecclaircissement was first made by Mr. Atkinson. In a letter, written a few months before his arrival at Charleston, after mentioning his increasing infirmities, and the difficulty of finding men with whom he could entrust his business, he added, "I sometimes think if my daughter were married to a worthy man, it would lessen my anxieties. I am known to be very rich, and she, although I say it myself, is very pretty. As soon as she is introduced into the world, which I have not yet permitted her to be, these advantages will be sure to attract a crowd of admirers. She has neither brother nor sister to guard or counsel her, and the restraints and advice of an old man are often, by the young, thought morose and selfish. You have frequently mentioned your nephew, Sidney Romilly, in terms of high commendation. Now, Brainard, what if we should contrive a match between him and Zemira? You, I know, will not object, and from your description of him, and my knowledge of her, I should think they would easily agree. My daughter is young; too young, indeed, to be married, scarcely sixteen; but my health is very poor, and I must either confine the dear child at home with me, for a nurse, during the bloom of her life, or let her go forth alone into a dangerous world, or give her a protector suitable to her age and feelings. What say you to my proposal?"

The answer of Mr. Brainard was in the affirmative; for such an offer, what rich man would refuse! A large estate always requires a balance of power, or the dignity of the wealthy party is terribly sacrificed.

They settled the business thus: Mr. Atkinson was to come, accompanied by his daughter, to Charleston, ostensibly in search of health, spend the winter, and renew his acquaintance with his friend Brainard. The intercourse once established, Sidney and Zemira would, of course, be often brought together, and their guardians flattered themselves mutual affection would soon ensue.

The plan was well devised, and could the impressio her first appearance would make on Sidney's heart hav been foreseen, would not many have wondered at th sagacity of these match-makers, who had even seemed t anticipate the intentions of Providence? And woul they not have pronounced the union to have been de signed by heaven?

They would have been mistaken, however.

Sidney, it has been shown, was already caught, an his attentions to Zemira soon became so pointed and pa ticular that she could not mistake their meaning. Bu still her pale cheek grew paler, and, except when beneat the eye of her father, whose glance always appeared to make her tremble, she was pensive or silent.

Sidney sometimes thought she was unhappy, and sometimes feared it might be from secret disappointment; but her father said she had never had a suitor; her reserve, therefore, was only bashfulness, and, in her lover's opinion, it constituted her most delicate charm.

Many a time had he sighed on beholding some fair lady, who, with glowing cheek and tender air, had been listening to his compliments, smile just as sweetly on the next admirer who approached her; and often had he repeated, that at the shrine he worshiped, others must not bow. And how rapturous to win the love of Zemira, so young, so inexperienced in the world, and make her soft, unhackneyed heart all his own!

The *denouement*, however, speedily arrived.

Urged on by the impetuosity of his passion, secure of his uncle's approbation, and certain, from pretty broad hints, he was favored by the father, Sidney thought he might dispense with such a scrutiny of the sentiments of the daughter as he had always determined to institute before making a formal declaration to any woman on earth.

How easily love leads captive the judgment of men! Many reasons, plausible ones, too, now occurred to Sidney, why a lady should never "tell her love;" no, not even let it be suspected by any, certainly not by the object of her partiality. It was a violation of maiden delicacy—a sacrifice of female dignity—and he would not marry with her who could "unsought be won."

And there was truth in all this. The mischief was, he did not consider the difference which would appear in one whose heart was touched with the merit of her lover, and in one who was indifferent or averse. And though every particularity on his part only added to the reserve or evident inquietude of Zemira, he still flattered himself her decision would be favorable.

At length he made his avowal. I cannot tell whether it was at a morning call, or an evening walk, in the parlor or garden—neither do I know the exact form of speech used on the occasion. And of what consequence would it be if I did?

There are specimens of this kind of eloquence already extant, sufficient to furnish the vocabulary of every pretty fellow who is incapable of wording his own petition; and lovers of sense and honor, why, they will not regret the omission, for they know the language which would express their feelings must be their own.

Sidney told her, however, of his affection, ardent, sincere, and undivided, and entreated a word or look to assure him he might hope.

Her color went and came like the gleams of an April day, but grief overpowered at last, and she burst into tears.

There have been tears of joy, but her lover saw these were not, nor was her confusion that of gratified surprise.

> "Not that the blush to wooers dear,
> Nor paleness that of maiden fear,
> It may not be."

He took her trembling hand.

"My dear Zemira, do not cast me off!"

She struggled to release her hand.

"Oh! Mr. Romilly, you know not whom you address, but I will tell you all—I am—I am—already a wife; I have been married these three months."

Sidney's feelings had been wrought up to such a height of expectation he hardly believed disappointment possible; certainly he never could have anticipated it in such a shape. Her words fell like an ice-bolt on his heart. He did not merely see, he *felt* his hopes annihilated. Cold drops of sweat started on his forehead—he trembled—her hand fell from his nerveless grasp, and leaning against a support, he groaned aloud.

A long and death-like pause ensued; at length it was broken by Zemira. Raising her tearful eyes to his, she said—

"Mr. Romilly, before you blame me, listen to my story.

If I have not mistaken your character, you have a kind, generous heart. You profess to love me—oh, do not prove my enemy! You can comfort, you can befriend me; and though I cannot return your affection, I will bless your kindness—I will accept your assistance—and if you really wish to contribute to my happiness, you now have it in your power. Say, will you not be my friend?"

"Your friend, Zemira, your friend! when you have thus pierced my heart?"

"Yet how could I avoid it? I endeavored to discourage your addresses, but you persisted, and my father favored you; he does not know my marriage. Oh, if he should learn it at present, he will cast me off forever! but he does not know it; and he gives you every opportunity to approach me, and I have no resource left but to throw myself on your humanity, your honor."

"Where is your husband?" said Sidney, in a tone of bitterness. "Your husband must protect you. Why does he not claim you? Were you my wife, I should not thus leave you to the casual interference of strangers"—And he walked hastily away, as if intending to depart.

"Mr. Romilly," said she, and the despair of her heart communicated itself to her voice—"listen to me one moment. Hear my story—I ask no other favor—and then, if you wish, publish it to the world;—I can but die." And she covered her face and burst into a hysterical sobbing.

Sidney hurried back, caught, and supported her to a seat.

"Forgive—forgive me, Zemira; I am myself again. You must not wonder at my unreasonableness; my disappointment——but I will mention it no more. Now tell me how, at your age, this strange marriage could have been contracted without your father's consent or knowledge."

After a few moments' silence she began; but her narrative was so often interrupted by her sighs or Sidney's questions and exclamations, that it would not be as intelligible to my readers as a connected story. And besides, there were circumstances she did not understand, and effects whose causes she had not developed. None but the author can know the hidden springs which move the world of his creation; and the scholar and philosopher who requires a reasonable apology for the unreasonable marriage of Zemira must read carefully the three succeeding chapters.

Every lady and every lady's man will surely peruse them, and without *skipping*, when assured they are all about love.

CHAPTER XVII.

ZEMIRA'S HISTORY.

Dost thou love me? I know thou wilt say *aye*,
And I will take thy word.—
Yet if thou thinkest I am too quickly won,
I'll frown, and be perverse, and say thee nay,
So thou wilt woo; but else not for the world.
ROMEO AND JULIET.

ZEMIRA ATKINSON was an only child, and her mother dying when she was an infant, the heart of her father seemed to rest on her alone. He did not merely love, he idolized her, and expected from her a return of the same extravagant affection.

She was a sweet-tempered, warm-hearted child, so gentle that restraint of any kind seemed almost unnecessary. Why need she be troubled with lectures, be taught she must sometimes control her inclinations, and that the world was fraught with disappointment! Her father never intended she should be exposed to temptation or sorrow. He had wealth to gratify her every wish,—he would select her friends, direct her affections to the high-minded and worthy, provide her amusements, encourage her studies, and in seeing her happy, he should ensure his own felicity. But

"There's a divinity that shapes our ends,
Rough hew them how we will."

The web of human life is never unmingled; and let no one fancy he or his shall be exempt from misfortune, or infallible to error. It is the height of folly to flatter our offspring with the hope of being good without exer-

9

tions or sacrifices; or that the whole universe will move in unison with their wishes and for their happiness.

Among the instructors Mr. Atkinson provided for his daughter was Mr. Charles Stuart, a young gentleman from Massachusetts, liberally educated, of fine talents, and whose prospects had once been brilliant. But losses and crosses occurred, and he found himself compelled, after leaving college, to earn money before he could complete his studies for the profession of law; his visit to the south was to seek employment as a preceptor in the languages.

Mr. Atkinson was highly pleased with his appearance, and satisfied with the credentials of character and scholarship he exhibited, and he employed him to instruct in French and Latin, his daughter and a boy whom he had adopted, giving Stuart a large salary.

Zemira, then not quite fifteen, was "gay as a lark, and innocent as gay;" one of those sweet, happy, laughing fairies, that so soon weave their spells around the hearts of the brave or wise when their lofty souls are saddened by care or misfortune.

Mr. Stuart instructed her with all the attention a faithful preceptor should do; and he soon loved her with all the ardor a young man of the most exquisite sensibility and entirely unengaged would do. It was his first love; he feared it would be hopeless, for he saw her father was a proud man, and expected a proud fortune for his child. Would he give her away to a Yankee school-master?

And Stuart considered it all, and he felt it was dishonorable to attempt winning her affection when thus committed to his care. A hundred times he resolved to leave the place and the employment, and Zemira and her father. These resolutions were always taken when absent from his pupil; a tone, a look of hers, altered his plans in a moment.

Then he remembered his engagement to her father, and fancied he had power to command his own passions, and that his secret would never be discovered; and a soft ray of hope would fall on his path—it might be, it might be she would be his.

He redoubled his assiduities to please and oblige Mr. Atkinson, but the more he won his confidence, and the better he understood his character, the less reason he saw to hope he would give him Zemira.

With Mr. Atkinson, as with many other men, wealth and success were criteria of merit; genius and learning being considered as appendages only, which should perhaps attract some notice, but which might be dispensed with easily, and without much inconvenience.

People who derive all their consequence from wealth, and have received their wealth by inheritance, are not usually very generous to encourage talents, or willing to acknowledge that, in conjunction with prudence and industry, they may soon obtain for their possessors even a higher station than themselves. Those who are rich can conceive of no happiness without riches; for they are ignorant of the satisfaction the exertion to obtain eminence or fortune excites. But moralize for yourselves; the reader who cannot, will never be wise. I must to my story.

Zemira, meantime, was as unsuspecting of the passion she had inspired, as she was of the one she entertained. She had scarcely heard of love, and never, in her life, thought seriously on the subject. Happy in the indulgent affection of her father, and charmed with the lessons of literature and wisdom imparted by her instructor, she did not think from whence arose the exquisite bliss she was enjoying. And when her father told her of his plans for her future felicity, she would press his hand, while the tear of delight trembled in her dark eye, and exclaim:

"Why do you feel so anxious about me? I never can be happier!"

She did not know why she so loved to have her tutor linger in the parlor where she received her lessons; nor why she so often studied questions to detain him; nor why it seemed so lonely when he was away; nor why she always counted the hours of his absence.

She did not think of loving him. He was her instructor, and her father's friend; she ought, therefore, to feel interested in his fortune; and he was so noble and amiable, she must admire his sentiments and conduct.

So she would have reasoned had she been called on to defend her partiality; but she was so insensible of her love for Stuart, that she never framed an excuse to justify or conceal it.

But suddenly his behavior altered. He no longer listened to her questions with a smile, or drew his chair nearer while giving an explanation; he came but at the stated moment, and staid only to hear her recitation.

He entered the room with a gravity of countenance bordering on severity, and often left it without once turning to give any directions for the next lesson. He grew pale, thin, and melancholy, and to all her inquiring and sympathizing looks, only answered with a suppressed sigh.

"What can be the matter with him?" was a question she repeated to herself a thousand times in a day.

She feared that she had done something to offend him, and taxed her memory for some omission of civility, some inattention to instruction, and redoubled her diligence—all was vain. He heeded no attentions she offered, no arts she practiced—he was cold and indifferent.

So she believed, yet she did not mention it to her father; for some how, though she knew not why, she shrunk from exposing her thoughts to him. And of what could she accuse Stuart?—he heard her lessons, he gave her the stipulated instruction. Should she complain his smiles were withdrawn?—would not her father say,—"Foolish girl, what are his smiles to the heiress of Atkinson!"

At length she felt so wretched she determined to come to an explanation, and know the reasons for his altered behavior. It was several days after this resolution was formed before she could gather courage to put it in execution. He left the apartment so suddenly she could not begin.

"The next time"—he came again and departed as before.

One day, when she had finished her recitation, she looked up and saw he had covered his face with his handkerchief, and she thought he wept. She burst into tears.

Stuart gazed on her, astonished. "Zemira, why do you weep?"

"How have I offended you?" said she.

"Offended me!" replied Stuart, incredulously.

"Yes, I know you are offended; you appear so differently from what you did. You are silent, and look so sad, and sometimes, I fancy, angry. Pray tell me what I shall do to make you happy and regain your favor?"

"Good God!" burst from Stuart's heart. He seized both her hands and pressed them to his bosom; all his resolutions of prudence were vanquished by her pathetic appeal, and he poured out his whole soul.

Zemira, abashed, confounded, scarce drew her breath; frightened at his vehemence of passion, yet rejoiced that he was not angry, that he loved her; yes, he loved her, and at that moment she did not think she could ever again be unhappy.

But the cloud soon returned on the brow of Stuart. He knew the obstacles to their union, and his nice sense of honor condemned the declaration he had made, as a violation of the confidence with which her father had entrusted this lovely girl to his instruction. He released her hands, started from his seat, and regarding her a moment, said, in a tone rendered touching by sorrow.—

"Zemira, I must leave you, even now leave you. Your father never will consent to our union, and to stay and endeavor to win your love and then be compelled to part, would only add to my sufferings. Farewell! I must go far and endeavor to forget you. The attempt, I feel, will be vain, yet I ask you not to regret me. You are surrounded with blessings; let not my remembrance ever prevent your enjoying them. I would not plant one care in your happy heart. Farewell, farewell!"

He was leaving the apartment. She started up. "Stay, Stuart, stay one moment, I entreat you."

He turned, saw her quivering lip, her pale cheek, sprung and caught her as she was falling to the floor.

"Zemira, Zemira," he exclaimed almost wildly, as he bore her to a window.

As he pronounced her name she opened her eyes, and looking up faintly said, "Do you still intend to leave me?"

"Why should I stay?" inquired he mournfully.

"For my sake," she replied, covering her blushing face with her hand.

Stuart could scarcely credit his hearing. The violence of his emotion shook his frame. He endeavored to reason, to reflect, but passion conquered.

Again he urged his love and found he was beloved. Zemira could not dissemble; she was artlessness itself; though nature had "wrought in her so," that she had never given him any suspicion of her attachment till his declaration demanded a return.

"Can I, Zemira, flatter myself with the hope you will be mine?" whispered Stuart.

Her smile might have imparted hope to despair itself, while she replied, "Ask my father; if he consents, I shall not refuse. And he will consent; for he has often declared he lived only to contribute to my happiness."

Stuart shook his head. "I am a poor man, my love, and the rich see no merit in such."

"You wrong my father," she replied; "he loves and respects you. He has wealth enough for us both, and why should he care from which party the abundance is supplied. Oh, when he finds his consent is necessary to my happiness, he will not withhold it."

The cold snows that wrap the frozen earth, like the shroud of nature, are not more unlike the soft dews which sparkle on the bosom of the summer rose, than are the feelings of selfish age and generous youth. The dews and snows are both exhaled from the same source, they descend from the same skies; yet who can discover their similitude?

Stuart felt their difference on his heart, as slowly he walked down the broad avenue to seek Mr. Atkinson, who had retired to his garden. He saw him in an arbor.

There are but few men, and I do not believe there ever was a true lover, but trembled when approaching the guardian of his fair one with an intention of asking consent. And Stuart trembled, but he told his errand like a man.

"Zemira," said the old gentleman, regarding the petitioner with an eye of lightning, "Zemira, you say, has accepted your suit if I will consent?"

"She has."

Mr. Atkinson paused a moment, as if to deliberate, and Stuart hoped, though the paleness of the father's face, the paleness of rage, forbade him to indulge it. But suspense was not long; Mr. Atkinson only paused to gather strength to express his wrath, and then it burst forth like the thunder of a torrent!

It is unnecessary, and would be painful to record his language—the ravings of a bedlamite are not more frantic. He poured his curses on the ingratitude and arts of Stuart, and on the weakness and simplicity of his daughter. Epithets the most opprobrious and contempt the most galling, seemed inadequate to convey the bitterness of his soul; and no efforts on the part of Stuart to appease or moderate his anger, were of the least avail, till exhausted by his own violence he was compelled to stop to recover breath.

"You have heaped your reproaches on me," said Stuart, when he could speak, "but they shall not move me, for God and my own conscience will witness I do not deserve them."

"You deserve the gallows," cried the furious father, "and I doubt not you will yet grace it. Such dissimulation and ingratitude will not go unpunished. But go, go from me; I will not listen to any apology. I owe you for your last quarter—there is the money; take it, and never let me see your face again. You may send for your clothes, but never presume to darken my doors yourself." As he ended he threw the money at Stuart, walked hastily out of the arbor and proceeded to the house.

Mr. Stuart was a man of strong and ardent passions, but they were usually subjected to the control of reason; and his own disappointment was forgotten while he sighed to think a man—an old man—should exhibit such an ungovernable and furious spirit.

"I pity him," thought he; "my own sun, darkened as it is by misfortune, is bright to his. There are scorpions in his bosom, whose sting is more keen than the gripe of poverty. My sorrows have arisen from casualties I could not avoid; his misery is the result of his own wilfulness and folly."

As Mr. Stuart could devise no expedient either to conciliate Mr. Atkinson or see Zemira again without encountering him, which he did not like to do in her presence, fearing unpleasant consequences might ensue, he had no alternative but to obey the bidding of his employer and depart.

The devoted lover, who has experienced a similar doom of banishment from his mistress, and only he, can conceive what his grief must have been. There are but few such despairing swains in our land of liberty and equality, and therefore should I draw the picture ever so touching and true, it could neither excite sympathy by its tenderness, nor admiration for its justness.

Stuart went to the house of an eminent merchant in the city, who had shown him many civilities, and on whose counsels he thought he might depend, and asked his advice what course to pursue.

Mr. Lee respected and loved Stuart; and besides, being a brother free mason, he felt bound to assist him.

After listening to Stuart's history of his love and grief, he said,—"If you have any hope of obtaining Mr. Atkinson's consent, there is but one course—you must acquire wealth, and a pretty large sum too, as that only will be a passport to his favor. It is strange," continued Mr. Lee,—"and yet it is true—that we usually find the greater a man's stores, the more inordinate are his desires, especially if he consider wealth necessary to rank and character. Property here has such an effect much more than at the north; because wherever slavery is established, to labor will be disreputable for a free white man, and while this prejudice operates on the minds of a community, the wealth that will exempt from exertion becomes absolutely indispensable. You must, therefore, endeavor to push your fortune; and were you willing to hazard the perils of the sea, I could employ you in a lucrative situation."

"I should not fear the danger—the distance might appal me more," replied Stuart; "but where would you send me?"

"My agent in New York is now fitting out one of my vessels for a voyage to the Mediterranean: I want a superintendent on whose capacity and faithfulness I can rely. If you would undertake the business, you shall have an opportunity of some advantageous speculations, and besides I will allow you a liberal compensation."

"And leave the country without seeing Zemira—without letting her know my destination and entreating her to be faithful?"

"Why no, my dear sir; for in that case, I fear you would be tempted to drown your sorrows, not in the flowing bowl, but in the briny deep. Yet, if Mr. Atkinson has really said and sworn you shall not see Zemira again, it will be very difficult for you to obtain an interview. He is one of those characters who always make it a point of honor and conscience to keep their word, thinking by that means to pass off their dogged obstinacy for manly perseverance. Now the man who tells me he never alters his opinion, I immediately set down for a very ignorant or a very obstinate fellow—certainly a very disagreeable one; and such has always been the social character of Mr. Atkinson."

"Then you are proving that for me to see and converse with Zemira is an impossibility?" said Stuart, thoughtfully.

"O, no," replied Mr. Lee, laughing: "who would ever attempt to prove impossibilities to a lover? I was only stating some of the difficulties you must encounter; then intending to offer my mediation in the affair, and should the issue be successful, the more credit would be mine. That, I believe, is the usual management of skilful diplomatists. I do not know what influence I might possess with Mr. Atkinson; our acquaintance has never been an intimate one. Yet, if you please, I will call on him, and shall doubtless learn something of his intentions, and perhaps be able to convince him of your merits."

Stuart gladly accepted the proposal; and after Mr. Lee had seen his guest accommodated to pass the time of his absence pleasantly, he departed on his embassy.

CHAPTER XVII.

ZEMIRA'S HISTORY CONTINUED.

——————— My dearest husband,
I sometimes fear my father's wrath; but nothing
(Always reserved my holy duty) what
His rage can do on me. You must be gone;
And I shall here abide the hourly shot
Of angry eyes; not comforted to live,
But that there is this jewel in the world,
That I may see again. CYMBELINE.

MR. ATKINSON received Mr. Lee with a profusion of civilities; for the man who has just fallen out with one friend is usually anxious to conciliate another, either to strengthen himself against the enemy he has lately made, or to demonstrate he has a heart capable of friendship whenever he meets with a worthy object. Few persons distrust compliments when paid to themselves, because but few distrust their own merits; unless, like Mr. Lee, they penetrate the motives of the speaker. But although he suspected Mr. Atkinson's uncommon flow of kindness proceeded from that revulsion of feeling from rage to complaisance which he had just experienced, and expected, should he mention the name of Stuart, to see a return of the storm; yet he determined to brave the tempest rather than betray the interest of the lover; and it is what but few men would have done, to offend a rich and powerful neighbor by appearing in behalf of a poor, friendless stranger.

But Lee and Stuart were brother free masons.

After some conversation, Mr. Lee introduced the name of Stuart by mentioning the proposed voyage, and inquired of Mr. Atkinson if he thought he might safely trust the young gentleman with such a responsible situation.

"I can't answer for your business," replied Mr. Atkinson, his anger rekindling, "but Stuart has betrayed my confidence most cursedly!"

He then proceeded to detail the matter as it appeared in his eyes, breathing denunciations against Stuart, and lamenting his own folly in employing him; "For," said he, "I might have known a Yankee pedagogue would stick at no means to gain property. I don't mean any reflections on you, Mr. Lee; you have been a citizen here a long time, and are naturalized to our customs, and have imbibed our generous spirit; and besides, you are not a Yankee, only from New York; but I do despise the people of the north that come like locusts to devour whatever they can find. To better himself is the first study of a Yankee; and heaven knows their situation needs *bettering;* but I have no intention they shall do it at my expense. My daughter shall never marry one of that canting, hypocritical race who are forever declaiming against slavery, and yet wish to reduce all the world to a dependence on themselves."

"But, Mr. Atkinson, I have often heard you speak in terms of the highest praise of your daughter's tutor."

"Ah! that was before I knew him. It takes a long time to find out the cunning of the race. Yet I might, if I had only had any thought, have found out Stuart before now. Why he was always walking and looking around my plantation, and inquiring about the management, and the income, and suggesting plans by which my estate might be improved; and I fancied it was all done to gratify me by showing an interest in my affairs;—fool that I was not to see that he was planning for himself! And my daughter is so young, it is no wonder she should be deceived. But his plans are blown now. He never shall see Zemira again, even though I should be compelled to confine her to her chamber till the day of her death."

"You don't confine that sweet girl, I hope!" said Mr. Lee, looking astonished.

"But I do, and I will, till that villain leaves this part of the country. Oh! 'tis here the ingrate has wounded me;" and he laid his hand on his heart. "He has stabbed my peace by robbing me of the affection of my only child, and I will never forgive him, even though I knew my eternal salvation would be forfeited by refusing."

"And did you not expect your daughter would love some man besides her father? Did you mean she should live in celibacy?"

"No, but I expected she would bestow her love on a man I could approve; and then the gratification of her wishes would fix another bond of obligation on her to respect me for thus providing for the continuance of her happiness. But now, Stuart has wheedled her out of her senses, and she thinks she must marry him or be wretched; and she regards me as a tyrant, and feels as if I were depriving her of every enjoyment. O! we shall never be happy again."

In spite of the knowledge that this misery was the effect of his own unyielding prejudices, Mr. Lee could not help commiserating the grief of the father, and he exerted all his ingenuity to convince him of his unjust accusations of Stuart, and persuade him to accept him for a son-in-law. But his arguments might as well have been employed in teaching self-denial to a Sybarite. His words, like oil poured on fire, increased the violence of the old man's anger, till his extravagant and irreverent language became too painful to Mr. Lee to endure, and he suddenly made his exit.

"There is no hope of appeasing or convincing Mr. Atkinson," said Lee to Stuart, after he had detailed in part the particulars of his interview. "He is in a more terrible rage, I presume, than you ever saw any one indulge. Your cool climate keeps your temperament cool; and the perfect equality subsisting in your society makes the controlling of the passions more indispensable than with us, where the overflowings of wrath may be poured out on the heads, and *bodies* too, of unresisting menials. But you will also find our virtues are proportionally more warm and ardent; this you will willingly concede, if you are a lover of Zemira, as no doubt you invest your charmer with every perfection under the sun."

"No," replied Stuart, "I only think her more free from the foibles which usually blemish such perfections and advantages as she possesses. She is beautiful, and yet neither affected, insolent, nor vain; she is rich, without being proud, arrogant, or extravagant; and she has always been indulged, and yet is neither petulant, wilful, or selfish."

"So you make her a paragon at last. I knew it would end there; and indeed I think she is well worthy your love. But now the only question is how to obtain her. I can contrive but two methods—either to elude the eyes of her Argus, and steal her away, or wait till they are closed in everlasting sleep."

"And before that event his cruelty will either have broken her heart or her spirit; she will be in her grave or in the arms of a rival."

"You are for expediting matters," said Lee, smiling. "Then suppose you contrive to steal her away? A clandestine marriage would be an affair of some celebrity in your history, as it is an event so seldom occurring in our country. Who knows but it might furnish a good plot for some dramatist? But it is uncertain yet whether the tragic or comic muse must be invoked; pray heaven it be not Melpomene. Yet we have some excellent characters for a tragedy. There's Mr. Atkinson very much resembles old Capulet; and if your fate should end like Romeo's——but I always thought his might have been avoided. He was too precipitate; you have his example before you, and would doubtless avoid his errors."

"And when was a lover ever made wiser by the mistakes or misfortunes of his ill-starred fellows?"

"O! never. You lovers are just like the girl in the Arabian Nights, who was in search of the talking bird, golden water, and singing tree; and would not turn back for warning, threat, or expostulation. She stopped her ears against the din; you are more courageous; you hear it, and yet go on."

"And she obtained the prize which a cowardly retreat would have forfeited. And true lovers always expect to obtain one. I am so confident of the worth of her I am seeking, that no hazard to myself would stay my pursuit. I only pause, fearing rashness on my part might involve her in distress. Could I only see her!"

"You can write to her," observed Mr. Lee.

"And how shall my letter be conveyed?"

"Easily enough. You know Tom; well, that fellow I purchased soon after I came here. He was such a faithful servant that about eight years ago I gave him his liberty. He afterwards continued with me some time, till Mr. Atkinson, hearing of his faithfulness, and always, by some means, being troubled to obtain good overseers, offered him such enormous wages, I advised him to accept. He has since resided there;—but still gratitude to me will prompt him to any service or sacrifice I require. He can carry your letters to Zemira, and return her answers: for he is cunning and dexterous as a juggler, and would outwit ——"

The offer was accepted, the letter written and despatched. It is due, however, to the good sense and real passion of Stuart to record, that his love-letter was not an unmeaning rhapsody—alternately fire and frost; now breathing out his affections, and now lamenting his destiny.

He addressed Zemira as his friend, and therefore entitled to his confidence—as a reasoning being, and therefore able to understand his situation, and assist him with her counsel. He explained his intentions and hopes, stated the offer of Mr. Lee, and asked her whether, in the event of his acceptance, she would still continue her faith, and at his return, allow him to claim her for his own.

Early next morning her answer arrived. It was so characteristic of the writer, so devoid of dissimulation or artifice, that it may be worthy of inserting as a *unique* of its kind.

It was written in pencil on a blank leaf torn from a book--(she was not allowed pen, ink, or paper)—and had been begun with "Dear Sir." This address she thought, possibly, too formal, and she substituted "Charles." But "Dear Charles" was too familiar, so she had tried to efface it, and wrote on it—

DEAR MR. STUART:

Your letter was the first consolation I have received since we parted. You have not then forgotten me; you will not then forget me, though my father has treated you so angrily. But he is my father, and has always been so kind, I must bear with his severity now without murmuring. He says I am too young and inexperienced to know what will most conduce to my own happiness; but I know my own heart, and feel that my affections can never be altered or divided. By your letter I perceive you judge it best to accept the proposal of Mr. Lee, and perhaps it is so. O! these cruel prejudices of my father, that make such a sacrifice necessary. Why should riches be thought so indispensable to happiness? I would rather live in poverty all my life, than have you exposed to the dangers of the seas to acquire wealth. Yet, if you think it best to accept your friend's offer, I will not urge your stay; only do not let time or distance blot Zemira from your memory or your heart. You need not bid me be faithful: I cannot be otherwise, for the idea of you is blended with every thought, every sentiment, and lesson you have taught me. And when I read over those passages in my books your pencil marked, I almost fancy I can hear your voice. I shall read them constantly during your absence; but what will remind you of ZEMIRA?

Postscript.—My father confines me closely to my chamber, yet allows me every indulgence I wish, except my liberty, and the means of corresponding with you. I suppose I am foolish to weep so much, and I endeavor to recollect all you have urged on the necessity of self-command; but thinking of your advice always makes me weep more. I wish I had more fortitude. When do you leave Savannah? Z. A.

Tuesday night, 12 *o'clock.*

The simple and pathetic letter of Zemira overcame Stuart's resolution, and he told Mr. Lee he could not embark in an enterprise that would take him so far, and detain him so long from that lovely and innocent girl; certainly not, if he must leave her thus exposed to the tyranny of her father, who would probably confine her till he could find a match which gratified his ambition, and then compel her to marry. "I cannot," continued he, "endure such uncertainty."

"Then why not marry her yourself—before you go?" said Mr. Lee.

"Marry her! How?"

"Why, as lovers of the olden time were in the habit of doing. Steal her away from the dragon that guards her. I will engage the parson. You may bring the fair lady here, and Mrs. Lee will protect her—with my assistance in times of imminent peril—till you return."

A spasm passed over the face of Stuart, as though he struggled with some deep agony of mind, some feeling he dared not entertain. After a few moments he raised his head, and said, hesitatingly—

"It may be the only way to save Zemira from being sacrificed to her father's hatred of me. And yet, how can I, as a man of honor, propose to this child—she is a child in her timid, clinging nature—to disobey her father, and desert him? I have no means of supporting her—and must leave her to the kindness of my friends. I don't doubt your friendship, Mr. Lee, but I fear your advice is wrong."

"Then don't follow it," said Mr. Lee, dryly. "You can go on this voyage; she says in her letter she will be faithful. You may return in two or three years——"

"And find Zemira lost to me!" exclaimed Stuart.

"Her father's threats, notwithstanding the sincerity of her affection for me, will overcome her resistance, or he will use artifice to persuade her I am inconstant—and when I return she will be lost to me."

The workings of his spirit displayed their power, and even his stern self-command could hardly restrain the violence of his emotion.

"If Zemira loves you as your merits deserve, and as her father's anger would imply, her happiness ought to weigh something in your decision," said Mr. Lee, earnestly. "I do not approve of elopements, nor would I counsel you to this course, only I know Mr. Atkinson, and know that your case is a desperate one. He would rather see his daughter in her coffin, than at the altar with you, even if you gain wealth, because he has sworn she shall not marry you. Now, you can live without her—men don't often die for love;—but poor Zemira will have a pitiful lot. She has never been disappointed; she has a very tender, loving heart; and I am sorry for her."

"What would you advise me to do?"

"To leave this place at once. Go to Augusta, and remain there two or three weeks. When Mr. Atkinson finds you gone, he will release his daughter. Mrs. Lee shall visit her then. My wife loves Zemira, and has her confidence."

"And then?"

"We shall see how this little Juliet, as my wife often calls her, because she has such an exuberance of love in her young heart, we shall see how she bears separation from her Romeo. Should she droop like a broken lily——"

"Oh! let me know it at once!"

The suggestion was acted on, and came very near proving a real tragedy. Mr. Atkinson, finding Stuart had actually left Savannah, was so overjoyed that he burst into his daughter's prison-chamber, told her she was free, for the villain had fled, never to return!

She heard the announcement calmly, as her father

thought; before the next morning she was in the delirium of a fever.

Mrs. Lee was sent for; Zemira loved her well, and Mr. Atkinson had no female relation in the city. At the first lucid interval, Mrs. Lee told the poor, broken-hearted child, that her lover had not forsaken her—he was then returned, privately, and waiting to see her as soon as she recovered.

It was wonderful, the effect of this simple assurance, and how suddenly Zemira's health improved!

Then Mrs. Lee tried her rhetoric on the father; but she found him in no melting mood. To all she could urge of the danger Zemira had just escaped, and how deeply her happiness was concerned in her union with Mr. Stuart, the father was utterly unmoved. He met every attempt to gain his consent, by a stern refusal, declaring that "Zemira might die! but she should never marry Charles Stuart!"

To reason was hopeless;—so the trio at Mr. Lee's resorted to stratagem,—Mrs. Lee justifying her course by her belief that it was the only way to prevent Mr. Atkinson from becoming accessory to the death of his daughter. The love of Charles Stuart overmastered his scruples of honor—yet his own passion was not so predominant as his terror lest Zemira, unless tranquilized by the assurance that she was his *wife*, should, on his actual departure, sink into a state of hopeless despondency.

Zemira's assent to the secret marriage was easily obtained—but not to the residence at Mr. Lee's. She would remain with her father. He might be ill and need her care; he always needed her caresses. In one of her letters to her lover, she wrote,—

"Do not, dearest Charles, ask me to leave my father. I will marry you; but while you are gone, let me stay with him. Perhaps he will relent. *Perhaps, in some* blessed moment, he will say,—'Zemira, when Stuart returns, you shall be his!' Oh! how such a permission from his revered lips would confirm my happiness. But should he retain his prejudices against you, and endeavor to compel me to marry another, and I find no other resource of escape, I will then confess my marriage, fly to your friends for protection, and there await your return."

So it was arranged. And when Zemira had recovered sufficiently to go abroad, her father permitted her to pass a week with Mrs. Lee. An easy opportunity was thus presented for the marriage; and she and Stuart pledged their faith at the house of Mr. Lee, in his presence, his wife's, and a lady, the particular friend of Zemira, whose affection and secrecy admitted not of suspicion.

A few days after his marriage, Stuart was obliged to take leave of his young bride, and actually depart. It was a moment that called for the exertion of more fortitude than he had ever before practiced, when, with her soft arm encircling his neck, she wept on his bosom her last adieu—it was one of those partings that "press the life from out young hearts." He was obliged to suppress his own emotion to soothe and encourage her; and he promised a speedy return, and faithful remembrance, and constant correspondence. His letters were to be directed to Mr. Lee, enclosing Zemira's, who could convey them to her without being discovered.

And thus they parted; he on a foreign destination, and she to weep his absence in her father's splendid but, *to her, lonely halls.*

The sorrow and desolation of such partings are not felt in their full bitterness by man. He plunges in business or resorts to amusements; new scenes attract his notice, new friends solicit his favor, and the smile he at first only affects, soon images the real gayety of his heart.

But woman, sad and secluded, sits alone and muses on joys that are past. In every dream of her fancy is blended the image of her lover; and every tear she sheds, hallows the remembrance of his friendship. She *must* be faithful—"she cannot choose but weep."

Zemira wept almost continually, though her father, more fond, if possible, than ever, tried every art to console and divert her. But her melancholy continued; her color fled, and her health seemed fast declining.

Mr. Atkinson, convinced it was the loss of her lover which thus affected her, thought the best method of dissipating her grief was to give her another; and he renewed his correspondence with his friend Brainard, of whose nephew and heir he had heard much, and on whom he had fixed as the future husband of Zemira. To accomplish their union with the least delay, was his constant study. The feeble state of his own health forbade him to expect a long continuance of life, and he fancied he could die happy if he saw his daughter the wife of Sidney Romilly.

So fondly does the world cling around the hearts of men! And when they can no longer enjoy it themselves, they labor to direct its enjoyments for others.

In pursuance of his plan, Mr. Atkinson informed Zemira she must make preparations to visit South Carolina, and spend the winter in Charleston. His health required journeying and change of scene, and he had many friends in that city to whom he was anxious his child should be introduced.

Zemira heard this declaration with dismay. She could not think of an introduction to the notice of strangers. She could not leave the place where she often fancied she heard the voice of her beloved Stuart; and she should be deprived of the dearest happiness she now enjoyed—the perusal of his letters, which arrived almost daily; for how could she receive them at Charleston where she knew no one to whom they might safely be directed? But her entreaties to relinquish or defer the journey, by making her father suspect she intended corresponding with Stuart, only made him hasten her departure, and she was compelled to obey.

She had just received a letter from her husband, detailing an account of his success in prosecuting the business entrusted to his care, and flattering his hopes with a fortunate voyage when he might return with wealth to support his sweet wife, claim her, and be happy.

"It will never, never be," thought she often during her journey, and after her arrival at Charleston. "I shall not live to see him again." But when she was introduced to Sidney, and discovered she was, by her father, destined to be his wife, fear and grief did indeed nearly deprive her of existence. She was separated from every friend on whom she had any claim for assistance. But one ray of hope yet remained—Sidney Romilly had a kind heart; he could sympathize in the sorrows of others, and more, he had the power to relieve them. She determined, whenever he declared his passion, to tell him the whole of her story, and rely on his generosity to forgive, pity, and assist her.

CHAPTER XIX.

IN WHICH THE HERO SHOWS HIS HEROISM.

But O, how bitter it is to look into happiness through another man's eyes! AS YOU LIKE IT.

"AND what do you expect from my interference in this business, madam?" said Sidney, with an air of petulant haughtiness.

Zemira uncovered her face; and, turning her dark eyes, bathed in tears, upon him,—

"O!" said she, "I hoped—I hardly dare tell you—I hoped you would be my friend, and conceal all from my father, and make him believe you did not wish to marry me; and"—— she grew paler.

"And what more?" said Sidney, trembling with suppressed emotion. "What more do you require of me?"

"Only—to receive Mr. Stuart's letters and convey them to me. My father will not suspect you, and I must hear from my husband, or my heart will break. Will you—will you do it? O, say you will!" and clasping her hands, she leaned towards him in the attitude of entreaty.

Sidney might, with old Norval, have complained, "Alas, I am sore beset." He professed himself her devoted lover, and yet shrunk from bearing the name of friend. "I must resign her," thought he. He looked at her, and his feelings overcame his resolution.

"O, Zemira!" exclaimed he, seizing her clasped hands in his, "why, why did you marry him? You say you esteem me—you wish me for a friend. Ah! had I seen you before this fatal connection, and could I have obtained a dearer title, my whole life should have been devoted to your happiness. Zemira, say, at least, if you were not the wife of Stuart, you might have preferred me."

"Mr. Romilly," she replied, with such an air of modest dignity as compelled him instantly to release her struggling hands, "I never thought of preferring any man to my husband. I said you were generous; but you are not like him. If you were acquainted with him, you would not wonder at my partiality. O, he is my pride, my preceptor, my friend! But I can convince you of his worth, nobleness, and superiority," she continued, her face glowing with animation: "I will show you his letters, and then you can judge whether he is not worthy of my confidence—my heart."

As she ended, she left Sidney, but soon returned with a small ivory box in her hand, and opening it, took out a bundle of letters, and holding them towards the discarded lover, said, with a sweet smile,—"Here, if you will only peruse these, you cannot, I am sure you cannot, blame my choice. But do return them; they are dear to me as my life."

Sidney took the letters, although he would willingly have been excused from seeing them; but he could not refuse such an urgent request, especially when made by such a persuasive voice. He took them, and without speaking, bowed, left the house, and, hurrying home, shut himself up in his own chamber, to deliberate what course to pursue. But his mind was all anarchy; and at last, as a refuge from his own thoughts, he took up the letters. They were all neatly folded, and each labeled with the date of its reception.

Although Sidney had no intention of analyzing the mind of his rival by a minute examination of the contents of the several epistles, yet he naturally opened the first in order, intending merely to glance over its contents, without expecting to be much edified by the morality or consistency of a love-letter. However, he made no pause till it was finished, and then laid it down but to take up another; nor did he once change his posture till the reading of the whole was accomplished.

The hand-writing was beautiful and very plain, which much facilitated the reading and comprehending too; for who can understand the connection of a sentence when obliged to pause and hammer and spell one half the words composing it. But Sidney thought not of the penmanship; it was the sentiments of the writer, so noble, so wise, so just, yet expressed with such simplicity, and illustrated and applied with such anxious, yet delicate tenderness to direct the mind and conduct of his pupil and bride. There were directions for the regulation of her time and temper; hints on the selection of books and the choice of company; on the advantages of a taste for literature, when kept in subordination to her duties, to the happiness and usefulness of a woman; and a recommendation of the heaven breathing spirit of piety, as the beautifier which added loveliness to the lovely. These were the topics introduced and discussed with all the knowledge of the philosopher, yet with all the suavity, feeling and delicacy that friendship and love could inspire.

"He is worthy of her!" exclaimed Sidney, starting from his seat and pacing the apartment with rapid steps. "She was right in saying I was not like him. I have worshiped her for her beauty and to gratify my passion; Stuart loved her for the excellences his intimate acquaintance showed him she possessed, and he is employing his influence over her mind to render her worthy of forever retaining his confidence and affection. He sought her not as a toy for the moment, but to make her his friend, his companion through life. For this she loves him as I shall never be loved. I may obtain a wife or mistress; wealth would gain either, though a man were deformed as Æsop; but a friend, a true love, who will "love on through each change and love on till we die," such a one must be deserved, and must be cherished. I am not worthy of Zemira, for I could not guide aright her gentle spirit, that would so entirely commit itself to mine to be directed. Yet why?" continued he, sitting down and leaning his head on his hand with a mournful expression of countenance, as if lamenting over the loss of long cherished hopes, "why am I thus inferior to Stuart? I was, in childhood, extolled as possessing uncommon genius, and flattered with the expectations of becoming a *great* man, and now I am—a *gay* one. Strange, that the expectation of being able to bestow a fortune on a child should lead those who have the care of his instruction to educate him only to spend it! As if they thought riches possessed the quality of imparting knowledge without the necessity of study or exertion. Had I remained in the old granite state and won my way from the plow to the honors of a college, as our greatest statesmen have done, I should not now be envying the superior acquirements of even Stuart. I know I could have equaled him. But luxury has undone me. Wealth all covet; yes, my good, sensible, and contented parents were dazzled by its lustre, and thought, by placing me in a situation to inherit it, I should of course possess the advantages which it is supposed to convey. But they erred, or I have wretchedly misimproved my opportunities. And is there then no privilege attached to the possession of riches? Yes, the power of conferring benefits on those less favored by fortune's smiles. It is there I can excel Stuart; and I will —yes—I will make him, learned and noble, and dignified as he is, confess himself indebted to me. I will go to New York, find out Stuart, and offer him such inducements as shall make him forego his intended voyage. I will restore him to Zemira, and by the influence of my uncle, reconcile Mr. Atkinson to their marriage. Then Zemira will be happy, and she will bless me, and acknowledge I have a soul capable of estimating worth; and I shall perhaps feel deserving of her gratitude."

Sidney was an enthusiast in whatever he heartily engaged, and he had no sooner taken this resolution than he hastened to put it in immediate execution. He communicated to no one whither he was going; but simply informed his uncle he wished to be absent a few days or an expedition from which he promised himself much pleasure.

His uncle consented, though not without endeavoring to ascertain whether his business had any reference to his nuptials, which Mr. Atkinson was anxious should be celebrated without delay.

"Mr. Atkinson," said his uncle, "told me Zemira had received your addresses. You will be a happy man if she loves you."

How often the face speaks a language foreign to the heart. Sidney suppressed a sigh and forced a smile, and Mr. Brainard thought he was happy.

Early the next morning Sidney took his seat in the New York stage.

Steam and telegraph have made a revolution in affairs of the heart as well as in business affairs. Space and time being annihilated, novel writers can no longer keep lovers in the purgatory of suspense. There is no possibility of delaying the meeting or the letter, as lightning can be used if steam is too slow, unless the author raises a tornado to break the wires, or blows up the steamboat, or runs the rail-car over a precipice. And these horrible accidents must be sparingly used, or the interest of the work will prove too painful for readers of amusing fiction.

But in the good old times of which we treat—say thirty years ago—neither steam nor lightning connected the South with the North. From South Carolina to New York, was a weary pilgrimage of nearly eight hundred miles, and many long days—more than now suffice to make the voyage to Europe—were required for the journey by land. It required, also, some heroism to undertake it solely for the benefit of others. Our hero, however pursued his way without interruption, and arrived in due time at the end of his journey safely, and in good health. No sooner was he set down at the hotel, than, directed by Stuart's letters to Zemira, he proceeded to his lodgings, and inquired if he were within. The waiter answered in the affirmative. Sidney then sent up his name, and requested an immediate interview on business of importance.

The waiter soon returned, saying, "Mr. Stuart is engaged, sir, but says he will attend to your business now, if it does not require long attention." Then motioning Sidney to follow him, he began to ascend the stairs.

This was a trying moment for the rejected lover. In the hurry and bustle of the journey, he had thought but of reaching the city in time to find Stuart before he embarked, without considering the consequences which might result from an interview with him. But now, when so near the completion of his wishes, embarrassments he had not anticipated, began to appear. What should he say to Stuart? and how introduce the particular business that brought him to the city? Should he tell the husband he had made love, serious, ardent love, to his wife? and how would he relish the intelligence?

Sidney ran over in his mind every dilemma to which unfortunate lovers had been reduced, but found no parallel for his case, and no precedent to guide his behavior. Once he paused, almost resolved to return back and leave the affair unexplained; but he was within three steps of the apartment, the waiter had already reached the door; "I must proceed now," thought he, "and my communication shall be regulated by the appearance of Stuart. Perhaps he is not so formidable as I imagine."

The servant opened the door, and Sidney entered.

"Mr. Stuart," said the waiter, motioning towards a gentleman who was seated before a table at the upper end of the room, then instantly retreating, he closed the door.

Stuart raised his head as the waiter pronounced his name, and fixed a scrutinizing gaze on the stranger; Sidney Romilly felt his heart beat, and his cheek flush, beneath the penetrating regards of the Yankee schoolmaster. He stood exactly fronting Stuart and a large mirror, and the view of his own face as compared with that of his rival, did not afford him much pleasure.

Sidney had often been told he was a handsome fellow; and it is not strange if he sometimes indulged a little self-complacency on his good appearance—but he now saw of how small account, especially for a man, is a "set of features or complexion" to the perfection of the human countenance.

Charles Stuart's features, examined by the rules of art, were irregular, and his complexion, though clear and healthy, had nothing of the delicacy or freshness that usually distinguishes students from men of business (the *freshness* can only be claimed by those who burn no midnight oil; remember that and be careful, ye dandy students.) His was the beauty of deep thought, the lofty expression of superior intelligence, giving to his countenance an irresistible fascination, while a gravity almost approaching sadness told the struggles he had to maintain with the world, which had always seemed adverse to his happiness. But the animation of his eye at once evinced he did not shrink from the contest; his eyes literally flashed forth the feelings and meaning of his soul, and seemed to read the thoughts and hearts of those who approached him, and few could meet their keen, searching, expressive glance, without feeling a sense of inferiority.

Oh! the eye is the index of the mind, and let Gall and Spurzheim examine the bumps of the cranium, one glance of the eye tells more than all.

"Your name is Romilly, I believe," said Stuart, examining his card. Sidney bowed. "You have business of importance, the waiter told me."

"Yes, yes," stammered out Sidney, and all was silence. "Would to Heaven," thought he, "some trapdoor would kindly open beneath my feet; I should care little where I landed if once freed from this awkward dilemma."

"I am in haste," observed Stuart, "and shall be

obliged to urge the despatch of your affairs with all convenient speed."

"Yes, sir, yes," said Sidney, and drew towards the table, then suddenly stopping. "I came here, sir, without considering the awkwardness of introducing myself or my intentions to a stranger; yet I came as a friend, to serve you, to make you happy."

"And really for a stranger you were very benevolent," replied Stuart, smiling; "but can you not explain the reasons which induced you thus to interest yourself in my fate?"

"Your *wife!*" exclaimed Sidney, resolutely raising his voice while pronouncing *wife*, as if determined to convey his whole meaning at once.

"My wife!" repeated Stuart, starting from his seat, while his face was crimson and his eyes seemed to emit fire; "my wife! what do you know of my wife?"

Sidney was now the calmest of the two, and certainly was relieved from a part of the feeling of inferiority which had so sensibly depressed him in the presence of the scholar and philosopher, when he found Stuart was also a lover. Nothing affords more self-complacency than seeing those whom we imagine exempt from human weaknesses, exhibit the like passions as other men.

"We will sit down, if you please," said Sidney, "and I will tell you a tale that might well grace a romance, were it not over-true for such a place. I hope you will listen with patience, and judge with candor."

They sat down, and Sidney began and related minutely the particulars of his meeting with Zemira, and told the tale of his love; but then he did not dilate, for the changing color and compressed lip of Stuart warned him to be brief, and he hastened to his last interview; and when he mentioned the delicate and noble conduct of Zemira on the occasion, her husband's eyes beamed with tenderness, while he unconsciously ejaculated, "What an angel!"

Then Sidney made his own generous offer of assisting the lovers, urging Stuart to accompany him back to

Charleston, and pledging himself, with his uncle's assistance, to remove every obstacle to his happiness.

"We will," said he, "either conciliate the old gentleman's prejudices, and he shall receive you as a son, which he may well be proud to do, or we will place you in a situation to support yourself and Zemira independently of his favor. Do not deny me the pleasure of thus deserving your friendship, for the man worthy of Zemira's love must be estimable as a friend."

He sighed, and Stuart pitied him; yes, pitied the man who was offering him assistance.

There is riches in reciprocal affection—there is wealth in superior intellect—which cannot be estimated or transferred, and the possessor of either has a jewel the man of gold can never purchase with gold.

Stuart held out his hand.

"I accept your offer, Mr. Romilly, with the same frankness it is made. Although I have oftener found deceit than kindness in the world, yet my heart is not chilled into suspicion; and if your countenance be an index to your soul, I have now no cause to fear being betrayed."

Sidney pressed the offered hand, and felt, at the moment, almost as gratified as if he were pressing Zemira's. *Almost*—self still held a sway, which reason and generosity were striving to extinguish. His love could not at his bidding retire, but by continued exertion he hoped it might be overcome.

There were circumstances which gave to the offers of Sidney the appearance of the design of fate, or rather, Providence—the term is more appropriate in a Christian country—to reunite the husband and wife. The agent employed by Mr. Lee to procure the cargo, had failed, and in consequence of his bankruptcy the vessel could not proceed on her voyage.

Mr. Stuart, therefore, was destitute of employment, and at the arrival of Sidney was anxiously meditating some plan to enter on business. Several had been proposed, considered, and rejected · and he was then actually employed in speculations on a voyage to China, the only one offering which afforded him a chance for pecuniary profit, and that demanded a length of time that almost rendered such a recompense valueless.

But now he might stay in his own country, with his beloved Zemira, and while he thanked Heaven in a transport of gratitude, he fully appreciated the noble sacrifice and disinterestedness of him who so largely contributed to his happiness. Everything was soon arranged, and the two friends, without any feeling of rivalry, commenced the journey which was to terminate the suspense of all parties.

If Sidney sometimes breathed a sigh that his fairy visions were thus dissolved, he never failed, on listening to the conversation of Stuart, to acknowledge that he who had robbed him of his love was worthy of the prize. There was a satisfaction in the thought—not that we like to be eclipsed—but the heart involuntarily pays a tribute to merit, and we are consoled with the hope of obtaining a like reward, when, like the favored one, we shall deserve it.

CHAPTER XX.

RECONCILIATIONS.

A death-bed's a detector of the heart.—YOUNG.

THE two gentlemen reached Charleston in safety, and were set down at the house of Mr. Brainard.

"Where is my uncle?" said Sidney to the servant who appeared.

"At Mr. Atkinson's," was the reply.

"When does he return?"

"Lack, sir, I don't know," replied the servant—"why, Mr. Atkinson is dying with a fit of the *artiplax*."

"Oh, my God!" exclaimed Stuart, "where is Zemira?"

"The old man's daughter I heard my massa say took on *desputly*, and he feared she would die too."

"Let us go, Romilly," cried Stuart, "perhaps we may save Zemira."

Silently and hastily they proceeded to the lodgings of Mr. Atkinson. In reply to their eager inquiries, the servant said his master was still living.

"And where is his daughter?" asked Sidney.

"In her chamber, I believe."

"Go to her and say Mr. Romilly wishes to speak with her immediately, if she is able to hear him."

"I will wait in the hall," said Stuart, as Sidney opened the door of the parlor, "till you apprise Zemira of my arrival; should I appear suddenly, the effect might, in her present low spirits, be overwhelming."

Sidney had not passed many minutes in the parlor before Zemira, pale, and her eyes swollen with weeping, entered, and, making an effort to speak, burst into tears.

"My friend," said Sidney, as he hastened towards her, "you have allowed me that title—I may not aspire to a dearer—I know your sorrow, and I need not tell you of my sympathy. Is there any service I can perform for you?"

"My father," sobbed Zemira, "wishes to see you he insists on pledging you my hand before he dies. O, what shall I say to him! How can I so deceive him at such a time, and who will protect me?"

"If your husband were here you would not feel so destitute," said Sidney, trembling almost as much as she.

"O! no, no; but I have heard nothing from him since I came to this city. He has, I suppose, sailed, and I fear I shall never"——. Here her agitation overcame her, and she wept aloud.

"Zemira, Zemira, be calm!" exclaimed Sidney. "You will see your husband again—I pledge my life to restore him to you."

"When?"

"Now, whenever you can have fortitude to support the interview."

"Is he come?—is he here?—I am calm; let me but see him, and I will be calm." And she gazed eagerly at the opening door.

Stuart entered: he had heard all, for the door was not entirely closed, and at her pathetic entreaties he could no longer restrain his impatience. He rushed forward and caught her, as faintly uttering his name she sunk into his extended arms.

Sidney did not dare trust himself to be a witness of their rapture. He felt sick, oppressed for breath, and hastened to the door with an intention of leaving the house. A servant overtook him as he reached the street, with a message from his uncle, requesting to see him. He turned back, and was conducted into an apartment adjoining that in which the sick man was confined, where his uncle soon joined him.

After a few hurried inquiries, respecting what had so long detained him, which Sidney evaded as well as he was able, Mr. Brainard described the melancholy situation of his friend, hinted the probability of his speedy dissolution, and finally ended by telling him he had engaged for his marrying Zemira.

"But," continued he, "the old gentleman is anxious to witness the performance of the ceremony, and I was about despatching a messenger to hasten your return."

"What a prize might have been mine!" thought Sidney; "but I have begun to act the part of the self-denying, philosophic lover, and must proceed." He then related to his uncle the story of Stuart, and the resolutions he had himself taken.

Mr. Brainard listened to the recital with astonishment and emotion; and when it was concluded, leaned his head on his hand and sat for some time in deep and evidently unpleasant reflection. Then suddenly starting up, he drew his hand across his eyes, as if to shut some unpleasant object from his view, while he said, in a melancholy tone,—

"Sidney, I applaud your conduct, though my example did not teach it. But you need not my praises, for I am convinced integrity always imparts its own reward, and your heart is now enjoying a happiness which the possession of Zemira could not bestow; at least not for any length of time. I know that connubial affection to be lasting, must be reciprocal, and that if we would enjoy felicity we must be able to confer it."

He sighed, and Sidney, who suspected his sadness arose from self-reproach for the ungenerous part he had acted in supplanting Reuben Porter, changed the conversation by inquiring how they might best communicate the affair to Mr. Atkinson, or whether it was not better to let him depart without a knowledge of his daughter's marriage. After some discussion, they concluded to visit the sick man, and consider what effect the intelligence might have on his weak frame and agitated nerves.

His disorder was a fit of the apoplectic kind; and although he had partially recovered from the shock, and now possessed his reason, his enfeebled constitution was sinking beneath the attack, and his wasted and livid features struck Sidney with horror. At their approach, he turned his dim, heavy eyes, upon them; death was already glassed in their sunken orbs, yet there was something like the lighting up of joy at the sight of Sidney, as if earth still held one object on which they might rest with confidence—one heart on which he might rely for comfort.

Mr. Atkinson raised his hand and Sidney extended his, although shuddering while he did so; for the hand he took was already cold, and the damps of death gave a clammy chilliness to the long bony fingers, and he trembled while involuntarily striving to release himself from their convulsive grasp.

"I thank God that I see you once more," said Mr. Atkinson, at length, in a hollow, rattling tone. "I can now depart in peace—you will protect my daughter."

Sidney could not answer.

After a moment's pause, Mr. Atkinson made an effort to raise himself, while he said with energy,—"Mr. Romilly, you know my partiality for you, and I think—I believe—I hope Zemira favors you also. Will you promise me, in the name of that God before whom I shall soon stand, to make her your wife, and by your kindness console her for my loss? Ah! she will soon be an orphan."

Sidney's eyes glistened with tears as he turned them on his uncle with an expression that supplicated his interference.

"My nephew," said Mr. Brainard, comprehending the appeal, "on account of some singular circumstances, is not able to give you a decisive answer. If you will consent he should retire, I will make the explanations, and then we will agree to whatever shall be proper."

Mr. Atkinson released the hand he had held, and by a motion of his head signified his assent; yet when Sidney was leaving the room he called him to return, and told him he hoped nothing had happened which would impede his marriage with Zemira; "for," said he, "my sick heart cannot brook such a disappointment."

"Oh! would to heaven she could be mine!" exclaimed Sidney, thrown off his guard by the mention of a union as possible, "but she is already"—— married, he would have said, had not his uncle caught his arm and hurried him from the chamber.

Then returning to the bed-side, Mr. Brainard, after much circumlocution, and many exhortations to the dying father to consider what was past and inevitable as designed by Providence, revealed the marriage of his daughter and the return of Stuart.

It was some time before Mr. Atkinson could believe the story; but when he learned the noble part Sidney had acted, and the praises he bestowed on his rival, he was conquered. Tears streamed down his cheeks, as he faintly said, "I am satisfied; may God bless their union—it was of his appointment." Then turning his face towards Mr. Brainard, continued, "My friend, the world is fading from me; its riches, honors, and pleasures appear now like the baubles that amused my childish fancy. They have been bright, but now I see their vanity; I wonder I could ever have prized them so highly. A death bed, Mr. Brainard, a death bed reduces the things of earth to their intrinsic value. I am passing the dark valley, but it is the world only that is shadowed. Heaven and goodness are bright and beautiful, and in the scrupulous practice of christian duties, I must acknowledge the superiority of Stuart. He bore my unreasonableness, my rage and rebukes, with the calmness of conscious innocence. I knew he was worthy of Zemira, but he was poor—his poverty was the objection I could not overcome. I thought a rich man would add lustre to my name, and my name will soon be known only on a neglected tablet of stone. I thought a rich man, by adding his wealth to mine, might make great improvements on my estate, and now my eyes are to be closed on everything below the skies. I was providing for an earthly eternity—ah! that is a provision no mortal need make!"

He had spoken so rapidly, Mr. Brainard could not check him, although trembling for the consequences; and his fears were realized, for Mr. Atkinson now sunk down exhausted and apparently dying, and it was not until after the application of many restoratives that he recovered sufficiently to express his desire to see his daughter and her husband.

"I will bless them," said he, "before I go hence; Zemira will live happier, and I shall die happier."

Mr. Brainard summoned Sidney, and acquainting him with the result of the conference, bade him go to Stuart and Zemira, and conduct them to their father.

Sidney said he rejoiced te hear all would be so amicably adjusted; yet his step, when proceeding to seek them, was not a "tripping on the light airy toe" of unbridled happiness. He lingered a moment in the hall, endeavoring to assume a cheerfulness of countenance, that he might not appear like a disconsolate lover; but when he unclosed the door and saw the beautiful cheek of Zemira resting on the shoulder of her husband, while with his face declined towards hers, and an arm encircling her waist, he was supporting her and soothing her grief, the image of mutual love, confidence, and tenderness was more than his disappointed feelings could endure, and hastily closing the door, he paced the hall in an agony of perturbation.

"And yet," thought he, "I knew it would be thus. I must control my passions—one effort of self-denial will not make me good, or my friends happy. I will be consistent—I have reunited the lovers, and now shall I mar their felicity, and blast my own, by indulging in weak and wicked repinings and envyings? I will not yield to the suggestions of imagination. Zemira never can be mine, but tranquillity may, if I do not foolishly waste my life in vain regrets."

He now again opened the door; the lovers were standing evidently in a state of anxious expectation.

Sidney approached them with tolerable composure, and related the approval of the old gentleman and his desire to see them. Sudden felicity is usually in its first tumultuous throb, more overwhelming than sorrow. Zemira had never dared to expect such a result. Joy and grief had been, for the last half hour, strangely commingled in her bosom. She had been folded to the heart of her husband, but she could not anticipate the happiness of enjoying his society for any length of time without associating it with the death of her beloved and only parent. She dared not think of the future, for on every side dark shadows were resting; but Sidney's intelligence dispelled them all, and she who had borne sorrows and separations patiently and calmly, now fainted in the sunbeams of prosperity!

As soon as she recovered sufficiently she begged to be conducted to her father. He had been strengthening himself to take a last farewell of his daughter—the world he had already shaken off.

Early independence, an ill directed education, and violent passions, had involved Mr. Atkinson in many inconsistencies, exposed him to many temptations, and it must not be thought strange if he had at times yielded to the allurements of pleasure and vice; yet of cold, premeditated cruelty or villany he had never been guilty. His impulses were usually on the side of goodness, when his passions did not interfere; and had he in youth been subjected to judicious discipline, or taught by necessity to govern himself, he would have been an inestimable man.

As it was, he had been prosperous, but never happy—rich, but never contented; and instead of studying himself and discovering from his disappointments the inadequacy of the world to afford real or permanent enjoyment, he had, by the failure of one ambitious scheme been stimulated to a more ardent pursuit of another, till they centered as the schemes of life usually do in age, in a desire of accumulating wealth, not for himself—for he was sensible he could not long enjoy it—but for his daughter. Such are the subterfuges of selfishness.

But the approach of death dissipated the illusions of earth. He saw the broken reed on which he had been leaning. His vices and follies sprung up like armed men when the field was sown with dragons' teeth, to threaten and destroy him. Oh! how gladly would he have given all he possessed for the peace of a quiet conscience!

But peace is not to be purchased; it is won only by goodness, or accorded to penitence. He could not claim it for the first; he had not besought it in the humility of the last. For some time he struggled to suppress his feelings and his fears; but an alarmed conscience is not easily hushed. His pride at length yielded to his terror, and a clergyman was sent for—a sensible and pious man, whose conversation and example were alike heavenly. He listened to all the confessions and complaints of the sick man with patience and pity, and gently as the dew falls on the drooping plant, he breathed the words of consolation.

Mr. Atkinson became convinced the Bible he had so long disbelieved, or at least doubted, was the only sure guide to immortal life; and that the Saviour he had neglected was indeed the kind physician who would heal all his sufferings by forgiving all his sins. How rich now appeared the promises of the gospel!—how glorious the love of the Redeemer and the joys of heaven! He believed; and while relying on the mercy of God, he felt a spirit of benevolence towards his fellow men, which he had never before cherished.

The pride which had so long elated him at the idea of his vast possessions, was now humbled by the consciousness of the little good he had performed with all his advantages, and the utter nothingness of wealth to purchase the favor of heaven.

He could now listen to the account of his daughter's

marriage with a poor man, who he knew was rich in merits, without feeling a degradation, and was eager to press her to his bosom and give to her union with Stuart the sanction of his approbation.

As they approached, he stretched forth his hand, saying, while an attempt to smile gave to his sunken and distorted features an unearthly expression.—"Ah! my daughter, my darling, do I see you happy before I die."

Zemira sprung from the support of her husband, and throwing her arm around her father's neck, burst into a passion of tears. It was more than his weakened frame could endure, and the attendants had to separate them. She was consigned to the care of Stuart, who succeeded in calming her agitation by representing the fatal effect it must have upon her father.

After a few minutes he again spoke and called on his daughter and Stuart. They knelt by his bed-side and took each a hand.

"My children," said he, looking on them tenderly while the difficulty of his respiration seemed increasing every moment, "I have much to say, but death will soon interrupt me. I feel his cold embrace. He is stealing on, and this heart and pulse will soon cease to beat. Yet do not grieve; my Saviour has interceded for me and God will receive me. But, oh! do not love the world as I have done. I could tell you—but I am going. God bless ye—God bless ye, my children! Stuart, forgive me—love Zemira—and be kind to my servants."

As he ended he fell back on his pillow; his eyes were raised and his lips moved as if in prayer; then drawing his hand across his eyes, as if to shut his weeping friends from his view, a low groan, a slight tremor, and the spirit had gone forever!

CHAPTER XXI.

FRIENDSHIPS.

And blest are those
Whose blood and judgment are so well commingled,
That they are not a pipe for fortune's finger
To sound what stop she please! Give me that man
That is not passion's slave, and I will wear him
In my heart's core, aye, in my heart of heart,
As I do thee.

MORALISTS and philosophers have consumed much time in advancing arguments to prove that disappointments are not always evils; but perhaps we might not yield our assent to such self-denying propositions did not daily experience confirm the theory. Even the annihilation of our dearest hopes, although fraught with keen agony at the moment, often proves in the end a precious blessing, and well worth the price we have been compelled to pay.

However Sidney might think the loss of Zemira could never be repaired, yet when he found himself the object of such unceasing regard, and saw the gratitude he had awakened in hearts so pure and noble, and now by his means, rendered so happy, he felt the delightful approbation of his own heart, the joy which the truly benevolent only can know, and which seems, more than any other happiness, to assimilate men to angels and earth to heaven.

The resignation of his beloved had been rewarded by the acquisition of *two friends*, and though he did not dare indulge in any intercourse approaching to intimacy with Zemira, lest his weak heart might rebel against Stuart, he indemnified himself for this constraint, by making him, excepting in some wandering dreams where his wife was yet concerned, the depositary of all his secrets and the oracle he consulted on every question.

Charles Stuart was just such a friend as Sidney Romilly needed; bold, ardent and enterprising, yet with a mind tempered and disciplined to caution and perseverance by the lessons of adversity (and more useful precepts are acquired in her school than ever were in that of Plato)—learned and accomplished, yet estimating his talents more by the benefits he might by their exertion render to his friends and society, than for the consequence they bestowed on himself. And thus, while his intelligence rendered him a most agreeable companion, his integrity made him a perfectly safe one.

In short, he was a man capable of true friendship; there are but few such. How can a selfish, a frivolous, or an ignorant mind, be actuated by that disinterestedness which sacrifices its own wishes when the welfare of a friend requires? or that steadfastness which remains unshaken in affection, when the world forsakes or derides the object of its choice? or that delicate propriety which seizes the fittest opportunities both to show its zeal in defending, or its love in advising a friend?

But if to the compact of friendship now subsisting between these two young men, Stuart brought a mind the best instructed, Sidney had undoubtedly as generous and warm a heart; and the knowledge that they were both natives of the same section of the country, had also an effect to increase their confidence in each other; for Sidney had never forgotten he was Yankee born, although half *raised* on a southern plantation. The green hills of New Hampshire still rose on his "mind's eye;" those frequent eminences swelling into an endless variety of forms, yet still retaining a character of softened grandeur, lofty but not inaccessible, and severe without being savage, they might personify the stern, steadfast, yet generous race their cultivation had helped to form.

The natives of a mountainous and sterile region are more enthusiastically attached to their place of birth, than those of a monotonous and fertile country. This attachment is naturally excited, partly by the degree of labor necessary to subdue a stubborn soil, which, making attention and care necessary, fosters a deep and exclusive attachment for the spot where they must be exercised; and then there are more distinct objects on which the eye rests at particular seasons and under peculiar circumstances—and thus conveys impressions to the mind, hallowing their appearance by connecting them with the emotions of our hearts or the events of our lives.

The Old Granite State has been often styled the Switzerland of America. In the vicinity of the White Mountains this comparison is most appropriate. Other portions of the State have less of the Alpine grandeur, and the softer features are more blended with the charm of life. There are very few dark frowning pinnacles of bleak, barren rocks;—forest trees climb up the steepest hills, and leaping brooks shout in their freedom, as they dash down mountain ravines, wind under the old woods, or linger in the lap of green meadows, where industry welcomes their freshness and their song. But the most beautiful scenery is in the neighborhood of the lakes and ponds; and hundreds of these, counting all the little lakelets, are found in New Hampshire. Embosomed among the green hills, or opening suddenly upon you by the wayside, as you journey on through the cleared country, these lakelets lie, blue, bright and clear, like earnest eyes looking from earth up to heaven in never-ceasing gratitude that God made all things good!

"The mountains are God's temples," and calm, sweet waters are like His mercies.

Sidney, while listening to descriptions, or viewing delineations of this scenery, which his friend executed in an elegant manner, would recall with wild rapture the sweet associations of his childhood, and almost fancy himself transported to the mountains and lakes, where he had spent its brightest hours. In spite of the luxuries surrounding him, and the fortune and flatteries he commanded, he still cherished the remembrance of his own dear home, and in reference to New England could truly exclaim:

> "There's none, ah! none, so lovely in my sight,
> Of all the lands that heaven o'erspreads with light."

Stuart employed the ascendency which his penetration soon discovered he had obtained over Sidney Romilly, to lead back the heart and mind of the latter from frivolous and pernicious pleasures, to the love of study, of quiet scenes, and calm amusements. Instead of rioting in the round of gay diversions which had lately appeared so necessary to his happiness, he now preferred a ramble with his friend, whose active and enlightened mind gathered subjects of entertainment and instruction from every object and appearance of nature. Or if conversation wearied, he was always supplied with a book, which would charm while it enlightened.

Thus gently, and almost imperceptibly, Stuart was loosening the chains which fashion had twined around our hero, and restoring him to the freedom of that rational enjoyment which his soul was formed to appreciate, but for which the Circean cup of luxury had nearly destroyed his relish.

The gay companions of Sidney were loud in their complaints of his abandonment, and tried all their wiles to lure him back to their society. They were his friends, they said, his old and tried friends, who would stand by him in all weathers, and now he was leaving them for the acquaintance of a day.

But when Sidney had once escaped from their atmosphere, he saw objects and motives through a very different medium from what he had while breathing the contaminated air of licentiousness. He could now discover the selfishness or thoughtlessness that dictated their lavish expressions of attachment. He saw they wished to indulge their appetites at his expense, or justify their follies by his example, and that their friendship, like the favor of the flatterers of Timon, would last no longer than did his means to gratify their whims and extravagancies.

"I am convinced," said Sidney to Stuart as they were about to separate, "I am convinced of the superior happiness of a life of usefulness over one of mere amusement. I was, in early life, educated to love study and activity; but the tempter came and would certainly have prevailed had not your advice and example again roused me to energy. Still continue my Mentor till I have acquired sufficient hardihood to face this formidable world with its host of enchantments, and when I note down my benefactors your name shall stand in conspicuous characters."

"And how shall I sufficiently honor yours?" returned Stuart, grasping his hand: "to you I owe my felicity—my Zemira!"

It was an allusion seldom made, for both felt the danger of awakening recollections which might lead to a discussion of past events.

There was a moment's silence. Sidney drew his other hand across his eyes.

"You have," said he, "sufficiently honored mine already, by thinking favorably of its bearer, although you have learned the weakness of his heart and the inconsistencies of his conduct."

"Friend of my soul!" exclaimed Stuart, "you have the best, the kindest of human hearts. It is only the excess of its generosity, of its goodness, I fear. There are so many insidious minds, watching like serpents every opportunity to twine themselves around the unwary, that a little precaution—*suspicion*, perhaps, would better define my meaning—is absolutely necessary, if we would escape being allured by their fascination and destroyed by their venom. This precaution is all you need; and could I, at the hazard of my life, impart it to you, it should be yours. But no man can grow wise by another's experience; it is only by exercising our own sagacity and discretion we can discover and avoid the subtle and powerful temptations which beset youth and fortune. Would you, my dear Sidney, be as true to your own feelings and reason as you are to your friends, I should have nothing to fear from you, nothing to wish for myself."

The earnestness with which he spoke penetrated the heart of Sidney. His eyes sparkled with the proud consciousness of determined resolution. "You shall not," said he, "from henceforth have cause to blush for me. I have always loved the right;—your example will embolden me to practice it."

* * * * *
* * * * *

After Mr. Stuart's departure, Sidney lived a very retired, and, to confess the truth, a very dull life. His mind and will had been so long undisciplined, that to refrain thus at once and entirely from the contemplation or the wish to pursue pleasure was impossible, and the attempt frequently threw him into the horrors.

However, he persevered in the course of reading and amusements his friend had recommended; and although he sometimes sighed to think so much circumspection was necessary, he was gradually acquiring habits of study and reflection, which, by unfolding new and noble sources of enjoyment, contributed to fix his heart more firmly in the resolutions he had formed to follow wisdom. A letter from Stuart came very opportunely to confirm his good intentions, and for that reason it shall be inserted.

"*Georgia*, *June* 4*th*, 18—.

My Dear Romilly,—When I tell you we reached home in safety, and are now enjoying excellent health, you will know that I, at least, am happy. But it is that kind of happiness which makes no figure in description. It is the quiet consciousness of peace, the calm security of reciprocated affection, in short, the 'sober certainty of waking bliss.' And for much of this felicity we must thank you; certainly for the final reconciliation, without which Zemira's mind never would have been at rest. And how shall we requite your disinterestedness?—your heroism? We pray daily that God would bless you, and assuredly He will, if to obey His command and do as you would be done by is holy in His sight. Property you do not want; yet, I will acknowledge my selfishness, I have sometimes wished you did, that we might show how highly we rate the favors you have conferred. But gold cannot gain friendship, nor can it requite the sacrifices you made for me. I will tell you how I propose to reward you—even by furnishing you with wise precepts for the better guidance of your sublunary course. You, I presume, will allow that those who have done us the most essential and generous services, are always most willing to pardon our officiousness. The inference is obvious. I feel secure of your favor although I should harass you with my old *saws* by way of advice.

There are but few who have the moral courage, or the moral rectitude, to speak undisguisedly to the wealthy and the powerful man. Either fearing to give offense, or hoping to profit by his errors, they abandon him to the guidance of his own heart or humor. And pray why should he not follow his own humor as well as others? It is not, my dear Sidney, that his inclination for pleasure is greater, but his facilities for its indulgence that constitute his danger. The universal necessity for constant labor or application to business, which yet happily exists in the New England States, contributes, perhaps more than any other cause, to preserve the purity of morals which distinguishes the inhabitants of that section of our country. Had the Puritans and their descendants been fed with manna and fattened with quails in their wilderness, they would, doubtless, long before this, have spurned the hand that bestowed the unsought favors.

And speaking of New England, I wish you would improve the first opportunity to visit your native state. There are sacred associations connected with the thoughts of home and parents, brothers and sisters; while their spirits seem, as it were, hovering around us, we are often deterred from the commission of some folly, or invigorated to tread with more firmness the path of rectitude and duty.

With your family I have not the happiness of being acquainted; but judging from your disposition and what you have related, I should not hesitate to say you will find them worthy of your warmest love. And notwithstanding you have drank so deeply of pleasure's intoxicating cup, and fancy, perhaps, that 'heaven, earth and ocean' have been plundered of their sweets to form the mixture, yet I cannot but hope you will hereafter find a more cordial drop than any yet tasted. In no society are the domestic affections cultivated, and the love of relatives more sincere and ardent, than in New England. Natural affection seems there to be expanded, or at least increased by the concurrence of external circumstances. There, children are not merely the heirs of their father's property, but frequently the means by which he acquires it. A Yankee farmer looks on his boys with affection as his offspring, with pride as his representatives, and yet he thinks of them, perhaps, quite as often as his assistants in his toil. There is an intimacy created by a participation in the same labors and hopes, and a confidence arising from a community and equality of interests. Ah, our lordly planter, surrounded by his host of slaves, has no such sensations of generous pleasure!

There is no telling how long I might have pursued the subject, for I was quite in the scribbling vein, but luckily, for you I mean, my servant—I say servant and even *slave*, so easily we yield to the dominion of custom, and adopt habits which once made us glow with shame and indignation—enters to say a gentleman wishes to see me, and so I must end this immediately or lose this mail. Write soon and tell me how you relish your studies, and whether the mathematicians have yet obtained grace in your sight, and whatever else you please; nothing from your pen will be uninteresting to

Yours, forever, C. STUART."

This letter was soon answered and a constant and confidential correspondence maintained through the summer; but the letters being very long their entire insertion would make this work too voluminous, and might not be sufficiently interesting to tempt the reader to such a frequent perusal as the friends alternately bestowed on each other's epistles, and such as they would still think they merited. However, in the autumn an incident occurred to Sidney which drew from him a letter necessary to be made public.

" *Charleston, Nov. 24th*, 18—.

MY DEAR STUART—I have made a new acquaintance, and one from which I promise myself much pleasure; yet for fear you should call me romantic, I will describe the man and relate the accident which introduced him, and then I think you will allow there is a necessity—I hope not a fatal one—for the present intercourse.

About a week since, arrived the brig Ann, from Liverpool, and among the passengers was a young English gentleman by the name of Frankford. He brought letters of introduction to some of our principal citizens, and among others to my uncle; but it happened that his trunk, soon after he landed, was rifled of its contents, and the introductory letters were among the spoil. The thief, who was also a foreigner, and a well dressed, bold faced villain, conceived the plan of passing himself off for the real 'Simon Pure,' or at least he resolved to take that opportunity of seeing, for once in his life, a little good company. While the legitimate Englishman was quietly refreshing himself at the sign of the 'Lion,' the newly patented gentleman arrived at my uncle's, and presenting his credentials, was received with a most cordial welcome and a pressing invitation to partake our dinner, which he accepted without hesitation. Why he was thus infatuated it is difficult to say. It is now generally thought he calculated more on the *plate* than the pudding; yet surely he must have expected detection.

Well, in the midst of our conviviality I was summoned to the hall, and there found the landlord of the house where the Englishman lodged and a couple of constables. It seems the police had received an inkling of our guest and were on the alert to apprehend him. I could hardly be persuaded he was an impostor, but finally, as the officers insisted on seeing him, I entered first and unfolded their errand.

Our guest received the intelligence with perfect *nonchalance*, and even the landlord was staggered when the villain offered to accompany him to the hotel and explain matters to his satisfaction. I attended him, but just as we entered the street, the fellow started, knocked down the constables on his right hand, overturned the fat landlord on his left, and was in a fair way of escape had I not —from an innate love of justice, some would say, but I think it is only the instinct which prompts us to secure the rogue lest his practices may injure ourselves—rushed forward, seized and held him till help arrived to secure him. It is needless to repeat particulars, suffice it to say, the plundered Englishman succeeded in recovering his baggage and establishing his identity, and the process bringing us together on very familiar terms, and he being profuse in his acknowledgments, an intimacy was soon established.

And besides, I find him a very pleasant companion; and one who would, under almost any circumstances, have gained an interest in my heart. He is about twenty-eight, liberally educated, and highly accomplished, both by an intimacy with the best society in his own country and by foreign travel. He intends spending the winter in our city and at Washington, and next summer will make the tour of the middle states. But though he stays here so long, you need not fear a rival in my friendship; nor have I, because my heart is wholly engrossed with him, employed so much paper in his service. I wished you to understand the causes which have thus, in a manner, forced me to an intimacy with a stranger and a foreigner, who is agreeable, to be sure, but whose principles and character I know you will think we have not yet had sufficient opportunity of ascertaining. Should the intercourse prove detrimental, may I not blame the stars and curse the waywardness of my fate, instead of lamenting the weakness of my folly?

Ever yours, S. Romilly."

Many letters attesting to the excellencies of the Englishman, were written by Sidney during the winter; some extracts from one of the number may be sufficient for our purpose.

"*Charleston, April 4th*, 18—.

"Friend Stuart,—Frankford certainly has, as you intimated, his prejudices against America; still he is a reasonable man, and although admitting conviction slowly and only on the most irrefragable proofs, yet I think he is becoming not only tolerant but liberal in his estimation of our character and customs. Neither is it strange that the aristocratical spirit of the old world should be alarmed and revolt at the democratical influence which the new is so rapidly obtaining. We cannot expect those who pride themselves on an ancestry, whose pure blood has flowed through proud veins for many hundred years, will forget at once this fancied superiority, and look on what they call our plebeian origin, without feelings of contempt.

* * * * * *

"My friend—I now call him *friend* without any misgivings—has deservedly a high place in my esteem, and if you knew him, you would, I am positive, approve the partiality. Besides those qualities which command respect, he has that indescribable fascination of manner which wit and talents, improved by strict intellectual culture, and graced by politeness and good humor, never fail to impart. By the way, I do think the real English gentleman has more of dignity, and less of arrogance, than our purse-proud citizens. The Englishman is more proud, perhaps, but is free from that puffing consequence which is the most offensive part of the folly in our own countrymen. This may arise from the superiority of the former being established and acknowledged, whereas our own gentlemen are continually striving to maintain their precarious honors, and seem determined, by making the most of what they happen to possess, to indemnify themselves for the transientness of its continuance.

* * * * * *

"Frankford is often pressing me to accompany him to England; and if, after visiting my parents, I can obtain their approbation and my uncle's consent, I shall assuredly go. We are intending, in a few weeks, to start for the north, visit Saratoga, and, after the establishment of our healths—no very difficult process—Frankford will proceed to Quebec, to arrange some business entrusted to his management, and I shall go to New Hampshire. Should our plans all succeed, we may probably embark together for Europe in the autumn.

"In the meantime, wherever I am, I am ever yours,

"S. Romilly."

Agreeably to the intention expressed in the foregoing letter, Frankford and Sidney set off on their tour, and after alternately admiring the works of nature, and censuring those of art, the Englishman always indemnifying himself for his encomiums on the former by his severe strictures on the latter, they arrived at Saratoga, the Bath of America, and sipped the far-famed Congress waters with many a delicate nymph and dashing dandy, both equally wishing it might prove a Lethean draught—to her of her faithless lovers, to him of his faithful creditors. Our travelers prolonged their stay rather beyond their intention, Frankford wishing to explore the country in the vicinity of Fort George and the works of Ticonderoga, as it was there one of his great uncles had fallen, in the same engagement which terminated the career of the young and gallant Howe. The picturesque shores of Lake George and its limpid waters, drew many an epithet of admiration from the Englishman, and even the dilapidated fortifications excited considerable interest, as he remarked they exhibited proofs that there had once been a martial spirit in the country which otherwise he should never have suspected.

After visiting the Falls of Niagara, and wondering, and rhyming, and repeating what hundreds have before repeated, they proceeded to Montreal, Sidney accompanying his friend thus far, and then intending to return to Saratoga, and bend his course to New Hampshire; but he was prevented by the illness of Mr. Frankford. The very next morning after they reached Montreal, he was violently attacked with a fever, the consequence of a cold caught by passing beneath the cataract at the falls; and, increased by his impatience, the fever, which was a slow typhus, soon raged to such a degree, his life was despaired of. For three weeks he was insensible, and during the whole time Sidney nursed him with all the watchfulness and tenderness of a brother; and, assisted by the landlady, a kind-hearted creature from the "States," he had at length had the unspeakable pleasure of hearing his friend pronounced convalescent.

The English residents in Montreal paid but little attention to their countryman; perhaps the house where he had taken lodgings might make him appear a renegade from their principles, as it was one always frequented by travelers from the "Union;" but whatever were their reasons, they neglected him, and their apparent indifference stung the proud and sensitive mind of the Englishman to the quick. There is no season when kindness or cruelty makes so deep an impression on the hearts of men, as that which is offered or inflicted in the hour of sickness; and Frankford, when reflecting on their conduct, and comparing it with that of the Americans, acknowledged that the virtues of benevolence and sympathy were not exclusively English.

It was three months before he was sufficiently recovered to travel; the lateness of the season and his own debility made a journey to Quebec hazardous, while advices from England rendered his return necessary. Abandoning, therefore, his intention of journeying northward, he concluded to repair to Boston and take passage from thence to London or Liverpool, and yielding to the urgent solicitations of Sidney, he agreed to accompany him to Northwood and see him restored to his friends.

Sidney had not apprised his parents of his intended visit, as he wished for the zest which a surprise would give their affection; and after his journey was so long delayed by the illness of Frankford, he rejoiced at his own forbearance, for he was sensible his mother would have been greatly alarmed by the delay. Thus they had arrived unexpectedly, and yet how welcome!

O, give me the welcome that waits the unexpected yet ardently wished friend! The loved countenance suddenly lit up with the surprise of wild delight—the agitation of unrestrained affection—the abrupt exclamation—the half uttered ejaculation, bursting warm from the soul to thank heaven for your safe arrival,—ah, these are dear pleasures, and such as the proud and mighty, who travel in state and send forward their couriers to announce their approach, never know!

And now we must return to Northwood.

CHAPTER XXII.

A MONEY LENDER AND HIS VICTIM.

Anthonio—I pray thee, hear me speak.
Shylock—I'll have my bond;—I will not hear thee speak;—
I'll have my bond, and therefore speak no more.
MERCHANT OF VENICE.

THE two weeks succeeding the departure of the Englishman were passed by our hero in a continued round of visiting and feasting, as every family in the village considered themselves entitled to at least one visit from the son of their much esteemed neighbor. Sidney could not refuse invitations thus pressingly made, yet had he consulted only his inclination, he would have confined his attentions to the families of Dr. Perkins and Deacon Jones; and now, notwithstanding his engagements, he generally contrived to drop in at those houses, especially the deacon's, almost daily. This ought to have excited no wonder, as his brother Silas was there; yet it soon became the theme of conversation among the ladies of the neighborhood, and several wise ones, who had undoubtedly given Annie Redington to George Cranfield, now confessed they felt that the suit of the young divine would be coldly received, should Mr. Sidney Romilly appear as his rival.

Perhaps some such apprehension stole into the mind of that young gentleman, for he became more particular in his assiduities, to the extreme regret of Annie, who sincerely esteemed him, and felt loth to wound his feelings by a rejection.

Ephraim Skinner, too, ventured to quit his store on those evenings he ascertained Sidney was at the Deacon's, and at the hazard of losing business, joined the party at the "conference room," where he was always graciously welcomed by the deacon; and although he never could succeed in obtaining a single smile from the fair lady whose bright eyes were the magnet that attracted him, he indemnified himself by indirectly displaying his consequence in sundry heavy complaints of the hurry of business, and some pretty significant hints on the profits a country trader, who attended closely to his affairs, might realize.

One evening while he was alternately dilating on this subject and on his religious feelings, and pitying those poor blinded creatures who seemed to take no thought for this world or the next, Deacon Jones, whose ears eagerly drank in such prudent and pious discourse, was casting many a glance at the party occupying the other end of the apartment. These were his daughter, niece, son-in-law, Sidney Romilly, and young Cranfield, and to judge by their lively conversation and frequent laughter, they needed not the happiness that gold could purchase; yet the deacon more than once reflected with chagrin, how very foolish Annie was, thus to lavish her sweet attractions on that fine southern gentleman, who had never a thought of marrying her, and neglect so shamefully the hopeful merchant who might easily be secured.

But his unpleasant cogitations, Skinner's wise remarks, and Sidney's gallant speeches, were suddenly interrupted by a loud rap at the door, and Annie, who was nearest, started so suddenly to obey the sound, her uncle had no time to utter his accustomed "walk in." As she opened the door, a man entered, whose appearance bespoke poverty and misfortune, and awakened Sidney's curiosity to learn by what accident he should be reduced to misery in a place where it was seldom seen or felt.

This person, whom Deacon Jones, coldly offering his hand, addressed by the name of Merrill, had a countenance clouded with anxiety and sorrow, yet the smile that momentarily lit up his sunken, care-worn features, as Miss Redington kindly offered him a chair, spoke a heart susceptible of gratitude and inclined to cheerfulness. As his eye wandered over the well-dressed company, he drew closer around him a rusty grey overcoat, as if to conceal the tatters visible in his own attire, and turning to Skinner, who had only remarked his entrance by a slight movement of the head, said, "I called to speak with you at your store, and they told me I could find you here."

"And what do you want with me?" inquired the merchant, in an imperative tone.

"I wanted to see if you would'nt allow that are execution to be stayed a spell. If my property is all attached now, my family must suffer, or come upon the town."

"I have already waited much longer than I ought," returned Skinner, haughtily, "and have nothing more to do with the affair. The business is all with the sheriff; you may apply to him."

"But, Mr. Skinner, you have often said you were willing to assist me; and you offered me the money in the first place, or I should never have thought of asking you. Old Col. Griper, bad as he is, would never use me so hardly."

"Such are the thanks I always get for obliging people," said Skinner, endeavoring to speak plausibly, though his face glowed with anger. "Your farm would have been forfeited before now, if I had not advanced the money. All I ask is to be repaid. You cannot surely call me unjust for wanting my own."

"I don't think hard of you, sir," replied Merrill, "for wanting your own, and I intend to pay you, but I cannot at present, without undoing me. My wife has been sick these four months, and three of my children are now confined to their beds. Poor little Nancy died last week; but I don't mourn for her;—she is better off than any of us."

The tears that gushed to the eyes of the father, however, gave evidence he lamented his child, notwithstanding he was assured of her felicity. Annie, turning hastily to the window, hid her face, and Sidney's as he glanced alternately at her, Skinner, and the petitioner, was red as scarlet.

Skinner, however, noticed not their emotion; he was intent on gain, and had not sufficient sensibility to imagine the abhorrence his display of selfishness excited in generous and feeling minds.

"Mr. Merrill," he retorted, elevating his voice, "I have heard enough of your excuses, but they don't pay a cent, and I want the money and must have it. If your family are sick, you needn't blame me for it; and really I don't see why you should always be telling me such stuff."

"Such stuff!" repeated Merrill, starting, and shaking his fist, while the tone of submission which conscious dependence had compelled him to assume, was forgotten in the anger roused by these insults:—"Such stuff! I tell you, Skinner, you are a mean, miserly, hard-hearted villain; and you flattered me to give you a mortgage of my farm on purpose to cheat me out of it. I know you did, or you would be willing to wait a few months. You shall have good security."

"I mean to be secured," replied Skinner, trembling, as he rose to seek his hat; but whether his trepidation was caused by fear of his tall, gaunt debtor, who stood with his clenched hand extended over him, or from suppressed rage, no one could determine.

He found his hat, and was hastening towards the door, when Merrill inquired, in a more humble manner, if there could not be some arrangement made.

"I have told you the affair was wholly with the sheriff," replied the inexorable creditor. "Good evening, ladies and gentlemen;" and closing the door hastily, they heard him walk off with a quick step over the frozen ground, as if he feared being pursued by further entreaties.

After the sound of his tread had died away, there reigned, for a few moments, in the apartment he had quitted so abruptly, the most profound silence. And the different expression on the faces of the group, might have furnished a good subject for the study of those who would attain to the art of divining the difference of temperament and character by the effect which the same occurrence had on the countenances of the several witnesses.

The old deacon had lit his pipe at the beginning of the dialogue, and through the whole scene continued to puff away most furiously, apparently indifferent to all that passed. He sat now with his eyes nearly closed, and a huge volume of smoke curling over his head. Ah! while his own mountain stands strong, he cares little who bides the peltings of the tempest;—he is selfish.

There was pity in the expression of young Cranfield's countenance, blended with an "I don't know what to do" air, that revealed the man of good intentions, but rather wavering in purpose.

Silas looked up with a wondering stare, half angry with Merrill for thus putting himself in the power of a villain, and half hoping matters would yet be adjusted without causing much trouble. He has lived secluded from a knowledge of the deceitfulness of the world—he is innocent, is happy, and imagines all men might easily be the same.

But our hero's countenance displayed the workings of the most powerful emotions. Nothing touched his noble feelings like the exhibition of cruelty or meanness; and perhaps the picture Dr. Perkins had drawn of Skinner now arose to increase the detestation he felt for the original. His dark eyes flashed with indignation and contempt as the little man disappeared through the door; then, as he turned their gaze on his victim, the expression suddenly changed to deep concern, mingled with a determination of manner, which, had the debtor noticed, he might have augured favorably for his own cause.

But he, poor man, was meditating bitter things. He must return to his home, and see it despoiled of all its furniture, and rifled of all its stores that the law permitted a creditor to attach. His cattle, too, would be driven away—and the cold winter was approaching—his sick family!—he could think no longer. Something between a sigh and groan burst from his full heart as he stooped to pick up his hat, which was lying on the floor. He placed it on his head, drew it closely over his eyes, and took one step forward.

"Won't you stop and drink some cider?" said the deacon, shaking the ashes from his pipe.

"I haven't much appetite for any thing just now," answered the other; "I can't eat nor drink now a-days; and I must hurry home, for the sheriff is there, and he would'nt promise to wait only two hours before moving off my property."

"And pray how have you got yourself so involved?" inquired the deacon, who liked to learn the causes of misfortunes, not, however, so much to relieve the sufferers as to suggest the way in which they might have avoided such a calamity. "Come, sit down and tell me all about the affair."

"I can't stop to sit," replied Merrill, "but will tell you something about it. You know I purchased my farm of Col. Griper; well, he was a hard man, but I think pretty honest; yet he drove me considerable hard for his pay, and sometimes it was tough scrabbling to get the money. But I got along till a year ago last January, when there was a hundred dollar payment, I could'nt make out unless I sold more stock than I knew how to spare. Skinner heard me one day complaining about the old colonel, and he offered to advance me cash enough to pay him all off at once, if I would give him the same security I did Griper, and I might pay him just when it was convenient. He talked so fair and the colonel had dunned me so sharp, I was glad to let him see I could have credit, and so, like a fool, I took the money and gave a mortgage and my notes to Skinner. The whole sum was three hundred dollars, and Skinner insisted on having it all in twelve dollar notes, on demand, because, he said, I could pay a small note every little while without feeling it, and he always did his business in that manner. I have found him out now; it is, when he intends to ruin a man, to bring as many actions and make the cost as big as possible—but I did'nt think of it then. Well, I was to have three years to pay it in, and pay a hundred dollars a year if I could. That was the bargain before evidence. I have taken up eight notes, and intended to have paid as many more this fall and winter, but last August my wife was taken sick with the *typus* fever, and she ha'nt never been able to do a *chore* since, and now can only walk from the bed to the fire; and all six of my children have had the same disorder. There's two of 'em are a little better, but the other three are very bad now, and poor little Nancy, our only daughter, the doctor could'nt save her. I ha'nt had off my clothes to lie a-bed as I used to for three months; and I have had to let every thing, out doors and in the house, go to destruction, for the sake of taking care of my family. I could'nt find help enough to do it, and the little ones would'nt let any body but me take care of 'em. Your niece and daughter knows how sick they 've been, for they have been up to see us several times and brought us nice things, and they'll be blessed for such kindness."

Here he paused a moment, and then added, "But I ha'nt told you yet how Skinner served me. I sent to his store to get my necessaries—and in sickness there's a thousand things wanted—and his bill amounts to something like fifty dollars; so he pretended he was afraid he should lose his debts, and he had twelve writs made out against me, the whole of which, cost and all, will be as much as two hundred dollars, and he has got the sheriff and ordered him to attach every thing he can find. I told the sheriff he might take every thing out doors if he would only leave my oxen and one cow and hay enough to keep 'em, and my household furniture; but he said he could'nt without Skinner consented, and so he told me to take his horse and come down to see him—but 'tis all in vain I see. My property will be sold at vendue and go for half price, and my family must suffer or I must apply to the town, and I had rather die."

"But why does Skinner drive you so hard, when he has security and knows he can be paid?" inquired George Cranfield.

"O, he calculates on distressing me so much by taking my stock that I ca'nt manage my farm, and so he thinks I shall be unable to make out the payment next year, and then he will get my land, either by the mortgage or at public sale, for half price."

"I wish there could be some way contrived to assist you," said George Cranfield.

"And I wish there could," said Silas Romilly.

"And so do I, with all my heart," responded the old deacon, solemnly.

Merrill walked slowly towards the door and turned partly round as he reached it, probably to bid them "good night," but he could not articulate a syllable.

"I will accompany you, sir," said Sidney, snatching his hat and springing after him.

Merrill started at the sound of a strange voice, and when he saw the gentlemanly figure that was following him his features wore the surprise of astonishment.

"I have not the happiness of knowing you, sir," he remarked in a low tone, as they walked through the gate.

"No, I presume not," replied Sidney; "but I have heard your story, and if you will go with me to my father's, to Squire Romilly's, I will try and assist you."

"And you are the Squire's son, then, that I have heard so much about?" said Merrill, stopping and gazing earnestly in our hero's face, now plainly revealed by the bright moon.

"Yes, I am," answered the other, half laughing at the critical survey he was undergoing.

"Well, you have a worthy father, and you look like him, and they say you are like him, and that's praising you very highly. I was just going to your father, for I knew if any one advised or helped me it would be him."

He then took his horse by the bridle, and leading him

along, walked himself by Sidney's side, and won by the kindness of his manner, he revealed so many particulars of the sickness of his family and the sufferings they must undergo if the property were removed and sold, that Sidney determined to prevent it at all hazards.

Sidney's attendance on the Englishman had made him peculiarly sensible of the horrors of a long and severe fever, and nothing makes the heart so susceptible of pity as a personal observation or experience of sufferings similar to those we are requested to relieve.

There were obstacles, however, which made the performance of his benevolent wishes difficult, and indeed impossible at that time, without the aid of his father. His journey had been longer and more expensive, owing to his long detention in Montreal, than he had anticipated, and his money was nearly gone.

He had twice written to his uncle, requesting a supply, and was now in daily expectation of receiving a remittance; yet this business could not well be delayed till its arrival, or at least Sidney did not like to entreat the forbearance of such a one as Skinner, nor could he think of assisting Merrill with promises only. He marveled much that his uncle should thus neglect to supply his wants, and when recollecting he had received but one letter from him since leaving Charleston, and that written evidently under great depression of spirits, he could not but fear some unpleasant or unfortunate circumstances were the cause of this delay.

When they reached the house, Sidney took his father aside, told him the situation of Merrill, stated his own wishes to relieve him from his embarrassments, and then asked his father if he could advance the money, "and I will repay you soon," continued he. "My uncle will certainly send me three or four hundred dollars. I started with six hundred, and have now but about fifty remaining; this Merrill shall have, and if you can furnish the remainder, I will take his note for the whole, and return yours when my remittance shall arrive. I will then leave the note against Merrill in your care, and let the poor man pay whenever he can without distressing himself."

Squire Romilly listened to his son's harangue, delivered with all the ardor and animation purposed benevolence inspires in youthful and generous bosoms, and his heart beat with proud delight to find him worthy the fortune he was to inherit.

"How I rejoice that wealth has not made you selfish, nor prosperity hardened your heart, my son," said the delighted father; "yet before assisting those who appeal to our compassion, we should endeavor to ascertain in what manner our charity will be the most beneficial. Many people, with really good intentions, bestow their favors so arbitrarily or inconsiderately, that they may injure those who receive their bounty, and it is not, therefore, to be wondered at if they miss the gratitude and popularity they expected to obtain. Yet these remarks do not apply to the present case; perhaps you may have been precipitate and a little romantic in forming a scheme for assisting thus largely a stranger, but your good genius has directed you to a worthy object, and saved you from the mortification of learning your generosity would have been misplaced. Merrill is an industrious, prudent, good man, and the cunning of Skinner and unavoidable misfortunes are the cause of his present distress. I think your assistance will enable him to surmount it, and there will not, I apprehend, be any danger in trusting him. I will let you have one hundred dollars, which is all I have on hand, and that I intended soon to pay Silas as a part of his portion; but you may take it, and, with your fifty dollars, I should think Skinner might be satisfied, or Merrill could turn out property to make up the deficiency."

This plan was adopted, the money produced, and Merrill informed all that would be required of him was a note, which he might consult his own convenience in paying.

His surprise, as he looked alternately at the money and then at Sidney, was extreme; but when he became convinced his difficulties were all to be removed, he betrayed more agitation than he probably would have done had he seen his property under the hammer of the auctioneer. His hand shook so violently it was some time before he could sign his name, and Sidney saw several tears fall on the paper as he wrote.

Then he silently placed the money in an old pocket book, which he deposited carefully in his pocket, buttoned up his coat, and seemed exerting himself to overcome his emotions so as to express properly the thanks he conceived due to his benefactor. But his exertions were of little avail. Nature and feeling could not be conquered; and when he arose to depart, instead of a long speech on unexpected obligations and everlasting gratitude, he took our hero's hand, shaking and pressing it with so strong a grasp the effect was really painful, bowed to Squire Romilly, and hurried away without uttering a single word.

Sidney rubbed his aching hand without speaking, while his father, smiling, remarked, he had insured his remembrance in one heart; "Merrill," said he, "will never forget you."

CHAPTER XXIII.

A REVERSE.

Thus, sometimes, hath the brightest day a cloud;
And after summer, evermore succeeds
The barren winter, with his wrathful cold:
So cares and joys abound, as seasons fleet.

KING HENRY VI.

THE story of Sidney's generosity soon circulated through the neighborhood, and produced what the fashionables would call quite a sensation.

Merrill was as much esteemed for probity and industry as Skinner was detested for his meanness and rapacity; and though riches gave the latter the means of purchasing many smiles, the situation of the former insured the sympathy of all hearts. Those who would not have felt it their *duty* to have assisted him, applauded his benefactor, flattering themselves, no doubt, that to appreciate charity was nearly as meritorious as to practice it.

There were, however, a few who felt rather mortified that a southern man, as they considered Sidney, should thus display his consequence—it seemed a tacit reproof of their own illiberality, or a convincing argument of his superior wealth. Either way it was mortifying. The old deacon was perhaps prompted by such feelings when he observed, very gravely, that

"Mr. Sidney Romilly knew nothing about getting property, and it was no wonder he thought little of spending it or giving it away. But I should like," continued he, "to see him work a few years as hard as his negroes do, and then I guess he'd keep his money, if he had any, in his own pocket."

But the sweetest praise Sidney received was from Dr. Perkins and Annie Redington. The doctor felt every word he uttered, and again and again congratulated Sidney on thus having an opportunity to exhibit the noblest virtue humanity can boast—disinterested benevolence.

Then came Annie with a blush, smile and tear, to thank him for the example of philanthropy he had so happily displayed. "We cannot imitate it," said she to him as he was sitting beside her a few days after the affair, "but we will admire it."

"If it secure the admiration of Miss Redington, I shall feel amply rewarded," replied Sidney, fixing his dark eyes on her animated face.

She felt her cheek glow, and angry with herself for blushing so easily, raised her eyes, intending to reply gaily to his compliment, but when they met his she forgot her answer, and might in her confusion have betrayed more sensibility than the occasion could justify, had not their *tete-a-tete* been luckily interrupted by the entrance of her uncle.

He told Sidney he had been to Skinner's store on business, and just looked into the post-office room, where the mail was opening, and saw a large packet for him taken out.

"I would have paid the postage and brought it along, said he, "only I hadn't any money in my purse. don't have money quite so plenty as you do, Mr. Sidney."

"You cannot be more destitute than I am at present, replied Sidney, smiling. "The witches might now hold their 'jig and reel' as conveniently in my pockets as the ever did in those of Burns; and if the packet you mention has not brought a supply, I must e'en solicit a loa to expedite my departure, or I shall be compelled t quarter with you through the winter."

"Well, that would suit our young folks well enough I guess," replied the old deacon, with one of his signi cant grins. "My niece, here, wouldn't be much sorry should you, Annie?"

Annie did not dare look up, while she observed, in as calm a manner as she could assume, "that she should be sorry to have any one compelled to stay, but in their limited society such an acquisition as Mr. Romilly was certainly to be desired."

Sidney, while warmly thanking her for the compliment, thought he never saw her look so beautiful, and on his way to his father's he recalled her words and manner, and almost fancied he could, if he pleased, rival George Cranfield.

"And yet," thought he, "I never can be so secure of possessing any woman's affections as Stuart was of Zemira's. He had no fortune to conceal his defects or add lustre to his excellencies; he was loved, well and truly loved. O, could I be so blessed as to gain the undivided affection of a pure and lovely being, how willingly would I, this moment, relinquish all pretensions to my uncle's fortune, and go forth, like Stuart, to conquer *fate* with a *ferule.*"

Immediately on reaching home, he despatched Harvey to the post-office, who soon returned with the letter.

"It is very large," said the little fellow, as he handed it to his brother. "Pray, Sidney, who gives you all your money?"

"My uncle—he always gives me all I ask for."

"Then I'd ask for a thousand dollars," said the boy.

"What would you do with it, Harvey?" inquired his father.

"O, give it to poor people, papa. Everybody is praising Sidney for being generous, and I mean to be generous."

Squire Romilly sighed as he looked on the animated face of his youngest son, and contrasted it with the noble countenance of his eldest.

"Your disposition," said he, addressing Sidney, "and Harvey's are almost similar; yet I must educate him differently from what you have been. Perhaps, however, his happiness through life will be as well insured as yours. If he never attain to your prosperity, he will not be in danger of those reverses to which you are exposed."

"I have never yet pondered much on the possibility of a reverse," said Sidney, while he pressed the rich packet between his fingers, as if to calculate something of the contents—and this might be pardoned, as he had been for a few days destitute of money. "I know there are casualties no human prudence can foresee or avoid, and they may occur to me; yet my philosophy teaches me it is the height of folly to anticipate evil. The man who does so commits suicide on his own happiness."

He then retired to his chamber to peruse his packet.

The envelope contained two letters; the one in his uncle's hand he opened first, and stared, astonished, when he saw it contained no money! What could it mean!

He broke the seal of the other, and a solitary hundred dollar note was all that appeared.

He laid it down, drew a hard breath, and pressed his lips closely together, as if nerving himself for whatever might be recorded, and again took up his uncle's epistle. It had no date, and the hand-writing was scarcely legible, yet Sidney soon made out what follows:

"MY EVER DEAR NEPHEW:—The sickness that oppresses me, and which is hurrying me to the grave, is on my heart. I am sick of the follies and vices of the world; I am miserable when reflecting on my own. I have longed and pined to write and confide to you all my troubles and griefs; but I could not persuade myself to damp the pleasures I hoped you were enjoying with your friends.

"My physician, however, informs me I cannot long survive. I shall never see you more, and I must write; yet my shaking hand will scarce be commanded—and my brain burns. Strange visions often pass before me; my mind wanders, and I see you and hear you speak, and say you forgive me. Will you forgive me? I never regretted I was not blest with a son since you resided with me. You have been all a child need be, and I was proud, justly proud of your merits and accomplishments, and intended to leave you a fortune to support the style in which I had educated you.

"Sidney, I am now a beggar, or soon should be, and I thank God that he is in mercy removing me from a world where nothing now remains which I can call my own. I would tell you the circumstances of this change, but my weakened nerves will not permit; and Henry Howard—you know him, he is a worthy man, and you may trust him—has promised to write you every particular, as soon as I am gone.

"Sidney, do not blame me too severely for your disappointment—I have erred, but I have been deceived. I suffer more than you can, for I suffer remorse and self-reproach—remorse for wronging you and my servants, whom I had promised to leave to your care. When they found they were to be transferred to a stranger, their lamentations nearly overpowered me. If you ever have it in your power, Sidney, remember them; they would all die to serve you. I am weak, very weak, and when I would collect my thoughts I cannot. I lie down and think of a thousand things to tell you, but when I begin to write they are vanished.

"Your father will advise you what to do; he has always walked in the paths of wisdom, while I have committed myself to the guidance of folly. Sidney, I know you will mourn for me, and you will wish you had been with me in my last moments; but I do not. It would increase my distress to witness your sorrow, and when the tribute is paid, which I feel assured your kind heart will give my memory, I hope you will endeavor to be happy. My sight fails me—farewell. O, it is the hardest pang in death to say farewell to those we love! God bless you, my son!—I have no inheritance but my good wishes to leave you, but may God bless you, and forgive me, YOUR UNCLE."

After Sidney had a little recovered from the first shock of the intelligence which this letter conveyed, he took the other. It was from a lawyer, a gentleman in whose probity and honor he could implicitly confide, and who he was certain would "nothing extenuate, nor set down aught in malice."

Perhaps the circumstances detailed in the letter will be best understood by inserting the whole; and though long, it will not be very tedious to those who feel an interest in the fortunes of my hero.

" *Charleston, Nov.* 1, 18—.

MY DEAR MR. ROMILLY:—Your uncle is no more; and his earnest request, must be my apology for addressing you, and detailing some of the unfortunate circum stances which have occurred to him since you left the city. It is an unpleasant office, and one I would gladly have been excused from performing; but I could not refuse Mr. Brainard, and I trust your good sense will not confound the narrator of evil tidings with the unpleasant intelligence he must communicate.

Perhaps you will recollect your uncle had not, for several months before your departure, exhibited his wonted cheerfulness. This melancholy proceeded, no doubt, partly from ill health; but more from the anxiety he was suffering on account of pecuniary embarrassments. He was not addicted to extravagance, yet the companions with whom he most associated had, by degrees, drawn him into expensive amusements, and he had engaged in hazards which proved unlucky, and—for I will omit a minute detail of circumstances, which can benefit no one by being related—in consequence he found himself involved to such an amount that he must sell a part of his estate to satisfy his clamorous creditors.

The reasons he gave me for not acquainting you with his embarrassments, were these:—He knew your generosity would consent to any sacrifice to save him from anxiety; but still he feared you would suffer a mortification in thus seeing your fortune diminished, and he loved you so entirely he could not bear to witness your vexation or melancholy. He knew, too, that you had not been accustomed to business, and could not endure your first lesson should be the humiliating one of studying to repair his errors and miscalculations. In short, by keeping you in ignorance he spared his own pride and your sensibility; and he therefore urged you to visit your friends, intending, during your absence, to settle his affairs, and hoping—when do we cease to hope? —that before your return he should devise some expedient to repair his fortune, or at least prevent you from feeling sensibly its diminution.

His whole estate you undoubtedly know he valued at two hundred seventy-five thousand dollars; one half of this estimate included his plantation and slaves; his city residence and a large tract of unimproved land the other. His debts, as nearly as he could estimate, amounted to sixty thousand dollars. He concluded to dispose of his city residence and wild land, pay his creditors, and, as he saw your predilection had of late appeared for the country, he hoped his plantation, servants, and a few thousands in ready money, would satisfy your ambition.

Accordingly he offered his elegant house in —— street and his city lots for sale, immediately after your departure, and soon found a purchaser. A Mr. Cox, a Philadelphian, well known here and considered rich and respectable, appeared and bargained for the property without a single demur at the price. The deeds I drew myself, and your uncle took his note for sixty days. Mr. Cox departed for Philadelphia to procure the money, and your uncle was arranging with his creditors and flattering himself he should leave you an unincumbered estate, which, though not so large as he wished, would yet insure your independence, and be sufficient for your happiness.

But who can calculate his destiny, or claim exemption from disappointment? Before the time fixed for the return of Cox had expired, another gentleman from Philadelphia arrived in our city and exhibited a deed of the property purchased from your uncle, and insisted on possession. The villain Cox had sold it him for twenty-five thousand dollars, taken the money, and absconded; and every effort to trace him has hitherto proved unsuccessful. Your uncle's creditors caught the alarm—creditors are a sensitive and sympathetic race, and the panic of one is communicated to the herd with electrical rapidity They brought suits by the dozen, and attachments were laid on the plantation—nothing could satisfy their rapacity. To prevent a public sale, your uncle, by my advice, consigned all his effects to Owen Dunbar, Esq. Every thing is to be valued by commissioners; Dunbar satisfies the claimants, and whatever remains is to be paid over to you, and you have one year to redeem your property by repaying what the consignee advances. I cannot, however, flatter you with the hope of receiving much; indeed I fear there will be a deficiency. The amount of debts, costs, and incidental expenses is more than we anticipated.

Your uncle's anxiety made his last days unhappy, no doubt, yet I do not think it hastened his death. He had been failing during the summer, but so gradually, he would not acknowledge it, and never consented you should be informed of it, or be recalled. It was not till the day before his decease he wrote the letter I forward with this. I saw him buried according to his desire, and in a manner I think you will approve. With respect to what course you can pursue, I feel incompetent to offer any advice; yet should you conclude to return here, my house shall be open to receive you. Whatever services I can render you shall be cheerfully performed, and any orders you transmit faithfully executed.

Your letters to your uncle, requesting a remittance of cash were received by him when confined, and happening to be present, he requested me to read them. The part relating to the money I omitted, as it would have caused him uneasiness, and I have taken the liberty of enclosing a hundred dollars, as a trifle to answer your present exigencies. I would have sent more, but am myself suffering embarrassments. I hope, sincerely hope, you will yet surmount your misfortunes, and that the time will come when they will merely serve, by contrast, to enhance more fully your prosperity. Those who have never experienced reverses are but half schooled in the discipline of the world, and know not the resources of their own minds.

I am still endeavoring to ascertain the retreat of Cox, yet from what I can learn of his habits and resources, there is but little hope that you will ever obtain any thing of consequence from him. He is a gambler and speculator, characters on which no reliance for probity can be placed. How we were so long deceived by such a one is now surprising, but villany so deliberate as his, is rarely anticipated or guarded against by men of integrity. I shall, however, be vigilant to trace him, and at least expose his baseness.

Let me hear from you soon, and believe me, sir,

Most respectfully, your servant,

HENRY HOWARD."

CHAPTER XXIV.

MEANS AND ENDS.

Though losses and crosses
  Be lessons right severe;
There's wit there, ye'll get there,
  Ye'll learn no other where.
BURNS.

THE first crush of pecuniary misfortunes is never felt in its full extent. Those who have been accustomed to command whatever they desired, cannot be taught, except by experience, how keenly they will miss their habitual indulgencies, nor how mortifying will be those petty inconveniences to which the poor are exposed. It is sensitiveness to these little deprivations that causes much of the misery of those who have fallen from opulence to poverty.

The factitious wants and appetites created or fostered by riches, are no farther essential to human happiness than, as by becoming habits, they are hard to be laid aside;—this truth, those who have the care of children and youth ought always to remember.

Happily for Sidney Romilly, he was, in childhood, inured to temperance and industry; and although his subsequent life of luxury had enervated, it had not wholly incapacitated him for exertion when exertion became necessary. He thought, therefore, but little, and grieved less for the loss of fortune; while tears, bitter and unrestrained, flowed fast down his cheeks as he again perused the letter of his beloved uncle, and reflected on the pain and sorrow that kind friend had suffered during the summer, while he had been seeking amusement and enjoying happiness in an expensive journey.

While he sat thus, indulging in tender and affectionate recollections, his father, with his usual pleasant face, opened the door, saying, "What news, Sidney?" but seeing the tears on his cheek, he added, coming hastily forward, "sad, I fear."

"Sad enough," replied Sidney, presenting the letters; and then retiring to a window, he sat down and leaned his head on the window frame, while his father perused them.

Squire Romilly cast many a glance at his son, even while reading; and when he had finished, he wiped the dew from his glasses, sat a few moments, and then gave a hem, which always indicated he was ready to enter on the discussion of the subject he had been considering. Sidney raised his head and fixed his eyes on his father.

"My son, for the death of your uncle you may well grieve; such an affectionate, sincere, disinterested friend as he, is seldom to be found, and his loss cannot, to you, be well repaired. Yet, though we may mourn, we are forbidden to repine. He is, I trust, removed to a better world; certainly he has gone to the presence of a Being who will judge in mercy, and the trials of earth, which he has of late found so severe, are at an end. But you, it seems, are fated to encounter some of them, in the disappointment of those expectations of fortune which he had taught you to form. Yet I do not consider your misfortune as irreparable. It is true, there are advantages attached to wealth, and I would not teach you to underrate them; yet our own happiness does not depend so much on external circumstances as we imagine. There is usually more enjoyment in the pursuit of fortune than in the possession; and that enjoyment, had you inherited your uncle's estate, you would never have known. You can now, with your talents and education, undoubtedly enter on some business that will afford you a competency; at present we shall rejoice to have your society; and though the first disclosure will be a little mortifying, yet I think you will not, among our people, experience any diminution of respect."

"Do you consider it best to disclose the matter?"

"Certainly; and the sooner the better. Deacon Jones is now below stairs, waiting to discover how much cash your packet contained; we will go down, and I will read both letters to him, and let the whole truth circulate at once."

"But why is it necessary?" returned Sidney, whose mind had wandered to the Deacon's niece, and to the effect the disclosure might possibly have on her smiles. "I shall injure no one by secresy, and why need my private affairs be matters of public discussion?"

"Because it is impossible to maintain a secret of this kind for any length of time, without a resort to mean subterfuges and expedients unworthy a man of honor. Neither could you keep the secret if you would, for our Yankees examine thoroughly every suspicious or unexplained circumstance, and they would soon unravel the affair; and in the meantime rumors and guesses would be circulating and giving a far worse coloring to the matter than the real truth."

"The truth is humiliating enough," replied Sidney, whose losses appeared to increase in proportion as he reflected on the estimation in which they would be considered by others. "To be thus, at once, reduced from independence to poverty, is not certainly a slight evil."

"No, it is not," said his father; "and yet, my son, the evils of property arise oftener from false pride than real wants. Dare to appear what you are. Say, I have, by circumstances I could not control, lost my fortune, but my merits are still, I hope, unimpaired. By seeming ashamed of poverty, we tacitly acknowledge that riches imparted all our consequence; and by soliciting the pity of the world for our pecuniary embarrassments, we always invite its contempt. Instead of complaining of Fortune's frown, look the capricious goddess boldly and cheerfully in the face, and she will either relax her severity, or lay aside her ugliness. Come, go down stairs with me, and we will make an experiment on the Deacon. He will be sorely surprised, no doubt; but if you exhibit that strength of mind which can only be displayed in adversity, and which I think you do possess, you will certainly rise in his esteem, as gold looks brighter the more it is purified."

He then rose and Sidney followed him, though rather reluctantly, to the sitting-room. The kind father felt keenly the mental sufferings of his son, but experience had taught him what Sidney could not well know, that the *sense* of such mortifications is most in *apprehension*, and that the longer the communication was delayed, the more painful, if not disgraceful, it would become.

Mrs. Romilly saw them enter with an exulting smile, as for the old Deacon, he had just replenished his pipe, intending to smoke away most vigorously and indifferently while Sidney was recounting his golden news.

After a short preface, the Squire unfolded the tidings of the decease of his brother-in-law; the trials he had been called to endure in his last sickness, and then read, in a loud, unhesitating tone, the whole of both letters Sidney had received.

The Deacon's eyes, at the mention of Mr. Brainard's death, rested on our hero with a squint very much like envy, but before the conclusion, they were opened to their utmost vision; and his pipe, which in his utter amazement he had taken from his mouth, actually dropped from his hold, and was broken, not in a thousand pieces, but only the stem a little shortened.

He observed, as he hastily snatched it up, "that it would answer very well yet; it was nothing at all when compared with Mr. Sidney's misfortune. He hoped the Lord would give his young friend wisdom to improve such crosses to his spiritual good. He wondered Mr. Brainard could take any man's note for such a large sum—he ought to have required bondsmen, or taken a mortgage of the property sold; and finally wished Mr. Sidney well, and should be very happy to have him spend a month or two in his family if he didn't find any business to his mind, nor a more agreeable offer." And then declaring he had not thought when he first came in, of stopping half so long, he hurried away to recapitulate by his own fire-side the intelligence he had just gathered.

Mrs. Romilly was sorely vexed; and while she wept for the death of Mr. Brainard, she declared she had no patience at all with such carelessness as he had been guilty of in trusting Cox.

"And everybody will hear of it," said she, "and there's some will be glad, I know. Oh, what can Sidney do!"

"Do!" repeated her husband, "why, there are a thousand things he can do; and he has not the least reason to feel discouraged. We will soon contrive some way to put him in business, and in the meantime, if there are any who rejoice at his misfortune, we will pity *them*. Those persons who cherish envy, or discard humanity, are more real objects of commiseration than the meanest beggar; theirs is that poverty of the heart and mind which the possession of the whole universe could not enrich."

Although Squire Romilly treated his son's loss of for tune with more than philosophical indifference, with true christian resignation, yet the circumstance gave him much anxiety. He felt there would be difficulty in inuring Sidney's mind to the idea of steady exertion and necessary dependence; and he was not without fears his son might do what thousands have done, plunge in dissipation to forget his disappointments. But he determined to watch over, advise, and assist him to the utmost, and not imitate the example of those parents who make one failure or disappointment, in what was expected for a child, an excuse for withholding further aid.

Meanwhile, Sidney's meditations were of a still more sombre character. The longer he reflected on his situation, the worse it appeared. He had been educated to inherit affluence, not to acquire it, and feared he could not succeed in business which required method, and a circumspection and calculation he had never been taught to practice. Neither could he endure to be a burthen on his kind parents, when they had so large a family unprovided for. We are created social beings, and perhaps it is generally the case, that in sudden calamities, the human heart, especially in youth, rarely depends on itself; it seeks the refuge of friendship.

Sidney had a host of friends in Charleston; but after a recollection of their several characters and pursuits, he felt compelled to acknowledge but little dependence could be placed on their assistance. They were his friends forever, when dining at his uncle's, or drinking at the club the wines for which he had paid, and his humble servants while he was heir apparent to a rich man. "But who will humbly serve the poor?" Sidney felt he could not and would not apply to them.

He then thought of Stuart. Stuart, for whom he had sacrificed his dearest wishes and conquered his love. And Stuart had been profuse in his professions, and yet had not, for a number of months, written him a single line. And Stuart, too, had correspondents in Charleston, and must have heard of his uncle's failure; and he ought to have written and offered his assistance. So Sidney argued, and he determined he would never become a beggar of one he had so much obliged.

Then came the Englishman, frank, noble and generous. He too had acknowledged deep obligations to Sidney; but he could not know of his misfortune. He ought to know it, and have, at least, the opportunity of being grateful.

"I will write him immediately," thought Sidney, "and shape my conduct by his answer. If he remember me, and offer his assistance, and urge me to visit England, I will go, and accept his aid; if not, I must seek some other resource. In the interim, I will remain here—here with my good parents; and parents, after all, are the surest friends."

On the following morning Sidney acquainted his father with the plan he had formed; it was approved, and a letter was accordingly written and despatched across the Atlantic; not asking assistance, however, but only detailing those circumstances which Mr. Frankford, as a friend, had a claim to be entrusted with.

Squire Romilly did not expect much from the Englishman, but he felt unwilling to damp his son's hopes. Hope seemed now all that was left him, and its fancies might soothe till his mind was strengthened to bear more composedly the buffets which those who struggle with fortune must endure. In the meantime he would be making arrangements to assist him to enter on business of some kind, should the answer of Frankford be unfavorable.

But several months were to be passed in suspense—long winter months—and Squire Romilly knew it would require more apathy than Sidney possessed, indeed more than he wished him to have, to pass that time pleasantly without employment, and engaged only in the amusements a secluded country village could afford.

"You will never be contented with us, Sidney," said his father, "if we do not contrive something for you to do. Nothing keeps the *hypo* so completely at a distance as employment. Now what if you should instruct a school a few months? Many very respectable men have engaged in that business."

"And have been successful too, much more than I should be," returned Sidney, who remembered that Stuart was thus employed when he won the heart of Zemira.

"But you could try," said the Squire; "and a failure would not involve you in any serious difficulties. Yet I think you would succeed."

"Yes, I know he would," said Mrs. Romilly, "and if he could only keep in this district, he might board at home. And he might have this school, only George Cranfield is engaged; but I heard Dr. Perkins say that George might have another."

Mrs. Romilly seldom saw any insurmountable difficulty to a favorite plan, and she argued George might easily be induced to relinquish the school, and finally she persuaded her husband—she could usually persuade him to whatever she wished—to go immediately to Perkins and get him to negotiate the exchange. No time was to be lost, as the school commenced on the following Monday.

Dr. Perkins had heard of Sidney's disappointment, and had been anxiously deliberating in what way he could serve him. He had not called to condole, for condolence was not his *forte;* but when he could devise some plan to assist him, how lightly he would go to be a messenger of good. He undertook the business with alacrity, and as he knew of a school Cranfield might have, doubted not but he should be successful.

George, however, listened to the proposal with evident uneasiness; and Perkins saw the praises of Sidney, although he assented to their justness, were far from giving him unmingled pleasure. Nor was he long in understanding the reason of this. Miss Redington had smiled on the stranger, and George was too ardent and sincere a lover to brook patiently a rival in her affections. He told Perkins he would answer him in a few hours, and they parted.

The doctor had now many fears that the young divine would not abandon his situation so near the abode of his charmer, in favor of Sidney; but had he known the resolution the former had taken, he would not have doubted the issue. George had determined to declare his love to Annie, and by her reception be guided in his answer to Perkins. If she favored him, he would not, by yielding the school, place Sidney in a situation to approach her; if she rejected him, he should wish to be gone as far as possible.

His fears rather outweighed his hopes; but he thought suspense worse than a rejection.

Annie was alone when he entered her uncle's, and musing on Sidney, whose story she had heard with deep concern; and yet she liked to think about it. It was something like her own disappointments, and the similarity seemed to excuse her for dwelling on his.

The emotions George Cranfield could not suppress at

hearing her name his rival, and lament his misfortunes, drew from her an inquiry of what disturbed him; and to her regret, she was compelled to listen to the protestations of his love and the proffers of his hand. It was not entirely unexpected, though certainly undesired. She knew his worth—she believed him sincere—she felt her own dependent situation; but her heart refused to acknowledge him for its lord, and in the kindest language a refusal could be conveyed, she gave him a denial.

His face was pale as marble, and the beatings of his heart might have been seen through the thick folds of his coat. There was a moment's irresolution, as if he almost determined to solicit, to conjure her pity; but the proud spirit of the man prevailed. He arose, and suddenly clasping her hand that was resting on the table, pressed it to his lips, and kissing it, repeatedly exclaimed:

"Annie, dearest Annie, farewell! I have loved you better than my life, but you are not for me. I acknowledge it all right. I should, I fear, were you mine, rest in the gift and forget the Giver. I shall go from this town till I can think calmly on your preference for Sidney Romilly. He may deserve you more than I, but he cannot, Annie, he cannot love you better. O! if he should, by a residence here, gain your heart, he will be richly recompensed for his loss of fortune. Farewell, farewell!"—and he rushed from the apartment.

Annie had scarcely recovered from the confusion which her lover's strange allusion to Sidney had occasioned, when the latter appeared. He had just encountered Dr. Perkins, who informed him George Cranfield had called and relinquished the school, and he might be installed in the magisterial office the following week.

How soon the mind accommodates itself to its situation. But a few days had passed since Sidney would have considered the proposition to instruct a school as an insult; but now he received the intelligence of Perkins with more real pleasure than had ever been conferred by the costly gifts of his uncle; and he could recollect none who would rejoice more at this arrangement than the family of Deacon Jones, so he dropped in to communicate his good fortune.

In spite of Annie's exertions to appear natural, she could not welcome him with her accustomed frank and easy gaiety. The words of young Cranfield made her fear she had testified more satisfaction in Sidney's society than she ought, and she was now silent and reserved.

Sidney noticed it, and immediately imputed it to his fallen fortunes. So sensitive are the unfortunate! He went home very wretched, reflecting on the selfishness of the world, and almost despairing of ever finding that generosity and disinterestedness which his course of reading and romantic feelings had made necessary to his happiness, but which he knew most prudent people considered chimerical.

He had not recovered his tranquility when Dr. Perkins, on the following day, called to see him. Mrs. Romilly, who was sorely afflicted at beholding the melancholy of her first born, entreated the doctor to use his endeavors to cheer him; and the good natured man readily promised his best services should be at her bidding. He visited Sidney in his chamber, where he had passed the forenoon, and, after the kindest and most friendly greeting and inquiries, succeeded in discovering the cause of his present dejection. Now he had, through the medium of his wife, who was intimate with Silas Romilly's wife, gathered most of the particulars of Annie's last interview with George Cranfield; and from what he had himself observed, he doubted not that the partiality of the fair lady was given to our hero; yet he would not for the world have hinted such a secret to him, had he not thought, under present circumstances, it was indispensable to his happiness—almost to his life.

The medical practitioner had not made pills and potions so entirely his study as to be ignorant of the human heart. He knew there was nothing, not even the possession of power, fame, or wealth, that imparted such a feeling of self-complacency and self-respect to the mind of a young man, as the knowledge that he was deeply, and truly, and exclusively, beloved by a lovely, innocent, and amiable woman.

He therefore, after a little raillery, unfolded what he had learned respecting the rejection of George Cranfield, and suggested that the reserve of Annie, instead of being the effect of indifference to Mr. Romilly, was but that sweet, retiring modesty, which is fearful of betraying its own sensibility, and even blushes lest its virtuous inclinations should be suspected.

The idea was rapture to Sidney, and he welcomed it with ardor; yet reflection presented so many obstacles to be overcome before he could, with propriety, be a suitor for her favor, that he almost regretted such an event should be considered possible, and his tone was still melancholy, while to the doctor's suggestions he replied,—

"And of what consequence would Annie's partiality be to me at this time? I must never think of a lady's smiles, till I can secure those of Fortune; and I am now completely out of her favor."

"You have basked in her broad sunshine till you are unable to bear the shadow of a cloud," replied Perkins; "but remember storms and calms are successive, and why should you always expect a lot more favored than your fellows? Yet, even now, I presume George Cranfield thinks you in a most enviable situation."

"Why should he?" returned Sidney, "when he knows that even if my affection for Miss Redington were similar to his, I should still be compelled to subdue it. You surely would not, in my present situation, have me make advances which might ultimately render us both miserable?"

"O! no, no," answered Perkins, eagerly; "I think there ought not to be a declaration at present; certainly not, if you succeed in procuring a situation abroad. Annie's feelings must not be trifled with, nor her confidence betrayed. But something may possibly occur which will induce you to alter your plan. You may even settle here among us, and be a clever, contented Yankee. Suppose you study my profession? I will assist you all in my power, gratis; and there are worse situations in life than being a physician. And then, what a sweet wife Annie would make! Yet I only wish you to think of her instead of praying to your saints, as I believe you have not one in your calendar more worthy of adoration. You see I suspect you of being inclined *to catholicism; but never—never bow at her shrine till* you come with a sincere heart!"

He spoke the last sentence with an air of solemnity Sidney had never before seen him assume, and after he had departed, our hero reflected long and painfully on his embarrassments, yet a gleam of light had fallen athwart his path that seemed the precursor of future felicity.

Was he, then, without fortune, beloved? and could his merits alone secure the heart of that beautiful and excellent girl? I have often, thought he, complained that I should never be happy in love, because my riches would prevent me from feeling secure of the disinterested attachment of a woman; and now shall I lament the loss of fortune when it removes that barrier to my happiness? I will exert myself to gain property, and if I succeed I shall doubly enjoy prosperity. If I fail I will solace myself that affection has been mine which gold could not purchase. Stuart was poor, and yet I envied him more than any man I ever saw. But Annie certainly exceeds Zemira in beauty, accomplishments, and intelligence: if I gain her love, I shall be more enviable than Stuart. I will despair no more.

CHAPTER XXV.

THE HERO IN A NEW VOCATION

From scenes like these *my country's* grandeur springs
That makes her loved at home, revered abroad;
Princes and lords are but the breath of kings;
"An honest man's the noblest work of God;"
And certes in fair virtue's heavenly road,
The *cottage* leaves the *palace* far behind. BURNS.

THE period at which Sidney Romilly was, for the first time in his life, to commence business for himself, arrived—a cold, boisterous December morning, for the winter had now commenced with extreme severity; and while he listened to the howling blast that came sweeping over the bleak hills, and shook the chamber in which he lay, while the frozen snow rattled against the windows, his blood almost froze in his veins as he thought of braving the tempestuous weather. He could not but moralize—it was an excellent time for moralizing—on the bitter change in his own prospects.

But a little time before, and he was sporting in the summer of prosperity; but the blight had fallen, the blast had swept, and he was now stripped of all, and could, in the language of the sweet but unfortunate poet whose lines adorn this chapter, exclaim,—

"The tempest's howl, it soothes my soul,
My griefs it seems to join;
The leafless trees my fancy please,
Their fate resembles mine!"

He arose and looked abroad, but the scenery was not at all calculated to raise his drooping spirits. Every object around was covered with a white shroud, even the evergreens on the mountains were loaded with snow, and

SYDNEY AS A YANKEE SCHOOLMASTER.

nature wore that cold, cheerless, monotonous appearance that chills the heart, and sends the warm affections and fancies, which love to revel amid the buds of spring and roses of summer, back to the social hearth for smiles, and beauty, and pleasures.

And in the kindred circle of the Romillys, warm affections and sunny looks were kindling and radiant the whole year round. Winter came not to chill the feelings of their kind and happy hearts, and Sidney, while witnessing their cheerful industry and the alacrity with which the younger members of the family prepared for school, and saw how lightly and joyously they bounded over the high snow-drifts, felt ashamed of his own effeminacy in thus shrinking at obstacles his little brothers were fearlessly braving.

The snow had fallen several feet during the night, and all the men in the neighborhood went abroad at an early hour to break the paths. This they effected by means of their sleds and what is called a drag, drawn by oxen, and using a shovel where the snow was piled the highest, and so thoroughly they performed their work, that Sidney found a tolerable road as he bent his steps towards his school-house. On his way he was frequently passed by some of his scholars, cunning, laughing urchins, who just paused to bow lowly to their *master*, and then sprung away like deer through the snow-wreaths, shouting with delight as they often purposely fell and rolled among the light, feathery particles.

Sidney smiled at their sports, while memory transported him back to the days and scenes of his own childish amusements, and he thought how little was requisite to constitute happiness when the mind was only contented to enjoy it; and before he reached the school-house, he had firmly resolved to be contented.

When he entered the house where the scholars had nearly all assembled and taken their seats, he found a comfortable room, warm fire, and smiling faces to welcome him; and a sensation of pleasure, hitherto unknown, swelled his bosom when he saw them all waiting his nod, and attentive to execute his commands, and discovered that although they were legitimate born and thorough bred republicans, yet they were very easily subjected to the monarchical authority of their rightful *master*. But Sidney Romilly was not one of those who, "drest in a little brief authority," appear like an angry ape, and pelt all subjected to their sway; his own kind feelings had taught him that kindness was the master key to the human heart, and so well did he manage to obtain the love of his pupils, and yet impress them with the fear of offending him, that his wishes were very soon all the laws he needed, and to express them was to insure their cheerful performance.

The duties of an instructor are always perplexing and often irksome, yet there are many agreeable passages in hours spent in imparting knowledge to the young and ductile understanding; and the exertions the employment required, were necessary to occupy Sidney's mind, and prevent him from indulging in useless regret, or yielding to consuming ennui. When his daily task was concluded, how dearly he enjoyed the tranquil domestic bliss that brightened his father's hearth; or the lively, intelligent, though sometimes whimsical gaiety that characterized the abode of his friend Perkins.

But there was one house whose attractions, although he did not, even to his own heart, dare to acknowledge the extent of their power, possessed a charm of tenderness more exquisite still. Yet it was not the conversation of the Deacon, although he always welcomed the *school-master*, and exerted himself to entertain him by proving the orthodox validity of his own faith, and attempting to convince his auditor of his utter sinfulness and ruin if he did not embrace the same religious tenets. These observations were generally introduced in the preamble that now was an excellent time for Mr. Sidney Romilly to examine himself, as he was released from the temptations of great wealth, and must have seen the folly of trusting in an arm of flesh; and they were always concluded by a libation from his pitcher of cider, which

Mr. Sidney was heartily invited to participate. Then the old gentleman usually retired to his own room to smoke his pipe and plan his business for the next day.

After he and his woman, as he commonly called his wife, had withdrawn, Silas Romilly and his wife were assiduous in offering every attention, and promoting every amusement they thought would contribute to their brother's happiness, and, assisted by Annie, seldom were they unsuccessful. Her acquaintance with polished society and the forms of fashionable life, gave him an opportunity of displaying his taste and sentiments on subjects with which he was most familiar, but which no other person in the village, except Annie, would have comprehended. Their favorite authors were the same, and thus their sentiments were every day more closely assimilating their feelings, and their intercourse and friendship ripening into intimacy and affection.

Annie sung, perhaps, like an angel, but that is, to us, an uncertain comparison; certainly, however, with one of the sweetest of human voices. Neither did she, by capricious refusals, endeavor to enhance the value of her condescension; but almost always complied with Sidney's first request for a song, with such winning grace, that even an indifferent execution would have delighted. How, then, could he fail to be enchanted by her harmony? Even the timid reserve that often stole over her in their gayest moments, and her occasional evenings of silence, were not unpleasing to Sidney. He well remembered what Perkins had told him, and though the universe would not have tempted him to have wounded her delicacy by betraying a consciousness that he was beloved, yet it was bliss to hope it. He had not formed any distinct purpose why he hoped it—it was like a sweet vision which he feared to dissipate by any attempt to ascertain its reality.

But the weeks passed rapidly away, and nothing occurred to mar the winter's enjoyment. George Cranfield came not by his melancholy to cast a shade over their happiness; his name, whenever spoken by Annie, was always mentioned with respect, and Sidney never heard an allusion escape her lips which hinted in any manner her rejection of that amiable young man.

Ephraim Skinner now seldom intruded his busy and important face among the cheerful group at the deacon's. In particular, he avoided meeting Mr. Romilly there; and though the old deacon always stoutly vindicated him, saying he believed him an *experienced* man—meaning pious—and that he only wanted his own, and that Mr. Sidney would find it necessary to look out a little sharper before he ever acquired any property; yet he never could, in his own family, make any converts to his opinion, nor was he much more successful in the neighborhood.

Benevolence is a passport to most hearts, and Sidney's generous sympathy for the misfortunes of the poor debtor, had created a lively interest for his fate in the minds of that unsophisticated people, which his subsequent losses, by reducing him nearer their own level, had contributed to increase. He was the magnet of the village. A school master in the country is always a personage of consequence; his relation as instructor of their children giving him a vast importance with the parents, and he was accordingly invited to all the dwellings in the district, and numerous parties and sleigh rides were contrived to amuse him, and testify their deep sense of his merits and services. At these parties the *schoolmaster* and Miss Redington were almost always associated; the good folks seeming, by common consent, to agree, that no lady, except the deacon's niece from Boston, was a fitting partner for the southern bred gentleman; and proud were they that they had amongst them so lovely and amiable a being to grace their drawing rooms and be the queen of their festivities.

Among those who insisted on, at least, a *call* from Sidney, was his *protogee* Merrill. When his family had nearly recovered, and he could go abroad without fearing for their safety, he came to visit and make his acknowledgments to his benefactor. He found Sidney at Deacon

Jones' and there poured out his gratitude in the strong, simple language of native feeling. His appearance was so altered that Sidney, at first, hardly recollected him. When he saw him before, his long black beard gave an almost savage look to his countenance; while the fatigue and anxiety he had undergone made his eyes appear sunken and his complexion sallow, and his neglected and even ragged apparel, affixed to his image, in the mind of Sidney, an idea of wretchedness which he never liked to remember.

But now he came arrayed in a neat and comfortable suit of *home made;* his beard was closely shaven, and his brisk eye and animated countenance had taken at least ten years of age from his former appearance; and there needed not the affirmation he gave of his present happiness to satisfy his hearers of its reality.

While he was, with tears of joy swelling in his eyes, relating that his family had nearly recovered, and how happy they were, and that every thing seemed now to go *right* with him, as he expressed it; and thanking Sidney again and again for his assistance, Annie wept unrestrainedly, and the old deacon wiped his nose often, which he afterwards ascribed to a violent cold; but which was undoubtedly the thawings of sympathy, so long congealed that the passages to his eyes were closed, and therefore it took another course.

Merrill knew of Sidney's present embarrassments, but delicacy forbade him to allude to them, except by telling the arrangements he was making to refund the money his benefactor had advanced.

"My wife and I are talking it over every day," said he, "and I will endeavor to pay it now, if you say so, though I sell all my stock, oxen and all. I can part with my oxen now better than I could a month ago, for I have been hauling up a pretty good mess of wood—I am determined never to be short of wood again."

Sidney told him he did not wish him to distress himself to refund the money; that was not the idea under which he had received it, adding,

"My assistance would be no kindness at all should I insist on payment now; you might just as well have satisfied the execution of Mr. Skinner."

"O! no," replied Merrill, "not by a great sight. My family are now nearly well, and there is a great deal of difference in our feelings about paying it to you, sir, or having it forced from us by the cruelty of that villain. But, Mr. Sidney Romilly, you must come up and see us—my wife will never rest easy till she sees you, and our baby, poor boy, is'nt well enough yet for her to go out, or she would have called and thanked you before now. Then my boys all want to see you. Do come up next week, and bring Miss Redington here, she's been as kind as an angel too. And your brother and his wife must come, and Dr. Perkins—the doctor has promised me already. Now won't you come up all together?"

Annie blushed and smiled, while Sidney gaily inquired if she would ride with him and call on Mr. Merrill; and finally the visit was settled for the Thursday evening following.

And a beautiful evening it proved, only very cold; but wrapped in buffaloes, and with good horses, they cared little for the "nipping and eager air," while the jingle of the sleigh-bells formed a concert by no means unpleasant, and quite appropriate with their rapid motion.

They soon arrived at the dwelling of Merrill, a small one-story house, the color of the wood, and only lighted by two glass windows, the apertures for the remaining ones being closed with boards. There was, however, a large, well finished barn and sheds a few steps distant, and Perkins remarked he always noted down the farmer as a thriving, industrious, economical man, who had a barn larger than his house.

A bright fire shone through the small windows and open door as they drove up, where Merrill waited to receive them; and, after shaking hands with every individual, and bidding them welcome, he ushered them into the only finished room, which served for every occasion, introduced them to his wife, and then went out to take care of the horses.

His wife instantly offered chairs, and assisted them to disencumber themselves of their bonnets and overcoats, and then they formed a circle around a fire that literally blazed like a furnace. Mr. Merrill, thinking one essential rite of hospitality in such a cold night, was to provide a good fire for his guests, had contrived, by placing a maple log, nearly three feet in diameter, at the back of his capacious fire-place, and then piling small wood almost to the mantel-piece, to have, on their arrival, what might very well represent a bonfire. The strong light displayed the neat room and furniture, bought for use not show, to the best advantage, every article looking as clean as if it were under the superintendence of those fairies who of yore presided over the department of the tidy housewife.

On low stools, by one corner of the fire-place, sat the four boys, their chubby cheeks well attesting their complete recovery from the sickness they had suffered; and looking like pictures of innocent happiness as their roguish eyes from time to time glanced on the good gentleman their father had told them they must love, and then turned significantly smiling on each other.

A cradle stood beside Mrs. Merrill, in which lay her babe, whose illness had been protracted by a fever-sore that now threatened to destroy the use of its limbs, and the history of which furnished her first topic of discourse, as it certainly was the one on which she had been pondering most intently.

Over the mantel-piece, suspended on a wire hook, hung a file of newspapers, and beside them an almanac, and Sidney, as he remarked it, could not but relate the anecdote of Zeb, and the mirth of Frankford.

When their host returned, he was accompanied by a stripling whom Sidney immediately recollected as the "Captain Luther" of the squirrel hunt, and whom the elder Merrill said was his brother, and that he had come there that evening just to see Mr. Sidney Romilly, and thank him for his kindness.

"But thanks are poor pay for what we all owe you," said Mrs. Merrill, the tears filling her mild blue eyes.

"I intend to be paying him something more substantial, by-and-by," said her husband, briskly. "I and my boys shall work like Jehus next summer. I have a good farm and a good wife, and if we only have good health, I'll soon get out of debt, and then we shall be independent, and I wouldn't swap with a king. Yet, we shall never forget who were our friends in the hour of trouble. Come here, boys, and make your bows to this gentleman."

The children all came forward, hanging their heads and looking rather silly; yet the pleasure their parents enjoyed while relating how well they could read and work, and what they intended to make of them, was so heartfelt that no one could witness it without sympathizing in the happiness that appeared so sincere and so virtuous.

"Now here's my John," said the exulting father, nodding significantly to Sidney, and pulling his boy closely towards him; "he is but twelve, and has never had a very good chance to school, but he'll read anything right off as fast as a lawyer. If I can only get out of debt, I believe I shall try and send him to college. I always take the papers, for I think every man who has the privilege of voting, ought to know what is doing in the world, so I take 'em, and John reads 'em all; and some of them congress speeches are plaguy long-winded, you know. I'm so tired when I've done work I don't read 'em half; but John, if he can get a book or paper, is never tired. But there's a good many hard words in them are speeches, and I couldn't tell John the meaning, for I didn't know, and he teased me till I bought him a dixonary last winter. John, bring the book here and show it to the gentlemen."

The boy obeyed with alacrity, and soon rummaged out his dictionary from a pile of school books, that together with a large Bible, were the ornament of an old fashioned desk.

"Now," continued his father, taking it from him and presenting it to Sidney,—"now see how nice he's kept it; and he's studied it too, more, I'm afraid, than his Bible, and his mother is pretty particular to make him read in that every day. Well, when Skinner sued me, I felt so poor I told John I guessed I mustn't take the papers any longer, and I must turn out his dixonary to the sheriff, and the boy cried in a minute. And he hadn't shed a tear in all his sickness, and had taken all his med'son without saying a word, but when I told him I must sell his books, he cried like a baby. And he said I might sell his new hat and welcome, if I'd only let him keep his dixonary. Then I thought I should never save enough by *skrimping* the children's books, and stopping the papers to make me rich; and I told my wife I'd work a little harder, or drink a little less rum in haying time, and I don't drink much now, before I'd make 'em cry so about their books. And then, Mr. Sidney, you were good enough to help me; so John keeps his dixonary, and reads the papers every week, and I don't think you can hardly pick out a word but what he'll tell you the meaning."

The company laughed heartily, and joined in commending John's perseverance, and predicting his future greatness and the speeches he would probably make in Congress some day, when Mrs. Merrill, who felt the mother's impartial affection for all her children, and could not bear that one should engross so entirely the attention, began to dilate on the excellencies of the others. In this she was soon heartily joined by her husband, and after they had proved that certainly, in their opinion, their children inherited every good quality ever bestowed on mortals, the kind father took up from the cradle his sick boy, and holding him with the most careful attention. declared he was the brightest of them all; "and," continued he, "though I don't expect he'll ever do a day's work in the world, I don't care anything about that. If he may only live, I'll take care of him, and make him a *minister* or a *doctor*, and then his lameness will never do him much hurt."

Mr. Merrill was standing, with his head a little declined over the pillow on which lay the little sufferer, who feebly smiled as he met the looks of kindness and sympathy thus bent upon him. Sidney gazed on the tall, muscular form of the father, whose large, sinewy hand and strong arm, that seemed formed for deeds of dexterity and daring, to heave the huge weight, or hurl the ponderous weapon, was now clasped around and supporting with all a woman's tenderness, a sickly infant; while his soul, that in accordance with the rough, gigantic frame it inhabited, might have been thought of a stern, rugged, and unyielding temperament, was all dissolved in sensations of compassion and love.

"O, these affections of the heart," thought Sidney, "how easily they subdue the lofty or the stubborn spirit, and make bosoms of flint gush with streams of feeling and charity, till the disposition of the man, proud, bold, and lion-like, is softened down to the tenderness and constancy of the meek-eyed dove."

As he finished his mental soliloquy, his eye rested on Annie's lovely and intelligent countenance, beaming with all the benevolence with which his own heart was overflowing; and at that moment he loved her better than ever he did Zemira. It was the affection of holy sympathy.

But these deep and engrossing reveries were soon dispelled by the jollity of Dr. Perkins. He always liked to see every one merry and sociable, and he related some of his best anecdotes, and insisted on a song from Annie, which was given, when assured the noise would not injure the poor babe.

The sweet and simple air she sung was listened to with breathless attention, and when she finished, not the *encore* of the fashionables at an Italian opera could be more expressive of approbation than were the smiles of her auditors; nor could Jenny Lind herself be more gratified at the applauses her "Bird Song" elicited, than was Annie Redington when her lover—he might well at that moment be called her lover—softly whispered,—"How charming!"

Merrill proffered around his cider with an unsparing hand, and the little boys followed with fine mellow apples, and they were careful to point Mr. Romilly and Miss Redington to the largest and fairest. These, with fried cakes and gingerbread, both as sweet as maple sugar could make them, minced pie, pumpkin pie, and cheese, constituted their treat; and after passing about three hours, enjoying besides the good cheer, what might well be called *substantial* happiness, as it was of a kind which could forever be reflected on with satisfaction, they prepared to depart.

Before they went, however, Annie found an opportunity to inform Mrs. Merrill of an excellent poultice and embrocation for the limb of her babe, and then kissing its pale cheek, she gave her hand to Sidney; and, followed by the good wishes of this grateful family, they entered their sleighs and were quickly whirled home.

Sidney, in spite of the din of the bells, found an opportunity to say to Annie, "What pleasure can be compared to the bliss of such domestic confidence and affections as we have just witnessed. I am a thorough convert to the sentiments of the plowman bard.

'If happiness hae not her seat
And centre in the breast,
We may be wise, or rich, or great,
But never can be blest:
Nae treasures, nor pleasures
Could make us happy lang;
The *heart* aye's the part aye,
That makes us right or wrang.'"

Annie did not answer, but her audible sigh breathed warm on the cheek of Sidney, as his face nearly touched hers, listening for her reply, and assured him she approved, indeed reciprocated his feelings.

CHAPTER XXVI.

GOING ABROAD.

"My native land, good night."

CHILDE HAROLD.

THE term, four months, for which Sidney had engaged to teach the school, was now expired, and he closed with the love and approbation of both parents and scholars. Not a murmur against him had been heard excepting from one individual. This man, it seems, agreed to furnish wood for the school during the season, for a certain sum, and he now complained of the quantity consumed.

"There had been a confounded sight burned," he said, "and he hoped the committee would never employ another master who had been used to living in a warm climate; they were all as cold as frogs, and couldn't live here to the North, without their house was kept as warm as an oven."

But no notice was taken of his complainings, and the district unanimously voted to employ Sidney the following winter, if he should be disposed to engage. To this proposition he could not return a definite answer. He was yet in uncertainty respecting his own fate. Recent letters from Charleston destroyed the hopes he had entertained of receiving at least a small sum of surplus money from the sale of his uncle's plantation; while they also expressly stated Cox could not be discovered. A return to Charleston, therefore, was not to be contemplated.

He was impatient for letters from England, not that he really wished to embark for that country; he now felt that to leave Annie would require as great an exertion of self-denial as he had practiced when resigning his hopes of obtaining Zemira; but as he knew not what plan to pursue, he was anxious for every item of information that would flatter him with the hope of success.

Sometimes he thought and talked seriously of commencing the study of physic, and he fancied Miss Redington listened well pleased to a scheme that would fix him near her. Then came the recollection of the long preparation requisite before he could commence business, and the strict application necessary to insure success, and how long he must struggle with poverty, never, perhaps, to be surmounted.

These were painful reflections to one educated as he had been, in the lap of luxury; nor did the hope of being beloved by Annie at all allay his inquietude. She, too, had been accustomed to elegancies. O! could he only command such, how rapturous it would be to confer them on her, and meet her smile of gratitude when again raised to the rank for which nature seemingly designed her. But now to take advantage of her partiality, and urge her to share his poverty and dependence, honor, generosity, love forbade it.

He passed two or three weeks in such uncertainty of purpose and struggles of mind as made him exhibit more dejection of countenance and manner than he had ever before worn, and his mother was seriously alarmed, lest he was inclining to a consumption, when the long wished for packet from England arrived, and opened once more a prospect of success and prosperity.

Mr. Frankford's offers exceeded in generosity anything Sidney had ever anticipated. After declaring he could not regret his friend Romilly's misfortunes, as they promised to afford him the satisfaction of displaying his gratitude, he bade his preserver welcome to share his fortune; but fearing his independent mind would revolt at receiving charity, he considerately stated an offer of a certain situation he had reserved for Sidney, which would insure him competence and respect, and he conjured him to embark immediately for London.

He also sent, with his cordial love, some small token of affectionate remembrance to each member of the Romilly family; but Sophia's, a beautiful string of pearls, was far the most costly and elegant.

Sidney, while perusing the letters, turned so pale that his father apprehended unpleasant intelligence; but after ascertaining the contents, he easily divined the agitation of his son arose from the necessity he found there was of relinquishing either his love or his ambition.

Squire Romilly was a man of kind feelings, and he prized the dear domestic affections and tranquil happiness of home as more inestimable than the treasures of Ophir; but he knew his son had been differently educated; he knew that riches and rank were essential to his felicity; and feared that should he now yield to his passion for Annie and forego for her the offers of Mr. Frankford, he would in a short time regret it as folly, while the obstacles to his advancement would then be insurmountable. But should he now depart and secure the smiles of fortune, and his love endure the test of absence—a severe trial of the affections—he might renew his intercourse with the lady at some more auspicious period. He therefore seriously, and even strenuously advised Sidney's acceptance of the Englishman's offers.

Mrs. Romilly wept at the thought of her child's departure, and going, too, such a vast distance, and across the boisterous ocean, but to the arguments and reasons of her husband, she yielded without clamorous opposition; and the voyage was in a short time fully determined upon.

It was now a question with our hero, whether he should, before his departure, declare his love to Miss Redington, and bind her by a promise to be his when he could return to claim her, or whether to delay expressing his sentiments till he reached his destination, and discovered what expectations of ultimate success he might rationally form. There were good reasons for both plans, but finally, after all his studying, he was, as men often are, compelled by incidents he could not control, to adopt a different course from the one he really intended.

When Annie learned his intention of departing in a few days, her mind suffered the most cruel agitation and disappointment. She felt what had been hitherto unknown to herself, the deep strength of her affection for him—an affection she had incautiously cherished, at first under the name of admiration of his talents and accomplishments, and then of sympathy for his misfortunes, or esteem for his virtues. But the certainty of a separation at once betrayed the tenderness of her feelings and the truth of her love; and in the hopelessness of her heart she accused Sidney of dissimulation and cruelty, in thus winning her affections and then leaving her to regret.

A little reflection, however, made her exculpate him; he had never adopted the language of a lover, though some of his compliments had been more ardent than mere friendship usually dictates; but she had misinterpreted his meaning—he was only, what he had professed himself, her friend; and there came such an humiliating sense of her own weakness, in thus indulging a partiality for a man who was, probably, totally indifferent to her, that she wept with vexation and shame, and firmly resolved never to see or speak with him again.

But lest such a proceeding might be noticed and excite inquiries she felt unable to satisfy or evade, she finally concluded to see him as little as possible, and on no account to allow him a moment's separate conversation, lest she should betray to him her emotions. Therefore, when Sidney called at her uncle's, which he did often, she was always engaged except when the whole family was present, and thus the time passed till the evening preceding the day fixed for his departure, and he had not spoken one word to Annie on a subject that occupied, at least, half his thoughts.

On that evening he repaired to the deacon's, determining to come to an explanation, for the nearer the time came for his journey, the dearer Annie appeared, and he felt an expression of her love and promise of her constancy, were indispensable to his enjoying peace of mind during his absence.

But when he arrived at the house he found her engaged in conversation with George Cranfield, apparently very willing to receive his attentions; and her affability to George, and reserve or even coldness to Sidney was so apparent, that the latter, indignant at what he thought unpardonable coquetry, for he was confident she must know his affection for her and certainly had given him encouragement to hope it was returned, addressed but little conversation to her, or indeed to any one, and soon rose to depart.

He was now to bid farewell.

The old deacon took his hand and made a long harangue, in which he failed not to bestow advice and warning and exhortation; his wife then offered her sincere and benevolent prayers for his present and future happiness. Silas said he would not bid "good bye" now—he would see him again the next morning; Priscilla's soft blue eyes swam in tears while she whispered "farewell" to her brother-in-law, and George Cranfield proffered his hand with frank and hearty wishes for the success of his friend—wishes certainly not the less sincere that their realization would detain Sidney in a foreign land.

Who could blame him when such a prize as Annie was hazarded, if not lost, should he stay much longer in New England?

Miss Redington sat last in the circle. Sidney paused a moment before her as she rose gracefully from her seat, and, without raising her eyes, extended her hand to his. It trembled like an aspen in his grasp, and her cheek was white as snow, but she spoke "farewell, Mr. Romilly," with a calm, steady voice, and when she looked up, the only form she wished to see was just quitting the apartment. She left it almost immediately; she had overacted her part, and felt wretched when reflecting he would probably accuse her of caprice, despise her for her inconsistency, and banish her from his memory.

George Cranfield went home sighing, both for himself and Annie. He saw she loved Sidney, and thought her affection unreturned; and he knew the sorrow of hopeless love.

Neither were Sidney's reflections of a much more serene character. His anger, however, soon subsided, and he imputed Annie's apparent indifference to her exertions to prevent a display of feeling which might have been suspected as favoring him; and this conclusion, which he drew while leaning from his window and gazing on the still landscape, now tranquilly sleeping in the soft rays of the moon, for a moment subdued his resolution, and he hesitated whether to undertake his journey. He was leaving the calm, certain enjoyments of sequestered life, to engage in the tumultuous scenes of a flattering but heartless world.

He gazed on the distant mountains, whose shadowy outline was just visible in the horizon, and he could trace the course of the stream by the wreath of light vapor that rested on its surface, looking in the calm moon beams like a soft pillow spread invitingly for the weary children of sorrow to come and sink to repose.

It was a delicious spring evening; and the young buds then swelling beneath the influence of the genial dews, would soon expand in beauty, the sweet flowers would come forth, but his eyes would not greet them; he would be far away—and would Annie, while straying through those fields, and reposing in those groves, ever wish him near her to twine a garland for her fair brow, or quote a sentiment expressive of the sensations of her heart?

He hoped it, and yet there were remembrances that convinced him a change in his own wishes might occur, and why not in hers? He had loved before, and yet had found it necessary and practicable to conquer his passion; and circumstances might soon arise which would render a connexion with Miss Redington incompatible with his duty, and, in the nature of things, impossible.

When reflecting thus he rejoiced there had not been a solemn engagement between them. If Annie really loved him, absence would increase her affection—it always did that of a true woman—and when he knew what his destiny was to be, he would write to her and his friends.

With such anticipations for the future, he at length reconciled himself with the present, and retired to bed beneath a roof which the morning sun would see him quitting, perhaps, forever.

CHAPTER XXVII.

DEATH OF A GOOD MAN.

The chamber where the good man meets his fate
Is privileged beyond the common walk
Of virtuous life, quite in the verge of heaven.
His comforters he comforts; great in ruin,
With unreluctant grandeur gives, not yields,
His soul sublime, and closes with his fate.

YOUNG.

SIDNEY slept till a late hour on the following morning, and was at length wakened from his heavy and somewhat perturbed slumbers, by a sound which he at first imagined to be a shriek; but listening a moment and hearing no further noise, he concluded it was the coinage of his own disturbed brain; and therefore again laid his head on the pillow, thinking before he rose he would arrange in his own mind the proceedings for the day, and summon fortitude to support his spirits in what might possibly be an eternal separation from his friends.

His friends—at that thought his fancy rested on Annie. He had bidden her adieu, but might he not call again, tempted by the beauty of the morning to a walk? He had not decided, when a loud and yet louder bustle below stairs made him again start to listen. He now plainly distinguished groans, and voices apparently in agony.

"What has happened?" said he, as his door was thrown open with violence by little Harvey, who, with pale face, eyes staring, and limbs trembling, stammered out, "Oh! Sidney, come down, come down, pa' is dying!"

"Dying!" repeated Sidney, springing from his bed and seizing his clothes, "what—how—what ails him?—is he sick?"

"He's killed!" shrieked the child in an agony of grief, that now, for the first time, found vent in tears. "He'll die! he'll die! and who will take care of me?"

"I—I will," said Sidney; "don't cry, Harvey," and the tears stood in his own eyes.

"But you are going away," said the child; "oh! Sidney, don't go!"—and he was proceeding to urge his stay, when the voice of their mother, calling on Sidney to come down, silenced, in Harvey's mind, every thought except of his father's danger, and he flew down stairs with the quickness of thought.

Sidney followed him in trepidation, and on entering the sitting-room, saw at once the confirmation of his worst fears. His father, covered with blood, and apparently nearly exhausted, was extended on the couch; around him stood his terrified, horror-struck children. His wife, although ready to faint with grief and terror, was bathing his temples, and endeavoring to hope he might yet be spared to their prayers and exertions. As Sidney, awed and silent, advanced to the couch, his father opened his eyes and endeavored to stretch forth his hand, while he *faintly said,—"My son, you must delay your journey for* the present—I am taking my departure before you. I am going to my long home—a journey I shall never tread back."

He paused, while his wife's tears fell fast on the hand she held in hers; and Sidney hastily inquired why they did not send for a surgeon?

"We expect Perkins every minute," said one.

"And he is coming now," said another.

"But he cannot save me," replied the dying man. "My bounds are set, and I have just reached the goal. I feel it;—I should—for my family's sake—have been glad

—to have lived—a little longer. But God's will be done. I am resigned to die."

The Doctor entered.

The apathy which familiarity with scenes of suffering and danger creates in the minds of those accustomed to wrestle with disease, and watch the approach of the king of terrors under every appalling form, was conquered when Perkins beheld that good and benevolent man, in whom every child of sorrow and trouble found a counselor and friend, now stretched on a bed of suffering, and read in the contraction of his features, and the ghastly appearance of his countenance, the probable issue of his misfortunes.

But his concern, although evincing itself by a half smothered groan and quick change of color, was not of a kind to induce despair or inactivity. He made immediate preparations for an examination of the wound, which Sidney now learned had been occasioned by his father's being thrown from his wagon while descending a steep hill about half a mile north of the village. He had been abroad at an early hour, on business, and was hurrying to reach home, on Sidney's account, that he might spend a little time with him before his departure, when his horse, while trotting very fast, chanced to step on a rolling stone, lost his footing and fell headlong, and the bolt that confined the wagon being forced out by the violence of the shock, Squire Romilly, with the body of the vehicle, was precipitated down a steep bank, and thrown on a sharp stick or root of a sapling that protruded near a foot above ground. The stick entered his back, just below his left shoulder, and it was probable had penetrated some vital part.

Fortunately, two pedestrians were descending the hill at the same instant; they saw the accident and hastened to offer assistance, raised the nearly inanimate body, staunched the bleeding wound, and the wagon, which had not been broken, being prepared, he was laid in it, supported by one man while the other led the horse, and thus brought back to the home he had lately left in health and cheerfulness.

Dr. Perkins requested the family would withdraw while he made the examination, fearing a sight of the wound and blood would draw forth lamentations augmenting the distress of the wounded man. The children all obeyed. Squire Romilly looked on his wife.

"I shall not leave you," said she, calmly.

"But you must," he replied; "it will overcome you. Go, Sidney, go and support your mother."

"My husband," she replied earnestly, "you must not bid me go; I cannot leave you. I shall not faint; I can endure anything better than to know you are suffering, and I am not by to watch over and relieve you. And it is my duty," she continued, seeing him about to speak, "and if you do not wish to make me miserable, you will not drive me from you."

There was no more said, and the doctor proceeded to examine the wound.

Mrs. Romilly appeared during the whole process with astonishing composure; she prepared the lint and bandages, watched every change in her husband's countenance, and administered cordials to support him, and it was not till from the agitated manner of Dr. Perkins she became convinced he thought the wound a mortal one, that her fortitude forsook her. She gazed on her husband, then turned her eyes on the doctor. Sidney saw her agony, and sprung to her support, but she fell senseless before he could reach her.

"My poor wife," said the Squire feebly, as Sidney bore her from the apartment. "My children, where are they? Death is coming like an armed man, and I would say a few words—my lips will soon be closed forever."

The doctor entreated him to be composed.

"You cannot give me any hope of life," said the wounded man; "and if you did, my own feelings would contradict your words. It is no time for deception—my race is run. Call my children, then, that I may give them my last advice—my dying blessing."

The doctor could no longer oppose it; from the symptoms he was convinced his recovery was impossible; indeed he thought his dissolution very near, and that to deprive him of the opportunity of bidding his family farewell, would be cruelty.

The news of this fatal accident had circulated through the village. Squire Romilly and his family were universally beloved and respected, and the sympathy which spontaneously burst forth on hearing the distressing tidings was sincere.

The Rev. Mr. Cranfield was one of the first who reached the house of sorrow. It was his office to comfort the afflicted; but his compassion needed not the spur of duty. His flock were his children; he felt all their calamities, and to comfort the mourners and bind the broken heart was not with him an artifice to gain popularity. Not that he might boast of his faithfulness, or complain of the pressure of his parochial duties; but he came to the bedside of the sufferer to assuage pain, strengthen hope, teach submission, and to prepare the dying for that world, where he hoped and prayed to meet all his congregation; while with the fondness of a parent bird, he

"Allured to brighter worlds, and led the way."

Mrs. Romilly engaged his first attention. He consoled her grief, he calmed her agitation; not by telling her of the uselessness of sorrow, and illustrating it by referring to the sovereign power of that Being who "killeth and maketh alive at his own good pleasure." No: he spake of the piety of her husband, of his fitness for the great change, of the glory and happiness awaiting him, of the infinite gain when leaving a world of change and sorrow for one of secure and unfading bliss, and of their reunion so shortly to occur. Why should a christian shrink at death? It is because faith is weak, and cannot look within the veil. Who can grasp the infinite, or comprehend the mysteries of that world which no created eye hath seen?

When Mr. Cranfield had, in some degree, succeeded in

calming the first torrent of grief which nearly overwhelmed this affectionate wife at the terrible certainty of being deprived of him who had been the light of her path, her guide and counselor and friend, Sidney informed her of his father's request to see them. She dried her tears, and endeavored by her composure to restore that of her children; and then, supported by Mr. Cranfield and her son, she again entered the apartment of death, followed by all her family.

Squire Romilly's countenance had undergone a great change. The severe pain which had, during the operation, distorted his manly features, was much abated; and something that at first had appeared like impatience or anxiety, was wholly past. All was now faith, hope and peace.

His high and expanded forehead, which time had but lightly touched, and where neither care nor grief had ever stamped a furrow, looked calm as a summer sunset; his dark expressive eyes were lighted up with the radiance of joy, so calm, so benign, that their glance spoke at once of heaven; and the smile of benevolence and love hovered on his parted lips, as if the dear affections and kind feelings he had cherished on earth were rendered dearer and kinder by the purity of the region which his spirit could even now anticipate.

Mr. Cranfield looked; and that look sufficed at once to inform him of the situation of his dying brother. Hope had till then whispered that he might be saved; and he entered the room with a secret belief of being able to impart the same confidence to the sorrowing family. But now he could only press the hand of the sufferer, and silently ejaculate—"God, thy will be done!"

Squire Romilly was the first to break the impressive silence. He cast his eyes around and saw those he most loved were all assembled. They surrounded the bed. The whole apartment was now nearly filled by the sympathizing neighbors, who came silently in awe and grief. The doctor, with a face of anxiety, leaned at the foot of the bed, steadfastly watching every symptom of change in his patient, and studying if there were any further means he might attempt for his preservation; but the dejection that clouded his usually gay countenance, declared he had no hope.

"You have come," said the Squire, addressing his pastor in his own mellow and placid tones, "you have come to witness my death, or rather my entrance on eternal life. A short, a very short time, and I shall be admitted to the society of the blessed. I know in whom I have believed," continued he, elevating his voice, and grasping closer the hand that rested in his—"I feel an assurance of heaven—and would my beloved wife, and these dear children but acquiesce in the dispensation of Providence, would they resign me without tears or murmurs—oh! how willingly, how joyfully should I, at this moment, yield my breath!"

He paused, and clasped his wife's trembling hand—the sobs and sighs of the children became audible; while the deep commiseration of the spectators evinced itself in that profound silence, maintained to prevent the expression of feelings which might augment the grief it would strive to tranquilize. Many shaded their faces, and many a heart-breathed prayer ascended to supplicate for his recovery, or, (and their tears flowed while anticipating such an event probable) if that could not be, that the immortal soul might be received to mansions of glory. Ah! the sight of death makes the spirit eloquent. Many prayed there who never prayed before.

Squire Romilly resumed. "I could have wished for a little space to have arranged some affairs, that I must now leave unsettled. The world still clings to the heart of the husband and father; but the Christian"—and his eye beamed upward with angelic lustre—"the Christian can trust in God. To his care I resign thee, my wife, my best beloved;—trust in Him and you will need no other protector. And, my dear children, if you have ever loved your father, I charge you to honor his memory by obeying and cherishing your mother, and living in peace among yourselves; Grave it on your hearts to treat all with whom you have intercourse as you wish to be treated. That is a rule you may always follow; a principle you can always apply; a command of God which if you do, in heart, and spirit and action obey, you may be certain of happiness, of eternal blessedness. O! it is not professions—I have been a professor these twenty-five years; but that recollection is of small importance compared with the thought that I have, to the best of my ability, endeavored to perform what appeared to be my duty in the several relations in which I have been placed. Yet do not mistake me—I plead no merits of my own; —I have done no more than my duty—nay, I have often come short—and I rely entirely on the mercy of my Redeemer for pardon and salvation. But I feel a sweet assurance of acceptance in his sight; and I feel a serenity while reflecting on a life spent in endeavors to serve Him and promote the happiness of my fellow creatures. O! the wealth of the whole world could not impart such consolation!"

Here a faintness came over him, and for several minutes they thought him expiring. The wild grief of the younger children, who were witnessing this awful scene, is indescribable; and their cries and sobs became so agitated that not a person in the room could refrain from tears.

"My dear, dear father!" shrieked the little girls, while Harvey, without uttering a word, clasped his neck, and kissing repeatedly the pale face he loved more than all the world, sunk nearly insensible on his bosom.

Mrs. Romilly had been lifting her soul to God in mental prayer for strength and resignation to endure what His will appointed her; but the sight of her children's grief overcame her anew; and for a little time such a loud wailing was heard as is only called forth when the spirit is broken with anguish, and wholly subdued by the suddenness and intensity of its sufferings.

The soul of the dying saint seemed arrested in its flight. Making a strong effort, he again looked around; a smile so sweet, so animated, lighted up his features, that in spite of their ghastly whiteness, those who gazed almost fancied he was reviving to life. He laid his hand on the head of Harvey.

"God bless you, my darling boy—my wife, my children, give me your hands once more;—there—Father in heaven, protect and bless them. You must not mourn thus for me—O that you did but know what joy, what unspeakable rapture is mine!—then your lamentations would be turned to songs. I see my Redeemer—he is extending his arms to receive me! Farewell, my wife! —Sidney, be a father to these little ones, and protect your mother. O Jesus! I come, I come. Farewell, earth; welcome, welcome heaven!"—and he expired!

* * * * * * * * *

"Pray how is the Squire now?" said Deacon Jones, with an impatient tone, as he came puffing up to the door where Doctor Perkins had retreated to conceal his emotion.

"He—he is gone forever," replied the doctor, taking his handkerchief from his eyes.

"Dead!" exclaimed the old deacon, with a convulsive start.

"Yes, he is."

"Dead! do you say," and he twisted his face into a variety of strange contortions, intending to express grief, while he looked on the doctor's manly face all bathed in tears. But tears were a melting of the soul in which the deacon had seldom indulged, and not a drop could he make start.

"Well now, I did'nt think of finding him dead. I have been up to Jerry Sprague's this morning to get him to come and kill a calf. He is the best hand I know of; and when I come home my woman told what had happened, and I started right off—hem! I have come so fast I can hardly breathe—hem. How did the Squire die? easy?"

"As easy as an infant falls asleep," replied Perkins.

"O! I don't mean his bodily pain. How was his mind composed?" inquired the deacon, eagerly.

"As heaven: if there ever were a saint he was one."

"Well, well, I hope he was," replied the deacon, with

a shrug; "but there was a few questions I should liked to have asked him before he died. He was a good man—but on some points a little too lax—hardly what you might call orthodox in principles."

"I don't know to what principles you allude," said the doctor, warmly; "but I do know there never was a more upright man, nor one who more scrupulously performed all his duties, than the Squire. If such as he are not admitted to heaven, I should doubt whether any would be. He lived like a Christian, and had you witnessed his death, you would have acknowledged he died like one."

"O! well," replied the other, "I'm glad on't; but I do wish I'd been here a little sooner, just for my own satisfaction."

"If you could feel dissatisfied with his life," observed the doctor, drily, "you would not probably have been more charitably disposed by what he said at his death."

"Why, yes I might," replied the pertinacious deacon: "I don't hold moral actions to be a sufficient evidence of grace in the heart. We must, doctor, be sound in doctrine. We must hold fast the faith once delivered to the saints, before we can feel assured of the pardon of our sins. And those who are thus rooted and grounded in the truth certainly live a life of godliness, for, saith the Savior, 'If any man will do his will, he shall know of the doctrine.'"

"But they must *do* the *will*, before they are to *know* of the *doctrine*," returned the doctor; "and so, according to your own principles, *practice* must precede *faith*. Or, in other terms, let a man talk as long and loudly as he pleases about conversions, and confessions, and creeds, yet, if he do not perform the requisites of a Christian, if he do not 'deal justly, love mercy, and walk humbly with God,' we have not the least reason to credit his assertions of his own superior sanctity, or believe him elected to be an heir of eternal salvation."

The deacon's little grey eyes flashed forth the holy indignation of his spirit at hearing these Arminian heresies; but Warren Perkins was an obstinate fellow, and one whom he did not like to provoke to argument; so he settled his lank visage with a most determined and dolorous expression of sadness, and walked forward to enjoy the spectacle of mortality, and impart his ghostly comfort and advice to the bereaved family within.

"I would," said Perkins, walking hastily along the avenue, and flourishing his handkerchief as if in derision of his adversary,—"I would, as a nostrum to fit me for heaven, give more for a single grain of Squire Romilly's *practice*, than I would for a pound of the deacon's *faith*."

CHAPTER XXVIII.

A COUNTRY FUNERAL.

But I have that within, which passeth show;
These, but the trappings and the suits of wo.

HAMLET.

THE death of Squire Romilly occurred on Tuesday morning, and the funeral was appointed to be observed on the Thursday afternoon following. The interval was not so long, perhaps, as is allowed in some countries, but is assuredly sufficient to testify respect to the dead or insure safety to the living.

The time was spent in preparing for the solemnity; as a full suit of mourning apparel, and every requisite which can be supposed to express the grief such an occasion should call forth, is seldom omitted by the Yankees. But with the present afflicted family it was not a *seeming* show; they needed no "inky cloaks" to tell of the sorrow that was weighing down their almost broken hearts in the dust, and which would totally have unfitted them for the necessary preparation, had not their kind neighbors assisted them to the utmost.

Everything which could be devised to express regard for the virtues of the deceased or commiseration for the mourning relatives, was performed by this compassionate and friendly people. The services were all voluntary and gratuitous. There are no undertaker's men necessary, nor are the funeral expenses of much consequence—nothing but the coffin is to be procured; the hearse and grave are provided at the expense of the town, and every other service is rendered by neighborly affection.

The women and girls in the village came and arranged the house, prepared the mourning apparel, and endeavored to anticipate or fulfil every wish Mrs. Romilly could have breathed. And yet all was done in quietness and decorum; not a smile was seen, nor was scarcely a loud word spoken in the house of wo. All felt and sympathized in the affliction of this worthy family, and joined in deploring their loss.

Goodness may live without exciting uncommon regard—it may even meet with ingratitude, and be treated with neglect; but when death selects such characters for his victims, their worth is instantly acknowledged, and they are praised with sincerity by the living when it can be done without envy or self-reproach.

Thursday morning came, one of those soft, sunny May mornings, when spring, breathing her sweet influence over the earth, disposes all nature to love and gayety and happiness.

Sidney walked forth to try whether the calm and enjoyment abroad might not tranquilize his tossed mind, and restore his composure, before engaging in the melancholy solemnities which duty demanded. Everything around was breathing of life and hope. The birds from the thickets, or while winnowing the calm blue air, poured forth their songs of gladness; and what can be more expressive of gladness than their spring notes, when they lift up their voices in concert, to rejoice that the winter is past and gone?

O, I never listen to their exulting strains without a feeling of gratitude to the good and glorious Being who hath formed all creatures capable of enjoying happiness.

Spring is the season of happiness for all, and Sidney saw the young lambs and cattle gamboling over the fields; even the green trees and shrubs looked joyful, as their young, fresh leaves and buds quivered in the breeze that came with such gentle breathings that but for their motion it would have been imperceptible. But his heart was sick within him, and his fancy could not dwell on the calm of nature he witnessed abroad, for he contrasted it with the sorrow which had entered the abode of his father. Spring could not wake its inmates to gladness; the morning of their year had been darkened by an awful calamity—the storm had swept, the sheltering tree had been prostrated, and dear affections were sundered, and fond hopes crushed, and warm expectations blighted.

Such were Sidney's reflections, as he pursued his way along the banks of the stream where he had walked with his father and Frankford, endeavoring to reason and conclude what course he ought to pursue. He could not endure the thought of leaving his mother while thus overwhelmed with grief, and saw he must, for the present, suspend his intention of going abroad; indeed, from his father's last expressions he could not but infer he wished him to continue at home. Yet how could he, without sacrificing every hope of success, and every aspiring of ambition.

His father had left no will, and after the allowance of the widow's right of dower, a division of the remainder of the estate among the children would give but a small share to each individual. And even this share Sidney did not feel it honorable to accept. He had never assisted his parents, and he knew, in permitting his residence with his uncle, they expected to have secured him an inheritance far beyond what their other children would have enjoyed. He had been disappointed, but not by any fault or miscalculation of his family; and he could not but consider it unjust now to exert a claim which would diminish the small dividends of his brothers and sisters.

Perhaps there are economists who would have censured his scruples, and told him he was too regardless of small gains, and that the most useful lesson he could learn would be, that farthings formed pounds, and mills dollars. But such persons will never be corrupted by his example, for they have not souls to understand his character. He was generous, perhaps, even to excess; still he was never extravagant or improvident in his own expenditure; and the keenest mortification he had yet experienced from the loss of his property was nothing so severe, as was now the thought that he could no longer exercise his beneficence. How he wished he had his estate, that he might provide for his dear, afflicted family! His mother should possess everything she could desire—his sisters should be educated and dressed like ladies. Silas was amply provided for, but he should have something as a remembrance; James should be a physician, he had not the health to labor; Sam and Oliver might, when they arrived at a proper age, share the farm between them; and Harvey, "ah! Harvey," exclaimed he aloud, "I will always keep him with me."

The earnestness with which he pronounced the last words broke his reverie, and he could not forbear smiling at the absurdity of thus bestowing ideal riches on others, when he could not provide necessaries for himself. Sadder thoughts, and images of cold reality soon arose, and throwing himself on the turf, exactly opposite the place in the stream where he had once so narrowly escaped drowning, he melted into tears while he sighed in bitterness.

"I am nothing, for I can do nothing; I am neither educated for a profession, nor have I habits of industry to gain a subsistence by labor—and he is wretched indeed, who, depending on his fortune alone for support and a favorable reception in the world, finds that resource suddenly and unexpectedly withdrawn. O! how I wish I had perished here—here in this calm stream, instead of living to weep the loss of my dearest friends, and endure the miseries of a life of dependence."

As he lay thus agitated by a whirl of contending thoughts, now hoping with all the ardor of youth, and now abandoned to wild despair, the violence of his emotions at length exhausted him, and he insensibly yielded to repose. He slept heavily, and his dreams were confused and terrific. Many changes came over his visions, but all were indistinct or disjointed; now the dying words of his father seemed repeated—then his uncle's form stood before him—and next he was bidding farewell to his friends and departing on a journey whence he was never to return.

At last he thought he was standing on the spot where he then lay, and gazing on the stream which appeared whirling and agitated as if some substance had just been dashed into its waters. Presently a child rose to the surface and sent forth a terrifying shriek. Sidney sprung to save it, but found himself rooted to the ground.

The child sunk—then rose again—another shriek, but fainter, it was almost spent;—how he strove to rescue it, and could not move one finger. It sunk again. "O God!" cried he, in an agony, "should it rise again, I must save it."

It did rise, and he saw it gasp—quiver—'tis gone!

No, a man burst through the thicket, and plunged into the stream—he has caught the child—he has reached the shore—he presses the little sufferer to his bosom! Sidney looked up in an ecstacy of joy to thank that generous man, and beheld his father!

"My son," said he, mildly, but most impressively; "it was thus I snatched you from death, and I then besought my God, that the life so preserved might be devoted to Him! I could only pray for such a consummation—you can accomplish it. Wisdom is not shown in repining at the past, or in planning for the future; but in improving the present. I know the difficulties sur rounding you; but I also know that energy and perse verance will overcome them. But remember, Sidney, whatever sacrifices it may cost you, and do your *duty;* then may you expect happiness. And you will be happy, happier than you now dare hope, happier than I now dare reveal; for were we sure of obtaining the reward, one of the most powerful motives for human exertion would be rendered nugatory. Think not that to give money is the only way in which you can express your generosity, or confer favors on your friends. Your time, your tenderness, your love, are treasures more valuable than the mines of Mexico ever produced. In short, let your heart and not your purse be the object of your solicitude. The bad may be rich, the good only can be happy."

As he ceased a strain of music stole by, so soft, sweet, and ravishing, that, uttering an exclamation of rapture, Sidney started from the ground, and gazed wildly around, expecting to see his father, and hardly doubting but he yet heard his voice.

"It was nothing but a dream after all," said he; yet so powerful was the impression of the scene on his mind that it was long before he could convince himself it was but a dream. "I will stay with my mother for the present," he continued, as he walked towards the house, "and I will stay cheerfully, and endeavor to assist her without a single murmur at my altered fortune."

The funeral services of the deceased were to be performed in the meeting house, as the numbers expected to attend would be greater than could conveniently be accommodated at his late dwelling.

A funeral in the country towns of New England usually attracts all who can possibly leave their business; it being considered a duty thus to evince their respect for the memory of the dead, and testify their sympathy with the sorrows of the mourners. The inhabitants of the village, and indeed of many neighboring towns, first assembled at the house of the deceased, where a fervent, solemn, and pathetic prayer was offered by the reverend pastor. The coffin was then placed on a hearse, and attended by six of the most respectable church members as pall-bearers, and followed by a procession consisting of the mourning relatives, then the members of the church and society, next of the elderly part of the assembly, and lastly the youth and children, was carried to the meeting-house; and there, being taken from the hearse by the pall-bearers, it was borne into the place of worship, and set down in the space before the pulpit.

The mourners were respectfully seated in pews as near it as possible, and the whole congregation having taken their seats, Mr. Cranfield arose, and after again invoking the compassionate regard of a God who doth not willingly afflict, he proceeded to the sermon. In a discourse from the text, "*The memory of the just is blessed*," he set forth the virtues of the deceased, and the certainty of blessedness to such humble and heavenly piety. At the conclusion he pathetically addressed the widow and children, suggesting so many reasons for their rejoicing, even under the severe bereavement they had suffered, and so many considerations which ought to reconcile them to the dispensations of Providence, that Mrs. Romilly, although she wept unceasingly during the whole service, was all the time resolving to repine no more.

When the service was concluded, the coffin was carried forth and placed on a bier, standing on the green before the church. Here repaired all who wished to look upon the face of him they were soon to behold no more.

There was a marshal appointed to order the procession, and superintend the proceedings; all were satisfied with the arrangements except Deacon Jones. He could not forbear secretly lamenting that his connexion with the Romilly family, in consequence of the marriage of Silas with his daughter, rendered it fitting he should take his seat with the mourners, otherwise he might have had an opportunity of securing the marshal's office to himself.

The mourners at length came forth to take their last farewell of the remains of their beloved and tender friend. Sidney supported his mother, and the others followed and circled around the bier.

Where is the person who can witness, unmoved, the sorrow of the widow and the fatherless, when their crushed hearts are pouring forth the bitter tears of the final separation? Those who do not pity them can hardly claim to be allied to humanity. The mourners gazed long, and wept in silence. There was no loud murmuring, no passionate exclamation; all was the solemn stillness of deep, sacred and resigned grief; sorrowing, yet not despairing: grieving for the wound, yet adoring the Being who had inflicted it.

"Dust to dust" is the sentence pronounced against all the children of men. It will be executed. Beauty and talents, riches and power, wisdom and majesty, all, all lie down beneath the clods of the valley. No one can escape; nor can subterfuge, or entreaty, or artifice, evade or delay the doom.

Look on that clay; it was but now inhabited by a noble spirit; it lived, it acted—ye saw its smile, ye heard its voice;—where has that spirit fled?

Could that question be truly answered, death would no longer be the king of terrors. It is the uncertainty, the darkness and doubt and shadows resting upon it that make the terrible in death. Yet who could gaze on that serene, manly countenance, so pale and so tranquil, and not feel the grave was a safe retreat from the storms of life—a resting place for the weary, a refuge for the oppressed, a place of repose, of sanctity and security?

The coffin was at length closed and borne to the church-yard, the procession still following; but when the coffin had been deposited in the earth, the family withdrew, as it was believed Mrs. Romilly would be too much agitated should she await the filling up of the grave.

Deacon Jones, however, remained behind to make the speech; after the officious assembly had, by taking turns, filled the grave, and laid the turf, he took off his hat, and his example being imitated by all the by-standers, he returned them, in behalf of the afflicted family, his sincere thanks for the assistance rendered on the melancholy occasion; and all then departed to their respective homes, musing on the solemn scene they had witnessed, or conversing on the merits of the deceased, and on the probable consequences that must ensue to his wife and children.

Most of the speakers joined in opinion that Sidney would still adhere to his plan of going abroad, as he could not, should he stay, be of much service to his family, not having been bred to labor; but Mr. Merrill, who happened to overhear the conversation, instantly put his veto on the matter without qualification.

"He'll not go, faith," said he; "I can tell you so much. Sidney has too kind a heart to leave his poor mother in her troubles. And what if he don't know how to work quite so well, he can oversee the boys; and while I can lift a scythe or a sickle, I'll lend him a hand in haying and harvesting with all my heart."

"And so would I," said one, "only I should be plaguey 'fraid he'd think he was driving his negroes again. Deacon Jones says he don't doubt but all Mr. Sidney's losses of property, and these troubles are a judgment from heaven, because his father allowed him to go and be a partaker in the sin of slavery, that abomination of the South."

"Deacon Jones," replied Merrill, in a very exalted tone, "had better clear his own eyes of the beam, before he pulls the mote out of his neighbor's eye. Squire Romilly was a saint on earth, and he is now a saint in heaven, and that is a place I guess the deacon will find it pretty hard to get to. But I don't mean to judge him, though I do think money is the god he has always worshiped yet."

"You speak your mind pretty freely, I think," replied the other.

"I tell the truth," retorted Merrill, "and that is more than Deacon Jones always does. I could tell of some of his tricks if I'd a mind; and faith I would, if I handn't promised the poor Squire not to mention it. I 'spose he wanted to keep the deacon's character as fair as possible after they were connected."

This intimation of a secret which would affect the deacon's character, awakened the curiosity of the man whom Merrill was addressing, and he exerted all his eloquence to persuade him to reveal it, and to prove that the information would be perfectly safe with him.

But Merrill was staunch to his word, and fearful of offending Sidney, whom he adored, and nothing further could be elicited from him concerning the affair.

CHAPTER XXIX.

THE DIGNITY OF LABOR.

Oh, friendly to the best pursuits of man,
Friendly to thought, to virtue, and to peace,
Domestic life in rural labor passed.

COWPER.

AMONG the crowded assembly who had witnessed the interment, perhaps there was no one who retired with such mingled sensations of sympathy and anxiety as did Annie Redington. She had not since the death of the Squire, repaired to the house of sorrow to offer assistance, for she felt unequal to endure the scene in the presence of Sidney; but she had made various articles of the mourning apparel for the family, and her reiterated and eager inquiries concerning them discovered the strong interest she felt for their situation, and her restless eye and colorless cheek betrayed the mental anxiety her heart was suffering.

The event which had cast a gloom over even the most thoughtless ones in the village, was peculiarly calculated to excite Annie's sensibility. Her mother had often described to her, most pathetically, the scenes which followed the death of her own father. The cold courtesies of those gay acquaintances, who, like swallows at the approach of winter, instinctively fly those who are threatened with adversity; the rapacity of the ruthless creditors, bringing forward every claim which ingenuity or fraud could bring to bear on the insolvent estate; the seizure and sale of the property, even those articles which dear associations rendered almost sacred;—all dispersed, sacrificed, and the unfeeling world looking on with apathy or exultation.

Ah, these were arrows whose barbs could never be withdrawn from the bleeding bosom of Mrs. Redington, and it is not strange she had imparted to the mind of her only child a shade of the deep anguish and sad forebodings their remembrance awakened!

Annie never could hear of the decease of a father, without instantly recurring to the misfortunes and privations the death of her own had caused, and weeping tears of pity and terror, lest the path of each fatherless child should be thorny as her own. But concern for the family of the Romillys was not now wholly unmingled with solicitude for herself. She could no longer disguise the interest Sidney had gained in her heart; and though pride and prudence, reason and delicacy, had all been summoned to aid her in the parting, which she strove to consider a final one, yet hope seldom entirely deserts our bosoms, and there had, in spite of all her struggles to overcome them, still been a secret belief that she should meet him again. In vain she endeavored to banish the idea; in vain her understanding told her it was weak and chimerical to expect that in the new and brilliant scenes to which he would be introduced, a remembrance of the lowly orphan, far, far distant, would dwell on his heart and influence him to return.

She loved—and when does hope vanish from the horizon of a true lover?

And Sidney had been detained, and she had seen him again—seen him piously performing his duty to the living and the dead. Never had he looked so interesting, so noble; never had she loved him with such fervent, confiding affection, as when she saw him stifling his own emotions, while he sedulously strove to calm the agitation of his mother, and watching over the little fatherless ones with all the tender solicitude of a parent.

"They cannot part with him," said she mentally; "he will not leave them!"

A blush warmed her cheek, her heart throbbed, and she pursued the subject no farther. She returned from the funeral in that state of anxious uncertainty, when hope and fear are so nearly balanced that the mind is only intent to gain evidence which may confirm its hopes or its fears, and impatiently awaited the return of her cousin, from whom she expected to learn something respecting the arrangements of Mrs. Romilly, and whether Sidney was still intending to prosecute his journey.

But Silas and his wife did not return till a late hour, and then exhausted by grief and fatigue, they scarcely spoke; the deacon and his wife had already withdrawn, and Annie dared not hazard a question on the subject nearest her heart, lest she should betray her own anxiety about an arrangement to which she wished to appear indifferent, and she saw them retire without ascertaining the future proceedings of Sidney.

When the family, the next morning, assembled at the breakfast hour—always an early one, as the deacon was fearful his workmen would lose time, and on that account he omitted family worship during the summer, except on Sabbath mornings—Silas was absent; Annie inquired the cause, and received for answer that he had gone to his mother's. "Some arrangements they have to make respecting Sidney," said the deacon, peevishly; "I wish they would let him go away—I don't see what good they expect from keeping such a gentleman to manage a farm."

Annie glanced at her uncle; his countenance was naturally ungracious, but she thought he now looked most enviously ugly; and yet his speech was music to her ear, for she had learned that Sidney's stay had been the subject of discussion, and long before the meal was finished—which certainly suffered no diminution on her account—she had settled that for his family to permit his departure was impossible.

The Romillys were all of her opinion. Sidney hardly knew why he was not sorry to be detained; but the secret was, his duty and inclination exactly coincided, and conjoined they easily overcame, though they could not entirely silence his ambition.

It was really a "heavy declension" for a young man, bred with the expectations, and accustomed to the ease and elegance he had been, at once to renounce all his towering hopes, and voluntarily lay his hand on the plow; and, at the age of twenty-four, resign himself, for life, to the retirement and occupation of a Yankee farmer. These were the dark shades of the picture. But then he would fulfil his father's injunctions, give joy to his mother's widowed heart, gratify his brothers and sisters, and "though last, not least," there arose the idea of Annie Redington—might not she be willing to relinquish the gay world and consent to share his retirement? He would then be satisfied his wife did not marry him because he was rich and distinguished; and the romance of love in a cottage was what he had always liked to contemplate; might he not at last realize it?

But these motives, or rather these thoughts, were confined to his own bosom. He told his mother, and sincerely too, that he would willingly relinquish all claim he might have to a share in his father's estate, and pursue his intention of going abroad if she would consent.

But this proposition she could by no means approve She had always been averse to the plan of a foreign destination, and would have seriously opposed it, had not her husband insisted that, considering all circumstances, he could devise nothing which promised so well for their favorite son; and his deliberate opinions were arguments she seldom attempted to controvert.

But he had, with his dying breath, expressed a different sentiment, and she would have deemed the infringement of his last injunctions almost a sacrilege. Still she knew the portion to which Sidney was, by law, entitled, was inadequate as a reward for the sacrifice he must make in foregoing all hopes of eminence by consenting to a residence in that secluded place; and she was meditating on the difficulty, when Silas approached to inform her he had been offering Sidney, if he would stay and reside on the farm, to relinquish all his claims on the estate, and James would do the same, provided he could have some assistance in boarding and clothing while pursuing the study of medicine, on which he was intending to enter, as his sickly habits made labor, for him, impracticable.

"And I tell brother Sidney," continued Silas, "he can portion off the girls when they are married, and put one of the little boys to a trade, and manage to pay all that will ever be required of him without selling much of the farm—one of the wood-lots, perhaps—but there is enough on the other to last these fifty years."

Mrs. Romilly doubtless thought fifty years was quite sufficient to anticipate the want of wood; if she did not, she was more provident than most of her countrymen appear to be; as the destruction and waste of fuel in the New England States cannot be accounted for on rational principles, and doubtless has proceeded from the conviction of their occupiers that the world would expire with themselves.

However, Mrs. Romilly declared herself well pleased with the generosity of her sons; and after a long consultation, and many protestations on the part of Sidney against his brothers' resigning to him their inheritance, they answered by declaring they considered it no sacrifice at all, if it would induce him to reside at home.

Everything was at last arranged apparently to the satisfaction of all parties that could have any interest in the decision—except the deacon. He protested in a most formal and spirited manner against the whole proceeding, as not only extremely absurb, but very detrimental to every individual.

He said it detained Sidney in an unprofitable calling, when his education qualified him to shine in a higher sphere, and make money in some easier way. And he thought the boys, under the superintendence of Silas, might manage better without him, as he never knew a man of learning good for anything when deprived of his books. Thus he advised Mrs. Romilly, and harangued Sidney, and lectured Silas; but all in vain—each one having determined on a course to pursue, his interference only served to confirm them more fully in the propriety of their arrangements by the arguments which they were thus compelled to advance in their justification. Silas knew, and his mother suspected that the motives of the deacon were entirely selfish. He had already more land than he could cultivate or superintend, but was not satisfied; and he calculated, if Sidney could be prevailed on to depart, Silas would eventually secure his father's estate.

The search after earthly happiness is not confined to the young and gay. The aged and the grave, those whose professions and callings would appear to place them above the temptations and vanities of the world, are often its most devoted slaves. It is not the love of pleasure, or the taste for amusements that most trammels the soul. Mammon was the lowest among the fallen angels—if Milton's authority may be trusted. The love of money is an insidious vice, for it often assumes the name and obtains the credit of a virtue. It is called prudence, foresight, economy, and good management. If property be obtained the end has sanctified the means; and the prosperous are deemed good, and the rich happy, or at least in a very desirable situation;—for what covering so effectually conceals faults and follies, as a mantle of gold?

But there is no vice more opposed to the benevolence and charity which the word of God represents as being indispensable to the christian character, than this worldly-mindedness.

"It is easier for a camel to go through the eye of a

needle than for a rich man to enter into the kingdom of heaven."

* * * * * *

Sidney was now, in all probability, permanently established; and the duties and labors consequent on his new vocation, gave him sufficient employment to occupy all his time, and consequently *ennui*, that demon of the idle, never approached to torment him. There was, to be sure, a strange contrast between the life he now led, and the one to which he had been accustomed while residing with his uncle. There, he had only to breathe a wish, and it was instantly gratified,—issue a command, and it was promptly obeyed.

Now, he must put forth his own strength, and depend on his own exertions. Yet, strange as it may seem to those who connect felicity only with wealth, splendor and distinction, he was never, in the proudest moment of his prosperity, when he was the star of fashion and minion of fortune, so cheerfully and equally happy as now, while confined to labor and living in obscurity.

Happiness can never be compelled to be our companion, nor is she oftenest won by those who most eagerly seek her. She most frequently meets us in situations where we never expected her visits; in employments or under privations to which we have become reconciled only by a sense of duty. There she meets us and infuses that peace and sunshine of the mind, that sweet serenity which a consciousness of innocence and rectitude can alone confer, and which is true pleasure, because we can enjoy it without remorse or regret.

That our hero was now in possession of this "sober certainty of waking bliss," some extracts from a long communication he forwarded to his friend Frankford, will demonstrate. After detailing the circumstances of his father's death, and his own resolutions to obey what he conceived his last wishes, he proceeded:

* * * * * *

"I have thus relinquished, perhaps forever, my intention of visiting your merry old England, and prosecuting those schemes of aggrandizement, in which you so generously offered me your assistance. That I have submitted to these disappointments with perfect equanimity I dare not assert; indeed, I confess I have often murmured at my wayward fate, and if the stars ever deign to listen to complaints from this dim sphere, they have undoubtedly heard me lay some grievous sins to their charge. Now really, Frankford, do you think there are many modern heroes who have experienced greater vicissitudes than myself.

As a fair parallel I will mention Napoleon, the Great. Like him I was taken from humble life, to be the heir of a sovereignty; make what exceptions you please to my use of the term sovereignty, the southern slaveholder is as absolute in his dominions, or plantation rather, as the grand seignior, and when I had become accustomed to command, and my mind was weakened by indolence and enervated by dissipation, I was suddenly thrown back to my former insignificance, and compelled to dig for my daily bread. "O, what a falling off was there!"

I must think no more about it; neither do I think so lightly as I have written. There is a pleasure in fulfilling what I believe were my father's last wishes that makes, what otherwise would be a sacrifice, a triumph. You may call it a weakness, but I feel as if his eye still regarded my actions; as if his spirit still hovered over those objects he so fondly loved.

And then my labor is not like the servile drudgery of the body, when the mind can exercise no volition and the heart enjoys no participation. When I return from the field, covered with sweat and dust—by the way, Homer's heroes were often in the same predicament, though not exactly from the same cause—it is so gratifying to be met with approving smiles, and see every thing prepared that loving hearts and ready hands can furnish to relieve my toil, and make me forget my weariness. And then exercise gives me such an excellent appetite; and you know we have plenty to satisfy its cravings!

I wish you could see with what deference and affection I am treated, when, at evening, we assemble in domestic conclave. Then our plans are proposed, arrangements formed, and successes congratulated. Even failures and disappointments are not mourned by us as inevitable evils. Neither do we waste our time in moralizing on such occurrences for the behoof of others; but like wise philosophers, endeavor to make them subservient to our own. We examine the causes which contributed to the reverse, and sometimes, like other theorists, are so fond of establishing a favorite hypothesis, that we consider any inconvenience tending to that result as a blessing in disguise.

There is, however, one sacred remembrance that binds all our hearts and minds in unison, a recollection of the excellent friend we have lost forever. We seldom mention him, and yet I do not believe his idea has scarcely, since his decease, been absent a moment from the minds of even the youngest of our family. Why is it that those recollections and ideas which most engross the soul are seldom communicated? Undoubtedly because we know they cannot be participated. Yet that is not our fear; but each individual struggles to stifle or conceal emotions whose expression would awaken that painful sympathy we cannot endure to see exhibited. And thus we converse with calmness and cheerfulness; sometimes, indeed, with gaiety when together, yet, were we with strangers, we should be silent and melancholy.

And the activity we are compelled by our situation to exert, also operates to dispel the gloom of grief. Employment is an excellent comforter, and fatigue the best opiate in the world. I never slept so soundly since my childhood, and my slumbers are most refreshing. I awaken in the morning without any solicitude save just the business of the farm. I have no appointments to keep, or engagements to escape; no punctilios of honor or intrigues of love. In short, could I fairly forget the last dozen years of my life, I think I might now enjoy the best felicity of which mortal men can, on earth, be partakers. And that I am not thus happy is owing no doubt to the prejudices I have imbibed, and those habits which long indulgence makes it difficult, indeed almost impossible wholly to alter. How often I wish I could, with the philosophical serenity of Anaxagoras, at once reconcile myself to the change from luxury to plainness.

You see I am deep in antiquity, yet deep learning, you know, was never my fault; and you will easily pardon this reference to the ancients when reflecting that I am deprived of all intercourse with the moderns. Plutarch was my father's favorite author, and I have lately been reading it most attentively, partly to imitate my worthy parent and partly because no better or more interesting books are within my reach; and the examples of heroism and lessons of self-control there recorded, often make me blush for my own pusilanimity. But, Frankford, I am confident those stern, stubborn old Greeks must have been furnished with nerves of the size and toughness of a cable, and mine, I know by actual admeasurement, are no larger than a whip-cord. What a degeneracy! Whether this superiority of theirs was imparted by nature or their gymnastics, I am now endeavoring to ascertain; pray heaven it prove the latter, and then I think my daily exercise will soon assimilate my firmness to their example."

* * * * * * * * *

"In your letter you insinuated a suspicion that my free spirit was yielding to the omnipotence that even republicans dare not resist. And do you really think, my dear Frankford, that Cupid's chains possess sufficient tenacity to bind a veteran? Have I not once cast them off like scorched flax? and will you not allow I found sufficient gall in the honeyed draught of love to make me temperate for the future?

Yet I frankly confess I never saw a woman more deserving of admiration than Miss Redington, nor one with whom I think life would pass so happily. But disappointment and experience have taught me caution; not enough to make me wise, but just sufficient to render me fastidious; and the suspicions I formerly entertained, that I might be accepted for my wealth, are now changed to fears that I shall be rejected for my poverty. True, Annie is as poor as I, and I am thankful for that. I should not like to have it thought I was influenced by pecuniary considerations in the choice of a wife, yet where such a possibility exists, the inference is usually made, the worst construction always being most obvious to the million.

But now I have begun the theme, I will be candid, and so I confess that although I did not stay in New England because I was in love, yet I shall be in love because I stay. Annie treats me just as she ought, if she intended to make me her captive. Her kindness has increased with my misfortunes, and since my father's decease and the consequent arrangements, she has shown such sympathy of countenance, and approbation of manner, and 'tis in her face and air her soul speaketh, that I have more than once been tempted to declare my affection, and solicit her to share my destiny."

CHAPTER XXX.

LOVERS.

If heaven a draft of heavenly pleasure spare,
One cordial in this melancholy vale,
'Tis when a youthful, loving, modest pair,
In others' arms breathe out the tender tale,
Beneath the milk white thorn that scents the evening gale.
BURNS.

SIDNEY ROMILLY seemed now fast approaching the crisis which, by the universal consent of authors, rounds the period of a novel hero's historic existence; and the sage reader, no doubt, anticipates his exemption from further trials, and that he is soon to be consigned to marriage and obscurity.

Whether such anticipations will be realized, time and this authentic memoir will finally decide; but certain it is that the whole village were sanguine in the belief an attachment between the young Squire Romilly, as by courtesy they called Sidney, and the fair Annie Redington, and that their union was considered as a matter certain as the coming of the Fourth of July; *not that* they ventured *positively* to assert that their wedding would be celebrated on that important day, though the probability of such an event was actually hinted.

Nor would one have inferred from the equanimity, not to say triumph, with which Sidney listened to the raillery of his friend Perkins, and the sly hints of his own family, whose smiles, whenever the subject was alluded to, spoke their entire approbation, that he was at all chagrined at bearing the appellation of a lover, nor that he had any aversion against assuming a still tenderer and more sacred title. But when he felt nearly secure of possessing the affection of Annie, and only waited a favorable opportunity to urge his suit, a circumstance occurred which again plunged him into perplexity and distrust.

The partner of Mr. Redington, Annie's father, died about this time, and on his death-bed made a disclosure of the fraud and villany he had practiced against the widow and infant of his friend. In his will he left seven thousand dollars as the sum to which Annie was entitled in behalf of her father, and three thousand as a reparation for the wrong he had done, in thus retaining so long, her just inheritance. Such an event was unparalleled in the annals of Northwood, and created matter of conversation, inquiry, and wonder, at every tea-party and gathering in the village for a long time after.

But the old deacon was the person most affected by the intelligence, even more than Annie. The letter bearing the glorious, or rather golden news, was directed to him, and in the first transports, occasioned by being invited to come to Boston and receive such a large sum of money, he forgot he was not the owner thereof. The disagreeable truth, however, soon occurred, and after meditating a while on the affair, he came to the determination to keep the management of the property in his own hands as long as possible. For this purpose it would be necessary to discourage the attentions of Sidney, and prevent his marrying the heiress; this he determined to attempt. It would, he feared look a little like selfishness, as he had of late expressed great partiality for the young man, and shown that he sanctioned the connexion that was to unite him to his niece. This approbation proceeded, not from a wish to promote the happiness of either, but because he should, in the event Annie's marriage, be freed from the *duty* of providing for her.

These things, however, he kept and pondered in his own mind; to Annie, he was all indulgence, frequently declaring he felt more gratified she should thus have an independence secured to her, than at anything which could have happened, except to witness another reformation, and see her and his own daughter both partakers of the outpourings of divine grace.

For neither Annie's sincerity nor gentleness, her unfeigned desire to understand her duties, and her scrupulous exactness in complying with every command, and enduring every sacrifice they demanded, were of any avail to satisfy the rigid requirements of her uncle's creed. She had never, as he could learn, (she was an Episcopalian,) been specially awakened, and could not tell the precise moment when heart was changed from stone to flesh, consequently she was still in the gall of bitterness and bonds of iniquity; and all her excellencies were only the effect of education, or

————————" a milder feature
Of our poor sinful corrupt nature."

Annie, meanwhile, was not indifferent to the prosperity which awaited her; but Sidney was connected with every plan of future happiness her bright fancy was industriously forming; and to meet the declaration which she hoped—hoped while blushing at her own hopes—he would soon make, with candor and kindness, was the sweet yet agitating thought which oftenest occurred.

"I must not now," thought she, "affect indifference; his sensitive mind would instantly ascribe it to the pride and vanity of newly acquired wealth—and what is wealth in the scale of one who truly loves! I never esteemed Sidney less for his accidental loss of fortune, and shall I wrong him by thinking its accidental possession—for I can claim no merit of acquiring it—will, in his estimation, add lustre to my merits, or ardor to his affection?"

Thus the lovely heiress reasoned and determined; but her lover was not in haste to avail himself of her partiality. In truth, however strange it may appear to the real fortune-hunter, he was sorry she had become an heiress. He felt humbled to think he should appear like one obliged by her acceptance; and the fear, lest she should entertain the same doubts respecting the purity of his attachment now there existed a motive which might possibly excite it independently of her merits, as he had done while possessing a fortune, made him feel a painful diffidence, a kind of self-reproach in proposing himself, which he could not well overcome.

Neither was this diffidence at all removed by the behavior of the deacon. He had, all at once, assumed an air of distance and even dislike to Sidney, so palpable and pointed that the latter could not misunderstand it; and though the good graces of the old gentleman were not greatly to be coveted, yet the thought that such rudeness might be sanctioned by Annie to discourage his pretensions, gave him exquisite pain. He never credited such fancies, yet to think them possible mortified him, and to complete his chagrin, Ephraim Skinner again commenced his regular visits to the deacon's, and fortified by his own impudence, and his interest supported by the authority and favor of the uncle, he was not without hopes of obtaining the smiles of the niece.

Annie's treatment of this intruder was as cold and contemptuous as common civility warranted, but still he persevered, and always being aided by the deacon, he usually, in spite of her ill-concealed disdain, contrived either to obtain the seat next to her, or prevent Sidney from occupying it. Indeed the agitation of the latter often utterly incapacitated him from offering those little attentions to Miss Redington which he could so gallantly have performed had she been totally indifferent to him; and thus his embarrassments, her delicacy, Skinner's impertinence, and the deacon's cunning, seemed every day to increase the difficulties of the lovers' coming to an explanation.

This state of things was soon penetrated by Dr. Perkins, but as he had discovered the state of Annie's affections, and knew that Sidney would ultimately be successful, he determined not to interfere, but let him manage to win the fair lady himself, who was certainly worth all his exertions. He was even a little mischievous, for he whispered to Sidney, in great confidence, that he fancied Miss Redington's accession of wealth had already begun to make her feel dissatisfied with a residence in that unfashionable place, and that he presumed she would soon depart for Boston; but when he perceived the serious dejection of her lover, and knew with his sensitiveness of feeling he was refining away both his own happiness and hers, the good natured physician, pursuing his vocation of relieving pain, thought it would be but charity to attempt a plan for bringing them together.

Sidney's daily occupation on his farm left him but little leisure for calls or visits; and during the month which had elapsed since Annie became an heiress, he had not once been to deacon Jones' without encountering Skinner, who would never depart till he saw his rival fairly off; and so, in all that time, there had never occurred an opportunity of private conversation between the lovers.

But now the doctor, having previously arranged who were to form the party, proposed a stroll, to visit a certain cave or den, where tradition reported a celebrated Indian warrior once resided. The company assembled and set off without Skinner's once surmising the excursion, as the doctor feared, should he learn it, he would join them, though he should come an uninvited guest.

They had, as such parties always have, a most delightful time, and on their return, while they were slowly pursuing the meanderings of that identical stream which has several times been mentioned in this history, Perkins by some specious pretense, contrived, when Sidney and his partner had walked a little before the company, to detain the others till the lovers were fairly out of sight; and then he proposed walking a little distance in another direction to examine and procure some water from a curious, boiling spring. He praised the purity of the water, and regretted exceedingly, Sidney and Annie were beyond call, as they must now be deprived of an opportunity of partaking it; and so well did he play his part, that not one of the party, not even his wife, suspected the motives by which he was actuated.

As for the lovers, they would not have regretted being deprived of the waters, had the spring been the genuine Helicon, or flowing with the *elixir vitar*, while, with her arm fast locked in his, they trod the flowery path, sometimes conversing with animation, but oftener yielding to that delicious silence, the heart's deep enjoyment in the presence of the beloved object.

They heeded not their separation from their party, till, on reaching a spot always sacred to Sidney, the place where he had dreamed of his father, and where, since his death, he had often retired, but always alone, he looked back and saw no one following.

"We will pause here," said he, "till they overtake us. Perkins is doubtless delivering some of his botanical or mineralogical lectures; but I do not, at this time, regret being deprived of listening to the display of his eloquence. Miss Redington, will you sit down? you must be fatigued with your long walk."

Annie assented, not by an answer, but by seating herself where he directed her. This was on the trunk of a tree close to the margin of the stream, and shaded by the wide spreading branches of a lofty elm, that threw its gigantic shadow nearly across the water, while beneath its shade on the bank where they sat, the herbage assumed that deep green color and softness of texture that it always wears in such sheltered situations.

The sun, though now fast declining, threw a rich lustre on the long line of forest trees, stretching to an almost interminable length in the distance before them; and the bold summits of the far off mountains shone like molten gold, while the blue mists already gathering around their sides, were softened in the distance till they resembled fine veils, spread to conceal the recesses in the dark cliffs from the intrusion of mortal eye.

The air was perfectly still, and a calm seemed reigning over all nature; and though from the adjacent thickets the voices of a few birds were heard at intervals, their notes were low and languid, compared with the full, sprightly, joy-inspiring chorus they pour in the season of spring.

Even the waters appeared to share in the calm of repose which nature was enjoying, as the stream, with scarcely a ripple, stole along, while the sun-beams seemed to sleep on its still surface. But one spot looked deep and dark; it was where the stream was suddenly compressed by a huge rock that projected into the bed of the river, and on that dark spot Annie's eye was resting, as Sidney, who watched her glance, observed, "I never look on that place without an involuntary shudder."

"And why? I see nothing very terrible in its appearance."

"Not in its appearance. The terrible is in the recollections it awakens. Perhaps you may have heard I was once very near meeting my doom in that water."

"I never heard the circumstance," said Annie. "Pray when did it occur?"

"Long, long ago; it is a remembrance of my childhood, and often comes over my mind like the impressions of a frightful dream. If you will permit me to be the hero of my own tale, I will relate the incident."

He sat down close beside her, while she looked up into his face with an expression that not only promised attention, but such an interest in his narrative, that for a few moments he forgot what he had promised to relate.

She reminded him at length, and he began and described minutely and pathetically, the thoughts and feelings which had agitated him when he felt himself drowning, and related the manner of rescue by his father; then his dream came so vividly on his fancy he could not but proceed to detail it. Never before had he mentioned it to mortal; it was one of those hallowed impressions, awful, mysterious, yet soothing, which the heart broods over in silence, and while watching for the fulfilment of the prophecy, feels the oracle must be incommunicable.

But Annie could understand it, and she listened with breathless attention, her color, and the expression of her beautiful countenance varying with every change in the story; now pale with terror—trembling with anxiety —eager with expectation—flushed with hope—and radiant with joy!

Had Sidney watched her changing cheek he would not have made the desponding observation with which he closed his history.

"And I confess to you, Miss Redington, weak as it may appear to give heed to an airy dream, that the assurance of happiness, my father, in that vision gave me, has supported my courage and lighted my path while pursuing the course which I fancied his injunctions suggested. But shadows are gathering, and lately hope has hardly deigned even to cheat me with the promise of future felicity."

As he ended he turned to gaze, and met her soft blue eyes glistening with tears of sympathy; the blush, the tremor of her hand, that unconsciously to himself he had taken, all conspired to awaken a sudden revulsion of feelings. His pulse throbbed violently; but the animation of hope and joy flashed from his dark eye and lighted up his fine features, as bending towards her he softly whispered,

"Annie—Miss Redington, O! would you but condescend to be my friend, my companion, life would indeed be a flowery path! Tell me, may I not hope?"

What answer Annie gave I have never been able to learn; but that it did not sentence her lover to immediate banishment may be inferred from the circumstance that although they passed nearly an hour on the same spot, yet neither thought of the progress of time, the protracted absence of their party, nor indeed of aught on earth, save of each other. From this dream of love and bliss, they were at length aroused by the loud, merry tones of the doctor, calling out, as he advanced, laughing, towards them.

"Well, Sidney, have you surveyed the stream with sufficient accuracy? or are you intending to wait the rising of the moon, and watch how sweetly her soft beams will rest on the waters?"

"We shall have to wait the rising of the sun, I believe, if we wait the coming of our party," retorted Sidney, with a face of such happiness that no one could mistake the feelings that inspired it. "Pray where have you been loitering so long? Miss Redington"—

"Has been impatient at our stay," interrupted Perkins, looking on her blushing cheek with a most provoking inquisitiveness; "and you have both passed the time in surmises on what could possibly detain us, and every minute has seemed an hour."

"No, no, you need not, Warren, imagine your presence so essential to our happiness. We have neither thought nor spoken about you," said Sidney.

"Nor of any subject, I presume; you have undoubtedly been in one of your musing moods, and though I would not undervalue 'divine contemplation,' yet I must confess a man, while under her influence, is dull company for me. I willingly resign him to the stars and his own fancies. And now Annie, I know by her countenance, is of my opinion; she must have found it tedious sitting there so silent and gazing on the water. Romilly, though you are inclined to be a Zeno, I beg you would not attempt to make proselytes to your sect; certainly we shall not permit Annie to be one. And I am beginning seriously to fear for her spirits, as she is nothing so gay and sociable as she was before becoming acquainted with you. I believe I must prohibit your access to her society; come, Annie, take my arm, and I will conduct you to our party, and let this philosopher follow at his leisure; he will doubtless prefer a lonely ramble."

"I shall ramble alone no longer, Warren," replied Sidney, putting back the offered arm of the former, and drawing Annie's closer within his own; "Annie has promised to share my journey—for life."

The doctor's face, that usually seemed the reflection of a merry heart, wore an air of serious and unaffected emotion, while he congratulated them on the happiness awaiting their path; and with fervency offered his best wishes for their permanent felicity.

* * * * * *

The intelligence soon circulated through the village, but nearly all who heard it declared they were not in the least surprised; that it was just what they had been expecting; and several asserted the engagement was made in the spring, when Sidney concluded to stay. One or two even hinted they had learned such an arrangement, at that time, from the parties themselves. And the approbation of the measure, with one two exceptions, seemed unanimous; the people agreeing that Sidney, for generosity and kind behavior to his family, merited as good a wife as Annie, and as rich.

Merrill was in ecstasies at the news. It was reported that hearing it while reaping, he instantly threw down his sickle, changed his dress, saddled his horse, and rode over to congratulate his patron; but Merrill always asserted he did a good day's work before he went.

Though for his own part, he said, he should not have valued spending a week in rejoicing, if it would have added to the happiness of the lovers; yet, as he knew it would not, and guessed they would much rather look at each other than at him, and feared the boys would be lazy if he was away; and so he didn't go over to see the young squire and wish him joy till just about sundown.

But the envy, rage, and thirst for vengeance of merchant Skinner were too potent for control, and he expressed his feelings in such unseemly language and unchristian wishes against both parties, and especially Sidney, that the deacon, although his own spirit was sorely vexed on the occasion, did feel it his duty to admonish him, warning him against the sin of wrath and ungodly swearing, and entreating him to consider the unprofitableness of yielding to such angry passions.

"Though," said he, "I am as much grieved as you can be, yet I consider it my duty to be still. Indeed, I mourn more for the child than myself, for Annie seems as near as my own daughter, and I always intended to be a father to her. But I have told her if she will marry Sidney Romilly, though I confess he has some good and agreeable things in his character, yet being brought up away there among slaves and papists, I think his principles are little better than the heathen, and so I told Annie, if she would marry him, and did ever come to want, as I thought most likely she would, she needn't apply to me. I had cleared my conscience in advising her, and I never would assist her with a cent."

And thus, in the midst of this happy and rejoicing family, the deacon maintained his obstinate opinion that Annie was throwing herself away; and if one of his favorite texts of scripture may be literally understood, namely, "that by the sadness of the countenance the heart is made better," he was certainly very fast progressing towards perfection.

Many philosophers have asserted that the earth has, ever since the creation, contained the same quantity of matter; what, at any time, appears like loss in one element or object is compensated by an equal gain in some other element or object.

If such be the equalizing principle in the material world, can we not imagine its influence extended and regulating the moral world likewise? From the misery and disappointments of one individual may, and indeed we know there often does, arise an increase of felicity and fortune to another, and the overthrow of a mighty kingdom shall prove the means of aggrandizement to a rival nation; and consequently it might be inferred there is, in every period, the same aggregate of moral worth and human happiness.

Could this position be established, the melancholy of the deacon would not demand our sympathy, because the increasing felicity of the lovers more than counterbalanced the pain of his chagrin. The happiness of Sidney will need no other confirmation than a letter which he wrote to Mr. Frankford immediately after his explanation with Annie, and a copy of which I shall insert, as his feelings and sentiments are much more vividly and touchingly displayed by his pen than mine.

"*Northwood, N. H., Sept. 10th*, 18—.

MY EVER DEAR FRIEND,—It is but a short time since I despatched you a packet so voluminous that it might undoubtedly claim the respectable name of *folio*, and I then promised I would not again intrude under, at least, a quarter; but I *must* write, for there are feelings impossible to be restrained when we are blessed with a friend to whom they may be communicated.

I recollect an old gentleman, a man versed in the wisdom of proverbs, once told me, if I ever meant to succeed in business, to acquire a habit of conveying my thoughts with brevity, especially when writing, as nothing was so abominable to your matter-of-fact people, who usually manage all active business, as receiving a long epistle, written in a flowery style, with plenty of dashes and parentheses, and, to finish the climax, penned in most vile and unreadable characters. He said he had known many such letters thrown in the fire by those who received them, when had they been written legibly and succinctly the petitions they contained would undoubtedly have been granted. Instructed by the wisdom of this sage, I shall make my letter short, as I wish it all perused, and attentively too, it containing the history of my happiness, and the fulfilment of your prophecy.

You already anticipate my tale. I am a lover—an accepted one—and happy as your fancy can make me. I told you in my last of the fortune which had fallen to Annie, and my fears lest it would prove an obstacle to my advances; I knew the suspicions I had myself entertained of interested attachments in the days of my prosperity. I trembled lest the sweet girl should yield to the same suspicions. But her nature was too noble, and her principles too pure; she had not seen human nature under the same aspects I had, and she trusted at once—and she shall not be deceived. All the affection, tenderness, and esteem, my heart is capable of entertaining, are hers, hers undividedly.

O, there is rapture undefinable in the thought of possessing such a friend, and feeling secure the attachment and connection will continue through life! Let the world change as it may, my heart's treasure is secure. And perhaps I prize this confidence more dearly than most men, for I have been exceedingly distrustful; but my doubts are all happily removed, and my anxieties richly compensated. My fortune is now, I think, settled; Annie has consented to give me her hand on our annual Thanksgiving, which is usually held the last of November. I urged her to name an earlier day, but could not prevail; and so to occupy the interval, I am making some alterations in our dwelling, to render it more worthy to receive her.

What vicissitudes have been mine within the last year, or since you and I explored the route to my father's house in that old wagon! How different now are my feelings and sentiments, my hopes and plans and pleasures! How distrustful was I then of woman, lovely woman—whose heart is fashioned in sincerity, constancy, and generosity; and if she ever appears artful, selfish, and false, it is a lesson imbibed by the corrupting influence of the world.

You will probably inquire the effect my vicissitudes and changes of sentiment have had on my character and happiness. Well, sir, I am metamorphosed from a gay man to a grave one;—not sad, only considerate—and instead of strutting the gentleman, with a score of servants waiting my commands, I am a plain farmer, *planning* business for my *help*.

Such are the outlines,—now the filling up of the contrast. I am more respected and less feared; better, far better beloved, yet less flattered; have fewer followers and firmer friends; enjoy better health, a better appetite, with less leisure, and no *ennui* at all. And so, if from the foregoing facts you can form a correct estimate, you will set me down as far happier and more useful in my humble retirement, than when parading the streets of Charleston, the reputed heir of two hundred thousand dollars.

Does fortune, then, when so universally the object of pursuit, confer no advantages? Yes, many; but men are seldom qualified to improve or enjoy them rationally, without that moral, intellectual, and physical discipline, to which the inheritors of wealth will not readily submit. Were I now to recover my fortune, how differently should I enjoy it from what I did in my prosperity! Yet I do not covet its possession, and if—why must there always be an if?—it were not for certain recollections respecting its disposal, I think I should feel perfectly happy.

My uncle was an indulgent master; he loved his servants with almost parental affection, and they worshiped him; and when I think of the change they are probably feeling, my blood runs cold in my veins. The change of masters is frequently a terrible evil to the poor slave, and that system must be evil, on the whole, which subjects them to the occurrence of such a calamity.

There was one negro, Cato by name—did you never think of the absurdity of *freemen* conferring the names of those ancient champions of liberty only on their *slaves!*—who was particularly attached to me. I have no doubt but he would freely have laid down his life to insure my happiness. He was a merry creature, and laughed the loudest of any person I ever knew; in a still evening he might be distinctly heard a mile. When I was about starting on my tour, I recollect saying to Cato, who was officiously waiting near me, 'Well, Cato, I hope you will be industrious and faithful while I am absent, and live merrily and laugh heartily.'

The poor fellow looked me in the face, and tears stood in his large, shining eyes, and there was an expression of deep sorrow in his countenance as he plaintively answered, 'Cato nebber laugh loud when mas'r Sidney be away.'

Frankford, if I am ever able, I intend to go south, purchase that negro, bring him to New Hampshire, and give him his liberty. Heavens! how he will laugh to see me. I almost fancy I can hear him now.

What an unmerciful letter to tax your patience with, and I only sat down to write a billet, informing you of my intended marriage. Well, excuses would only, by lengthening it, add to my offense, so health and happiness attend you. Farewell!

S. ROMILLY."

CHAPTER XXXI.

A YANKEE SIBYL, AND OTHER MATTERS.

She dreams on him that has forgot her love.
TWO GENTLEMEN OF VERONA.

IT would be impossible, by description, to do justice to the joy and bustle pervading the habitation of the Romillys. That Sidney, their pride, and hope, and stay, should be thus blessed and fortunate, seemed like a particular interference of Providence, to reward him for his virtues, his cheerful sacrifices to the wishes and happiness of his friends.

There was but one shade in the picture—the father no longer lived to rejoice in the felicity of his son; but it was a consoling thought, that he would have approved his choice—and he was then rejoicing in a state of bliss and glory far beyond what any earthly pageant or transaction could bestow.

And Mrs. Romilly, though she fondly and faithfully dwelt on the memory of the deceased, yet felt, in witnessing her son's prosperity, that gladness might still become her.

Thus passed a few weeks, when one day, as Sidney was sitting in the house, conversing with his mother on the improvements they were about making, a gentlemanly looking stranger, ushered by Harvey, entered; and as soon as the civilities of the occasion were exchanged, requested to speak with Mr. Romilly alone. They retired to Sidney's apartment, and after the absence of more than an hour, which Mrs. Romilly passed very unquietly, fearing, she knew not why, or what, her son returned, and informed her the gentleman was from the south, and had brought information which rendered an immediate journey to Charleston unavoidable.

The mother, with the quickness of apprehension natural to her sex and character, eagerly inquired the news.

"I cannot now impart it," answered Sidney, smiling; yet his mother saw he was agitated, and fancied he was affecting gaiety to conceal trouble. "You shall hear from me as soon as I can arrange the business I go to perform, or see me, perhaps before a letter could reach you. But I must start immediately."

"Not till you have seen Annie," said the mother.

"No, no, I am going to call on her now. Sophia, do do put my clothes in my trunk; and mother, will you see the gentleman has refreshments, while I am gone to bid Annie adieu. We must be off soon, or we shall lose the stage."

Mrs. Romilly felt more than a woman's inquisitiveness, a mother's yearning, to know the business that was, at so important a time, taking her son on a long journey; but the delicate considerateness of her feelings forbade her questioning the stranger on a subject which her son had intimated was a secret; and though she made several inquiries which might have been designed as an opening to any communication he was inclined to make, he did not appear to understand her hints, and gave her no satisfaction.

Meanwhile Sidney reached the house of the deacon, and found Annie, with her aunt and cousin, busily engaged in preparing some bed-quilts; and though his affairs demanded haste, when looking at her he forgot his hurry, and only thought they must part, and might it not be forever? He could not tell Annie "farewell," in the presence of witnesses, and entreated her to walk in the garden for a few moments; she complied, and there, while she was innocently and sportively detailing the history of a plant whose rearing had been a source of vexation to her, Sidney, who was attentively gazing on her, but heard not a word, said, abruptly,

"Annie, I called to bid you good-bye, I am just starting for Charleston."

"Indeed!" said she, looking up, while her cheek waxed pale, and her lip trembled, "your resolution is very suddenly taken."

"Yes, it has been, and it must be as suddenly executed. I must go, but I shall, I hope, return in a short time. At any rate you shall hear from me soon; say four weeks. You will not in that time forget me, love," passing his arm around her waist and pressing her to his bosom.

She tried to smile, while she faintly inquired if he went alone.

"No, a gentleman from Savannah accompanies me, and he is now waiting at my mother's, I must be gone. Annie, keep this kiss sacred till we meet," and he pressed her to his bosom, kissing her cheek and lips, a freedom he had never before attempted. With an expression of countenance where a tear, smile, and frown, were equally blended, she broke from him.

"Go, go now, I entreat you."

"Yes, I must go now, Annie, farewell;" and he hurried out of the garden.

She gazed after him till the distance shut him from her view, and then retired to her chamber in wonder and perplexity. What could have induced him to take such a sudden journey? was her first inquiry. She could not answer it. She lamented she had not asked him. She thought his mother might probably know; and after wearying herself with conjectures, she put on her bonnet and walked to Mrs. Romilly's. But there she learned nothing, or at least nothing to quiet her, as she plainly saw his mother felt more anxiety on his account than she would express. However, as there appeared to be no better remedies than time and patience, Annie tried calmly to wait the explanation of what she could not but think was a mystery of some importance.

All the family spoke cheerfully and encouragingly on the subject, excepting her uncle. He certainly tried to augment her fears by hinting that it was not for any good Sidney was thus suddenly summoned away. These remarks were usually spoken to Mr. Skinner, who had again begun to drop in to the deacon's occasionally.

But Annie heeded not Skinner; her mind was constantly with her lover, fancying his situation, employment, even his thoughts—and she blushed while believing them fixed on her. At the close of each day she rejoiced the hour was drawing nearer for his return.

This looking and waiting for the return of an absent friend, is a sickness of the heart in which man can seldom sympathize, as he rarely feels. He could not endure it with the patience of woman.

The four weeks had nearly expired, when one fine day Mrs. Watson entered the store of Skinner to make some trifling purchases, and remarked she was going to Deacon Jones' to make an afternoon visit.

"And I haven't been invited there this many a day before," said she. "Miss Annie heard something I said last winter about her liking young Mr. Romilly too well; and so they pretended to be angry, and quite neglected me. But the story I told was a true one, and now he is gone, they are mighty good again. And Miss Redington sent over word for me to come and drink tea to-day; but I can guess the reason why."

"And what do you guess?" inquired Skinner, always interested when Annie was the subject of conversation.

"O, she wants me to tell her when her spark is coming back! You know, Mr. Skinner, the young people say

I can tell fortunes; and may be I can guess right sometimes; but I don't intend now to tell her one word. They'll make a good dish of tea, and I'll drink it, and say 'tis against my conscience to tell fortunes; and so it certainly is; and Annie is such a tender-hearted chicken she'll never urge me, if she thinks it will make me feel bad afterwards."

So far the conversation was overheard by Deborah Long, a girl who resided with Mrs. Perkins, and then Skinner, under pretense of showing a fine piece of premium linen, drew Mrs. Watson to a far part of the store, where they conversed for some time in a low tone, but apparently with great interest.

* * * * * *

Mrs. Watson was the gossip of the neighborhood; that term, in her case, implying a person who gathers and retails all the news of the town, occasionally making alterations where they can be done to evident advantage, and even adding items to fill any hiatus which threatens to spoil a good story. She was not naturally malicious, but the love of tea and of talk made her often guilty of saying evil, or at least uncharitable things about those to whom she bore no ill will, or none except what was created by her own slanders; it being morally impossible for the person who thus injures another, to feel a perfectly complacent, friendly temper towards the individual they have villified.

Yet Mrs. Watson had her good qualities and kind feelings too. She was an obliging neighbor, and an excellent nurse; whenever there was sickness she was sure to be wanted, and seldom did she refuse to watch by the bed of pain and affliction; it being indeed her pride to exhibit her skill on all such melancholy occasions. Some good women who never could leave their families to officiate as watchers or nurses, endeavored to depreciate the credit Mrs. Watson thus obtained, by saying her chief motives in going were to gather news and eat good things.

However, though such accusations were frequently

made, and perhaps generally by the villagers when they were in sound health, no sooner did sickness occur than her credit was instantly restored, and she was welcomed as a comforter and a friend; people usually assent to the proverb, that "a friend in need, is a friend indeed."

While this habit of making herself useful recommended her to the notice of the elderly part of her acquaintance, she had other qualifications which ingratiated her with the young. She was an oracle in all affairs of the heart, and a living chronicle of every courtship and marriage which had occurred in the vicinity since her child hood. And, moreover, it was asserted she could, when she pleased, tell fortunes as well as a conjurer; and many a good cup of tea was made by the young maidens, to treat her, that so they might have an opportunity of "turning up a cup" and hearing her, after an examination of the tea grounds, explain their future destiny.

As she is introduced in the important character of a sibyl, the reader may probably wish to know something of her personal appearance and habits of life; but I feel much diffidence in attempting a description of either. She was, indeed, a very *unclassical* priestess of futurity; very unlike, also, the witches of Macbeth, or the more modern Nornas and Megs of popular romance. Those remarkable women are represented as enormously tall—stature being an essential requisite—with long, skinny arms to match; sunken features; weather-beaten, sallow, shriveled skin; black or grey eyes, exhibiting flashes of a demoniac spirit; and then their hair, such a frightfully grizzled, disheveled, matted mass! How I have wished the ingenious authors, rich as they are in invention, could have afforded them a comb!

Neither is their dress in a more seemly style; but "haud ye there," I'll not repeat the description of a costume, the like of which no Yankee woman ever saw, and the like of which our fortune-teller would not have picked up in the streets, unless she saw it contained some cotton or linen articles which she might have converted into paper rags.

Indeed, truth compels me to record that in taste and

dress, habits of life, and personal appearance, Mrs. Wat son was totally unlike her celebrated sisterhood. She was a short woman, stoutly formed, and inclined to corpulency; and though her arms might, by wearing her sleeves tucked up when engaged in her dairy, or housework, have been a little tanned, yet they were plump, round, well-shaped arms. Her hair, as she was past fifty, was doubtless grey, but it was never exposed, being combed and confined on the top of her head, and always covered with a neat, fashionable cap, she being very particular about her dress, and reputed one of the neatest women and best managers in the village. And many wondered how it happened that though she went abroad so much, she generally contrived to have her own work done in season, and quite as soon as her neighbors. But she always enjoyed good health, and was very strong; and those women who have neither her *sleight* to work, nor constitution to endure fatigue, must not imitate the worst part of her example—gadding.

She had quite a fair complexion for a woman of her time of life, light blue eyes, regular features; and the only mark of her superior sagacity, or divining skill, was a very knowing wink, and a ready nod, which she had always at command, and which she had practiced so long and often, it sometimes gave her the appearance of trembling. She would, too, when listening—which she never willingly did—to the discourse of another, betray a restless agitation; this was not caused by the inspirations of the goddess of Fortune-telling, but merely by the chagrin she endured to be one moment debarred from the free use of her tongue. She was, indeed, an everlasting talker, and never, as I could learn, in the whole course of her life, was known to have a fit of musing, abstraction, or obstinate silence.

Such was the woman now in close conference with Mr. Skinner; and though I am aware the present wise philosophers of the old world may ascribe the difference between her and their own race of sibyls to the effect of that depreciation of character, and even *size*, which many of their elder brethren maintained was inseparable from the climate of America; yet I am confident Mrs. Watson would not have exchanged situations with those *cummers* their writers have so elaborately described to have been as tall as a light-house, with arms like a windmill, and the hair of a Medusa. How her decent pride would have revolted to have been seen in their mean habiliments!—as with a significant toss of her head she tied her new green bonnet in a faster knot, drew her handsome red shawl closer around her shoulders, smoothed down her rich black lutestring that rustled at every step, while her new morocco shoes replied in creaking chorus, drew on her gloves that she had thrown aside to examine the texture of the linen, and giving Skinner half a dozen winks and as many nods, said, as she turned to leave the store,—

"Never fear; I'll manage the matter, and call and look at that cloth again, some day."

The merchant gave a most malicious grin as she disappeared; and then drawing up the corners of his cravat with a sudden jerk, as if meditating the pressure his neck deserved, returned smirkingly to his counter to receive the orders of Miss Deborah Long.

Deacon Jones' wife was a woman of few words; and neither her daughter nor niece cared a fig for the conversation of Mrs. Watson; so they minded their work and let her talk, and she had an excellent visit. When they had nearly finished drinking tea, she said, turning suddenly to Annie,—

"Come, Miss Redington, if you'll turn up a cup I'll tell you when that handsome man is coming back, that you want to see so much. You needn't blush so, my dear; I am sure you ought to wish to see him. Come, shake it well, and turn it round and round, and then over quick, and wish for what you want most."

Annie, laughing, did as she was directed. It was indeed her intention when inviting Mrs. Watson. Many had asserted she could reveal the future, and though Annie had not any faith in such reports, yet the mystery that overshadowed her lover's motives for his journey, and the uncertainty respecting his return, kept her mind in such a state of feverish anxiety as made her resort to means her reason told her were absurd, to remove it.

"Now," said the fortune-teller, taking the cup, "I'll warrant you good news. La, what a looking cup! I'm sure you might have turned a better one. There's no good news here."

"O, tell me the bad then," said Annie, carelessly smiling.

"The bad—well—I don't know. Here's your sweetheart; but he aint a coming home very soon, as I see. There is something hinders him, and it looks to me like a woman, and a sick one too."

"Will he not write?" inquired Annie, earnestly.

"O, yes, yes, there's a letter; but that is not such a one as I like. And you have no good wish neither. Poh! 'tis an ugly cup, and you shall turn up another, and see if you can't have better luck."

Annie willingly obeyed, and her heart beat quick as she earnestly and silently breathed a wish Sidney might either write, or return within the month.

"Well," said Mrs. Watson, "now you hav'nt done a bit better. Your cup is all hurly burly, and there is something looks like a disappointment. But, la! you must'nt mind what I tell you; for I don't know much about fortune."

"It will not trouble me in the least," said Annie. But her cheeks, that all the afternoon had looked like damask roses, now wore the hue of the lily.

"These cups may mean what is past," continued the sibyl. "They say it is a sickly place away there to the south, and like enough you worry a good deal about your sweetheart; I warrant I should in the same case. So I'll just call these two cups nothing at all, and you shall turn up another. Come, Priscilla, do shake the tea-pot, and turn out some more grounds. I call you Priscilla yet, for I can't think of Mrs. Romilly half the time, though every one can see you are a married woman."

The face of the young wife blushed like scarlet, and she obeyed the directions of the gossip without looking up.

"There now, that's a plenty. La! you needn't turn out the whole tea-pot. Now, Miss Redington, be pretty particular, and I'll warrant I'll tell something to please you."

She looked peeringly in the cup for some time, turning it round, and examining every speck with scrupulous attention. Annie sat watching her in silence and trepidation; anxious to hear her tell a good fortune, and angry with herself for the weakness she was indulging.

"You are not in luck to-day, Annie," said the sibyl, in a tone of more solemnity than she had hitherto spoken. "You will have a letter though; but it won't be such a one as you expect; and you won't see the person you wished to very soon; I don't see as he thinks of coming back, and there's somebody, and it certainly looks like a woman, hindering him. But, la! what does that signify? I guess you won't care much about it; there's plenty more men in the world; and you'll find a good fish yet as ever swum in the sea."

"You need not tell me any more," said Annie, reaching out her hand, that trembled like an aspen, for the cup. "I am quite satisfied."

Mrs. Watson resigned the cup, and endeavored to maintain her usual volubility, but the depression felt by the others evidently embarrassed her, confident and careless of the feelings of others as she usually was when an opportunity of talking occurred; but silence was a worse penance for her than any of the Romish ritual could have enforced, and she soon took her leave.

"How foolish I was," said Annie to her cousin, "to allow any one an opportunity of thus exciting my emotions. And then it was flattering Mrs. Watson too, with a show of dependence on her skill, as if heaven would permit such a one as she to know those secrets of futurity the good and virtuous cannot penetrate. I deserve to be punished. But she was malicious and meant to tell me a bad fortune, and I will not allow her nonsense to trouble me. I am now satisfied she knows nothing."

"Well," said her cousin, "I hope we shall not be honored with another visit from her at present, she is so bold and loquacious, I think her a most disagreeable woman."

But though Annie intended not to feel troubled, she could not forbear thinking of what Mrs. Watson had told her, and she waited for the arrival of intelligence from Sidney with an intense anxiety that deprived her of sleep by night and quiet by day. That some fearful calamity was impending over her or Sidney, was impressed on her mind. She tried to think her fears were excited by Mrs. Watson's foolish hints, or her own weak fancies; but if they were, she had not the mental strength to shake them off. She could trust unwaveringly in the promise that "all things should work together for good, to them who loved God;" but she knew earthly prosperity and happiness were not, *certainly*, implied in that promise. Her path had hitherto been through the valley of humiliation and suffering, and she had pursued it unwaveringly, with the submission of a Christian; but a bright scene had lately been disclosed; and O, how she did tremble, lest it was about to be involved in gloom! And how earnestly she entreated she might be spared a trial she felt unequal to sustain.

As she was sitting, one day, by the window, wrapped in such meditations, Silas came merrily along, and raising the sash, threw a letter in her lap saying—"There is yours, Annie; and I have one for mother also. I shall carry hers over, and see what Sidney is about, as yours will have too many honeyed words to be exposed to vulgar eyes." And he ran off to carry the letter to his mother.

Annie was pale, but her eyes shone with joy, as seizing the letter, she exclaimed:

"What a treasure! Priscilla, you must rejoice with me, yet you cannot feel the same happiness; you have not known the same fears." She had broken the seal.

"How briefly he writes!" she continued, "I expected a full sheet; but he is no doubt coming soon;"—and she eagerly applied herself to read the contents.

Priscilla turned from her a moment to examine some work; she heard a deep sigh, started to look at her cousin, and saw her falling from her seat. With a wild shriek she sprung to save her, and the family, alarmed by the noise, all rushed in. The deacon groaned most grievously when gazing on her pale face and apparently lifeless form; and gathering from the exclamations of Priscilla that the letter had caused the swoon, he soon picked it up from the floor where it had fallen, and sat quietly down to learn what terrible things it contained, leaving the care of Annie to his wife and daughter. By the time she recovered he had managed to make out most of the letter, though some of the long words puzzled him sadly; and turning to her while she was inquiring for it, he said—

"Here, here's your paper; I've made bold to read it, and I think Mr. Sidney has just shown himself out; but I never thought any better of him, though."

"O, father," whispered Priscilla, seeing the agitation of Annie, "don't say anything. She cannot bear it."

"Well, well," said he, in a very loud tone, as he was leaving the room, "I can hold my tongue; but when a man shows himself a villain, it is against my conscience to say a word in his favor. I like to do justice."

He did not recollect that "in the course of justice none of us should see salvation."

"What has Sidney written?" inquired the soft-hearted Priscilla, her tears flowing as she gazed on her weeping friend. Annie held out the letter. Her cousin took it and read as follows. There was no date.

"MY DEAR MISS REDINGTON,—I hardly dare write what necessity compels me; and yet I know, in my situation, sincerity is the most atoning virtue I can practice. Let me then spare all circumlocution, and briefly state that our connexion must, from this time be at an end. Circumstances which I cannot explain make it impossible I should ever visit New England again, or not till a distant period. I lament I ever saw you; I lament our engagement. But these reflections are now too late. Write not—forget me—or think me unworthy your affection. May heaven bless you. Farewell!

SIDNEY ROMILLY."

Priscilla had just finished the perusal when her husband, accompanied by his mother, suddenly entered. Mrs. Romilly came for comfort. She could not believe Annie's letter was like hers; it must, at least contain some excuses, or expressions of sorrow for thus leaving them; something that would palliate—justify it he could not—his conduct.

But when she saw the agitation of that fair, innocent creature, she burst into a violent passion of weeping; sobbing out, as she rocked herself backwards and forwards in her chair, "O, Annie, Annie, what shall we do? Sidney says he shall never return; and the boys may take care of the farm, and have all his part, for he has money enough. I wonder what he means!—I wonder who that man was, and what he told him to make him go away. I wish that fellow had been in the Red Sea before he came to make us all so much trouble. Sidney, I know, would never have staid away of his own accord; he would be afraid it would break my heart—and so it will, it will; I depended on him. He was my pride, my darling; and he has been so kind since his father died; and so 'fraid I should be worried! And now he says he shall never come back! O, what shall I do—what shall I do!"

Silas saw the grief of his mother was overcoming Annie, and fearing she could not endure such emotions without serious consequences, he kindly bore her to her chamber, where she passed several days in seclusion and sorrow. To be parted thus from the man she expected so shortly to marry, would in any case have been a mortification; but her grief was not the repinings of mortified disappointment. It was the deep throbbings of a tender heart, whose dearest affections were suddenly torn from the object to which they had fondly clung; it was the dark melancholy of the lone spirit, feeling it had forever lost the society and friendship of the being more prized than all the world beside; it was the bitterness of reflecting she had given her confidence and heart to a man unworthy her trust, that caused the acuteness of her anguish. She could not excuse the part Sidney had acted towards her, nor reconcile the mystery in which he appeared to wish to involve his affairs, but by admitting he had before he came to New Hampshire, been guilty of some breach of confidence or honor which he was now compeled to repair.

"Had he but died," she said to herself a thousand times—" O, had Sidney but died, I would not have murmured; I could have resigned him, had it been the appointment of heaven. I should then have reflected on his virtues; I might have cherished my affection for his memory without a blush; I might have wept his loss without self-reproach. Now, nothing, nothing is left me but to lament his infatuation and ruin, and mourn my own folly and deception."

Sidney Romilly's letter to his mother was a counterpart of the one Miss Redington had received. He just briefly said his return was impossible; wished his brothers to share his property; and desired his family not to think about him, or disturb him by letter or expostulation.

But they were not thus to be silenced. His mother, Silas, Dr. Perkins, and George Cranfield, all wrote and despatched their letters immediately, conjuring him to return, or let them know the cause why he had thus abandoned his friends. These letters were most pathetically written, and Mrs. Romilly comforted herself with the hope that they would be successful. Annie did not write—she could not; but she awaited almost in an agony of anxiety the application of the others.

Meanwhile the affair made a terrible bustle in the village, and the report thereof went forth to the ends of the whole town. Sidney appeared fated to make a *talk* for the neighborhood. Ever since he came to Northwood, there had been a quick succession of singular events occurring, and seemingly connected with his destiny. Most people thought he had now run his race, and though pitying his mother and Miss Redington, they generally came to the conclusion he had better not return. They allowed he had some good in him, but he had been badly brought up, and they feared his principles were not very strict; and finally they declared, every individual of that fickle crowd, those who but a few days before had called Sidney a pattern of perfection, that they always mistrusted he would turn out bad at last.

But in this general defection one honest heart still retained its faith in the integrity of our hero. His own mother and affianced bride trembled and doubted and mourned; but Merrill stood firm, and repelled with scorn and indignation, every insinuation urged against his benefactor.

It was a few days after the affair had become public, and when it was literally in every one's mouth, that the sturdy farmer entered the store of Mr. Skinner. The merchant had, for some time, treated Merrill with particular civility; and though the latter had, in his anger, declared he never would trade with him again, yet his was not a temper to retain resentment after the provocation which had excited it was removed, and he had of late purchased some articles, always paying *down*, however, and qualifying his meaning of not trading with him into a resolution never to get in his debt again.

And well would it be for many a farmer in our country, if they would imitate the example of Merrill, and after a merchant has once sued them, keep out of his books.

The farmer had now an inducement to call often, for his brother Luther, a shrewd, subtle, spirited lad, had lately entered the store as clerk. When the elder Merrill stepped into the shop, he heard Skinner, who did not notice him, descanting eloquently on the unpleasant affair which had occurred, concluding with, "I have heard many other conjectures, gentlemen, but the most probable one is, that Mr. Romilly was arrested for counterfeiting. Some think it was a love affair. You understand me. Others say he is already married, and his wife sent for him; but I think there's no doubt but the person who took him away was an officer, and that he has been guilty of some crime."

"But I think there's some doubt of it, sir," said Merrill, loudly, and coming forward; "and I should like to know who tells all them are stories."

"O, I hear them every day," replied Skinner, stepping backward as the other advanced. "Mrs. Watson said here, yesterday, that Mrs. Greene told her that Colonel White heard that Mr. Holmes, the landlord, saw the warrant for Sidney Romilly's apprehension in the strange gentleman's hand."

"I heard," remarked a by-stander, "that it was a paper folded just like a warrant."

"And what else could it be?" said Skinner, triumphantly laughing. "It was certainly something that made the fellow step pretty quick. I suppose he made no resistance that the matter might be kept a secret."

Mr. Merrill was perhaps as prone to give heed to the testimony of that viperous slander that "rides on the posting winds and doth belie all corners of the streets," as his neighbors, and he might, by the list of very respectable names quoted as aiding to give currency to the report, and the appearance of credence among the by-standers, have thought it, at least, a politic thing to believe it, had not every feeling of his grateful heart revolted at such a charge against Sidney. And as he could think of no arguments or facts to disprove the opinion and authorities of Skinner, he elevated himself to his full height, which was plump six feet, shook his brawny, clenched fist, and exclaimed in a voice like thunder,

"'Tis a devilish lie, the whole of it; and the first man

I hear say Sidney Romilly is a villain, why, I'll knock him down, if he's big as Goliah!"

Merrill was close to the counter as he ended, and Skinner as far back as the space permitted; and his face was pale as marble, but whether it was caused by fear, rage or guilt, no one could determine. The by-standers could not but admire the farmer's bold defense of Sidney. It was dictated by gratitude, a virtue all men applaud, and so in deference to his feelings, or in fear of his fist, they urged the matter no further, and the conversation soon glided to other subjects.

But those who talk most, feel the least. It was not the villagers who lamented the faults or fall of Sidney. It was his mother in her home, now seeming so solitary and deserted, and where the name of that beloved, lost child, was seldom mentioned, never with invectives; it was his own Annie, sitting lonely by the window where they had so often sat together, or on the seat by that soft-stealing stream where he had first talked to her of love. How beautiful then was the landscape! how cheerful every creature around! how happy her own fond heart! But beauty had fled from the prospect, and cheerfulness from the grove. It was cold October; the leaves were falling, the birds had flown; and her own hopes were withered as the one, and sad as the other. That place was now her daily resort. There, gazing on the water, and apparently lost in abstraction, she would sit whole hours. But she was thinking of her lover; recalling every word he had there spoken, or reading again and again the cruel letter which had forever blasted her happiness.

"Why could he not have written more kindly?" she often thought. "He does not even seem to lament the separation; O, he never did love as he professed! I could not thus carelessly have wounded him."

Annie Redington had loved Sidney with more than the usual devotedness of the female heart, for there was no earthly being to divide her affections. She had neither parents nor near friend; and her tender sensibilities and ardent feelings, which had long been chilled and checked, found in him, as she fondly believed, a congenial object, and they had clung around and hovered over him with all the joy, tenderness, and constancy of the dove, when received to the ark after her lonely, unresting banishment.

Man never gives his whole heart, even to the object of his choice, with the entire, unreserved devotedness of woman. It is not in his nature. His soul is abroad in the world, seeking its employments and riches and honors. He has his cares and companions, his pursuits and pleasures, independent of the idea of her.

She sits at home and thinks of him the live long day. All her arrangements are made in reference to his return; and she feels that without him the world and her history would be a blank. And life looked indeed like a blank to poor Annie. Her friends, among whom the kind physician and wife ranked first, tried every method their hearts could suggest, to divert her mind from dwelling on her disappointment; they urged a journey to Boston, offering to accompany her, and used so many persuasions she at length reluctantly consented. This acquiescence was wholly caused by her sense of duty; for the society and amusements of the "literary emporium" had now no charm to which she could look for happiness.

She felt the sin as well as weakness to which she was yielding in thus indulging a passion she knew to be hopeless, and allowing her mind to become a prey to grief, for the desertion of an inconstant—she would not say criminal—man; and she resolved to exert the fortitude her mother had so often warned her she might find indispensable in her earthly pilgrimage.

"O, my mother!" said Annie, mentally, as she had finished her reflections and arrangements, "your lot was bliss to mine."

The evening before she was to depart she went to her favorite seat beside the stream, hallowed to her heart by a thousand tender recollections. It was the last time she ever intended to allow herself the indulgence, and she sat long, as if she could not tear herself away. The evening was cold and raw, the stream, swollen by the rains, looked deep and dark, and a damp fog was rising from the waters; but she thought not of danger to herself while weeping for him. The next morning she was to start on her journey; but her throbbing head and aching limbs, made her departure impossible. She had caught cold, and combined with the agitation her spirit was suffering, it soon threw her into a fever. This did not, at first, appear violent, yet the doctor feared, as he saw his medicine could not check its ravages. He attended her with the most vigilant care, and her case exciting universal sympathy in the neighborhood, all the young ladies offered themselves as watchers by night, or attendants by day.

The readiness of those services was no doubt prompted mostly by the tenderness of their natures; but there was a lurking curiosity among these rural fair ones to see a lady who was, as they firmly believed, dying for love; and they secretly hoped she would impart to them her sorrows; and how delightful it would be to see her weep, and sympathize in her distress! But they were disappointed. Miss Redington had never been heard to mention her lover's name during the four weeks of her confinement. She had been endeavoring to devote her heart to heaven; and though she often thought of Sidney, and prayed earnestly for his happiness, her hopes no longer centered around his idea when anticipating her own; and in her sick chamber she passed many an hour of perfect peace in meditating on the calm, blessed kingdom she expected shortly to inhabit.

The Rev. Mr. Cranfield made her several visits, and was always accompanied by his amiable son, who joined his father in his pious conversations, with the feeling and enthusiasm of a Christian. Annie never saw the young gentleman's excellencies in so fair a light; still such reflections only made Sidney dearer, by increasing her anxiety that he should, like his friend George, follow righteousness. How often she thought, "O, if Sidney

Romilly had only possessed religion, he would have been a pattern of perfection—it was all he lacked."

Mr. Skinner also seemed much moved with the event of Miss Redington's illness, which indeed appeared to affect every one, and he daily sent her some present of fruits or wine. He was often assured she could not take them, yet he would persist in sending, just to show his good will; for though, as he frankly declared, he was glad Sidney had been brought to justice, he pitied her.

Dr. Perkins had never, till within a day or two of the expiration of the four weeks, despaired of Annie's life; but then he found her disorder had many fatal symptoms. He called at the deacon's one Wednesday morning at an early hour, and the report of his wife, who had been watching there, made him tremble. He ascended to the chamber and softly approached the bed. The pale, emaciated girl, looked up with a sweet smile.

"How do you find yourself, this morning, Annie?" he inquired.

"Happy, happy," she softly answered. "I am going—and I go willingly. One earthly remembrance alone dims my felicity. Sidney Romilly—I have loved him too dearly—I love him still;—but it is the affection of benevolence, the wish to see him happy. You have been my friend and his—will you, when I am gone—will you send him this ring?"—and she took it from the trembling, wasted finger, and reached it to Perkins. "Send it after I am gone," she continued, "and write, and assure him of my forgiveness, my entire forgiveness; and when you tell him of my death, do not dwell on the grief his faithlessness caused me. This poor heart will then be still and cold. Tell him, my daily prayer, on my sick-bed, was for his happiness on earth and in heaven."

Perkins and his wife wept like children. And after depositing the ring in his pocket-book, he gave his patient a composing cordial, while he said, "Annie, your wishes, in the event to which you allude, shall be complied with;

but you must not indulge this depression; you will recover."

She shook her head. He saw she was nearly exhausted, and after preparing some medicine, and telling his wife to tarry till some of the family arose to watch by Annie, and then she had better return home and endeavor to procure some rest before their children awaked, as he was obliged to go to a distance that morning, he left the chamber.

As he reached the street-door, the old deacon popped his lank, wrinkled face out of an inner apartment, saying, "How d'ye do this morning, doctor—pray how is Annie!"

"Very sick," replied Perkins.

"O, yes, we know that well enough; but will she live?"

"Why, I have fears—many fears; but I have some hope."

"Well, I can't say I have one bit," said the deacon, in an awfully solemn, lengthened tone. "I have been thinking ever since I heard you go up-stairs, how cruel it was to make that poor child take so much medicine. It can do no good, and I *raly* think you'd better let her die in peace. I have given her up, and feel truly reconciled to the Divine will."

As he ended, he caught the doctor's glance; suspicion, contempt and anger were flashing from his kindling eyes. The deacon's sunk beneath them—he drew back his head and closed the door.

Perkins bit his lip, pressed his hand on his forehead a moment, as if in anxious thought, laid down his medicine-bag, and hastily re-ascending the stairs, beckoned his wife from the room.

"Do you feel able to stay here through the day, Mary?"

"How can I leave the children?" was her answer.

"O, I'll go home," said he, "and see to them, and charge the girl to take good care. You are an excellent nurse, Mary; just such as a physician's wife ought to be.

and such a one as Annie needs now; her life hangs on a brittle thread. I have left her some medicines which will help her, if anything will; but they must be given with great exactness. Do stay till I return, which will be by noon; and don't leave Annie alone one moment. We must save her. I'll go home now and see the children."

"Then I will stay, for I love Annie like a sister."

Her husband left the house, saying to himself, "Well, Annie shall live if care can save her, and enjoy her property herself; and then we'll see if her old avaricious uncle is reconciled to the Divine will!"

CHAPTER XXXII.

A FRIEND IN NEED.

The bridegroom may forget the bride
Was made his wedded wife yestreen;
The monarch may forget the crown
That on his head an hour hath been;
The mother may forget the child
That smiles so sweetly on her knee;
But I'll remember thee, Glencairn,
And a' that thou hast done for me. BURNS.

LEAVING Miss Redington to the care of her devoted friends, such as every person in her critical condition needs, you and I, kind reader, will go South, and learn what has befallen her recreant lover.

How suddenly Sidney left his farm and his fiancée has been already related. The gentleman, with whom he departed, was from Georgia, and brought letters causing Sidney much astonishment. The first he opened was from his friend Charles Stuart, who had, he fancied, forgotten him. The startling intelligence it contained, will be better understood by the insertion of the letter than any explanation I could give. It was dated at

"*Charleston, S. C., August 20th*, 18—.

MY DEAR ROMILLY,—This is the third letter I have written you since the misfortunes and decease of Mr. Brainard, your excellent uncle. To the two others I have received no answer: had they reached your hand you could not have neglected me, so I flatter myself; and I must believe they miscarried. To obviate all possibility of a like fate befalling this, I have engaged Mr. Tracy, who is on a tour to Boston, a friend of mine, and one well entitled to your confidence, to take a trip to New Hampshire and deliver it into your hands.

The manner of your late uncle's failure you know; and also the arrangement he made with the gentleman to whom his estate was consigned. In those letters I forwarded you were enclosed drafts on a bank in Boston to the amount of four hundred dollars, two hundred in each letter. The money I conjured you, in the name of our friendship, to receive, and entreated you to come to Savannah, and consider my home as your own. But when I received no answer, I sometimes feared you were offended at the liberty I had taken. I knew your independence of spirit; I knew from experience how mortifying are pecuniary obligations to a mind of nice and delicate honor; and I thought the most acceptable services I could render you, (and I owe you all I can perform) would be to attempt the discovery of the retreat of Cox, and the security of the vast debt he owed your late uncle's estate.

All my efforts were, however, for a long time unavailing; but a few weeks since I heard of him, and that he was at New Orleans. I hastened to Charleston, and consulting with your agent there, we despatched a trusty person to ferret out the villain if he were above ground. The man we employed hastened to New Orleans, and, the goddess of chance being propitious for once to honest men, he found Cox at a gaming-table, where, by an extraordinary run of luck, he was literally 'lording it over a heap of massy gold;' and he satisfied your whole demand, not only without grumbling, but even with exultation; saying, 'that he liked, at times, to clear scores with the devil by an act of honesty.' And thus your fortune is now once more at your command.

I need not say how much I rejoice at this; how much I want to see you, nor with what unfeigned congratulations you will be welcomed back to our section of the country. Do come immediately; your presence is necessary on account of your own interest; and it is indispensable to the happiness of your friends. Your agent writes, and therefore it is needless for me to detail those particulars which must, with your benevolent feelings, induce you to visit Charleston with the utmost despatch. I shall wait here till the twenty-fifth of September, in expectation of embracing you.

Zemira is well, and I am the father *of a fine boy.* We call him Sidney Romilly.

Yours, forever, CHARLES STUART."

The other letter was from H. Howard, Esq., and ran thus:

"*Charleston, S. C., August* 21, 18—.

MR. ROMILLY,—Sir, we have traced Cox to New Orleans, and recovered the money. It is all safe in my hands, waiting the disposal you shall order. I hope it will be convenient for you to come here immediately; indeed, it is absolutely necessary if you intend to redeem the estate of your late uncle. Dunbar was a good man, but he has transferred the property to another; subject, however, to the articles of redemption he entered into with your uncle.

The man who is now in possession, is one of those cruel, unfeeling wretches, whose actions are a libel on the name of man. Beneath his iron sway, your uncle's servants are groaning worse than the Israelites did in Egypt. They are looking for you as their Moses, and I need say no more. Your heart is their guarantee of release from their rigorous bondage. Should I recount the cruelty of this monster, your blood would chill; come, then, and fulfil the anxious desire of your late uncle, and gratify the wishes of your numerous friends here, by fixing your residence among us. To judge by the anxiety now expressed for you, there is not a man of respectability in the city who would not be happy to serve you; and though a part of this extraordinary civility may undoubtedly be ascribed to the recovery of your fortune, yet you are, independently of that consideration, very highly prized by your acquaintance, and you have *one* such faithful friend as but few men ever obtain. I allude to Charles Stuart. He has been indefatigable in his endeavors to serve you; it was by his efforts that Cox was finally discovered, and all the expense has been borne by him, as he would neither allow me to contribute, nor will he receive any repayment from the money he has thus recovered. He is, indeed, a tried friend; and long may you both enjoy the prosperity you equally deserve.

With the most profound respect,
I am, sir, your obedient servant,
HENRY HOWARD."

"P. S.—You must be here before the twenty-fifth of September, or the bond will be forfeited, the year expiring at that time; and the fellow now in possession, being loth to relinquish his bargain, he will take every advantage possible. The delay of one day beyond the stipulated time will bar your claim forever. H. H."

Such was the tenor of the intelligence that decided Sidney Romilly instantly to visit Charleston. He thought it not best to communicate the particulars to his betrothed or his family until after he had, from actual inspection, adopted some plan of conduct. If the servants were thus miserable, he should, at all events, redeem the estate, but to say so would cause his mother unceasing anxiety during his absence; she would anticipate his own removal to the south; and he knew too well how highly he was prized at home to think they would willingly resign him. He would not thus trouble them, unless absolutely necessary, and it might be, some other arrangement would, on his reaching Charleston, appear more fitting. And when all perplexity and uncertainty respecting his affairs was over, he would write or return, and his friends, finding matters actually settled, would acquiesce, especially when they found how liberally he was enabled to provide for them.

On his arrival at the city he found Mr. Stuart waiting to welcome him, and the pleasure of embracing that estimable friend, and meeting his former acquaintances, was as exquisite as sincere; and yet the meeting with the servants of his late uncle was far more touching to his heart. When he arrived at the plantation, they crowded around him, and their tears, exclamations, and almost frantic gestures, formed a picture of wild joy that cannot be intelligibly described. To be understood, it must have been beheld. And an examination of their condition determined him at once to redeem the estate. The wretch who had purchased it under an impression Sidney would never return, was highly enraged; but, after much altercation and the interference of many friends, he was at last brought to terms, and everything settled to the satisfaction of Sidney and the servants at least. Their countenances and manners underwent a complete transformation when they found he was again their own *mas'r!* Their tears were literally turned to songs, and their groans to such loud peals of laughter as made the whole neighborhood ring. Cato, in particular, justified Sidney's encomiums on the tone of his lungs; at the sight of his young mas'r, he would laugh so obstreperously that he incurred some serious reproofs; and the servants reported he was heard the night after the articles concerning the estate were settled, to laugh in his sleep, if he slept, nearly the whole night.

After all arrangements were completed, Sidney wrote to Annie and his mother, detailing the particulars with exactness, but dwelling most minutely on the situation of the slaves and the events which had made his repurchase of his uncle's estate necessary, indeed indispensable. He also entreated Annie to be in readiness to give him her hand immediately on his return, which would be in a few weeks; to his mother he sent two hundred dollars, to procure the children apparel for his bridal solemnity.

Why these letters were never received, will be explained hereafter.

He did not, in either of the letters, directly mention that he designed residing at the South; but he hoped, from the tenor of his remarks, they would infer it; and that when reflecting, as they must do, it was necessary for the comfort of his servants, and would conduce to his interest, their scruples might be overcome. He found, indeed, the measure more congenial with his own feelings than he had imagined, while residing in New Hampshire, it ever would be. But it was in Charleston his habits had been formed, opinions imbibed, and friends selected; and though he had yielded to necessity with philosophical firmness, and had labored with his hands without much repining, yet but few voluntarily subject themselves to the penalty of Adam; and I confess my hero felt very willing to lay down the spade when he found to dig was no longer necessary. He was intending to work in another way.

The inhabitants of Charleston have always been distinguished for their urbanity and hospitality, and their city as a pleasant place of residence; and in the first circles, in which our hero moved and now found himself flatteringly caressed, there was that union of intelligence, politeness and refinement which constitutes the charm of social intercourse, and which was so congenial to his taste.

It was true his fondest affections were centered in New Hampshire; but he thought if Annie would consent to accompany him to Charleston, and perhaps some of his own family also, he then should enjoy independence, and the advantages and pleasures of elegant society, combined with that dear domestic bliss which makes the heart's best, truest felicity. He thought, too, that such was the happiness his father's predictions had indicated; and he renewed with eagerness his acquaintance with many excellent families, who he knew were worthy his confidence, and to whom he anticipated, with proud delight, the introduction of his lovely and beloved bride. And many a dream of future happiness floated round his pillow by night, and brightened his smiles by day.

At length he was ready to begin his homeward journey, or rather to visit the home of his friends; his own he considered already settled at the South. The night before his departure two letters post-marked Northwood, were handed him; he recognized the writing of Annie, and instantly opened hers, smiling as he did so, while anticipating the sweet congratulations on his prosperity it must contain. But judge of his consternation when reading as follows:

"SIR—I have received your letter, and am glad of your good fortune; but I think it my duty to inform you our correspondence must be at an end. I know you will want me to reside at the South; but to go there and be a partaker in the sin of slavery is what I will not do. You can doubtless find, in Charleston, some fair lady more worthy your love, and more congenial to your manner of life than my education and principles would permit me to be. You need not write, for my resolution is taken.

Farewell, ANNIE REDINGTON."

Sidney gazed wildly on the paper—re-read it—tore it in a thousand pieces and crushed it beneath his feet; and then, pale, and trembling with contending passions, he sat down to peruse the other letter. It was from his mother, and briefly said she rejoiced he had recovered his estate, and thought best, all things considered, he should reside at the South. The boys had found they could manage the farm, and he had too much money to want to work, &c. &c.—and finally, she added that George Cranfield was very attentive to Miss Redington, and it was thought they would soon be married.

Such a confirmation of Annie's perfidy he could scarcely support. He was nearly frantic with rage, jealousy, and a thirst for vengeance; but when his angry passions, by exhausting his strength, had partly subsided, the recollection of his love, the thought of her tenderness, now no more to be cherished, overcame him, and he wept like a child. The disappointment of his wishes concerning Zemira was nothing like this. Then he never received assurance; now he had indulged the confidence of reciprocated affection. He had thought of Annie as his wife; he had associated her idea with every plan of earthly happiness; he had even hoped her piety would, like the pure-falling tears of an angel's tenderness, blot out his transgressions, and her example strengthen his weak faith and guide his erring steps in the way to eternal life. She had disappointed, cruelly disappointed, deceived, betrayed him. She had not only destroyed his hopes of happiness, but his confidence in human virtue, for could he ever expect to find more seeming purity, sincerity or piety, than she had exhibited, when "all was false and hollow?"

How he cursed the fickle, faithless, cruel sex; and vowed never again to trust their smiles, or seek happiness from their affection. He would not return to Northwood; and to remain at Charleston would inevitably subject him to the humiliation of having his disappointment made public; as he had openly revealed his engagements, and indeed boasted of the lovely, amiable, intelligent bride he was intending to introduce to his friends. O, it was too much! now that the cup of happiness was seemingly within his grasp, thus to have it dashed from his lip. But he would go far, where no one knew his story—he would go to England, visit Frankford, and, plunged in the whirl of dissipation, forget his home, friends, love, every thing! Such were some of his wild ravings.

At length he became more calm; but then he could form no plan so likely to succeed in restoring his serenity as a voyage to Europe. He determined on it; arranged his affairs, and took leave of his friends. To them he stated business made his visit to England necessary, and that, in consequence, his marriage would be delayed till spring. How few have courage to tell the whole truth to the world!

Sidney wrote a tender letter to his mother, for he would not part with her in anger, though he felt wounded by the indifference she had manifested in hers concerning his change of residence, and in his letter he enclosed another two hundred dollar note as a present to herself. To Annie he did not write—he thought her conduct merited silent contempt. He then took passage on board a packet ship bound for London, and ready to sail the first fair wind. It soon blew a favorable gale, his baggage was already on board, and followed by his faithful Cato, our hero ascended the vessel that was to bear him to a distant region; but he could no longer flatter himself with the hope of there finding felicity.

How the dissolution of one single tie will loosen our grasp from the world;—the disappointment of one expectation darken the sun of our prosperity! But a few days had passed since Sidney thought the whole world smiled upon him, for Annie loved him. Now there was "none so poor to do him reverence," none to lament his fate should he throw himself headlong into the dark waters beneath. He shuddered as the temptation to do so rushed powerfully on his mind, almost bearing down the instinctive dread of death implanted in our nature, and for a moment entirely sweeping away the mounds of prudence and principle.

But the thought of his father, so calm and happy, came over him. He felt reproved for such sinful and violent indulgence of his passions. He knew his father would have told him that the trials and temptations of men were mercifully allotted for the perfection of their virtue, and that to endure unavoidable misfortunes with firmness and resignation, was their duty, and one which, if they did perform, they might enjoy, if not happiness, certainly tranquillity. He turned from the contemplation of the deep waters, and pacing the deck, inquired, in an impatient tone, why they did not sail? and received for answer, they were waiting the arrival of some articles expected every moment, and then they should weigh anchor immediately.

But Sidney at last grew weary of pacing the deck, and gazing on the bright heavens and dancing waters, and hearing the laugh of the seamen; these objects were all too placid and happy to accord with the tone of his feelings, and he retired to his state-room, and there, seated in gloomy reflections, he waited impatiently for the vessel to depart. While he sat thus, Cato entered with his usual laughing look, to say a man wanted to speak with mas'r.

"Who is he? what does he want?" inquired Sidney, in a stern tone, that for a moment awed the smile of the favorite servant, and he bowed his head like the humble slave while he answered.

"Me don't know what he want; but he say he must speak wid mas'r. He look queer."

"Look! why, how does he look?"

"O, he great, rough, dirty fellow. No gentleman, mas'r."

"I won't speak with him, Cato. Tell him I am engaged."

Cato departed, but soon returned, saying, "He no go away till he see you, mas'r. He must see you, 'cause he big news to tell, mas'r."

"Well, let him come, then," said Sidney, roused by the mention of intelligence. "But then," thought he, "there can be no joyful news. I am at least freed from suspense. I know my fate." He sat with his eyes fastened on the door. Cato threw it open.

"Here be de man, mas'r."

"Heavens!" exclaimed Sidney, starting up, and rushing forward with such a look of amazement as actually frightened his servant. Cato thought his master was

THE MEETING IN THE STATE ROOM.

angry with the man thus introduced; but he was undeceived when Sidney caught his hand.

"Merrill, my good friend Merrill, can this be you? Where in the name of wonder did you come from?"

"Why, from home, from Northwood, to be sure," replied the genuine Yankee, returning the pressure and shake of his patron's hand, with more than lawful interest. "And I look as if I had, I guess. It's a pretty long road, I call it, and most of the way darnation dusty." And he brushed the dust from his sleeve, and shook his hat, as he seated himself in a chair Cato officiously offered—for Cato began to think, from seeing his master shake hands so familiarly with the stranger, that he might be a gentleman.

Sidney sat trembling with a thousand anxieties; at last he said to Merrill, who was still brushing his clothes, as if he had nothing else to think of,—

"Why, Mr. Merrill, what could induce you to come such a journey?"

"O, I came to find you, Mr. Sidney Romilly; all the way to find you. And, God be praised, I have found you, and my fatigue is now nothing at all."

Our hero could not inquire why he had thus been sought; an indefinite feeling, compounded of hope, wonder, and incredulity, took possession of his mind. He sat like one in a stupor, hardly crediting his own eyes, or acknowledging the identity of Merrill; and then to think he had made the journey solely to see him.

Merrill broke the silence. "Well, now I 'spose you'd like to hear about your folks; and they are all pretty well, only very *moloncholy*."

"And what should make them melancholy?"

"O, because they think you an't a coming home."

"Did they send you after me?"

"O, no, sir, no—they didn't know I was coming, nor any body else for that matter, only my wife and brother Luther."

"And what do you want with me?" asked Sidney, beginning to doubt the sanity of the farmer.

"Why, it's a long story, the reasons that made me come; but I'll tell you all, only I should like to ax you a few questions, and have you answer 'em right up and down."

"Well, ask away; I'll answer as many as you please."

"Did you ever write to your mother and Miss Redington that you wa'nt coming home, and didn't intend to marry her?"

"No, never to Annie; I wrote to my mother I should not return, but it is only four days since, and the letter has not yet reached her!"

"Ah! there it is now—just as we thought! But did you write to them that you had got back all your money and was coming home to be married, and in your mother's letter send some money to buy fine things?"

"Yes."

"Well, now I'll tell you all about it." He then related what the reader already knows; the arrival of those cruel letters, the consternation they caused, and the conjectures they excited; and then he proceeded to narrate —I would give it in his own language, but fear the reader would feel something of Sidney's impatience— that his brother Luther, who was a clerk of Skinner's, had seen him, instead of putting the letters of Mrs. Romilly, Dr. Perkins and George Cranfield into the mail bag, deposit them in his desk; and afterwards saw him write and superscribe some letters to Sidney Romilly. The lad, who, his brother affirmed, was a hawk-eyed chap, suspected foul play, and watched till he found an opportunity of obtaining the key, and then, on searching the desk, he found those he had mistrusted were there, and two others from Sidney, directed to his mother and Miss Redington. The remaining part of the story shall be given in his own words.

"And in them letters was all about your good fortune, and then Luther hnew the whole trick; and he took the letters, and as soon as Skinner was gone to bed, he came posting right straight up to my house, and called my wife and me both out of bed and told us the whole affair. And when we read the letters, we knew Skinner had kept back the right ones, and forged others, on purpose to keep you away; he always hated you ever since you helped me so much. And there was your mother a' most crazy, and Annie, poor girl, sick and like to die."

"Die!" exclaimed Sidney, starting up, while his face was white as marble, and his knees smote together.

"No, no," replied the farmer, eagerly, frightened at the lover's agitation; "no, she won't die, I don't think; but she's some sick with a fever. But she'll be well again as soon as ever she sees you."

There was that in the conclusion of the honest man's speech, that sent the warm blood through Sidney's heart with such a gush of tenderness, that hardly able to support the tide of hope rushing thus at once upon his mind, he sank into his chair and covered his face with his hands. After a moment's pause, he again looked at Merrill, who was watching him anxiously, and said in a low tone, "Go on, go on, I can hear you. You concluded to come after me."

"O, yes, I did. We talked the matter all over and over, and my wife said something must *sartinly* be done. And if we sent a letter to the post-office Skinner would destroy it; and if I carried it to some other one it might miscarry, or you might be sick as Annie was."

Sidney groaned.

"O, she'll live, Mr. Sidney Romilly. It can't be, as my wife said, but that this villany is all brought to light to make you happy. And so I concluded to start right off. We did'nt like to tell of the matter till I'd got you home, and then we thought Skinner would feel pretty blue. And I happened to have fifty dollars that I'd just sold some cattle for that very day. It seemed like a providence; and Luther made me take six dollars of him, 'cause he said you gave him so much, about a squirrel hunt, and he never forgot it. I didn't like to take it, for it was all the money he had, and he'd been saving it up a long time; but I thought I might be sick on the way. My wife was a little afraid I should get into trouble, and she warned me to keep clear of disputes, for she had heard your gentlemen here made no more of killing a man in a duel, than she would of killing a chicken for dinner. Howsomever, I told her not to fret. I guessed I knew how to shoot as well as the best of 'em. And I started on foot, for I thought folks would wonder if I took the stage; but I rode in the stage most of the way, only when I was too tired; and I got here at last, safe and sound, but black and dirty enough."

"How did you learn where I was?" inquired Sidney, who felt a restless anxiety to learn every particular.

"O, when I got to the hotel, I spoke to the landlord, and he sent a man where you used to lodge; for I felt a little queer in such a fine city, about going out till I had taken off my beard, and brushed up a little; but just as I was beginning, in came the fellow to say you had gone on board the vessel, and so I got him to come down and show me the ship pretty plaguy quick. I was afraid you would be off to sea."

"And what would you have done had the vessel been actually sailing away?" inquired Sidney, half laughing, while he anticipated what would have been the honest fellow's distress.

"What!" repeated Merrill, opening his eyes with a wide stare, at the proposal of a dilemma he had made no provision to obviate. "What!—why I suppose you must have gone. I am no Peter to walk on the water; I hav'n't faith enough for that. But I had enough to think I should find you on the land."

"And we will be on the land soon," replied Sidney, rising. "Cato, see my baggage unloaded and sent back to the hotel. I am not going to sea, Cato; you are glad, I presume."

"Yes, yes, Mas'r; me berry glad you stay in de land ob liberty," replied Cato, grinning with joy as he sat about executing his master's orders.

Sidney then, after arranging matters with the captain, left the vessel, with feelings at his heart very unlike those with which he had entered it, and accompanied by Merrill, proceeded to his lodgings in the city. There was a mingling of many emotions in his mind; but hope, sweet, love-whispering hope, predominated; and while the recollection of Annie's danger made him hurry his departure for Northwood, he had caught a portion of the faith of Mrs. Merrill, and could not believe he was now to be mocked with the phantom of happiness. He made Merrill relate minutely every particular he had heard concerning Miss Redington's illness. It was by the blunt farmer, ascribed entirely to pure, pure love, and Sidney very complacently listened to his opinion on the nature of her malady; and though pitying her, and cursing Skinner, yet he felt, were all things once more happily settled, he should, from the trials he had endured, find his felicity more perfect.

"And this," thought he, "is the true art of being happy; to be able to extract good from evil, and trace the bow of mercy still resting on the darkest cloud that dims our horizon."

Early on the following morning they left the city. Merrill said he should *raly* like to stay a few days and look about the country; he thought the place and the people too looked pretty smart, much better, and more civil than he expected, and he *raly* liked them both very well.

Sidney thought he had better stay a week and rest himself, and then follow in the stage; but Merrill would not see his friend depart without him. Besides, he said "he must be at home; he feared his wife would work too hard, and women had never oughter do anything out of doors." And then he wanted to see the *blow up* of Skinner, and much he anticipated from the exposing of that consummate villain.

The travelers never halted, except with the stage, Sidney being too anxious to reach home to think of fatigue. As for Merrill, in accomplishing so happily the object of his journey, he had entirely freed his mind from care, and he slept as comfortably, and snored as soundly—except when receiving a kick from some fellow traveler, who doubtless envied him his somnolency—in the stage as he ever did in his own quiet dwelling.

On the way, Sidney, while meditating what method would most unequivocally detect the guilt of Skinner, recollected the bank notes enclosed in those letters he had sent his mother. These notes the merchant would undoubtedly offer at the bank on which they were drawn, to be exchanged; and Sidney determined to call there and leave a description that would lead to the detection of the person presenting them. Accordingly, on his arrival at Boston, which was without accident of any kind, he went directly to the Suffolk Bank, and describing the notes, inquired if they had been presented.

The cashier replied in the affirmative, adding, "they were presented here, sir, about half an hour ago."

"How unlucky!" interrupted Sidney.

"Not all, sir; they were not changed. I was engaged, and the gentleman proposed calling again after dinner, or in about two hours. You can procure a warrant and officer if you think proper, and be here at that time."

Sidney made further inquiries, and became convinced the person presenting the notes was no other than Skinner himself; and Merrill was so overjoyed at the near prospect of *blowing him up*, he could scarcely eat his dinner. Everything was arranged, and the proper officer, with Sidney and Merrill, were stationed in an inner apartment. Presently they heard some person enter the counting room; and in the next moment Sidney recognized the voice of Skinner, speaking in his most insinuating tone.

"There," whispered Merrill, laying his hand on Sidney's shoulder, "there, just so palavering the rascal spoke when he flattered me to give him the mortgage of my farm. I'd rather hear a man speak as loud as thunder."

The cashier made some inquiries relative to the manner in which he obtained the notes; and Skinner answered they were a present to him from a brother residing in New Orleans.

"That may be," replied the cashier, "but here is a gentleman claims these notes as his property."

Skinner started quickly around as the triumvirate advanced from their hiding place. Had he beheld the Gorgons he could not have appeared more like a statue of stone than when his eyes met those of our hero. The officer instantly arrested him, and told him he must go before the magistrate to be examined.

Sidney's heart beat quick to hear from Annie, but he could not bring his tongue to make the inquiry of Skinner, so much he detested him. As for the prisoner, he maintained a dogged silence, nor would he deign a reply to a single question proposed by the magistrate. Sidney identified the notes, and his and Merrill's testimony were sufficient to establish a conviction of the prisoner's guilt in the minds of all present, and the magistrate ordered Skinner to recognize in the sum five thousand dollars, or he must stand committed for further trial.

It was then, for the first time since entering the court, that the culprit appeared to feel a sense of his situation. His countenance underwent several changes, but finally a deadly paleness overspread it, and his voice trembled as he said,

"I am guilty, I confess it; but I was not prompted by the desire of gain. It was envy and revenge against you, Mr. Romilly. I knew you were beloved by Miss Redington; I loved her myself, and I intercepted the letters to prevent your union. They contained money —this I was obliged to keep or destroy. I brought it here, and now I am detected. But you, sir, will suffer as well as I. If I must lose my liberty, you have lost your love; for Annie Redington is dead."

"Dead! is she dead?" exclaimed Merrill, "is she dead?"

"Yes, she died the day before I left home."

"O, God!" said Sidney, in a voice that thrilled the hearts of the hearers, as gasping for breath he leaned against a table for support. "O why did I not reach home sooner! Skinner, it was you that destroyed her, and your soul will answer it."

"I'll risk that," replied the villain, with an insulting laugh. "I am glad she is dead. She was not for me, and I rejoice she can never be yours."

"Wretch!" vociferated Sidney, seizing Skinner by the collar and shaking him as if he had been a rag, "wretch! you have murdered her, and I am tempted to dash you to atoms!"

"Hurl him to the devil, Sidney!" cried Merrill, fiercely, "where he should have been years ago. I wish I had hold of him."

The magistrate and by-standers were obliged to rescue Skinner, or Sidney in the wrath of his roused spirit, might have fulfilled the bidding of his faithful Merrill, who would indeed have gladly lent him a hand to avenge the wrongs the unfeeling monster had inflicted. After they were separated, Skinner still continued his taunts till Sidney was forced from the room, and supported by those who saw and pitied his emotion, conveyed to his lodgings. There he passed the night in a kind of sullen apathy, refusing all refreshment, and only replying to the inquiries of Merrill by a motion of his hand or a monosyllable. The next morning, though scarcely able to sit up, he resolved to proceed, seeming to imagine if he could only reach Northwood he should see Annie again.

Merrill drew many a sigh during their ride, and wore a most dolorous expression of countenance, which did not become his visage at all. And all he could say, which he thought would be acceptable to his patron, was, that "this was a world of trouble, and it was the duty of every one to prepare for a better. For his part, the only comfort he had was that Skinner would *sartinly* go to the State's prison."

But there was no comfort for Sidney, and he continued sunk in the deepest dejection, and scarcely spoke from the time he left Boston till the stage stopped at the well known tavern of Landlord Holmes.

CHAPTER XXXIII.

THE PRIZE IS WON.

The rose is fairest when 'tis budding new,
And hope is brightest when it dawns from fears;
The rose is sweetest wet with morning dew,
And love is loveliest when embalmed in tears.
LADY OF THE LAKE.

DR. PERKINS was half reclining on his horse before the door of the tavern, as the stage drew up, and conversing with the landlord, who held his horse's bridle, as fearful the man of physic would depart before answering all the inquiries which had been proposed to him. The most important were those a physician is always bound to answer—questions relative to his patients; and Perkins had been of late more strictly catechised than usual, as every person who ever heard of Miss Redington appeared interested in her fate.

The penetrating reader has doubtless surmised, the tender hearted one must have hoped, that the story of her death was a sheer fabrication of Skinner's to torment his rival. She was still living, and Perkins, to the inquiries of the landlord, stated he had some hope, though but very faint, of her recovery.

"I left her this morning early," continued he, "with my wife to watch and tend her till my return, and I must hasten to see her."

"What a cruel hearted fellow that young Romilly is," said Boniface, still holding fast the bridle, "to leave such a sweet lady, and so in love with him too! Don't you think he'll never come back?"

"How can I tell?" said Perkins, peevishly, and striving

to free the rein from the landlord's grasp that he might not listen to further invectives against Sidney, whom he could not justify, and yet to hear him condemned always went to his heart. "I should never have thought of his going away so, and he may return as unexpectedly. And there—by Jupiter!—there he is now!"

"Who?—where?" cried the landlord, jumping round as briskly as the weight of a quarter of a ton of flesh would allow.

"Why, Sidney, Sidney Romilly! Heaven, I thank thee!"—and the next moment he had vaulted from his horse and was grasping the hands of his friend! Sidney returned the pressure, but his wo-begone countenance sufficiently testified to his heart's sorrow; yet Perkins did not notice it while loudly exclaiming, "O, Sidney! how welcome you are; how joyful we shall all be; and Annie—Annie will recover!"

"Recover!" echoed the despairing Sidney, while his whole soul seemed rushing forth in his eager accent. "O, Skinner said she had died—she was dead!"

"No, no; she is not dead—she is alive—she will live!" said Perkins.

The truth flashed at once upon the heart of our hero. He wrung the hand of his friend with almost as violent a pressure as Merrill once did his own—tears of joy gushed to his eyes—while his expressive countenance was lighted up with such a glow of surprise, gratitude, and rapture, that the farmer, who had just alighted from the stage, cried out, "Well, well, Mr. Romilly, I'm glad to see you look alive again; I *sartinly* hav'nt seen you smile before since we left Boston. But there's that Skinner—hanging is too good for him."

"Why, Merrill, are you here?" said Perkins, offering his hand. "I did not notice you before. Why, where have you been?"

"O, I've been a plaguy long jaunt, I can tell you that; and glad I am to see New Hampshire again; as cold and rough as 'tis, it looks warm and pleasant to me. Though I like away there to the South, too, better than I expected; but here are all my friends and family, and now I've got Mr. Sidney Romilly back here, I guess you won't catch me away from home again in a hurry."

This speech led to inquiries and explanations, equally satisfactory to all parties; and then, borrowing a horse from the landlord, Sidney departed with his friend Perkins, after charging Merrill to call on him as often as possible, and assuring him, that though intending to reward him liberally for the services he had opportunely rendered, yet he should always consider him entitled to his warmest gratitude.

The farmer, however, disclaimed all merit in the affair, declaring, with an emphasis as sincere as Deacon Jones ever used, he had only done his *duty*, and that all the reward he desired was the opportunity of being present at his patron's wedding.

"And now," said he, "I must step home and see my wife and boys, and I guess they'll be as glad to see me as Miss Redington will you, only may be they won't be quite so surprised, as they never thought I was gone clear off."

On their way to his mother's, Sidney asked his friend what motives, he thought, induced Skinner to torture him with the report of Annie's death.

"O, he meant to make you suffer Purgatory before enjoying Paradise, I suppose," returned Perkins, laughing; "or, perhaps, he was even more malicious, and calculated on keeping you in Purgatory forever; as your despair would probably lead you to take the lover's leap; and the person guilty of *felo de se* is, I believe, by the universal vote of mankind, excluded from all hope of mercy."

"I cannot tell what I might have been tempted to do," said the other, "had I found Annie was actually in her grave. Though I never doubted the report of her death; indeed, how could I disbelieve what was so positively affirmed! yet I still felt as if, on reaching Northwood, I should see her alive. My mind was in that state of indefinite horror which a frightful dream sometimes occasions, and which, while yielding to its influence, we know is but a dream, and strive to awaken that the phantoms may disappear. But I—I have awoke to hope, joy, life!"

The meeting of Sidney with his family was a scene very touching and affectionate. They had been suffering for him the most intense anxiety and keen mortifications, and yet love and pride had forbidden them to complain of his conduct or seek sympathy for their sorrows. And they had smothered their feelings, or only indulged them in secret. But Sidney came—every suspicious circumstance was explained—every fortunate occurrence related—and he was still the same noble, generous, exalted being; their hope, and pride, and boast; and their tears, so long restrained in grief, now burst forth in floods to express their joy.

Annie he was not permitted to visit till the following day; the Doctor and his wife in the meantime having apprised her of everything she could desire to exculpate her lover, and finally informed her of his arrival.

Their first meeting was too affecting for description, especially in the last chapter of a work that was designed to leave none save agreeable or useful impressions on the mind. But the visit, though tender and tearful, was a cordial to poor Annie's heart, and she appeared through the whole day so evidently better, that even her uncle took courage, and in his evening orisons, returned his solemn thanks for the unexpected and undeserved mercy vouchsafed them in her amendment.

It was, indeed, curious to see the management of the Deacon, and how easily he transferred his favor and his conscience from the falling to the rising fortune. Our hero's merits were no longer equivocal. One hundred thousand dollars established the worth of his character beyond suspicion; and though the Deacon lamented the total depravity of human nature, yet he acknowledged Skinner's crime could plead no extenuation on that score, and he *raly* hoped he would receive exemplary punishment. And an event soon occurred which entirely reconciled him to the loss of the merchant's society.

The store of Skinner being closed, the villagers expe

rienced much inconvenience in procuring those articles he used to furnish; and Sidney thought the opportunity a favorable one for his brother Silas to commence the same business. Silas was a very ready accountant, and by exertion, and the aid of Luther Merrill, might soon succeed in understanding its details sufficiently for a country trader. He offered to advance his brother four thousand dollars, on condition he would pay the interest yearly to his mother, during her life, in such articles as she required; and at her decease the principal to be divided among all the remaining members of the family; Silas to have two shares, and the other individuals one each.

This offer was too liberal to be rejected; but the difficulty was in obtaining a room suitable for their purpose. Skinner's store was not then to be procured, and they wished to go into business immediately, before any one should anticipate their design. Finally, Deacon Jones offered his Conference Room, till a more convenient one could be erected; and they proceeded forthwith to make such alterations as were deemed necessary to fit it for the accommodation of their intended business.

The Deacon remarked, that though "folks might *talk* about it, he had fully answered his conscience in providing so long for the meetings of his brethren, and now it belonged to the others to fulfil their *duty*."

The store was completed, goods purchased, and a large sign, bearing the inscription of "Silas Romilly & Co.," in flaming letters of gold-leaf, displayed over the street door, opening into the Conference Room, within less than a month after Sidney returned. So well did Silas manage to please his customers, that not a desire was ever uttered for the return of his predecessor. But many wished the term of Skinner's confinement to hard labor in the state prison could be doubled, like that of Jacob's servitude, and then, instead of seven years—the time for which he was sentenced—he would be kept safe fourteen.

The "Co." on the sign was generally supposed, in the

neighborhood, to include the Deacon; yet whenever such a hint was suggested to him, he always would shake his head, look grave, and say he had enough of this world's goods already, and should let the young folks manage the business; it was all done to please Mr. Sidney, who had been so kind and generous to his family, they felt bound to do pretty much as he wished."

Sidney did, indeed, appear to his friends like their guardian angel. None were forgotten by him. He made ample provision for James to pursue his studies; and hired a steady man to manage the farm, with the assistance of Sam and Oliver, who were, if they did well, to share it between them. Sophia and Lucy were to be placed, for two years, at a celebrated school for young ladies, in Hartford, Connecticut; and after their education was completed, the two younger girls were to enjoy similar advantages. Harvey was to accompany his brother to the South; and the widowed mother had, indeed, everything bestowed on her she could wish for.

Nor while providing thus amply for his own relatives did Sidney forget his faithful Merrill. He canceled the note the latter was owing him, and bestowed on him a sum of money sufficient to clear every debt he had incurred, and the farmer declared he was "independent, and wouldn't swap with a king." And, moreover, Sidney left funds in the hands of Dr. Perkins, to furnish all the little Merrills with an ample supply of books; and should any one of the number exhibit sufficient genius to make it probable a liberal education would be for his advantage and happiness, he pledged his assistance to enable him to attain it; at any rate, he should consider the fortunes of one of the boys as depending on him for advancement.

Miss Redington, too, when she had sufficiently recovered, ordered a variety of presents for Mrs. Merrill and the children, till this worthy family, from being universally pitied, as they were but one year before, now became as universally envied. The favor of the lovers was really a matter of mighty consequence to all who wished an opportunity of attending the wedding, for which preparations were making on a magnificent scale. Mrs. Romilly said she was willing the invitation should be extended to every person in the town, except Mrs. Watson. To be sure there were some others who had credited and reported the stories about Sidney and joined in the censure against him, but they were deceived; whereas, Mrs. Watson had combined with the villain Skinner to tell Annie a frightful fortune, and propagate the slanders which he forged.

The sibyl urged in her own defense, that she did not know the design of the merchant; that she told him she was going to visit Mrs. Jones, and should probably tell Miss Redington's fortune, and then he offered, if she would tell that young lady her lover was not intending to return, and was probably engaged to another woman, he would give her the nicest shawl which could be purchased in Boston, and a pound of his best Gunpowder tea! That she did tell her so, and after the thing seemed actually to come to pass she was so frightened she did not dare reveal the secret. However, her plea was not admitted as a justification of her offense, and she received no call to the marriage-feast; which mortified her so sensibly she was heard to declare, to the deep regret of all the young ladies of the village, that she never would interpret another dream, or tell another fortune, if she lived as long as Methuselah.

New-year's day was appointed for the wedding, and a happy and proud day it was for the Romillys. The celebration was got up in far the most splendid style ever witnessed in Northwood, or its vicinity; and long furnished topics of discourse for all who had the privilege of attending it. The noble countenance and rich attire of the bridegroom, and the sweet face and elegant ornaments of the lovely bride, were themes that could never be uninteresting to those who beheld this amiable pair, when standing before the holy priest, they plighted hands and hearts in a union as dear as their affections, and indissoluble as their lives.

Mr. Merrill, whose agency in accelerating this happy *denouement*, gave him an undoubted right of exultation, could not conceal his triumph. He whispered his next neighbor, that "the bride was *sartinly* a very beautiful creature, but then she was none too good for Mr. Sidney Romilly, for *sartin* he didn't believe there was his equal in the United States."

And what does not often happen to eulogists of living merit, his praises of his patron were listened to, not only without a single shrug of incredulity, but his sentiments warmly responded.

George Cranfield again officiated as bridesman, with Miss Lucy Romilly for a partner; and to some inquiries, why her sister, who was the eldest, was not associated with him, it was whispered that Lucy was his favorite. And here I will just mention the surmises that floated among the young ladies of the village, after the Miss Romillys had departed to their boarding-school.

"That Miss Lucy was educating for the wife of the young clergyman; but that Miss Sophia would never find a beau to her mind unless that grand Englishman should return, which, as her brother kept up a constant correspondence with him, it was pretty likely he had engaged to do, as soon as she was sufficiently accomplished to appear like a grand lady."

Soon after the solemnization of the nuptials, Sidney having made every arrangement which he thought could conduce to the comfort and happiness of his mother and her children, and followed by their affectionate blessings, and the good wishes and kind adieus of all his Yankee friends and acquaintance, departed with his bride for their home in South Carolina.

A constant correspondence was mutually promised, and the young couple engaged to make a visit to New Hampshire every two years; and thus, with such flattering expectations for the future usefulness and rational felicity of her son, Mrs. Romilly was reconciled to the separation that duty and convenience seemed alike to impose, and she consigned little Harvey to the care of his brother without one bitter sigh, though tender tears she sought not to restrain. And she even tacitly consented to Sidney's proposal, that when, with his wife, he made his contemplated visit to New Hampshire, one or both of his sisters, whose education would then be completed, should accompany his return.

The good people of Northwood then thought, what the kind readers of this story are, probably, now thinking, that Sidney Romilly had attained all he could wish to make him happy. Still there was *one* heavy anxiety resting on his mind. A solemn responsibility, he could not evade rose before him. How this might be met and fulfilled, in the right manner, was the question? The way he solved it will be hinted in the next and last chapter.

CHAPTER XXXIV.

PLANS FOR THE FUTURE.

Oh! love of loves! to thy white hand is given
Of earthly happiness the golden key!
Thine are the joyous hours of winter's even,
When babies cling around their father's knee;
And thine the voice, that on the midnight sea
Melts the rude mariner with thoughts of home,
Peopling the gloom with all he longs to see.
Spirit! I've built a shrine; and thou hast come,
And on its altar closed—forever closed thy plume!

CROLY.

AND now they are at home;—Sidney and Annie Romilly are at *home!* To them the word is full of meaning—significant of Love, of Hope, and of Happiness. By the light of Love they will be able to look Truth steadily in the face; Hope shall make them strong to do the Right; and the crown of their work shall be Happiness for themselves and for others.

"Two are better than one; because they have a good

reward for their labor,"—that is, sympathy with each other. This implies full, trusting confidence, between the wedded pair. They must be friends as well as lovers.

Sidney Romilly had reflected much on this; for he had a most uncomfortable impression of the domestic discord between his uncle and Aunt Brainard. It had not troubled him much while he was expecting to reside in Northwood, because there his manner of life was known to Miss Redington; but after he had resolved to settle at the South, he could not help the intruding thought—that Annie might feel a repugnance to the measure. She had never been in a Slave State; she knew their peculiar institutions chiefly by the reports of those who sketched from fancy, or colored with fanaticism; and Sidney knew, from the example of his Aunt Brainard, how difficult it was to overcome such prejudices. He resolved, therefore, to have a clear understanding on this subject, and wrote the following letter soon after his return to Northwood—as soon, indeed, as he thought Annie sufficiently recovered to read and reply.

Putting the letter in her hand, he said, gravely, yet with deep feeling in his voice,—"I have made a full confession. I hope, dear Annie, you will be as frank in expressing your own views. Let us begin by an unreserved confidence; if we do not maintain it we may *live* together, but we can hardly be happy together!"

The letter, that Annie read with eagerness, ran thus:

You know, dearest Annie, that I am a *slaveholder*—perhaps I shall continue one—for I cannot desert the duty imposed on me by my late uncle. Mr. Brainard left his servants to my care, to support and protect. I am responsible before God for the charge; and you, my love, would not counsel me to abandon it. I have, to be sure, plans for the future welfare of these negroes which my uncle never entertained. Still I may not be able to do what I would. I never shall execute my plans unless you, dear Annie, aid me.

Enclosed is the Journal of my father, that I found in his desk after his decease. It was directed to me, and evidently written at intervals, when any thought, bearing on the subject of my welfare, had moved his mind. You will find in it his opinions on the momentous subject of slavery. I would draw your notice to two points, particularly, "What the Bible says of servitude," and "Religious instruction for the slave." Dear Annie, if this teaching is ever done, to any purpose, with my servants, (will they not soon be *our* servants?) it must be done by my *wife*.

You will see how highly my father estimated the religious influence of woman in her family. He illustrated this to me, only a few days before his death, in a very interesting way. You know he was a Congregationalist, and that this denomination do not kneel in prayer. I had never, when I left home for the South, seen my father on his knees in family devotions. When I returned, after twelve years' absence, I found he used this posture altogether. He told me the cause of the change was this: "Your mother," said he, "after your departure, united herself with the Methodist Episcopal Church. She had been brought up in that faith—converted, as she trusted, under that ministration—and she desired to be baptized by immersion. This our clergyman, Mr. Cranfield, would not consent to do; and he advised her to join the church to which her conscience inclined. I willingly gave my consent," continued my father, "and your mother became a member of the Methodist Church, though usually attending public worship, except on Communion Sabbaths, with me. But one change was apparent: she knelt at prayers; and soon the little children, following her example, knelt around her. I stood upright for some time—your mother never making a remark or breathing a word to induce me to change—but, at last, I can hardly tell how, from sympathy probably, I sunk down on my knees among them."

To my inquiries, which posture he thought the right, or most consonant with the Bible?

He replied,—"Both are consonant with Scripture, but neither is material to salvation. It is the heart that prays—not the knee nor the lip. And in this heart-worship women are more pure—more sincere than men. We arrange forms—they mould affections; we give rules—they set examples; we command in the household—and they govern; for the influence of love is mightier than the power of law. Therefore, Sidney," said my father, in conclusion, "be sure, when you marry, that your wife is a real believer in the Word of God. The woman who takes the Bible for her guide, will be a true light in the house of her husband—leading him and her family on gently but surely to happiness and heaven."

I have given you this long story, dear Annie, prefatory to the task I must beg you to undertake. I have a household, including the plantation hands, of *one hundred and forty-nine servants*;—more than a third of these are under fourteen years of age. This great family is to be fed, clothed, and instructed. The latter duty will, I fear, fall chiefly on my *wife.* I am not fitted for the task; and it has been sadly neglected.

Will you, dear Annie, help me in the plans of improvement I intend to begin immediately on my return South? With your aid, and the blessing of God, we shall succeed.

This letter had the effect Sidney had hoped for. Annie's reply was brief, but warm with sympathy for his feelings, and assurances of her co-operations.

And now they are at home with hearts overflowing with love, hope, and happiness.

"Mas'r Sidney" has been welcomed with such loud demonstrations of hearty joy as mark the return of the beloved friend. And their new "Missis" has shaken hands with every individual negro, old and young. And she has opened her week-day school for the children, taking, as her assistants, two of the most intelligent among the young colored women. And a Sunday-school for all the negroes is also established, where Sidney assists the good chaplain he has brought from the North, in teaching the men servants; while Annie and her assistants have care of the women and children. Then, when the school is over, all together, form a congregation, and kneel in worship of that holy God who is Lord over bond and free; and responses of prayer and songs of praise are participated equally by master and servant; and the sermon, from the servant of Christ, announces to both, on equal terms, the Great Salvation.

Sidney Romilly was not mistaken in the way he took to promote the good work of freedom. It is not, as some would counsel, the tearing up of the whole system of slavery, as it were, by the roots, that will make the bondman free. The life-blood of the Union might flow in such a struggle, but the black man would still be, in our land, a servant.

Never will the negro stand among men as a man, till he has earned for himself that title in his own country—magnificent Africa—which God has given him as a rich inheritance.

These ideas were enforced in the Journal left by Squire Romilly; and Sidney and his wife read it with the reverential attention such a memorial of thoughtful benevolence for the improvement of society and affectionate interest for his son, could not but inspire. A few extracts are all we can give.

Of Faith.—There are two kinds of faith—one in God—the other in man. Some people of undoubted piety, having faith in God, do yet despair of the progress of mankind in goodness. On the other hand, we have, even in our Republic, philosophers and reformers—so called—of both sexes, who put their trust in humanity alone. Those who deny the authority of God's Word, and claim to be governed by other moral laws than those the Bible sets plainly forth, may be zealous in their way of reform—we may admire their genius and enthusiasm

—but we cannot recognize them as Christian philanthropists.

Of Reform.—One cheering proof of the world's progress is the earnestness of those now working in the cause of humanity. Men and women are seeking for light in the path of duty. In our country the most dangerous hindrance of true progress is—activity wrongly directed. Those who urge onward the car of change, should bear in mind that moral reforms cannot be made as physical improvements are—by the power and skill of the agent that acts: there must be, also, spontaneous movement in the subject acted upon.

Even God, reverently speaking, could not, by force, compel His rational creatures to be, *in heart and soul*, obedient to His law. Therefore He sent His beloved Son to die for us, and thus, by His love, to move us to love, which includes obedience in return.

In short, as the Creator placed in the firmament but two orbs of light to dispel the darkness of the physical world, so in the moral world there are but two sources of real soul enlightenment, viz.: Love and Truth; and Truth borrows its radiance and holiest beauty from Love, even as the moon does her light from the more glorious sun.

All real reforms in society must be grounded on these two principles of Love and Truth, acted out and brought to bear in daily life and through the influences of moral and religious instruction.

Of Slavery and its Reformers.—The great struggle now going on for civil and religious liberty is, in our Republic, complicated by the system of negro servitude, established here by British power, before the true principles of freedom were understood anywhere.

To overthrow this system by any means, and at any cost, is the avowed intention of some Reformers.

Slavery is, no doubt, a great evil; so is despotic power; yet anarchy is worse than despotism; and to kill prisoners of war, or allow the poor to perish of hunger, is worse than servitude.

Domestic slavery was, probably, first established to remedy greater evils,—when these are removed, that should be abolished; yet not in a manner to cause more ills than it cures.

Can Christians, pious men and women, favor the employment of *fraud*, *falsehood*, or *force*, rather than wait God's time for the liberation of the slave?

What the Bible says of Slavery.—Taking for granted that a true Christian believes the Bible to be the Word of God, that in it He has prohibited, expressly, those acts which are absolutely in their own nature sin, let us see if slaveholding is included.

It is not forbidden in the Moral Law; therefore it cannot be sin in the sense that *image-worship*, *profane swearing*, *Sabbath-breaking*, *murder*, *theft*, *adultery*, and *false witness*, (or *slanders of brethren*) are sins.

To hold slaves is not, in any part of the Bible, denounced as sin, though *servitude* is threatened as a punishment for sin.

Men established domestic slavery, as they did all human institutions; and in all things ordained by men, there is more or less of evil; but as this particular institution was allowed and *regulated* by the authority of God among His chosen people, it could not, at that time, have been a sin to be condemned.

The Hebrews, when settled in Canaan, had bond-servants or slaves, and we will give the exact ordering of the matter by Divine authority. See Leviticus, chap. xxv., from verse 39 to the end.

"And if thy brother that dwelleth by thee be waxen poor, and be sold unto thee, thou shalt not compel him to serve as a bond-servant:

"But as an hired servant and sojourner he shall be with thee, and shall serve thee unto the Jubilee.

* * * * * *

"Both thy bondmen and thy bondmaids, which thou shalt have, shall be of the heathen that are round about you: of them shall ye buy bondmen and bondmaids.

"Moreover, of the children of the strangers that do sojourn among you, of them shall ye buy, and of their families that are with you which they begot in your land: and they shall be your possession."

Thus this chapter goes on, *regulating* slavery, and not a word in condemnation of the system as it then existed, is recorded. The "*possession*" spoken of must have meant the right of *property*, in servants as truly as in land, or any other thing.

Again in Deuteronomy, chap. 15, verse 12, the *selling* of the Hebrew men and women into servitude is *regulated.*

* * * * *

But the abolitionists exclaim—"All these wicked laws were set aside, and the holding men in servitude became sin immediately on the promulgation of the gospel!"

"Love your neighbor as yourself"—and "Do unto others as ye would they should do unto you," are indeed gospel principles, bearing on every phase of the Christian life, applying equally to our treatment of master and of slave, and giving no countenance to the bitter denunciations breathed against the former, nor to any fraudulent or violent means of freeing those who are held in bondage. The gospel is one strain of "peace on earth, and good will to men." The Saviour lived in the midst of a slaveholding world; he never denounced this particular form of evil; but he did denounce *hypocrisy*, *covetousness*, *evil speaking*, and all violent means of reform. He taught but one way—that of overcoming evil with good.

* * * * *

The Apostles preached before slaveholders and their servants; both classes received the word of divine truth, and became Christians. Did the Apostles order the believing master to free his bondman? or tell him, even, that the gospel required it? Consult St. Peter, 1st Epistle, 2d chap., verse 18, to the end.

"Servants, be subject to your masters with all fear; not only to the good and gentle, but also to the froward.

"For this is thankworthy, if a man for conscience toward God endure grief, suffering wrongfully.

"For what glory is it, if when ye are buffeted for your faults, ye shall take it patiently? but if, when ye do well, and suffer for it, ye take it patiently, this is acceptable with God."

Then turn to St. Paul and read his injunctions to both master and servant—not breaking the relation between them, but *regulating* its duties.

"Servants, be obedient to them that are your masters according to the flesh, with fear and trembling, in singleness of heart as unto Christ;

"Not with eye service, as men pleasers; but as the servants of Christ, doing the will of God from the heart;

"With good will doing service, as to the Lord, and not to men;

"Knowing that whatsoever good thing any man doeth, the same shall he receive of the Lord, whether he be bond or free.

"And, ye masters, do the same things unto them, forbearing threatening: knowing that your Master also is in heaven; neither is there respect of persons with him."—*Ephesians, 6th Chap.*

Then turn to Colossians, 3d chapter, 22d verse, to the end, where the same obedience of servants is taught.

Then read the charge to Timothy, 1st Epistle, 6th chapter; but this is so full and seems so pertinent to the solution of the gospel doctrine of peace and love, that I give it entire.

"Let as many servants as are under the yoke count their own masters worthy of all honor, that the name of God and of his doctrine be not blasphemed.

"And they that have believing masters, let them not despise them, because they are brethren; but rather do them service, because they are faithful and beloved, partakers of the benefit. These things teach and exhort."

Also, in the Epistle to Titus, 2d chapter, verses 9 and 10, a similar charge of teaching obedience to servants, is enforced; and nowhere did the Apostles attempt to disturb the relations they found existing between master and slave. They preached the gospel of peace, believing its truth, through divine love, would overcome the errors, wrongs, and evils of society.

Is American Slaveholding sinful?—Every age must be judged by the light it has received, and every nation by the opportunities it enjoys. The American Republic is favored, above every nation, ancient or modern, with civil and religious liberty; her people should, therefore, lead the world in diffusing these blessings.

Holding slaves is a great hindrance to the diffusion of American principles; this the true patriot must deeply lament.

Though *slaveholding* is not, in God's Word, denounced as sinful, like *Sabbath-breaking*, *profane swearing*, and the other flagrant sins forbidden by the holy Law, yet, from the system of slavery in our land, evils and sins of awful magnitude do result; and though no Christian has any Bible warrant for denouncing his slaveholding brother as criminal, yet all should unite in diffusing the true spirit of the gospel—its Truth and Love—which will, eventually, break every bond.

How the Slave is to be made Free.—That the system of servant and master is not the best for Christian advancement, is indicated by the great Apostle in his Epistle to the Corinthians, chap. 7th, verse 21st.

"Art thou called, being a servant? care not for it: but if thou mayest be made free, use it rather."

Mark the words—"*if thou mayest be made free:*"—the Apostle does not counsel the escape or even the discontent of the servant. Freedom may come to him—it is the *best condition*, because he can "use it;" therefore it is to be desired.

Christian slaveholder, is it not your duty to place, so far as you are able, every Christian servant in this *best condition?*

And what shall the Christians in the Free States do? How help their brethren, both master and servant? Thanks be to God, the way is clearly indicated. The Bible is the oracle to consult when, apparently, conflicting duties are before us. Read St. Paul's Epistle to Philemon, whose servant, Onesimus, had escaped and fled to the Apostle. It appears that this runaway slave had been converted under the teaching of the Apostle: Philemon, too, was a believer; and thus runs the letter that the returned slave bore to his Christian master:

"I beseech thee, for my son Onesimus, whom I have begotten in my bonds:

"Which in time past was to thee unprofitable, but now profitable to thee and to me:

"Whom I have sent again: thou therefore receive him, that is, mine own bowels:

"Whom I would have retained with me, that in thy stead he might have ministered unto me in the bonds of the gospel:

"But without thy mind would I do nothing; that thy benefit should not be as it were of necessity, but willingly.

"For perhaps he therefore departed for a season, that thou shouldest receive him forever;

"Not now as a servant, but above a servant, a brother beloved, specially to me, but how much more unto thee, both in the flesh and in the Lord?

"If thou count me therefore a partner, receive him as myself.

"If he hath wronged thee, or oweth thee aught, put that on mine account:

"I, Paul, have written it with mine own hand. I will repay it."

* * * * * * *

Let the pious friends of the slave imitate the example of the Apostle, teaching those who come to them for aid their duty, as the BIBLE sets it forth, first to God, then of obedience to their own masters; then, turning to these masters, entreat them, in all kindness and brotherly love, to deal tenderly with the returned servant; and, should it be necessary, and these northern friends of the southern slave are *real Christians*, will they not, remembering the promise of St. Paul, rather *pay* for the slave, and thus free him, than connive at *stealing* him, or even *concealing* him from his master?

Of the Bible and the American Constitution.—There is a remarkable agreement between them in some important points. Neither *established slavery*—both *regulate* it. The Bible authority we have quoted; here is that of the Constitution; all that it says of slavery, except to appoint the time when the slave trade should cease in 1808, and regulate its political power.

CLAUSE III.—"No person held to service or labor in one State, under the laws thereof, escaping into another, shall, in consequence of any law or regulation therein, be discharged from such service or labor, but shall be delivered up on claim of the party to whom such service or labor may be due."

The Bible, in the gospel, establishes the law of brotherhood, which will finally, by its influence break the bonds of servitude in every land.

The American Constitution makes imperative the law that "guarantees to every State in the Union a republican form of government;" a brotherhood. Also in the "Preamble" is set forth the indefeasible rights of humanity. These principles must, in time, blot slavery from our escutcheon of liberty.

Slavery among the Hebrews was permitted and *regulated* by Divine authority, to prevent greater evils.

Negro slavery in the United States was permitted for a similar reason. Without this—evil it may well be called—the union of *eight* slave-holding states, and *five* free states could not have been effected; the very existence of popular freedom would have been periled by the strifes and wars of brethren, and this Republic, now the asylum for the oppressed of Europe, would never have spread her protecting banner of stars.

The gospel humanizes those who live within its sound, though they may not participate in its hopes or privileges.

American institutions are imbuing the minds of our slaves with the true principles of civil and religious liberty; these they will yet carry to their fatherland, and there teach and exemplify, till that dark continent shall become radiant in the white lustre of truth and the warm beams of love.

Heathenism never looks so foul as when contrasted with pure Christianity.

Slavery in America seems monstrous because the true freedom is here. Letting in the light shows the dust—when the sunbeams are excluded, as in Russia, for instance, where all are slaves, no one heeds the filth. But the first and indispensable step in purifying an apartment or a people is to let in the light.

Of instruction for the slave.—Religion is the one thing needful for all mankind. Instructed in Christianity the slave on earth has the key of heavenly freedom; and the one who is really a Christian should bless God for the privileges that American slavery has conferred on himself and on his race. The slaveholders have an awful responsibility resting on them. The souls of their servants, will they not be required at their hands? And the sins these poor, ignorant creatures have committed, which the master might have hindered, as well as those he has stimulated, for these sins will not the just Judge hold him responsible? Oh, it is a thought to freeze the blood—this of responsibility!

Every gift, every privilege possessed and misused will rise up in judgment against the offending soul.

The acquiring or holding property is not sin—but "*the love of money is the root of all evil*," and through the temptations thus arising from wealth, it may be all but impossible "for a rich man to enter into the kingdom of God."

Thus the system of slavery increases the temptations to sin, and only the most resolute courage in duty and humble reliance on Divine aid can struggle on successfully against the snares of evil around the slaveholder.

Remember that on the conduct of one master or one mistress hangs, perhaps, the immortal destiny of a hundred souls! To teach the slaves their religious duties, must be insisted on, as the imperative obligation of every American slaveholder. It is not indispensable that the servant should read in order to be well taught, though it would be much easier to teach such an one. Three hundred years ago there were no books; all Christendom had been taught orally; and now, in three-fourths of Christian (so called) Europe, very few among the masses ever *read*, or even *see* the Bible, and a large proportion cannot read at all. Therefore those nations need not taunt us with the ignorance of our slaves, who, at least, see the Bible, and hear it read, and are often able to repeat texts and chapters with the greatest facility.

To instruct the slave in his Christian duties is the best means of fitting him for freedom, indeed the only way to insure that he will not, by his liberty, injure himself or others. When Israel was freed from Egyptian bondage, it took a long and weary pilgrimage in the desert to train the people for their religious duties—all the adults died in the process: Americans must take warning by this example and train their servants to worship the true God before their emancipation.

In this soul education pious women are the most efficient instructors, because they, more often than men, enforce their lessons by examples of goodness and disinterestedness. They have, too, that sympathy with the young, and patience with the ignorant, which the other sex often lack. And then they *love* the Saviour more trustingly, and the angels are with them to help their humble efforts, when men are proudly relying on their own strength.

The Bible, history, experience, all show the mighty influence of the mother's teachings; the religion of the household and of society is mainly woman's. How finely that Shakspeare of Christianity—John Bunyan, illustrates this. His hero Christian, with all the man's power, knowledge, and force of will, could hardly hold on his way to the "Celestial City." What doubts beset him! What dangers, and delusions! He went *alone*, and only one soul joined him on the long pilgrimage. But when the *woman*, Christiana went, *she took the children with her*. She drew nearly all she met to join her, and angels led them on through pleasant ways to heaven and eternal life.

Nearly three years are gone since Sidney Romilly and his wife first read together the Journal I have just placed before you, kind Reader. They read it with resolves to do what they could for their servants and the cause of freedom—and they have done much.

And now they are returned from their first visit to Northwood, whither they went to witness the twin marriages, as it were, of both sisters, Sophia and Lucy Romilly. For the Englishman had proved his admiration of America, or of one of her fair daughters, to be sincere, and had come over the wide ocean to claim his Yankee Bride.

It seemed to him that the New World, as if to welcome his coming, put on her bridal robes. The Old Granite State that, when he saw it first, had looked like a fortress of rock-ribbed hills keeping guard over the dying forests around, was now, in the "leafy month of June," Nature's Green-house, carpeted with flowers and roofed by the sky.

But the change in his bride was more astonishing still. He had, or he thought he had kept the image of Sophia Romilly in his heart—he had sent her his own miniature and received hers in return six months previous to his arrival; and he fancied he could see exactly how she would look when he met her. He knew she was beautiful, exceedingly—tall and sylph-like, with a slightly bending figure that seemed so charmingly to woo his support. Such she was in his fancy. She appeared now in another guise. The slight, drooping form of the girl had rounded into the graceful majesty of womanhood. Her mind had been developed and disciplined, and its pure free light seemed to irradiate her face with intelligence, and gave a lustre to her eyes that made their deep tenderness, as they met his passionate gaze, seem less of earth and more of heaven than mere mortal love.

Mr. Frankford was absolutely awed as he approached; and he did not dare do what he had intended—clasp her in his arms and kiss her sweet lips—he bowed before her, took her offered hand, and pressed it softly between his own. He felt in his secret soul that he must *honor* as well as love her—and strictly guard his own life to be worthy of her love; and that he should be a better man for the companionship of a woman so pure and noble.

A few days afterwards, the "Old Granite State Gazette" announced the marriages of "Spenser Frankford, Esq., of London, England, with Miss Sophia Romilly"—and of "the Rev. George Cranfield with Miss Lucy Romilly—both brides being daughters of the late James Romilly, Esq., of Northwood." It was further announced that the newly wedded left on the morning of the marriage—the first named couple for England, the other for Detroit, where the Rev. George Cranfield had lately been settled as pastor over a Congregational Church." A hint was added, "that England, now despairing of conquering the sons of America, was planning to capture and carry off her fairest daughters; therefore the Republic must be on its guard."

The weddings were strictly private, as poor Mrs. Romilly could not bear any bustle, being quite overcome with the parting from two daughters at once. It is doubtful if grief would not have preponderated over the thankfulness she felt that they were both so happily married—to good men, as she hoped—if Sidney, Annie, and their dear little boy, Charley Stuart, a babe of a year old, had not remained behind to comfort her.

Sidney Romilly passed the summer in New England, traveling through the country, examining the improvements, and collecting the best implements for agriculture, and all the new labor-saving machines, both for household and out-door work, that could be used at the South. He also engaged a living labor-saving instrument, an ingenious Yankee machinist and practical farmer, who was to reside with Mr. Romilly and see, experimentally, what could be done to improve and facilitate the labor on a Southern plantation; and also, for the introduction of white laborers.

The plans, then, that Sidney and his wife are now discussing, this second time we find them in their own beautiful Southern home, relate to these improvements, and to the number of servants they hope to be able to free by this mode of emancipation. They have resolved that every slave whose services are not needed to keep up the present income of the estate, shall be well fitted out and sent to Liberia. And thus, gradually, without disturbance to society, or danger of suffering to their servants, they hope to make them all, eventually, free, and prepared to do good by and with their freedom.

These plans had, in part, been suggested by Charles Stuart, Sidney's friend in Georgia, with whom he kept up a constant correspondence. A few extracts will show Stuart's opinions and doings.

"You inquire *if I am intending to emancipate any of my slaves?* Yes, I say, but not till I can fit them for freedom, and send them where they will be free. Two races, who do not intermarry, can never live together as equals. Frame laws as you will, the white race, being naturally superior to the colored, in all that constitutes moral power, the Anglo-American will be master over the Negro, if the latter is near him. So I am intending to help colonize Liberia. What a glorious prospect is there opened before the freed slave from America! If he has been religiously instructed—as most of the slaves are in this State—he goes forth a priest, bearing the Ark of God's Covenant mercy to Ethiopia. Millions on millions of his black brothers will bless his name. And if there is a country on earth where some future hero, greater even than our Washington, may arise, it is Africa. The real negro has never yet done anything for himself or for humanity; but in the future, as a Christian, he may win the palm from the world."

* * * * * *

"*What am I doing to prepare my slaves for freedom?* Well, on week-days, I am careful that they *work*. Industry is the lever to move the world, and Hope the propelling power to uplift the soul. I have found the way to educate and elevate my people. I have opened an account with all my field hands, over twenty-one years of age. Each has a daily allotted task; for every hour of over-work, I pay a stipulated sum; this is returned to me and credited to the individual. I also allow for conduct; good behavior through an entire week, entitles a servant of either sex to a premium of twenty-five cents; extraordinary merit may claim fifty. I pay the money on Saturday evenings, into the hand of each, that they may have the pleasure of looking on the present reward of their labor—I think this a material point—then I keep it for each, as his or her banker, to be accounted for when they shall have earned their own freedom, or to be paid over to whomever, among their fellow-slaves, they wish to free.

"In this way I am not only preparing my servants for freedom, but insuring it. All know their price; indeed, nearly all priced themselves. In many instances I cut down their own valuation, telling them it was more than they were worth. By this increase of industry and faithfulness, I shall be able to realize profits to fit them out for Liberia, as they become free, without much loss; and the negroes will be immensely benefited by this course of training in self-exertion. On Sundays everything is done for their moral improvement that my chaplain and I can devise. My wife is as zealous as I, and instructs the female slaves most faithfully. In short, we are working earnestly, and trust that, before many years, the majority of the planters will follow our example."

* * * * * *

"*Will Slavery ever come to an end in America?*—Yes; because, wherever established it has proved a burden and a curse on the general welfare. It lowers the tone of morals; checks learning; increases the ignorance and helplessness of women and the idleness and dissipation of men; in short, it injures the white race more than it benefits the colored—so that there is an actual loss of moral power in humanity. Let me illustrate by the single example of *language*. The negro is imitative and capable of speaking the English language correctly; as a *slave*, he will never be taught to do so—but allowed to go on in his own idiomatic jargon. This he communicates to the children of his master, and thus our noble tongue is vulgarized and rendered disgusting to the scholar and people of refined taste. I have met southern ladies, elegant looking women, whose manner of speech and intonation were so "*niggerish*," that it required a knowledge of this peculiar dialect fully to understand them.

"These are the mothers of our great men, the inspirers of Southern chivalry! Men free themselves, in a greater measure than women do, from this early vitiation of speech, because of their more liberal education. But they return from their college course, where they often give promise of great talent, to smoke cigars in a veranda, or lie in the shade reading *cheap* novels!

"It is the curse of slavery that it crushes the talents and dwarfs the soul of both master and servant. Never will the native genius of our noble Southern people be developed till the system of free schools, which cannot be carried out to much purpose, where slavery exists, is established, and the masses are educated.

"There are, in this old State of Georgia, founded by philanthropy and guided by philosophy, where Learning was to have her seat: there are here thousands of free white persons more ignorant and far more degraded and miserable than any slave. *Forty-one thousand white adults who cannot read!* and the number of children, whose parents are not able to send them to school, is upwards of *thirty-eight thousand!*

"While in New Hampshire, there are only *forty-one* persons in the whole State who cannot read and write—and these are foreigners.

"Such is the difference between freedom and slavery in our land!"

And now, kind reader, we part in friendship, I hope. Mine is no partizan book, but intended to show *selfishness* her own ugly image, wherever it appears—north or south: and, also, to show how the good may overcome the evil.

"Constitutions" and "compromises" are the appropriate work of men: women are conservators of moral power, which, eventually, as it is directed, preserves or destroys the work of the warrior, the statesman, and the patriot.

Let us trust that the pen and not the sword will decide the controversy now going on in our land; and that any part women may take in the former mode will be promotive of peace, and not suggestive of discord.

The reverend clergy have an important work to do in this crisis; to promote brotherly love and Christian progress is their especial vocation. They can teach the way of peaceful emancipation, and help to provide the means. One mode might be this. There are in the United States about forty thousand churches: on the Annual Thanksgiving Day, let a collection, for the purpose of educating and colonizing free people of color and emancipated slaves, be taken up in every church in our land. If the sum averages but *five dollars* per congregation, the aggregate would be *two hundred thousand dollars!* And if this mode is found productive of beneficial effects, as it surely would be, the sum raised could be annually increased, the slave holding states and the general government would after a time, lend their co-operation; till, finally, every obstacle to the *real freedom* of America would be melted before the gushing streams of sympathy and charity, as the ice of the polar seas yields to the warm rains of summer.

Africa—word of wonder, fear and mystery, telling of a land where nature is an Eden run wild, and man darkens under the shadow of chains and death; where science has never softened the primal curse, nor the sun of righteousness broken the gloom of sin!

"The night cometh, and also the morning." Is not thine, sad Africa, near? Over thy western shore the day star of liberty has risen with lustre caught from the stars of the New World. God grant that the light may spread, and the millions of thy heathen children may find true liberty through the ministry of those who have in the house of bondage, learned to know and worship the true God. Liberia has solved the enigma of ages. The mission of American slavery is to Christianize Africa.

THE END.

www.ingramcontent.com/pod-product-compliance
Lightning Source LLC
LaVergne TN
LVHW020057110826
845151LV00001B/6